A Show for Two

Books by Tashie Bhuiyan
available from Inkyard Press

Counting Down with You
A Show for Two

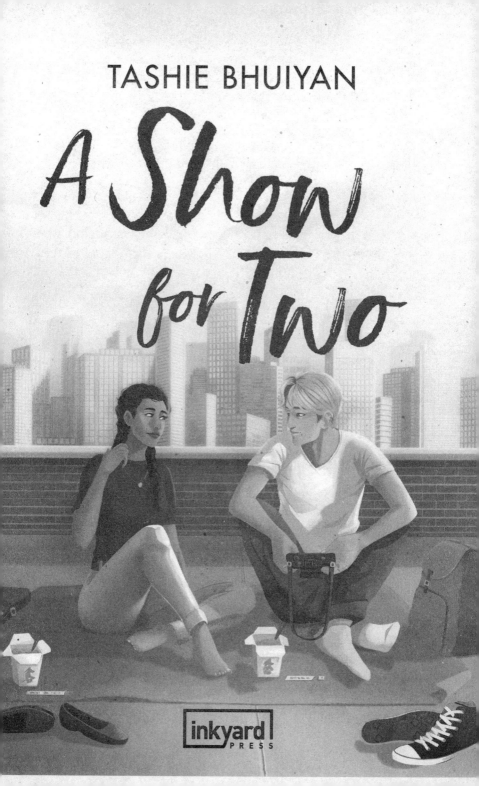

ISBN-13: 978-1-335-42456-3

A Show for Two

For questions and comments about the quality of this book, please contact us at CustomerService@Harlequin.com.

Inkyard Press
22 Adelaide St. West, 41st Floor
Toronto, Ontario M5H 4E3, Canada
www.InkyardPress.com

Printed in U.S.A.

To New York City, for loving me first.

author's note

Dear reader,

Welcome to part one of my author's note: the inspiration behind this book. Just a few years ago, the wildest thing ever happened to me. During my senior year, Tom Holland secretly enrolled in my high school, the Bronx High School of Science, as an undercover student to learn more about American high schools for his upcoming role as Spider-Man. I was lucky enough to meet and talk to him during his time there (literally still reeling in shock if we're being honest because w h a t), and I've always treasured that experience. Since then, an idea has lingered in the back of my head—wouldn't this be such an incredible concept for a book? So when the chance to write it came along, I knew I couldn't pass up on it. While the love interest, Emmitt Ramos, is undeniably *very* different from Tom Holland, I'd like to believe Tom would be friends with Emmitt in another life. It's the bestie agenda!

The second part of this author's note talks about something

a little more serious: the heart of this book, beyond just the inspiration. This book follows the main character, Mina Rahman, on her journey as she grapples with her mental health, being diaspora, and navigating complicated familial relationships, all of which is very in tune with my own experiences. While this story is very fun and chaotic and just a little bit ridiculous, this is also a story about gaining agency and survival and making the best of what you have. It reflects one singular experience—because we are not a monolith and we never will be, which is why it's important to read widely and expansively, to get a whole scope of everyone's different experiences—and one girl's path to finding herself. At the end of the day, I believe this is a book about hope and perseverance and love, love, love. The love you have for your family, the love you have for your friends, the love you have for your significant other, the love you have for your home, and, most importantly, the love you have for yourself.

So as you embark on Mina's journey, I hope you know that you are loved. You are fiercely, tenderly loved. As someone once told me when I was a teenager: *There are people you may not even know yet who are waiting for you with open arms, and they will love you unconditionally. Trust me. Keep your head up.*

And I did. I hope you will, too.

All the love,

Tashie

opening

"I'm not a bad person for wanting."
—MINA RAHMAN
(SCREENWRITER, *COUNTING DOWN WITH YOU*)

1

The world looks better when it's caught on film. It's an indisputable fact. With the right lighting, the perfect angle, and a filter or two thrown in, something ordinary can become phenomenal.

As my younger sister puts on an impromptu fashion show in my bedroom, I itch to record it, to keep this memory forever rather than just in this one moment.

But when I give in to the urge, pressing Record on my phone, I come face-to-face with a scowl.

"Stop filming me, and tell me what I should wear to school," Anam says, shoving my shoulder and jostling my phone. My sister prefers to live in the moment, shaking her head in exasperation whenever she sees me recording, but that's never stopped me before.

"I *can* multitask," I say, making a face at her. She sticks her tongue out, and I roll my eyes, though we both know I don't mean it. I've never been able to hold a grudge against her for more than a few hours.

Anam nudges me again, so I set down my phone on my bedside table, beside a stack of unfinished scripts. When I turn back to my sister, I take in her maxi dress and high heels combination with appraising eyes.

Then I shake my head. "Nice try, but it's too fancy," I say, waving toward the door. "Again."

Anam sighs long-sufferingly. *"Fine."*

She heads for her room across the hall, and I watch her go with a small smile on my face. Everything about her is so loud, from her voice to the way she dresses to the music she blasts every morning without fail. Even from my room, I can hear "#LoveSTAY" by Stray Kids blasting from her laptop.

The next time my sister comes back, she falters in the doorway, her nose wrinkled. I pause midway through packing my bag for school. "What happened?"

Ma's voice carries from downstairs, making both of us flinch. "Samina, come downstairs *now.*"

"What happened?" I ask again, edging toward the doorway, where Anam is glaring over the hallway's banister. "Why are they calling me Samina?"

"They opened your mail," my sister says, looking back at me. "It's addressed to Samina Rahman, so they're being extra as per usual."

"They could *at least* say Mina if they're going to be dramatic," I say, but then the rest of her sentence sinks in and I tense, my shoulders stiff. "My mail?"

"Something from USC," Anam says, chewing absently on a lock of blue hair. I reach forward, batting it away, and she offers me a grateful half smile. "I didn't realize the mailman would do his rounds so early, or I would've snagged it before Baba could."

Again: *"Poppy!"*

Well. At least it's my dak nam now.

Still, I pinch the bridge of my nose, hoping to stave off the headache I feel forming between my brows. "It's too early for this."

Anam grunts in agreement. Even though we're a year apart, our brains are eerily in sync. "I don't know how they're not tired," she mutters, crossing her arms over her chest. "Have you given any thought to my brilliant idea about stuffing me in your luggage when you move out for college?"

"I wish," I mutter, tucking my binder into my bag before swinging it up over my shoulder. "I'm guessing they're upset."

"When are they not?" Anam asks, rolling her dark eyes. We're often mistaken for twins, our facial features near identical—thick eyebrows, upturned noses, full mouths. Only Anam's home-dyed blue ombré distinguishes us at this point.

I tie my own black strands back into a loose braid before snagging my phone off its charger, sticking it in my back pocket. "Maybe we can sneak out without them noticing."

"As if Baba isn't guarding the door," Anam says with a grimace, but disappears into her room across the hall to get her own bag. "Give me a minute!"

I'm long used to mornings with my parents screeching at the top of their lungs. It's basically tradition at this point. Their nitpicking is relentless, especially when it comes to school. It's been this way for years and it's only gotten worse in the last few months.

Ever since I announced I was planning to double major in business and film at the University of Southern California, I've been subjected to nonstop lectures about making terrible life decisions. Why pursue the arts when I could be a doctor, an engineer, a rocket scientist? Clearly I've lost my mind.

I almost feel bad for Anam, who has to hear them by proxy, but I've had to sit through our parents scolding her enough times that it evens out. Most recently, because of the debacle of the bleaching her hair at home without any supervision.

Anam comes out of her room wearing a tank top and leggings. "Ready?"

I smile despite myself. "You look cute," I say. "But you're going to freeze to death. Late January is still January."

She shrugs, the strap of her top sliding down her shoulder. I lean forward, tugging it back up. "Thanks, Apu," she says before hip-checking me. "Let's grab breakfast from the deli?"

"Sounds good." Sitting at the dining table long enough to scarf down a roti and egg isn't feasible with the mood my parents are in. With that in mind, I toss a wool sweater at her. "Take this. You can take it off when we're at school if you really want to."

Anam grumbles half-heartedly, pouting as she tugs it over her head. "Happy?"

"Don't give me that look," I say, flicking her forehead. "I'll pay for your bagel."

Her face immediately brightens. "Okay."

I hasten down the stairs, even as my father says, "Poppy! Come here!"

I stay silent, maneuvering around my mother's extensive vase collection littering the foyer. The wall is covered in family photos, and with every step I take, it's almost like I can see the progression of me shifting from loving my parents to tolerating them.

Then again, it's not exactly one-sided.

At four years old, I offer the camera a toothy smile. At eight years, my mother's hand grips my shoulder tightly, wrinkling my shirt. At twelve years old, my eyes are bright, but my jaw is clenched. At sixteen years old, Anam and I stand stiffly to one side, our expressions blank, as our parents try not to glare at us.

And on and on it goes.

Some days, it feels like Ma's love for home decor outweighs whatever affection she holds for her daughters. Those days, I consider smashing each and every single piece of furniture in this house, then striking a match, letting it all go up in flames. The rest of the time, I'm just tired.

Today, my bone-deep weariness is winning over my blood-boiling anger.

Baba calls my name again, and I don't bother to raise my voice when I say, "Maybe later. We're going to be late for school."

Behind me, Anam stifles a giggle, and I give her an exasperated look. If anything, we're going to be early, even with our stop at the deli, but that's neither here nor there.

Anam raises her hands above her head in a general gesture of surrender, but not without smirking. I flip her off after making sure neither of my parents are approaching from down the hall.

"Anam, you too!" Ma says from across the house. The smell of fresh suji halwa wafts through the house, making my stomach rumble. I ignore it, grabbing a puffy jacket off the coatrack. "And bring your sister!"

"As if," Anam mutters, on her knees digging through the closet as she looks for a pair of shoes that aren't my mother's.

It doesn't take a genius to know what awaits me in the kitchen. Another lecture about how I'm setting myself up for disappointment because I'm never going to get into USC. Another lecture about how I should be reasonable and focus entirely on business, since a degree in the arts will never pan out.

I've heard it all before and I'm not eager to hear it again at seven in the morning. They can run me a check if they want to waste my time.

"Hurry, before she starts yelling about how we should've made our own breakfast this morning," I say, slipping my feet into a pair of black boots.

"Poppy," a voice says over my shoulder, making me jump half a foot into the air. My mother is standing behind me, her lips curled in disapproval. In her hand is a postcard with *VISIT USC* and *SAMINA RAHMAN* printed across the top. "Both of you need to start waking up earlier. You're old enough that you should be making *us* breakfast instead of the other way around. These are skills you will need in the future. You know, your cousins all wake up—"

"No, they don't," Anam says, her eyes narrowed on my mother. "Bristi is always late to school. I'm supposed to believe he wakes up early to cook Chachi *breakfast*?"

Ma turns to look at Anam, her teeth grinding. "I'll deal with you later," she says, before looking back at me, grabbing my wrist with her free hand. "How many times have we told you, Poppy, that you need to stop with this USC nonsense?

We're just trying to look out for you. You know it's never going to—"

"We have to go," I say, refusing to meet her gaze. An anchor ties itself to my heart, weighing it down to the pit of my stomach. Is it too much to ask for one single day without this? "We're going to be late."

"You can make time for this," Ma says, tightening her grip until my bones feel brittle, ready to snap at a moment's notice. "This is some stupid fantasy you've built up in your head, and you need to wake up—"

I pull away from my mom roughly, then tug open the front door and hop down the steps leading up to our porch without another word.

"Poppy, you're being childish," Baba says, appearing over Ma's shoulder. He looks vaguely distressed as he scratches his beard, but that doesn't garner any sympathy from me. Not when my wrist is red. "You say you want us to treat you like an adult, but then you continue to run from your problems."

"I have no idea what you're talking about," I say, my voice cold. I don't know how they're not tired of repeating themselves. I'm certainly tired of hearing it.

Silently, I hold my hand out for Anam to take as she slips out in the space between my parents, hurrying down the steps after me.

I'm halfway down the driveway when she interlaces our fingers, grinning at me. My mom glares from the doorway and my dad sighs, but neither calls after us, not for the fear of shame riding them too hard if our neighbors happened to overhear.

It's always *what will people say?*

It's never *what will make you happy?*

★ ★ ★

It's not until we're a few blocks down that I breathe easy, pulling my phone out of my pocket to check my notifications.

There's two from my best friend, Rosie, complaining about the lack of snow, despite the forecast last night, and one from the film club's technical director, Grant, asking about competition dates for the upcoming Golden Ivy Film Festival.

I grimace, wondering why that's even a *question*, and Anam peers down at the screen, reading over my shoulder.

"You're too hard on him," she says, tugging on my hand once the traffic light turns red and we can walk across the street. Our neighborhood is relatively quiet, but as we move closer to the subway, the loud bustle of the city increases. "Not everyone is as anal about film club as you are."

"Then he shouldn't have joined in the first place," I say, although I don't really mean it. As co-president of the film club alongside Rosie, I'm grateful for every single club member. Even Grant.

Anam can tell, judging by the way she looks at me, but she humors me anyway. "Didn't he have a crush on you freshman year? Maybe that's why he joined."

"Don't remind me," I say under my breath, rubbing my eyes. I want to go back to bed, and maybe stare despondently at my ceiling for a few hours. That, or carve out this God-awful feeling in my chest, this black hole that *devours*. It's not always there, but when it is, it smothers everything else.

"I mean," Anam says, "maybe you could—"

I shake my head. "Forget it, Anam. I'm pretty sure the actual reason he joined is because his dad is some big-shot film producer. Familial pressures and all that."

"We wouldn't know *anything* about that," Anam says dryly, and I offer her a noncommittal hum. "Well, maybe you should cut him some slack, then."

I huff a quiet breath. "Like you cut the girls' volleyball team any slack?"

Anam shoves me, and I shove her back. "I have to show Coach that I'm capable of being captain next year," she says, jutting out her bottom lip.

Something flashes through her eyes, and if I weren't her sister, I don't know if I'd catch it. But I am and I do.

I squeeze Anam's fingers. "I'll fight Coach myself if he gives it to anyone but you."

When I let go of her, it's only to open the door to our neighborhood deli. The girl behind the counter, Nazifa, smiles at both of us, and Anam offers her a brief fist bump.

The Ali family lives next door to ours. Nazifa's parents own the deli, so we often see her behind the counter in the early mornings, before school starts. Anam is closer with her than I am, both of them obsessed with volleyball, even though they technically go to rival schools.

I give Nazifa a smile in return as we pass through, heading for the fridge in the back to grab drinks. Anam harrumphs as she picks out a bottle of Snapple, picking up our conversation where we left off. "You won't be here to fight Coach anyway. You'll be off in California, chasing your dreams."

"I'll book the first flight back, just for you," I say and ignore the pang in my chest. I won't know for another two months if I'm accepted into USC or not, and the cruel voice that lives in the back of my head keeps insisting on the latter.

Anam wraps her fingers around my wrist as I reach for a

bottle of orange juice. "Hey. I know that look. Stop it, all right? You're going to get in."

Sometimes I forget she knows me as well as I know her.

"Inshallah," I say under my breath.

"Inshallah," Anam repeats, digging her thumb into my pulse point.

Both of us are more on the non-practicing side when it comes to being Muslim, even though we both firmly believe in Allah. It's natural for us to say words like *inshallah* and hold true to the meaning behind it—to believe that Allah is the one who wills things into existence—even if we aren't as religious when it comes to other things.

I know a lot of it has to do with my specific experience growing up as a child of diaspora and my fraying relationship with my parents. I have the utmost respect for those who have a better and healthier relationship with their religion and culture, but I'm not there yet. Maybe I never will be.

But I hope that isn't the case.

When I leave this city behind, there will be infinite room for me to figure myself out. I just have to wait until then.

By the time we get back to the counter, Nazifa has already prepared both our breakfast orders. I slide her the money and pass Anam her bagel, which she takes eagerly.

"I'll see you guys this weekend at my mom's party, right?" Nazifa asks, absently playing with a loose thread in her hijab.

I salute her with my croissant, some of the heaviness in my chest easing. "Absolutely. Wouldn't miss it."

"Can't wait!" Anam says, waving cheerfully as the door shuts behind us.

When we get to the subway station, there are two other

kids from our school waiting there already. I don't know either of them that well since they're freshmen, but I nod anyway before turning back to Anam.

"Are *we* still on for our movie marathon tonight?" I ask, mentally working out what time I need to be home by. Some days I test my parents' patience more than others, but considering this morning's events, it might not be worth pushing my luck today. "Or do you have too much homework?"

"Bold of you to assume I'm going to do my homework before Sunday night," Anam says, biting off a piece of her bagel. Through a mouthful of mush, she adds, "Yes, we're still on."

For one painful, heart-stopping moment, I remember I'm going to leave this behind if I go to California. Mornings with my sister will be a thing of the past.

Then I shove that thought away. My future is at stake—I can handle a sacrifice or two.

"I'll come home straight after film club," I say, smiling thinly as I wipe some cream cheese off Anam's chin.

She offers me a thumbs-up. "Sounds like a plan. Don't be late."

I give her a sidelong look as the R train pulls up. "When have I ever been late?"

2

There are three things that people applying for the Golden Ivy student film competition should know.

One: film transitions can make or break you.

Two: casting yourself in the film is as good as accepting defeat.

Three: having a celebrity make some kind of ridiculous guest appearance *always* wins points with the judges.

While our short films always have great transitions, and Rosie and I live strictly behind the camera, we've never had a celebrity make an appearance, ridiculous or not, in one of our films.

"Every single time," Rosie says, running her hands through her auburn hair, nearly wrenching out the curls. The rest of the seniors aren't much better, alternating between various stages of distress.

I frown, leaning an elbow against the desk. It's our first film club meeting after winter break. More importantly, it's our first film club meeting where we're actively working on our short film after the literal hell of submitting college applications.

The projector is broadcasting last year's winner on the classroom's whiteboard, one of the many short films we're watching for research purposes.

The freshmen sitting on the floor look bemused at our coinciding irritation. One of them, Brighton, looks imploringly at Rosie and hesitantly speaks up. "Every single time...what?"

Rosie is too busy pulling her fingers down her face in frustration to answer, so I point at the whiteboard. All of the freshmen follow the movement with wide eyes.

On the screen, some random popstar is smiling at the camera, as if mocking us for our inadequacy.

"Almost every year without fail, the winner of the competition snags a celebrity endorsement," I say. "And as all of you know, we have yet to manage such a feat."

Brighton blinks before turning her head toward the back of the room, where Grant is sitting. "What about Grant?"

I snort, and Grant sticks out his tongue at me. "Grant doesn't count. Being the son of someone famous isn't the same as being famous."

"Still more famous than you," he points out, but there's no heat behind his words.

Rosie leans against my leg, seated down below with the freshmen. I pat my best friend's head in a weak attempt at reassurance.

"Our film concept is strong," I say quietly, in part for myself. "There's still a chance we could win."

We have to is what I don't say.

She groans, burying her face in the rough material of my jeans. "This is our *fourth* year trying to win."

"Yeah, but this is our first time in charge," I say, flicking her hoop earring.

Astoria Academy of the Arts and Sciences has been applying to the student film competition at the Golden Ivy Film Festival for many years now, long before either of us enrolled.

When Rosie and I joined AAAS's film club as freshmen, we sat here just like this, watching the previous winners' films. Since we're co-presidents this year, I'm responsible for writing the screenplay while she's responsible for directing.

Planning the film wasn't that hard. Accepting our inevitable defeat to some random school in Los Angeles with connections to half a dozen celebrities is proving to be a lot more difficult.

It's been my dream—and Rosie's dream—for four years now. Winning means everything, starting with a scholarship and ending with visibility in the film community.

But as important as all of that is, I need to win for an entirely different reason. If we win, I'll finally have proof that choosing to double major isn't a mistake. My parents will be forced to accept that I'm capable of standing on my own two feet and making a path for myself.

And more importantly, they'll honor the agreement we made months ago and pay for me to attend USC in the fall.

If I get accepted.

"Next one," Rosie says, waving a hand in Grant's direction. "If I have to watch one more second of this, I'm going to *scream*. I still don't understand how we lost last year. This film isn't even that good."

I shush her. "You're going to set a bad example for the freshmen," I say, before offering the rest of the room a reassuring smile. "This just means we have to work that much harder when we're putting together the film. We still have two months left. Everyone has March twenty-nine marked in their calendars, right?"

The thirty-five people in the room nod. I pretend not to notice as half the freshmen discreetly take out their planners and mark the date.

Our supervising teacher, Ms. Somal, has long since checked out of the meeting, sitting beside Grant with her earphones in, flipping idly through a graphic novel. She looks up once in a while to make sure we haven't set the classroom on fire, but aside from that she seems more than content letting us do what we want.

Grant clicks into the winning film from two years ago, and we all fall silent as the opening credits begin rolling. I try not to grimace, in full agreement with Rosie. Our film was better than the winning films the last three years, but we've still never gotten past semifinals.

We watch around three more short films before the bell rings at five, signifying the end of after-school activities. I stand up, stretching my sleeping limbs. My entire body feels jittery with the anticipation of finally starting this project after months of prepping and planning.

One of the freshmen walks over to Rosie, shyly asking her a question. I leave her to it, gathering my things instead. My earphones are loosely splayed across the desk beside a scattering of different colored pens, three different journals labeled by project, and a planner filled to the brim with Post-its. My phone buzzes, and I glance at it briefly.

ANAM RAHMAN: hurry homeeeee I don't wanna deal with ma and baba by myself anymore

I type out a quick response. sooooon!

As I'm setting my phone down, Rosie wraps her arms around my neck, pale white skin contrasting against light brown. "Mina. I'm going to die."

"Hm?" I ask, glancing at her over my shoulder, meeting her blue eyes. "Why?"

"The Nutritional Science lab," she says, dropping her arms so she can lean against the desk. "Do you think you could help me? My dad will be here soon, but he can wait—"

I shake my head, eyes flicking toward my phone again. "Anam needs my help fending off the parental figures, so we might need to take a rain check. Maybe we can FaceTime later?"

Rosie grimaces and tugs on my dark braid. "I have a thing tonight with my dad's girlfriend. Maybe tomorrow? It's due Monday, right?"

I shake my head. "I have a community party on Saturday," I say, but I'm already rearranging my schedule to make room for a call. With only a few days until casting begins, I've been making final tweaks to the script in my free time. "How about Sunday afternoon?"

Rosie smacks a kiss against my cheek. "Perfect."

I wrinkle my nose, wiping away the leftover strawberry lip gloss residue on my skin.

She rolls her eyes and blows me another mocking kiss as she packs up her own things.

Rosie and I have been best friends for four years now, bonding over a shared love for Studio Ghibli films during freshman year. We've been attached at the hip ever since. Last year, instead of running for president of the film club individually, we both agreed to run as co-presidents, even though it wasn't *technically* allowed. But we made it happen, because we refused to do it without each other.

As we both leave the classroom, waving to Ms. Somal, Grant catches up to us, running a hand over his buzzed head. "Yo, so I was thinking—"

I slant him a look. "What?"

Grant pouts at me, and Rosie giggles. "Why are you like that? You're always so quick to jump the gun for no reason. Rosie never does that."

"You never hit on Rosie," I say offhandedly.

"I'm *not* hitting on you," Grant says, but he has the good sense to look slightly ashamed.

At the same time, Rosie says, "Because I'm gay, dumbass."

I shake my head at both of them. "What do you want, Grant?"

"Ignore her," Rosie says, nudging me out of the way. "What's up?"

Grant smiles at her, white teeth flashing bright against his dark skin. "About the famous celebrity, my dad—"

"I know your dad's famous, but he's not a celebrity," I cut in before he can finish. During freshman year, Grant attempted to impress me by bringing up his father every five seconds. The man's Wikipedia page is practically seared into my brain.

Speaking from past experience, it's best to cut this topic off at the root. "Producing the next big blockbuster film is cool and all, but I don't think it's going to win us brownie points."

Grant grunts. "That's not what I was going to—"

I sigh, my shoulders slumping with exhaustion. This isn't worth bickering over. Not when I've had my fair share of arguments this morning. "Fine. What is it?"

He stares at me for a long moment before he shrugs. "You know what? It wasn't that important anyway."

"Hey," Rosie says, tugging Grant's sleeve. "Ignore Mina. You know how she is."

I give her an affronted look in response but don't argue. Between the two of us, I'm admittedly the more standoffish one, but I wasn't trying to be rude. I just—I'm *tired* and I don't want to deal with this right now. Is that a crime?

"No, it's fine," Grant says, shrugging her off. "Never mind. I'll see you guys in class on Monday."

He walks away, slipping on his hood, and I can't help but feel distinctly unsettled. I didn't mean to upset him.

Rosie turns a look on me. "Seriously? What if he was trying to tell us something important?"

I try not to squirm under her gaze. "Like what? Was he going to offer to produce a celebrity out of thin air?"

Her lips thin. "You're always doing this, Mina. You know this competition is just as important to me as it is to you, but it's not the only thing that matters. There are other things in life that are also important."

I look away, tugging the collar of my turtleneck. "That's not—we have to win this competition, Rosie."

"I know," she says softly, laying a hand on my arm. "But we have to accept that there's every chance we might lose."

My throat is suddenly tight. Rosie needs to win as much as I do. Without the scholarship, it's going to be a lot harder for her family to pay the tuition for NYU.

But at least her family supports her dream of becoming a film director. At least her family believes in her.

I cough and paste a smile on my lips, turning back to my best friend. "Yeah, definitely."

Rosie scans my expression and huffs a quiet breath. "You're a terrible liar, Mina." She saves me from responding by grabbing my arm, pulling me in the direction of her locker. "Come on, before your parents kill me for making you late."

I follow her, all the while trying to push her words to the back of my head.

We have to win the competition. We *have* to.

If I have to spend another year at home, if I have to spend another year with this awful weight on my shoulders—with this tiny, familiar voice in the back of my head taunting me relentlessly—I'm going to lose my shit.

You're never going to win. You're never going to be good enough.

Sometimes I can't tell whose voice it is.

And sometimes…it sounds like my own.

3

The weather is absolutely atrocious outside. A strike of lightning makes me jump, knocking my elbow into Rosie's. Our school is tucked away in Astoria, and I can't imagine the East River's proximity helps when it comes to storms.

"Jesus, it's bad out here," Rosie says, shivering as she runs her hands up and down her arms, trying to get rid of goose bumps.

"Want to share my umbrella?" I ask, trying to hold it higher to accommodate her height, but my attempt results in both of us being assaulted by the rain.

Rosie shakes her head, tilting her head toward the end of the street, where a cute little blue car is waiting for her. "I'm good." She leans over, offering me a quick hug. "Love you! Get home safe."

She runs toward her dad's car, holding her tote bag above her head. I shake my head, almost certain she has an umbrella tucked in between her binders.

Rosie's dad spots us and rolls down the window to wave at me, even though it means stray raindrops splatter onto the car's leather seating. "Mina! You okay out there? It's coming down pretty hard."

I wave back, but the movement feels stiff and listless. "I'll be fine, Mr. Hardy."

He frowns at me, presumably because my umbrella is one gust of wind away from falling apart. "Are you sure? Where do you live again? Maybe we could…"

Rosie slides into the passenger seat on the other side, wringing out her wet curls. "I've told you like ten times, Dad. She lives in Forest Hills."

"Oh," he says, scratching his head. "I see. Are you taking the subway home?"

I nod, hitching my thumb in the opposite direction. "The R train is only a few minutes away."

He glances between his overworked windshield wipers and me. "If you want…" He falters, lips pressed together.

I immediately shake my head. Rosie lives in Brooklyn, which is a drive in the absolute opposite direction. Taking me home will mean double the trip. "It's fine," I say, forcing my mouth into the shape of a grin. "My sister is waiting for me at the subway anyway." It's a lie, but it's a believable one. Rosie doesn't think so given the way she rolls her eyes, but she knows better than to argue.

If nothing else, it clears up the remaining guilt on Mr. Hardy's face. "If you're sure."

"I'm sure," I say and half-heartedly catch the kiss Rosie blows my way. "Bye, Rosie. Bye, Mr. Hardy."

When the blue car disappears from sight, I roll my shoulders, attempting to relieve some of the lingering tension from earlier.

I start down the road, pulling out my phone to text Anam my ETA. Instead, I see three missed calls from my dad.

I furrow my brows but ignore it for the time being, instead texting my sister a quick: heading home rn, have the popcorn readyyy.

And then my phone starts ringing again, my dad's face lighting up the screen. I press my lips together but slide my finger across the screen, answering the call. "I'm on my way home, Baba," I say, turning the corner. "Calling me ten times doesn't make my commute any faster."

My dad grunts on the other end of the phone. "Go to the supermarket on your way home and pick up some bell peppers."

"You called me four times because of bell peppers?" I ask tightly.

"And be home by six," he says. "Or else."

Then, without warning, the call drops.

"What the fuck," I say to my phone, staring at the time with an uneasy sense of dread slithering through me. *5:33 p.m.*

I'm never going to make it in time.

And even worse, I'm going to be late for my movie marathon with Anam.

"Shit," I whisper, immediately dialing my dad's number. It goes straight to voice mail. Something starts building in my chest, rising up my throat and choking me slowly.

"Goddammit," I mutter, my eyes suddenly burning. Why is it that when one thing goes wrong, a million things follow in suit?

I go to call my dad again, but clearly the universe is plotting against me because I crash headfirst into someone instead. My umbrella goes flying one way, my iPhone the other.

"What—" I stare at the wet pavement in dismay, my bottom lip trembling "—the fuck."

There are hands wrapped around my forearms, keeping me from falling over, but that doesn't do much to protect me from the torrential downpour.

Then I look up at the person holding on to me, and my brain comes to a sudden halt. Even the insistent pressure behind my tear ducts eases up, my entire attention focused solely on the boy in front of me.

He's beautiful.

And familiar?

I struggle to place him in my memories. I'm certain I'd remember meeting someone who looks like him.

The boy lets go of me abruptly, his eyes dropping to the ground below our feet. I follow his stare, my gaze trailing along the sidewalk, until I see another iPhone, this one half-drowned in a puddle. Google Maps lights up the screen, but the spoken directions are barely coherent, his speaker sputtering.

Oh my God.

I open my mouth to—to—*apologize*, maybe, even though it's just as much his fault as mine—when his brown eyes flick back up to meet mine, narrowed. The words stumble over my tongue, and suddenly I have nothing to say at all, even though everything inside me feels alert, on edge, *alive*.

"Is this meant to endear me to you?" he asks, his voice

deep and slow, like warm molasses. "Because it's doing quite the opposite."

I blink, trying to make sense of the words, some of my adrenaline fizzling out. He has a British accent, lilting the vowels of his sentences, only further throwing me for a loop. *Do* we know each other? It would be just my luck to forget his existence.

I ignore the goose bumps spreading across my arms in favor of scanning him for clues. Nothing is clicking, even as I take in the black hair spilling across his forehead like wet ink, the jawline sharp enough to chisel granite, and the faint moles scattered across his neck. Something about the three piercings in his left ear tugs at my memory, but it's not quite enough.

"I don't believe we've met," I say finally, and the words are lifeless, even though I don't mean for them to come out that way. Maybe if I was a little less exhausted, maybe if his stare was a little less harsh, maybe if the world had been a *little* kinder today, I could offer this boy as a smile.

But I can't.

The boy's mouth presses into a thin line, a dimple indenting one of his cheeks. "You're going to lie to me?"

I stare at him in bemusement. "*Excuse* me?"

"I know you're angling for a picture," he says darkly. "You could've been straightforward about your intentions, instead of pretending to bump into me." He leans down, picking up his phone with a disgusted look on his face. "It would have at least saved me the trouble of purchasing a new phone."

Something shifts in my chest, uncomfortable and obtrusive, leaving me distinctly off-balance. "Right. It's not as if my phone is also currently lying on the wet sidewalk. Let me go ahead and take a picture of you with my brain. *Click.* How was that? I'll save it to my folder of random strangers I've never met in my life."

The boy raises a perfectly groomed eyebrow at me. "You recognized me earlier. I could tell. Are you going to pretend otherwise?"

"I don't know who you are," I say flatly, unable to put forward any other emotion.

An unfriendly smirk tugs at the boy's mouth, familiar and yet somehow not. "Are you sure, love? Because you're still standing in my way. You could stand to be a little less desperate—"

"What?" I ask, lips moving without permission. His words are slowly sinking in, but they still don't make any sense. What is *happening* right now? And why is he being such a condescending ass? Is the entire world taking a shit on me for fun?

He falters, blinking at me. "I said you could stand to be a little less desperate—"

"*Seriously?*" I ask. Now that the initial shock is fading, I'm left with nothing except irritation. It wasn't enough to be cold, wet, and on the brink of tears, but now there's a random boy *patronizing* me? Because he thinks I recognize him when I don't? He might be drop-dead gorgeous, but my bad mood doesn't care much for objective beauty—especially if it comes with a shitty personality. "Don't talk to me like that. I don't care who you are."

Almost deliberately, the boy looks me up and down, his eyes trailing across my skin like a whip. "If that's what you have to tell yourself to sleep at night. But we both know the truth."

I blink at him, my brain buzzing faintly. He's still staring at me, a wisp of a condescending grin on his face, as if to say, *I caught you.*

"Do we?" I stare at him for a long time, my gaze listless. "Do you?"

The boy's brows draw together, but the arrogance continues dripping off him, as unrelenting as the rain around us. "Of course I do."

I tilt my head. "Okay."

The longer I stare at him, the more his certainty seems to fade. "I do," he says again, his voice icy.

I blink slowly, a mocking smile parting my lips. "You're right. You do."

The boy straightens, some of his confidence returning. I can't help the resentment that slithers through me, wishing I could recover like that from a blow. Then maybe my family wouldn't have this much control over me. "I knew it—"

"I know exactly who you are," I say, cutting him off. "A dickhead that takes pride in belittling others. The kind with an inflated sense of self-importance, who thinks he's better than everyone around him." I mimic his earlier behavior, looking him up and down pointedly. "Though I can't imagine why."

The boy's gaze turns cold, his mouth cutting a cruel line. "Are you always this rude to strangers? Who raised you?"

My entire body stills. *My parents,* I think, the thought sharp and jagged. *My parents are the reason I'm like this. Is that what you want to hear?*

I don't say that. I couldn't even if I wanted to.

Instead, I say, "Leave me alone," and reach down to grab

my phone and umbrella. The umbrella is more or less a lost cause, but my phone miraculously survived the fall, unlike his.

I feel a brief pang of regret, but it fades when I see a text from Anam, promising to keep my seat warm. I'm going to be really late at this rate. The thought heightens the unpleasant heat simmering low in my stomach. It doesn't help that my clothes are sticking to me like glue now. Again, the urge to just sit down and *cry* hits me, but I push it back, ignoring how my throat is slowly closing.

"What's wrong with you?" the boy asks, drawing my attention back to him. "You don't have to be…" He trails off, his eyes narrowed, sharpening his beauty beyond words.

"Such a bitch?" I ask roughly. "No, go ahead. Say it. Say it with your whole chest."

A muscle slides in the boy's jaw. "I wasn't going to say that. I happen to have manners."

I laugh, but the sound falls flat. My brain is too sluggish to even attempt to continue this awful conversation. First my parents, then Rosie, then Grant, and now this? Can this day end already? "I'm sure you do."

The boy huffs, crossing his arms. I keep my gaze focused on his face rather than the rivulets of water trailing across his bare forearms, the sleeves of his hoodie rolled up. He doesn't even have a jacket on. It's *January*.

God, I don't have time for this.

"Get out of my way, would you?" I give the boy an unimpressed look when he doesn't move. The nearest deli is around the corner, and I can only hope they have umbrellas in stock—and maybe, just maybe, some bell peppers.

The boy keeps staring at me. Is he really not going to

move? The longer I stand out here, the more likely I am to *snap* and lose my shit. Or maybe just burst into tears. I swallow past the lump in my throat, forcing down the grief attempting to choke me.

"I have better things to do than stand around arguing with you," I say, my voice surprisingly even. "If you won't move, I will."

I shove my shoulder into the boy's, pushing past him. It becomes clear that he towers several inches over me, but I focus more on the sudden inhale that escapes him and the way his entire body seems to tense. A rush of vindication spreads through me, and I almost smile despite the heavy feeling weighing down my bones.

Sometimes taking pride in the small victories is all one can do. I know that lesson far too well.

4

A few minutes later, I stand in front of the deli, my hands shaking from the cold. Two girls from AAAS are lingering outside, underneath the deli's awning, shielding themselves from the rain. One of them gives me a sympathetic look as I head inside, which does nothing for my awful mood.

"Do you have bell peppers?" I ask the man behind a counter.

He nods, pointing me toward the back of the store. A rack of umbrellas hangs behind his head—something to come back for.

"Thank you," I say, relief rushing through me. I ignore the buzz of my phone in my pocket. I don't need another reminder of how late I'm running.

The bell above the door rings again as I make my way toward the produce aisle, but I don't look over my shoulder, focused on my task—not until I hear a British accent ask, "Do you have a map?"

I swivel around in disbelief. Is he *following* me?

But the boy is focused entirely on the man behind the counter. It almost looks like he's trying to hide, his hood pulled up and his sleeves rolled all the way down.

I turn back around, resisting the urge to grumble as I pick out a handful of bell peppers. As if I wouldn't be able to tell it's the same person.

The boy's voice echoes through the store. "Can I have this, then? And this?"

I glance over again, unable to help myself. The boy is fidgeting with his sleeves and keeps glancing toward the storefront, where the AAAS girls are. They're giggling loudly enough that I can hear it over the sound of the storm.

At least someone is having a good day. I can only pray mine will improve once this boy buys whatever is on the counter and *leaves*.

I turn back around, facing the opposite shelf. After a moment's hesitation, I grab a pack of Oreos for Anam. It's a thinly veiled apology, but it'll have to do.

A strange clicking sound goes off, and belatedly, I realize it's the sound of a camera shutter. Slowly, I face the front of the aisle, counting down from ten to keep from throwing something at the boy who's still somehow here.

"Are you taking *pictures* of me?" I ask, grinding my teeth together.

The boy blinks, setting down the disposable camera to look at me, his eyes flashing in recognition. Then he scoffs. "As if. I was taking a picture of the sign."

My gaze narrows. "What sign?"

The boy gives me a dark look and points behind me. I glance over my shoulder to see a handwritten sign that reads:

CUSTOMERS WELCOME
(FAMILY AND FRIENDS BY APPOINTMENT)

Oh.

An irrational wave of irritation rises up inside me at him pulling one over on me, and I promptly decide I am *not* dealing with this today. I've hit my threshold of bullshit.

I turn on my heel, taking the long way around the aisle to go up to the counter. I set down the Oreos and bell peppers without a word, and the man behind the counter raises his brows but rings them both up.

Naturally, the boy shows up at my side again. "Bag an umbrella for her, too. I'll pay for it."

"Piss off," I say, the words hissed. "I can buy my own umbrella."

The boy smiles, an edge to the curve of his lips. "I said I'll pay for it," he says, before pointedly looking down at his hands, where he's holding the disposable camera in one hand and his water-damaged phone in the other. "I take responsibility for my mistakes."

I bristle at the implication and open my mouth to snap at him, but one of the AAAS girls comes inside the store before I can.

"Do any of you know where Astoria Bookshop is? Hannah's phone just died and I'm not getting any service," she says. There's something strange about her tone, but I don't care enough to mull over it.

Instead, I nod, gesturing up the block. "Yeah, absolutely. Go up until you hit Thirty-First Street and then walk down the avenues. You should see it on the way there. It's a block off from the NW train at Broadway."

"Thank you," she says brightly, then casts a look toward the boy. "Hey, you probably get this question a lot, but are you—?"

"No," he says, his tone leaving no room for argument. He's turned away, his face mostly hidden by his hood. "Goodbye."

The girl blinks. "Okay then. Jeez." She offers me a more toned-down smile. "Thanks again."

I offer her a grimace, all too familiar with how rude the boy beside me can be. "No worries."

Once the door closes behind her, I turn back to the counter. "Just the bell peppers and Oreos. I don't need an umbrella," I say, half out of spite. I might regret it the moment I exit the store, but I'm not giving this dickhead the satisfaction.

"You're being ridiculous, love," the boy mutters.

I don't bother with a response, grabbing my bag and leaving without a single glance backward. Knowing my luck, the subway is probably delayed, too.

Before I can get halfway down the block, fingers wrap around my wrist, slippery against my wet skin. I stare at the boy's hand incredulously, half a dozen rings splayed across his fingers. "What," I ask quietly to keep from *screaming*, "are you doing?"

The boy drops my wrist, but the cold imprint of his rings

lingers on my skin. He shifts almost uncomfortably before he says, "I was wondering if you could give me directions to—"

I hold a hand up, cutting him off midsentence. He falters, but the way his brows are arched reeks of arrogance, as if he can't believe I have the nerve to interrupt him.

What an asshole.

"Here's a direction," I say hoarsely, before pointedly lowering four of my fingers. "Get fucked, *love.*"

Then I turn around and walk away without another word. I can almost feel the heat of his glare on the back of my neck, but I couldn't care less. I have a movie marathon to attend.

By the time I get to the train station and swipe my Metro-Card, I'm shivering uncontrollably and considering a lawsuit against the boy from the rain. Screw that dude. Seriously.

A homeless guy sprawled out on one of the benches gives *me* a pitying look, confirming that I look like a wet rat.

I sigh, dropping five dollars into the jar beside him before walking down the platform, tugging off my jacket as I go. Even though the thick air in the subway is absolutely disgusting, at least I'm drier than I was outside.

God, I hate New York City. The weather is so shitty, strangers are so goddamn entitled, and the public transportation is *never* on time. Everything about this city drives me up the wall. The day I finally leave this place behind is going to be the happiest day of my life.

I stand there for a minute, dripping onto the platform, the heels of my palms digging into my eyes. No tears. Not today.

Just two more months. *Just two more months.*

"Ugh," I say out loud, resisting the urge to text Rosie in

a half-hysterical fit. Instead, I pull up Anam's contact and say: pick the movie w/o me.

ANAM RAHMAN: shouldn't you be here by now tho??

ME: I'm running late I'm sorryyyyy

ANAM RAHMAN: what happened to never being late !!!

ME: shut upppp I said I'm sorry ok just pick anything that DOESN'T have british actors!!! if I have to hear another british accent today I'm gonna lose my mind

I take a deep breath as the R train approaches and attempt to blow out the negative energy encasing my heart. I squirm into a packed car and ignore my phone buzzing against my thigh, since I don't have the elbow room to text anyway.

ANAM RAHMAN: again??? wdym

ANAM RAHMAN: also how tf am I supposed to know if an actor is british or not

ANAM RAHMAN: apu I'm not googling every single actor in these movies

ANAM RAHMAN: WHY AREN'T YOU RESPONDING I'M SERIOUS I'M NOT GOOGLING THEM

ANAM RAHMAN: ok I'm googling them

ANAM RAHMAN: bro wtf there are so many british actors,,,,

ANAM RAHMAN: wait u still haven't told me why we can't watch stuff with british accents?? what is going onnnn

ANAM RAHMAN: fuck this let's just watch tangled for the 50th time

ANAM RAHMAN: ...taking that as a yes?

ANAM RAHMAN: the snapchat map says you're literally ten minutes away TEXT ME BACK

ME: sorry sorry

ME: also. uhhhhh

ME: I'm outside and forgot my keys

ANAM RAHMAN: I can't stand you

ANAM RAHMAN: omw

The moment our family steps into Nazifa's living room on Saturday night, my mom shoots Anam and me a look dark enough to make a lesser man shrivel. I ignore her, but Anam glares back, crossing her arms over her chest.

I don't have to read minds to know why my mom is upset. Anam and I came to the party wearing sweaters and jeans— Nazifa and her sister are wearing beautiful fatuas. Nazifa offers me an apologetic smile and I shake my head. It's not their fault.

"As-salaam alaikum," I say to the room at large. Half a dozen brown aunties are sitting around—though none of them are related to me, they're considered my aunties all the same—and they all say some variation of a cheerful "Wa-alaikum salaam" in return.

"Poppy, it's so nice to see you," Mishti Auntie, Nazifa's mom, says. She's serving jhalmuri to the guests but stops to smile at us. My mouth waters at the sight of it. The food at Bangladeshi community parties is inarguably the best, and it's always what I look forward to most. "Anam, I heard your volleyball team won against Bronx Science last week?"

Anam grins, grabbing a puri off the coffee table in front of us. "We destroyed them."

"Mashallah," Mishti Auntie says, grinning back. "Nazifa said you two are playing against each other next month. Are you excited?"

"I am," Anam says, leaning over to poke Nazifa's shoulder with her free hand, wiggling her brows in challenge. "Are you planning to come, Mishti Auntie?"

"Wouldn't miss it," Mishti Auntie says, and none of us look at my mom, who's quietly seething with rage.

It's common knowledge that Ma and Baba never come to Anam's volleyball games.

"We should go upstairs," I say, grabbing Anam's hand, pulling her away before she can cause a scene, because I have no doubt that's where this is heading. "*Please* save me some jhalmuri, Mishti Auntie! I'll come back for it later."

Anam sighs but follows me to Nazifa's bedroom. Nazifa's older sister, Syeda, closes the door behind us, but not without snatching a plastic box full of jilapi.

"You are such a troublemaker," I say to Anam, throwing myself onto one of the bean bags on the floor. Syeda joins me, offering me a consoling pat on the head. "You know we're going to be yelled at when we go home tonight."

"Well, screw that," Anam says, sitting down on Nazifa's bed with a grunt. "Can we trade families, Nazifa?"

"Absolutely not," Nazifa says, snorting as she takes a seat beside Anam after stealing a jilapi from her sister. "Your mom is *terrifying*."

"Cheers to that," I mutter, digging the heels of my palms into my eyes. My brain is still sluggish, trying to recover from the disaster of yesterday. Watching *Tangled* (2010) with Anam helped, but there's still a strange tension in my gut, and thinking about the inevitable fight with my mother tonight doesn't help.

"I don't get why she has to be like that all the time," Anam grumbles, breaking off a piece of Nazifa's jilapi and shoving it in her mouth. "She could take a night off once in a while."

Syeda snorts, her eyes bright with fond amusement. Nazifa is Anam's age, but Syeda is the oldest out of all of us, in her sophomore year of college. I've always struggled to comprehend why she would want to live at home and commute to college—but then I have to remind myself Syeda is majoring in fashion design and her family *encourages* her to pursue her dreams.

If I think about it too long, I get overwhelmingly sad. I wish my parents didn't care so much about appearances. I wish our happiness was enough.

"You guys truly won the lottery," I say, and I can't help how wistful I sound. "How come everyone has amazing parents except for us?"

Syeda sets down the box of jilapi, squeezing my shoulder.

"Hey, everyone fights with their family. It's a normal part of growing up."

"But this doesn't feel like a fight. It feels like a war. And Anam and I somehow *always* lose." I lean my head against the wall, looking up at the ceiling. "I bet if you murdered someone, your mom would help you hide the body."

"I don't know about *that*," Nazifa says, but I can hear the soft smile in her voice. "Ma and Baba are wonderful, but we still have rules to follow, you know? Murder might be out of the cards."

"Okay, maybe not *murder*, but your parents love you guys more than they love their rules," Anam says bitterly. "Which is how a family *should* be, but whatever." She shakes her head, her blue curls bouncing erratically as she pastes on a forced smile. "What's the plan for tonight?"

Both Nazifa and Syeda give us sympathetic looks but roll with the subject change, which I appreciate more than I can put into words. Talking about any of this at length always makes me want to curl into a ball.

"Apu has to finish up a project for school," Nazifa says, nodding her head toward Syeda. "So I thought we could just watch a movie while we wait? Baba said dinner is around ten, so we have some time to kill."

"What are you working on?" I ask, turning toward Syeda.

Syeda's expression lights up. "We have to design an article of clothing for one of my classes using techniques from a different time period. I've been working on a line of hijabs using techniques from the 1920s. My professor thinks it's a great idea, so I'm pretty sure I'll get an A, but I still have to finish writing up my research paper for it."

"That sounds amazing," I say, my lips curving up. Just a few more months, and I'll be in Syeda's place, working on all kinds of film projects that I'm passionate about. "Can I see some of them?"

Syeda jumps to her feet with a grin. "Of course."

When we leave the room, I feel like I can breathe easier, finally leaving behind any tendrils of the conversation about my parents.

Syeda leads me down the hall, and we pass a handful of aunties on the way, all of them cooing over how grown-up we are, as if we hadn't seen them only two months prior. I let them ruffle my hair with a fond shake of my head, and Syeda bats them away without any real intent, laughing the entire time. When we finally get to Syeda's room, there are clothes strung up all over the room, draped over the furniture and cheap mannequins. A line of hijabs is hung above Syeda's desk and I immediately gravitate toward them, eyes wide. "These are beautiful."

Syeda smiles. "This one is made from silk, this one from satin, this one from cashmere, this one—"

"I have absolutely no idea what the difference is, but keep talking anyway," I say, reaching out to touch one of them, the fabric soft against my fingers. "I have no idea how you do it. I could never make something like this."

Syeda snorts. "You stick to films, I'll stick to fashion."

I point finger guns at her. "Perfect." I look back at the hijabs, considering them. "It's so cool that you're following your dreams. Mishti Auntie and Farhan Uncle must be so proud."

She nudges me with a shoulder. "Give yourself some credit.

It'll be you soon enough. College is honestly amazing, Poppy. I know you'll love it."

I shrug, dropping my hand. There's a cloud hanging above my head, and the last thing I want is for her—or anyone—to see it. "Yeah, well. I'll let you get back to your essay, but you've got to let me borrow one of these hijabs for the Eid jamaat, okay?"

"Only if you promise to let me borrow your Netflix password," Syeda says back, but she's grinning again as she considers her own work. "Or else I'll have to bother Anam when you're at USC."

"It's a deal," I say, and turn away before my own smile can fall.

A few minutes later, I come back to Nazifa's room to see her and Anam crowded around a laptop. I wrinkle my nose, trying to get a good look at the screen. "What did you guys choose?"

Anam rolls her eyes, but her smile is more earnest now. "Don't worry, we picked from your preapproved list of films."

"As you should," I say, and join them on the bed, wiggling in beside Anam. "So which one is it?"

"Something called *The Silent Clock*?" Anam shrugs. "Nazifa picked it randomly from your list."

"Oh! Yeah, it's a British indie film, about this boy who finds an ancestral clock in his attic. He think it's broken, but… well." I grin, finally at ease. "You'll see."

"Already over your British-accent aversion?" Anam asks, raising her brows. "That was quick."

"Well, it's not like—" I cut off, staring at the screen as the main character shows up, walking down a busy London street. It's only his back, but something about it looks… "No. Holy shit, *no.*"

I scramble for the laptop, trying to bring it closer, but the sheets slide under me and I fall off the bed instead, hitting the floor with a loud thud. My head bangs against the bed frame, but I barely process it.

"Oh my God," Nazifa says under her breath. "Are you okay, Poppy? What—?"

"Give me the laptop right now," I say desperately, clawing at the sheets to sit back upright. My mind feels like it's on the edge of snapping in half. *"Give it to me."*

Anam is watching me with wide eyes but she passes me the laptop regardless. "What's wrong with you?"

"Shut up for a second," I say, sliding my finger along the mouse pad, taking us to the halfway point of the movie, trying to find a scene where the actor is facing forward.

"Don't tell me to shut up," Anam says half-heartedly, but she's looking over my shoulder with rapt awareness. Nazifa is staring at me like I've lost my shit, and she's not wrong.

There's no way this is happening. There's *no way* this is happening. The world has to be playing a cruel joke on me. Someone is going to jump out at any point and announce that I'm being punk'd.

"Oh my God," I say, as the movie finally pauses on a scene where the actor is looking straight at the camera, a familiar smile on his lips. "Oh my *God.*"

The boy in the rain yesterday was Emmitt Ramos.

Emmitt Ramos, the indie film star. Emmitt Ramos, half Chinese, half Spanish, grew up in London, slowly rising in the film industry for his international work. Emmitt Ramos, known for being a heartbreaker on set and an asshole during press junkets.

Emmitt Ramos, who I told to get *fucked*.

"This isn't happening to me," I say, half-hysterical. *"This can't be happening to me."*

"What is going *on*?" Anam demands, shaking my shoulder roughly. "Are you okay? What the fuck is wrong with you, Apu?"

"That—that's the boy I ran into yesterday," I say, pointing at the screen with a shaking finger. "Shit. *Shit.*"

"What?" Anam's head snaps back to the laptop. *"What? Are you joking?"*

"Do I look like I'm joking?" I ask, nearly screeching. "Oh my God, I'm going to *end my shit.*"

"What is going on?" Nazifa asks, looking between us, bewildered. "You met this actor dude yesterday?"

"Oh no," I say again, dropping my head onto the bed with a loud groan. How could I not realize who he was? I *knew* there was something familiar about him. His three earrings should've tipped me off. It's a known staple of Emmitt Ramos. And he—*that's* why he thought I wanted a picture with him. He thought I crashed into him on purpose so I could— Oh my God."

And worse…if I had been just a little more vigilant, I might have been able to ask him if he'd consider a brief cameo in our short film. Instead, I called him a dickhead to his face.

How could I be so *stupid*?

"This is the worst week of my life," I announce, my words muffled by the sheets.

Anam pulls my head into her lap, combing her fingers

through my hair. Her voice is soothing when she murmurs, "It's okay, Apu. You never have to see him again. Just pretend it never happened."

I just groan again.

After a long beat of silence, Nazifa says, "So… I'll pick another movie, then?"

"*Please.*"

5

After a weekend of moping in my room and avoiding my parents like the plague, school is a welcome reprieve on Monday morning. That's how I know my life is miserable—I actually look forward to sitting in a desk for seven hours a day.

I part ways with Anam at the door, watching as she runs off to find her volleyball teammates the second I let go of her.

As I pass through the cafeteria, I wave at some of the underclassmen from film club, and they eagerly wave back. I try not to think about how I potentially blew an amazing opportunity for the entire club by letting my bad mood get the best of me on Friday. It doesn't help anyone to be remorseful now. I can't exactly change the past.

"Rosie is looking for you!" one of them calls.

I nod, gesturing to my phone, which has seven unread texts from Rosie, most of which are keyboard smash. "So I've heard."

When I reach Rosie's locker, her head is buried inside of

it. I gently poke her arm, trying to gain her attention. She doesn't move but acknowledges my presence with a low groan. "Kill me," she says.

"What's in it for me?" I ask, leaning my shoulder against the locker beside hers. When she only groans again, I nudge her. "What's wrong? I'm usually able to decipher your texts, but these were just pure chaos."

She finally pulls her head out of her locker, her hair in disarray. I lean forward, picking a red curl out of her mouth. If I didn't know better, I'd think she heard about my celebrity encounter. As it is, I'm pretty sure Rosie would be trying to kill *me*, rather than asking me to kill her, if that were the case.

"Mina," Rosie says, her voice frighteningly solemn. "I'm going to die."

I pause, waiting for more information to come forward, but Rosie seems content to leave it at that. "Why?"

"Sofia asked me to *run lines* with her," Rosie says in the same awful voice I used Saturday night to explain the Emmitt Ramos situation to Nazifa and Syeda. Their response was to laugh at me while I pouted.

With that in mind, I try to be a good friend instead and consider Rosie's situation seriously.

"Sofia from drama club?" I purse my lips. "I guess it makes sense she'd want to be in our film. She was a good Rizzo in *Grease* last year. Are you worried that running lines with her might be unfair to the other people auditioning?"

"What? No," Rosie says, giving me an incredulous look. "Forget the film. She asked me to *run lines*."

I frown at her. "Am I missing something? Does run lines mean something different to you than it does to me?"

Rosie shakes me slightly. "Mina, it means she wants to spend time with me *alone*. I'm going to die."

The pieces finally click together in my brain. "Oh my God, Rosie, come on." I flick her forehead. "Get it together. Just run the lines with her."

"You don't understand," Rosie says insistently, her blue eyes wide. "I can't. Have you *seen* Sofia? She—she has pink hair! She's like a bubblegum fairy princess come to life! She's literally the most beautiful person I've ever laid eyes on. I can't spend time with her. I'll have a gay panic attack if I even breathe the same *air* as her."

I shake my head. "Just run the lines with her. She asked you to. Plus, she's bi, isn't she?"

Rosie moans pathetically, shoving her face in my shoulder. I stumble back in surprise before managing to regain my balance. "Yeah, but she only broke up with her ex-boyfriend like a *month* ago."

"Okay, then maybe it'll help if you just focus on the film," I say, patting her head absently. "Keep your feelings out of it."

"We can't all be like you," Rosie mumbles into my sweater.

My hand stills. For some reason, the words sting. I'm not sure why, since she's not *wrong*, but hearing it aloud feels like sucking on a sour lemon.

I force myself to laugh. "The world would be a much more productive place if everyone could channel my energy."

"Productive, maybe," Rosie says. She doesn't say it, but I can hear the *Happy? No.*

I pull away, nudging her upright, and try not to feel hurt. I know she didn't mean it like that, but it's not as if I chose to have depression. If I could get rid of gut-wrenching sadness that weighs most of my actions, I would. There are better weeks and there are worse weeks. This week is somewhere in the middle.

My obsession with winning the competition is the only way I know how to get through the day right now. It gives me something to keep reaching for. It gives me a purpose. Most importantly, it gives me hope.

"Productive, definitely," I say with a flimsy smile. "Listen, I need to go to my locker, but I'll meet you at Italian."

I turn away before Rosie can read my expression, certain that she'll pick me apart in less than a minute if I linger.

Given the last few days, I don't want to know what she'll find hidden in the lines of my face.

I'm the first person in the classroom aside from Miss Turano. Her eyes dart to the space beside me instinctively for Rosie before returning to me, a curious look in her eyes.

I don't say anything, offering her a nod and taking my seat in the front.

Miss Turano squints, but she doesn't press me for details. As disruptive as Rosie is—and I am, by association—we're both arguably the best students in her class, and she adores us. She even wrote one of my college recommendations.

Eventually, she turns back to the whiteboard and I take out my script, once again looking through for any lines that might need tweaking. There are still ten minutes before first period starts, and I plan to spend it doing what I do best.

My only distraction is the sunlight streaming through the second-floor window, almost too bright. I pull my hood up, shielding my eyes moderately, before I continue reading through the script.

I barely notice time passing by until the bell rings and Rosie slides into the seat beside me, dropping her binder with a loud thunk. I instantly look up, my hood falling down with the sudden movement.

"I thought you were running late," she says, furrowing her brows at me. "We usually meet outside."

I gesture to the pile of paper on my desk, ignoring the way my skin is prickling. "Sorry, I was just reworking some lines."

Rosie nods, but there's still a hint of a frown at the corner of her mouth. But then her eyes flicker behind me and she leans in, whispering, "Did you notice the new kid?"

"The new kid?" I repeat. We're in AP Italian, and it's the second semester. How can there be a new kid?

I turn around in my seat, trying to pick out which one of our classmates Rosie is talking about. I spot him in the back, sitting next to Grant. His face is turned away from us but his messy golden-blond hair is distinct enough that I know Rosie is right. He's not from our class.

"Does Grant know him?" I ask, unable to resist leaning farther out of my seat to catch a better look at the stranger.

The boy in the seat behind me, Kevin, perks up in interest. "Grant knows the new kid?"

"I have no idea." I wonder if Miss Turano would be upset if I launched something at Grant's head to grab his attention.

I already know Rosie will nag me all period if we don't find out more about the new kid. I'm willing to throw a paper ball if it saves me in the long run.

The girl sitting across from me diagonally is also eyeing

the back of the room with raised eyebrows. In fact, *everyone* is more or less looking at the back of the room.

Maybe in a calculus or history class, it wouldn't be as obvious, but in our class of seventeen, it's easy to spot something amiss. Our class has had the same students and same teacher since freshmen year, as our school offers only one Italian course. This is highly unusual.

And then the blond boy faces forward, and a collective silence floods the room as we all see his face for the first time.

Or, for me, the second time.

Emmitt Ramos.

Emmitt Ramos is sitting in the back of my Italian classroom.

Emmitt Ramos dyed his hair blond and is sitting in the back of my Italian classroom.

"Rosie," I say in a panicked hiss, prior dejection all but forgotten. What is he *doing* here? "Do you know who that is?"

"Am I supposed to?" she asks, equally as quiet. Her eyes are wide as they dart between Emmitt and me. "Do *you* know who that is?"

I turn around, scrawling Emmitt's name on the corner of my script and pointing at it deliberately.

Rosie inhales sharply. "Holy shit." Her head snaps up, turning to look at Emmitt again, taking in his features with a more critical eye. "Holy shit."

"So you guys know who that is?" Kevin asks, looking between us.

"No," I say immediately, even though I'm now regretting every life decision I've ever made. After Saturday night, I felt so ashamed about the whole situation with Emmitt that I decided to keep it to myself. Anam, Nazifa, and Syeda were enough witnesses to my stupidity. I didn't want to add anyone else to the list.

Not that it matters now.

"No, we don't," Rosie says, backing me up without a second thought, but she's nearly vibrating in her seat.

Kevin doesn't seem to believe us, but I couldn't care less.

Across the room, Emmitt finally catches sight of me, and whatever he was saying to Grant dies on his lips.

His features draw tight as he clenches his jaw. Then he gives me this look—this awful, condescending, arrogant *look*, like I'm the worst kind of human being, like he's appalled we're even sharing the same breathing space.

I flinch internally, but a different part of me flares up with irritation. I may have been rude to him, but he wasn't any better.

I consider the twist of his mouth and I'm reminded of last Friday, of nearly being in tears while he stood there and *smirked* at me. And all at once, the built-up resentment in me rises in the form of a reckless idea.

But what do I have to lose? After all, he's already made it clear I haven't endeared myself to him.

"Miss Turano," I say, raising my hand. When she nods, I take it as an invitation to continue. "I can't help but notice we have a new student. Since we're in an AP course, I think it'd be great if he could introduce himself in Italian. It'd be good practice for all of us, don't you think?"

"Mina, what are you doing?" Rosie whispers, but I'm too busy watching Miss Turano hopefully to notice.

Miss Turano looks bemused but offers me a smile. "That's

a great idea." She looks at Emmitt, making an encouraging gesture. "If you will?"

Emmitt's dark brown eyes flicker around the room, as if he's hoping the answer will present itself to him. I *knew* it. Of course he doesn't know Italian. Why would he?

He must have an ulterior reason for being here. The question is: what is it?

Grant whispers something to him and Emmitt clears his throat. "Mi chiamo Ezra Rivera."

Oh my God, he's even faking an American accent. This is ridiculous.

I clear my throat. "E? Di dove sei? Quanti anni hai? Conosci Grant? Come?"

And? Where are you from? How old are you? Do you know Grant? How?

Emmitt's hands curl into fists, gripping onto the edge of his desk, his knuckles turning white.

"Puoi rispondere?" I ask quietly when only silence prevails.

"I'm sorry, I think I'm in the wrong class," Emmitt says, getting to his feet. If heat vision existed, I'm certain I'd be set aflame from the daggers he's aiming my way. As it is, I remain impassive in the face of it.

Emmitt grabs his things hastily, shoving them into his bag, before moving toward the door. I watch him go, leaning my chin against the back of my chair. He turns for only half a second as he leaves, and I offer him a wave. He stumbles in the doorway, a scowl taking over his handsome features, before he disappears into the hallway.

Almost immediately, Grant runs after him, saying, "Sorry, Miss Turano, sorry!" as he leaves the room.

Miss Turano stares at the closed door, clearly at a loss.

A beat of silence passes.

Kevin mutters, "You definitely know him," and I loosen a deep breath, turning back to face the front of the room.

Another beat of silence.

"What," Rosie whispers emphatically, "the fuck?"

6

Rosie doesn't have a chance to corner me until lunch. When she finds me at my locker, the look on her face makes me want to run in the other direction.

"Stop looking at me like that," I say, pointedly turning away from her to find my economics textbook. My locker is covered in screencaps from my favorite films, organized randomly with *Pride and Prejudice* (2005) hanging near the top, and *Om Shanti Om* (2007) taped near the bottom.

Rosie flicks my nose, making me sneeze and consequently knock my head into *Moonlight* (2016) and *Train to Busan* (2016). They both flutter to the ground.

I sigh, reaching for the tape in the back of my locker while Rosie picks up the pictures with an apologetic look on her face.

"Sorry," she says, but then holds the pictures out of reach when I move to take them back. "Hey. Listen. We need Emmitt's help."

"For what?" I ask, playing dumb. It's pointless because what transpired between us is going to come out sooner or later, but I'd like to put it off as long as possible.

Rosie gives me an incredulous look. "What do you mean for what? I'm surprised you didn't think of it first."

"Think of what?" I ask, refusing to meet her gaze.

"You know what—forget that for a moment. What even *was* that this morning?" Rosie says, poking my shoulder roughly. "He looked like he knew you. How could he know you?"

My nose wrinkles. Well. That was nice while it lasted. "I… might have run into him on Friday, after your dad picked you up."

Rosie audibly gasps. "*What?* And you didn't say anything?"

"I thought I was imagining it," I mutter, resisting the urge to stick out my bottom lip. The few people lingering in the hallway don't even give us a second glance, used to associating the film club with dramatics. "What are the odds he's in New York City just casually taking a walk in the rain near our high school? Come on."

"Well, apparently the odds are high!" Rosie throws her hands up. "What happened? Did you talk to him?"

I wince and finally recount the whole situation to her. Rosie's jaw drops lower and lower until she's nearly on the floor, holding her head in her hands. "Mina, are you actively trying to ruin our lives?"

"He deserved it!" I say. I was expecting a *little* more sympathy from Rosie, so this is throwing me for a loop. "Come on, Ro. He treated me like I was the dirt beneath his feet. That's an asshole move."

"It is," Rosie says in agreement, which mollifies me somewhat. "If this were any other situation, I'd agree that he deserves to choke."

I sigh, already knowing what's coming. "But?"

"*But* he's a celebrity!" She rises to her feet, reaching out to shake my shoulders.

"I know," I grumble, pushing her off. "It's still not an excuse to be an absolute dickhead."

"I agree," Rosie says again, and I consider banging my head against the lockers. "But he's a celebrity. In our school. And in case you forgot, we are in *desperate* need of someone famous to be in our film."

"I didn't forget," I say under my breath. "I just… I didn't recognize him until later. And then it was too late."

"What about this morning?" Rosie asks, running her hands through her hair in distress. "I know you recognized him then! And you *embarrassed* him in front of our entire Italian class."

"Did you see the way he looked at me?" I protest. "It's not my fault!"

Rosie shakes her head. "You have to go apologize. Like, as soon as possible."

"*Apologize?*"

"You have to," Rosie says, looking at me through a curtain of red curls. "You have to, Mina."

"He's not going to say yes, Rosie," I say, holding back a scowl. "He barely promotes his own films. He's not going to agree to be in a student film where he's not even getting *paid*."

"Then you have to convince him!" Rosie says, finally dropping the pictures of *Moonlight* and *Train to Busan* into my locker, though both of them are crumpled now. I'll have to reprint them. I try to focus on that rather than the nonsense Rosie is spewing at me. "Put on your game face, dress up for battle. Whatever it is you have to do, just *do it*. This is life or death."

"Why can't *you* do it?" I ask, turning my glower on my locker instead of her, grabbing my Nutritional Science notebook from the back.

This isn't fair. The last thing I want to do is apologize to Emmitt Ramos.

She gapes at me. "Because I'm gay!"

"So *what*?" I turn to her incredulously. "You can't use that as an excuse to get out of everything."

"Yes, I can! What if you have to seduce him to get him to agree? I can't seduce him! It has to be you!"

"*Seduce* him?" I repeat hysterically. "You think I'm going to seduce him? Are you out of your goddamn mind?"

Rosie shakes her head. "I'm being absolutely serious right now. If you have to seduce him, you better go in there and fucking seduce the shit out of him. You already insulted him *multiple times*! You have to take one for the team!"

I open my mouth to protest, but Rosie slams my locker shut, startling me. "Think about the competition! Think about the judges! You *know* having Emmitt in our movie will make waves in the film community. I checked his IMDb, and he's supposed to be in the next Firebrand Studios movie, *Mina*. *Firebrand*. They're almost as big as Marvel and DC. He's going to blow up and become mainstream in no time. I bet you regretted losing your temper at him the moment you realized who he was. Don't lie to me!"

I take a deep breath to keep from screaming incoherently. She's right. Of course she's right.

The minute I got home Saturday night, I also checked his IMDb page and followed up by searching Twitter for mentions of his name. The results were half people mentioning his role in the Firebrand Studios movie and half people keyboard smashing about how they want to have his children. I spent all of Sunday mourning the missed opportunity. I know I should have been more levelheaded this morning, but it's hard when I have to stare at Emmitt's *stupid* face and his *stupid* hair and his *stupid* smirk—

Calm. I have to stay calm.

Emmitt might just be an indie film star right now, unrecognizable by the general public, but a year from now...

A year from now, the internet will devour him.

And having him in our short film will put us one step closer to victory.

Rosie and I both know it.

I swallow uncomfortably, weighing my wants versus my needs. Even though I want the earth to swallow Emmitt whole, I *need* to win the Golden Ivy Film Festival.

Goddammit.

"Does it have to be me?" I ask in a small voice, my shoulders slumping with resignation.

Rosie nods, but her face softens. "Listen, just do your best, okay? If he says no, at least we know we tried. Just say sorry and try to win him over."

Ugh.

"I hate you," I say, but both of us know that's far from the truth. "And I hate him." Not as far from the truth.

"Hate him as much as you want," Rosie says, looping her arm with mine and pulling me in the direction of the cafeteria. "Just make sure he doesn't hate you."

I wish I could tell her that's a lot easier said than done.

7

When I walk into my statistics class, Grant is at the front of the room with Mr. Ogarrio, gesturing to Emmitt and whispering in low tones.

I falter in the doorway, wondering if I should try to make amends now, but then the bell rings, and I take my seat with a sigh. I'll catch him after class.

As soon as I sit down, my partner, Kaity, turns to look at me with a conspiratorial look. She's in the drama club as well and we've worked together in the past, so it only made sense to partner up when we spotted each other in the beginning of the school year. "Have you seen the new dude? He's so hot."

I nod, trying not to let my gaze wander from her freckled nose and warm brown eyes. "Yeah, he was in my Italian class this morning."

"Did you talk to him?" Kaity asks, raising her brows. "What's his name?" She whips out her phone, already pulling up the Instagram app.

I stare at the screen for half a moment, wondering what's going to come up if she searches Ezra Rivera. Did he create a fake account to go along with his undercover identity? No one is going to believe that he doesn't have social media in this day and age.

"Uh, I forgot," I say, tugging on the end of my braid. "Something with an E."

Kaity nods, clicking into Grant's Instagram instead and looking through his following with an intense look in her eye.

As she's doing that, she passes by Rosie's username, reminding me of something important. Maybe *one* thing can go right today. "Hey, Kaity, you and Sofia are best friends, aren't you?"

Kaity doesn't look away from her screen as she nods. "Love her to death."

"Are you guys going to be auditioning for our short film?" I ask, hoping I sound neutral.

Kaity nods again, giving me a brief glance, before returning her attention to her phone, which is covered in Baby Yoda stickers. "Yeah, auditions are next week, right?"

I hum in agreement. "Is the drama club running lines together?"

"Some of us, yeah. I think Linli is running lines with her boyfriend," Kaity says, referring to the president of the drama club, who's almost definitely my pick for the lead role in our film.

"Oh," I say, trying not to smile at the opening. "So you and Sofia are also running lines with your boyfriends?"

"Unless the blond guy over there wants to date me, I don't think so," Kaity says with a rueful grin. "And Sofia would rather die than spend time with Matt after their breakup. It was *messy*, to say the least."

So Sofia isn't hung up on her ex. Rosie has a chance. I have to tell her as soon as I can—maybe it'll make up for this morning.

Instead of letting any of that show on my face, I shrug. "From what you've told me, Matt is an asshole. Who can blame her?"

Kaity laughs. "Not a single person."

The rest of stats goes by normally. Mr. Ogarrio talks more about his dog than actual numbers, Kaity looks up cute brunch places on Instagram, and I scroll through Letterboxd reviews. A particular review of *Hereditary* (2018) makes me raise my eyebrows—poorly rating the movie because of a bird decapitation doesn't sit right with me when the whole point of a horror film is to be *horrifying*, but I don't have the energy to fight a random reviewer about genre expectations, so I scroll past it—and that's about as wild as class gets. Life as a senior in second semester is oddly boring.

Now that college apps are done, most of the seniors have mentally checked out of all of our classes. Senioritis is rampant in the hallways, clear in the way none of us seems to do much other than lounge around at every possible opportunity.

I'm not exactly as laid-back as some of my other classmates, since the Golden Ivy Film Festival is still occupying the back (and most of the front) of my mind, but I'm grateful that my classes don't require as much work as they did in the previous years. I can't imagine having a full course load *and* having to organize everything for the short film.

Thankfully, Mr. Ogarrio is more than happy to indulge

the class with yet another tale about his dog. I keep expecting him to ask Emmitt to introduce himself, but he doesn't, even though some of the people around me are shooting Emmitt furtive looks.

I don't raise my hand and call attention to it this time, but when the bell rings, I immediately pack up and head in Emmitt's direction.

Kaity raises her eyebrows at me but mouths, *Good luck!*

I try not to grimace in reply. I need the luck, but not for the reason she thinks I do.

I catch up to Emmitt outside of class. He's at Grant's side, looking all but immovable. He walks down the hallways as if he owns them, a confidence in his gait that is completely unearned given the *six hours* he's spent here. Even his expression is cool and unaffected, his eyes roaming the hallways with a lazy ease.

Then he catches sight of me and a crack shows in his armor. He trips over nothing, steadied only by Grant's hand on his arm.

"Bro, are you good?" Grant asks, eyes wide.

"I'm fine," Emmitt says, still using his American accent.

I make my way through the crowd, sidling up beside them until I can step in front, stopping both of them in their tracks.

Grant looks at me uncertainly. "What's up? Did our club meeting get pushed from tomorrow?"

I observe his expression, trying to measure how much of it is earnest, before coming to the conclusion that Emmitt hasn't mentioned our rendezvous in the rain.

Which means Grant thinks I was just being a Good Samaritan this morning when I asked Emmitt to introduce himself.

Not exactly true, but I can work with it.

"No, sorry. I was just wondering if I could have a moment alone with Ezra," I say, taking in the way Emmitt's expression grows sharper. "I wanted to apologize for this morning."

"Oh," Grant says, scratching the back of his neck. "Yeah, of course." To Emmitt, he says, "Meet me in the cafeteria," and points down the hall, where the entrance to the cafeteria is. "We have lunch right now."

"We," I echo, looking between them. So that's why Emmitt was in AP Italian this morning. He's following Grant from class to class...how *interesting*.

Grant blinks at me, his mouth opening and closing, before Emmitt cuts in.

"It's fine. I'll meet you there, Grant," Emmitt says, leaving no room for argument in his tone.

I wave at Grant as he walks away from us, casting us a curious look over his shoulder.

"What do you want?" Emmitt asks coldly, British accent back in place.

I cock my head in the opposite direction. "Join me for a walk, please?"

Emmitt doesn't look particularly inclined to agree, so I start walking, hoping he'll follow along anyway. After a moment, he does.

"So..." I tug on my braid. "Last I checked, your name is Emmitt."

A muscle jumps in his jaw. "So you do recognize me."

I press my lips together for a few seconds, willing myself

not to respond with antagonism. "I do now," I say, hoping that's a good enough answer.

The corner of Emmitt's mouth twitches. "And is there an actual reason you're bothering me? Don't beat around the bush. Just ask."

God, talking to him is *impossible*. Manners, my ass. "Okay. Why are you here?"

He casts me a sudden look of suspicion. "Why? Are you going to leak it to the tabloids?"

Oh my God. First he thinks I want a picture, and now he's accusing me of trying to rat him out to the *press*?

"I could have already exposed you," I say wryly.

Emmitt doesn't look appeased. "You might as well have this morning."

"Right," I say and force my pride down my throat, past each of my ribs until it's buried deep inside me. *Do it for the short film*, I remind myself. "I wanted to apologize for that. I'm sorry for poking fun at the situation. It was rude and un-called for. I also apologize for my behavior on Friday. I know you think I bumped into you on purpose, but I swear I didn't. I was having a bad day and I wasn't watching where I was going. I shouldn't have taken it out on you."

He stops walking, watching me with a hooded gaze. I patiently allow him to work through whatever internal dilemma he's having, doing my best to keep my expression steady.

When the silence stretches too long, I repeat, "I'm sorry," and resist the urge to throttle him. He keeps *staring* at me, his brown eyes sharp and too aware.

"You want something from me," he eventually says, turning away from me and strolling down the hallway, his hands tucked in his pockets.

My lips part, and I stare after him, struggling to comprehend how he could have picked up on *that* just from looking at my face. "That's a bold statement."

"Is it?" he asks, a hint of cruel amusement in his voice. "So you don't want something?"

I glare at his back. "Okay. Fine. It's a small favor and I'm willing to repay you with a favor in return."

He doesn't say anything, still walking like he doesn't have a care in the world. I've never been more certain that I'm looking a homicide charge in the face.

I can't help but miss when he was flustered because of me. I vastly prefer that version of Emmitt to the one who just looked me up and down and dismissed me without a second glance once *again*.

"Our school is applying to the Golden Ivy student film competition," I say after a moment, giving in to the silence. "You might have heard of it."

He raises a brow. "Your point being?"

The urge to throttle him grows infinitely stronger. "My best friend, Rosie, and I are the co-presidents of the film club, and we'd be really grateful if you'd consider making a brief cameo in our film. I know it isn't *Firebrand*, and no one is running around to get you a hot water bottle, but it's important to us and we have a role that we think would suit—"

"No."

I hesitate. "No?"

"No," he says again, his jaw tight.

I blink slowly. "But you didn't let me finish."

"My answer is no." Emmitt turns around without another word, heading for the cafeteria.

I watch as he leaves, wondering if it's worth losing more of my dignity to chase after him. Then I remember the film competition is at stake.

I curse under my breath and hasten down the hallway. "Wait! Wait. I'm sorry. Was it the hot water bottle comment? I shouldn't have said that. Emmitt, *wait*!"

He doesn't even turn at the sound of my voice. Of course he doesn't.

I catch up to him and reach out, wrapping my fingers around his wrist. He falters, looking down at his arm in a way that's eerily similar to our first meeting.

"Please just hear me out," I say, forcing my voice to remain level. If he knows how desperate I am, he's never going to say yes. Clearly he has some type of superiority complex. "I can help keep your identity under wraps. Or I can help you with whatever undercover project you're here for. Or I can help you with something else, it doesn't matter. You don't have to be in a significant role. It can just be a brief cameo. Thirty seconds, tops."

"I said no," Emmitt says darkly, shaking me off. "Leave me alone."

My hand falls to my side limply, and I watch whatever hopes we have of winning the competition fade to dust as Emmitt walks away.

Shit.

8

Anam and I are sitting in the dining room, working diligently on our homework—by which I mean I'm rereading the script for *Gone Girl* (2014) and she's watching some K-pop music video on repeat—when Baba takes a seat at the head of the table.

He was in the kitchen for the past hour, cooking something that smells delicious, though neither Anam nor I were inclined to actually investigate what it was.

When we were younger, Anam and I used to hound Baba when he was in the kitchen, poking and prodding at him to give us a taste of whatever he was cooking at the moment. Given the disconnect between me and my parents, I don't know as much about Bangladeshi culture as I might have if we were closer, if we talked more, but food is one of the few things I *do* know about.

But now Baba doesn't really talk to us about anything that isn't our impending futures.

I don't look up at my dad when he sits down, too used to tuning him out, until he pointedly clears his throat.

I painstakingly look away from my MacBook. It's the only thing keeping me sane right now. If I don't keep focused, my brain is going to start replaying my latest encounter with Emmitt on a constant loop. It seems every single time I talk to him, I somehow make a fool of myself. "What?"

Baba looks less put together than usual. He's wearing a ratty band shirt, stained green from mowing the front lawn, and pajama pants with a hole in the knee. An apron hangs on the back of his chair.

"What is it with you?" my dad asks, shaking his head. "You're turning eighteen in a month and you continue to act like a child. We can hardly have a conversation with you these days."

I raise an eyebrow. Does he want me to make a list of references for why I have no desire to speak to either of my parents anymore? Because I could easily put one together, citations and all.

It starts with *you think I'm too incompetent to take care of myself* and ends with *you're incredibly dismissive of my passions.*

"What do you want?" I ask, tapping my fingers against the tabletop. Anam looks up at the motion and starts at the sight of our father, pulling out her headphones quickly and pretending to be invested in her AP Physics textbook.

"What I want is to speak to you like a normal human being," he says, looking between us with furrowed brows. Anam nudges my foot beneath the table and I nudge her back. "Your behavior is stressing out your mother. You know she has bad migraines."

I level him with a glacial stare. The guilt-tripping isn't going to work on me. I hate when they try to manipulate me into feeling bad for them, only to scream at me the next day. I used to fall for it, but I'm past that now. "Then I'm sure she'll be happy to have me out of the house in a few months."

My father sighs, scratching his beard. "God, Poppy. You're being ridiculous. We want you to be close by because we love you, not because we don't trust you."

"Whatever," I say, turning my attention back to my laptop. I'm not in the mood to have the same argument for the fiftieth time.

"Anam?" Baba asks, looking to her for guidance. I press my lips together to keep from snorting. I might dislike my parents, but my sister *hates* them.

My parents tend to gaslight her a lot more than me, thinking declarations of "love" will convince her to fix our fraying relationship with them. *We love you, we would never hurt you, we're doing our best, please work with us, all you have to do is hear us out.* As if we haven't listened to them say it a million times over. The words are always empty.

"I'm studying," Anam says sharply. "The SATs are coming up. I have to get a high score like Apu if I want to get in Stanford."

"Stanford," my dad repeats blankly. "In California."

"Yes, Stanford," Anam says, lifting her chin, her dark eyes blazing with determination.

I offer her a small smile. I'm immeasurably proud of her, even if my parents aren't. "I wouldn't worry too much. I'm sure you'll get a volleyball scholarship."

"*Volleyball* scholarship," my dad repeats, holding his head in his hands.

"Are you a broken record?" I ask him darkly. "Why are you just repeating everything we say?"

He can be as dismissive of me as he wants, but the second he starts in on Anam, my claws are out. I went through all of this so she wouldn't have to. I don't get why nothing we do is enough for them—whether it's being in film club or being on the volleyball team, our parents insist on seeing it as a "distraction" to our studies. Over and over, they tell us to focus on things that will guarantee us a good future. It doesn't matter that I'm the co-president of the film club. It doesn't matter that Anam has won several volleyball championships. None of it fits their definition of success.

My dad stares at me for a long moment before huffing loudly, pushing back his chair and going to the kitchen. He's grumbling something under his breath, but I don't care enough to decipher it.

Instead, I squeeze Anam's fingers once and return my attention to my work.

Ten minutes later, my dad leaves the kitchen, holding a cup of warm chai and a bowl of payesh. He passes by us entirely without a word, and I frown at his back. He usually offers us some, too, but even that is too much to ask these days.

Anam looks similarly bemused so I sigh, getting to my feet and wandering to the kitchen to make us both two cups. I'm not going to risk going near the stove, though, certain I'd set a house fire. The smell of warm payesh wafts past my nose, and I try not to glower at missing out on it.

Fine. If that's how it's going to be in this house, then *fine*.

I'm more than happy to Cold War the shit out of my parents.

It started innocently enough.

Junior year, we had a college fair. Rosie and I wandered for a few hours, trying to suss out which schools would be best for our respective interests. We spent almost an hour at the NYU booth with fifty other students, and Rosie came out with a starry-eyed look and a dream.

Then we got to the USC booth. The Queens representative was a young man who went by Dr. Stewart, and the moment he started talking about the School of Cinematic Arts, I *knew*.

I went home that night with an armful of pamphlets, Dr. Stewart's business card, and high hopes.

I remember sitting down at the dining table with a wide grin. "The University of Southern California," I told my parents.

They laughed.

And then they realized I was serious.

And they laughed again.

I left, slamming the door to my room shut. And then I spent days watching YouTube videos of USC students giving tours of their rooms and campus. And then I spent days looking up USC's famous alumni. And then I spent two and a half days crafting a perfectly worded email to Dr. Stewart.

His response was far more enthusiastic and encouraging than my parents', telling me that I was an ideal applicant and that I had a bright future ahead of me, and it settled the remaining doubt in my heart.

I was going to get into USC, even if it killed me.

Soon afterward, the fights started. It's not as if it was exactly *new*. It's been years since my parents and I have gotten along well—it's hard to look at families like Nazifa's and still maintain respect for my own. But for most of my childhood, I kept quiet about it. Even if I didn't agree with their methods, I never said anything about it to them.

But my future isn't something I'm willing to compromise on.

It began small, with my parents finding stray USC flyers lying around the house. And then it got bigger and bigger as I started doing more and more research on the school, meeting up with USC alumni for coffee and watching informational videos every spare minute I had, until the day before my USC interview at some fancy hotel in Midtown.

"You're *not* going," Ma had screamed.

I remember I sneered at her. "Who's going to stop me? You?"

"This is ridiculous! Fahim, tell her!"

Baba gave me an awful look, one burned into my memory—as if I was his biggest disappointment. "What's the point of being interviewed, Poppy? You're not going to get in."

The words were a slap in the face. "Why wouldn't I get in?"

He and my mother shared a knowing look. "You know why, Poppy. Stop deluding yourself. Business is a sensible enough major on its own, and there are hundreds of great business schools in New York City. We love you and want you nearby—"

"I'm going to get in," I said in reply, cutting them off. My words were fierce, if slightly unhinged. "I don't care what you say. I'm going to get in and I'm going to move to California."

Ma had laughed. "The day you get into USC is the day pigs fly, Poppy. It's as likely as you winning that stupid little film competition of yours."

Something broke between us in that moment. Something beyond repair.

A fissure that my parents will never be able to overcome.

But maybe it was already breaking. Maybe both sides have been chipping away at it, day by day, for the last seventeen years of my life.

"And what if I won?" My eyes were stinging, tears prickling at the corners, but I held them back by some miracle. "Would you let me go to USC then?"

Ma gave me a smile, something condescending and cruel. "If you won, I'd pay for you to go to USC myself."

My laugh was choked. "Is that a promise?"

"Do you want it in writing?" Ma asked, raising her brows at me. "Is that what it will take to get it through your head this is *never* going to happen?"

I still went to the interview. I just went with a signed piece of paper tucked into my back pocket—a weight even Atlas would prefer to leave behind.

Their words had been a challenge.

And I'm nothing if not determined to win.

Even now, the piece of paper is folded in between the flaps

of my wallet. When I need motivation to keep going, I unfold it, reread the words in Ma's smooth scrawl, and run my finger over the indent of her and Baba's signatures.

I'm going to get out of here. I'm going to leave all of this behind and start my life somewhere new.

No matter what it takes.

9

After hours spent scouring the internet because of Emmitt's refusal to participate in our film, hoping to find *something* to distract me from the overbearing buzzing in the back of my head, I stumble across something that brings on deeply violent urges. Grant's father, Elijah Njoku, is producing the Firebrand movie Emmitt is going to star in.

No wonder Emmitt is at our school. He must be undercover, shadowing Grant to learn what it's like to be a New York City high school student for his upcoming role.

"I'm going to strangle Grant," I say, struggling to break free from Rosie's grasp. I'd hunted her down as soon as the bell rang for lunch. "He fucking knew, and—"

"And he was likely going to *tell* us on Friday, if you hadn't shut him down so quickly," Rosie says, but I ignore her rationale, my eyes locked on Grant across the hallway.

"So he should be helping us convince Emmitt!" I say, finally stilling in Rosie's arms, turning to face her with a scowl on my face. It's been three days since Emmitt said no, and I've taken to glaring at the back of his head to satisfy my murderous rage. "You have to go talk to Grant, because if I do, I'm going to hurt his feelings."

Rosie studies my expression before she sighs, gathering her auburn curls in one hand and pulling them back into a bun. She uses her other hand to wrap a hair tie around it. "Fine. Just don't kill anyone until I get back."

"No promises," I say under my breath. At the very least, this new information has helped ease me out of my latest depressive episode.

I carry the weight of my sadness and exhaustion every day—I think I always have, even if I didn't realize it until high school—but some days are much easier than others. This week is an easy week, where the voice in the back of my head is only a murmur.

I long for a future where there are more easy days than hard ones.

As Rosie leaves my side, Kaity, Sofia, and Linli walk by, whispering to one another, but they falter at the sight of me. They're carrying a handful of props, from horse heads to fairy wings, reminding me that the spring play is *A Midsummer Night's Dream*. "Hey, Mina!"

Some of the tension seeps out of me, and I offer them a subdued smile. "Hey."

Sofia's attention seems to be elsewhere, her eyes straying across the hall to where Rosie is, but Linli is looking at me, a wide grin on her face as she nudges me with a fake branch. "Looking forward to auditions?"

"Looking forward to yours," I agree, and her expression brightens further. "The drama club never fails to impress."

Linli laughs, jostling the props tucked underneath her arm. "You're too kind, as always."

Before I can reply, Kaity leans forward conspiratorially. "So did you end up talking to Ezra the other day? I was telling Lin and Sofi about it, and we all agree you guys would be a cute couple."

I barely withhold the urge to gag. I would sooner die, but I don't want to be rude in the face of Kaity's kindness, especially with auditions coming up. "I don't think he likes me," I say instead, toying with one of my pigtails.

Linli frowns, and suddenly, I'm being pulled into a hug, the horse head pressing into my ribs. "Well, he can fuck off, then."

I huff a fond laugh into her silky black hair. "Thank you, Linli."

Kaity, however, is stroking her chin. "Maybe Lin and I could work some magic…"

"No, no, it's fine," I say quickly. God forbid they interfere. "If it's meant to be, it will be."

Linli sighs, pulling away. "Well, if you need anything, let us know."

I nod in agreement just as Rosie returns. Both Linli and Kaity perk up at the sight of her, sharing a knowing look.

I raise my eyebrows, considering their expressions and the warm look in Sofia's eyes.

"Hi, Rosie," Sofia says quietly, curling a strand of pink hair around her finger. "How are you?"

Rosie blinks, clearly at a loss, and I pinch her wrist. She

starts at the touch before letting out a high-pitched laugh. "Hi, Sofia. I'm—I'm good, thank you. How are you?"

"Good," Sofia says, and the two of them just smile at each other serenely, not saying a word.

Ya Allah. These two could give anyone a cavity.

"As sweet as this is," Kaity cuts in, a mischievous glint in her eye, "we should get going. Make heart eyes at each other some other time."

Sofia's lips part in disbelief as she slants Kaity a dark look, but Kaity and Linli are too busy laughing, running down the hallway.

"Sorry," Sofia says, unable to meet Rosie's eyes. "Uh, are we still running lines after school today?"

Rosie nods, her cheeks *blazing* red.

"Cool," Sofia says, and I watch Rosie's soul leave her body as Sofia ducks forward, pressing a quick kiss against Rosie's cheek, before rushing after Linli and Kaity.

I open my mouth, and Rosie hisses, *"Not a word."*

I raise my hands in surrender. "I wasn't going to say anything."

Rosie harrumphs, but it's hard to take her seriously when she's turning into a tomato. "Grant said he'll help us figure something out after school."

"Perfect," I say. My soul feels slightly appeased, so I swing an arm around Rosie's shoulder and tug her in the direction of the cafeteria. "I think they have chicken nuggets today."

"How am I meant to *eat* right now?" Rosie bemoans.

"I'm sure you'll find a way," I say dryly, but my brain is busy wondering how Grant is going to help us. He must know more about Emmitt than the internet does—there has to be something Emmitt wants, something we can strike a bargain for, something we can *do*.

We have to find a way to salvage our chances of winning the film festival. Even if it means sacrificing my pride even more than I already have.

10

The next day marks a week since my first encounter with Emmitt—not that I'm counting the days. It's just hard not to be hyperaware of the fact a week ago I inadvertently fucked up our chance of winning the Golden Ivy Film Festival. When the bell rings after ninth period, signaling the end of the school day, I sit in my seat for a few extra beats, absolutely drained by the world around me.

I almost want to tuck my tail and go home instead of to the film club meeting, where Grant will most likely deliver *more* terrible news. Yesterday, Rosie and I brainstormed with him for nearly two hours only to come up with absolutely nothing. It turns out that Grant and Emmitt met for the first time only last week, and he also knows little to nothing personal about the indie film star.

At this rate, I'm half tempted to perform a ridiculous skit in the middle of the cafeteria in the hope it'll convince Emmitt how serious we are about the short film.

Just two more months, I remind myself for the umpteenth time. Then all of this will be over. I'll know whether I got into USC, and our application for the Golden Ivy student film competition will be turned in.

I finally drag myself out of my English classroom and cross the hall to my locker. For a moment, I don't even bother opening it, leaning my head against the sea-foam locker and sighing quietly.

"Mina?"

I turn around immediately, recognizing one of the freshmen from film club.

"Christina," I say, offering her a tired smile. "What's up?"

She scratches her head, looking unsure. She's one of the more outgoing freshmen in the club, so her withdrawn expression pings a red flag in my brain. I soften my expression, hoping it comes across kinder.

"Is something wrong?" I ask quietly.

Christina looks down, muttering, "Rosie told me to come find you. She said you might have some advice? My dad doesn't want me to come to film club anymore. He says it's pointless, and I just… I don't know what to do."

I frown, leaning my shoulder against my locker. I wish Rosie would have warned me before sending Christina my way. This isn't the first or last time one of our club members is going to deal with this situation, but it never gets any easier.

"I've been there. It's rough when our parents aren't as supportive of our dreams as they should be." I level her a serious look. "If you keep coming to our meetings, are you going to be in an unsafe situation? Or are you going to face mild disapproval? Or maybe something else entirely? Don't downplay it. I'm asking because I don't want to give you advice that could hurt you in the long run."

Christina blinks at me, clearly taken aback by the graveness of my voice. But after a moment, she shakes her head. "Mild disapproval. He won't stop me. But he'll be upset with me."

I blow out a breath, nodding. "Okay. We can deal with mild disapproval. Listen, you love film, right? That's why you're a part of the club?"

"Yeah," Christina says, chewing on her bottom lip. "It's my favorite thing in the world."

"Mine, too," I say, reaching over to squeeze her hand. "I think you should keep coming. Sooner or later, he's going to understand what it means to you. That, or he's going to keep being unhappy, but he'll learn to live with it. I sincerely hope it's the first, but either way, you shouldn't give up on something that you love for someone who isn't trying to meet you in the middle."

Christina gives me a long, searching look. "Can I ask you something?"

"Of course. Anything," I say, and it still doesn't feel like enough. I wish I could do more, but I can barely do enough for myself some days.

"You've been in film club for four years, right? Did your parents ever come to support you?"

I grimace. I know better than to lie. "Not yet."

Her expression falls, but she nods as if she expected that. "But you still love film?"

"More than anything," I say and force myself to swallow past the lump in my throat. "Maybe more than everything."

"I figured," she says before shaking her head slightly. "One last question?"

"Of course," I say again. "Ask away."

"Why do you love it so much?" Christina asks and then winces, like she regrets the words.

I falter, unsure how to answer. For my college applications, I went on and on about escapism and being transported to another world, but I don't think that's the answer Christina is looking for.

After mulling over it, I finally land on an answer that's as close to the truth as I can manage. "I love film because it's layered," I say slowly. "It allows us to cover up the truth, to disguise it with lighting and angles and filters. Nothing is ever quite what it seems. There's a hidden depth to every single shot."

Christina blinks at me. "Wow. I've never thought about it like that."

I shrug, offering her a hesitant smile. "It means something different to every single person. But that's what it means to me. I've always thought the world looked better captured on film, so I could never give up on it."

"Thank you, Mina," Christina says, her eyes a little too bright. "I still have to think about what I'm going to do, but this conversation helped a lot."

"I'm glad," I say and open my arms, offering her a hug. She immediately wraps her own arms around my waist, squeezing me tightly. "No matter what you decide, we'll always be here for you and support you."

Christina murmurs her gratitude and then leaves in a haste, probably to stop me from seeing the tears threatening to spill down her cheeks. I stare after her for a long moment, my shoulders slumped.

It might be only two more months left for me, but it's years and years for other people. There are so many of us drowning in plain sight, and so little the rest of us can do to help.

I turn back to my locker, exhaling a deep breath. As I start to spin the dial, *32, 15, 41*, footsteps echo in the hallway, someone walking up to me slowly.

I glance to the side and I miss *41* completely, my heart skipping an uncertain beat.

Emmitt is watching me, his eyes calm and appraising. His British accent is back when he says, "We need to talk."

"We do?" I ask, forcing my expression into a blank slate. My feelings are still raw and this is the last thing I was expecting. "About what?"

"Your offer."

"My offer," I repeat dubiously and turn back to the dial, spinning it until I hear a *click*.

In my peripheral vision, Emmitt nods, inclining his head toward my locker. A film club magnet sits below my lingering fingers.

I drop my hand entirely and turn to face him, crossing my arms. "I don't know what you're talking about."

There's something strange about his expression, something a little too honest and grim. Did he overhear me talking to Christina? The thought of him witnessing such a vulnerable conversation makes my skin crawl.

But then a sliver of a smile passes across Emmitt's face, patronizing enough that I dismiss the thought. No. There's no way he would have sat through that entire conversation without offering unsolicited advice. "You were begging for my help five days ago."

"Begging is a stretch," I say mildly, although it's more spot-on than I care to admit. "If you're here to antagonize me, keep it moving, dude. I'm not in the mood."

Emmitt leans a shoulder against the off-white wall beside the row of lockers. "And if I'm here to help you?"

My eyes narrow, and I observe him. There's an ease to his countenance. Sunlight streams through from my English classroom, setting his dyed hair alight, as if a halo of gold is crowned upon his head. It's unfortunate that he's as attractive as he is. "Is that right?"

"I'll be in your film," he says, and I blink in surprise. "But you have to help me in return."

I don't like the sound of that.

"Help you how?" I ask, brow furrowed. "Did Grant talk to you?"

"No," Emmitt says. "I'm here because you promised me a favor in return for my participation."

So he wants to strike a bargain. "What favor?" I ask carefully.

In response, Emmitt takes out his phone, flicking through his screen with ringed fingers, before holding it out for me to take a look.

5 weeks.

5 photos.

1 winner.

Over the next five weeks, a prompt will be posted across social media every Monday. Applicants will have until Saturday night to upload a photo in accordance to the prompt that will be ranked by a team of confidential judges. Rankings will change week to week, as the previous weeks' scores are averaged. At the end, one final winner will be chosen to intern alongside Shana Torres.

"Who is Shana Torres?" I ask, frowning at his phone.

Emmitt gives me a deeply unimpressed look. "A famous photographer from Spain. One of the best."

I raise my eyebrows, turn back to my locker, and put away my English notebook and folder. "Right. What does that have to do with me?"

He pinches the bridge of his nose. "Your help. I require it to win this contest."

"Wait, what?" I glance between him and his phone. "You're entering a photography contest? For what? You're already famous."

Emmitt looks down at me, his gaze icy. "Are we stating the obvious now?"

"Do you get tired of being a condescending prick?" I ask, unable to help myself. I wince internally, already imagining Rosie's horror if she heard me say that.

"I'll pretend you didn't say that," Emmitt says, and I just barely resist the urge to flip him off. "Will you help me or not?"

I grimace. "What do you need my help with? I don't know anything about photography."

"No, but you know New York, don't you?" he asks, running a hand through his hair and looking off to the side instead of meeting my eyes.

The hallway is practically empty except for us. Far down, there are two girls sitting beside a set of lockers, commiserating over their English homework. Even farther down, a boy is drinking from the water fountain. Near the bathroom at the end of the hall, a few boys linger, looking at their phones.

At any rate, no one is close enough to eavesdrop on our conversation.

Not that they would understand any of it, since I clearly don't.

"Yes," I say slowly, trying—and failing—to make sense of what he's getting at. "I've lived here my whole life. What does that have to do with anything?"

He sighs deeply, as if it pains him to even say the words. "I need five locations for my photographs. The shots have to be perfect and tell a story. I don't know enough about New York City to do this on my own."

I know I shouldn't look a gift horse in the mouth, but when my lips move, the first words that come out are "Why not Grant?"

The voice in the back of my head yells at me immediately. I should be leaping for joy that he came to me for help. Not making him reconsider.

But it just doesn't make sense. Why *me* of all people?

Emmitt presses his lips together tightly. "Grant can't know about this contest. *No one* can know about this contest."

I stare at him for a long moment. "Is this illegal?"

"What?" He gives me an aghast look. "No, it's not illegal. What—why would you even think that?"

"You're being awfully suspicious," I point out, worrying my bottom lip between my teeth. "It's a photography contest, not a crime ring. Why can't anyone know about it?"

"It doesn't matter why," Emmitt says, his tone sharp.

I blink, leaning back against the locker beside mine and observing him. "It sounds like it matters."

He blows out a long breath, apparently at his wits' end. For some bizarre reason, it makes me want to smile. "Do you agree or not?"

"What would I have to do?" I ask instead, even though I already know I'm going to agree. I have to, for the sake of the film competition.

"You'll have to help me choose locations and accompany me to them for the next five weeks," he says, but his mouth is curled in distaste. It's clear he's as reluctant to partake in this deal as I am. "And I'll participate in whatever film things you require for the duration of those five weeks."

"I have to accompany you?" I ask wearily. I can try to stifle my distaste for the sake of the short film, but I don't know how *long* I can keep up the act if I have to spend extended amounts of time with him.

He nods, one tilt of his head. "And you will have to keep my identity a secret. Only Grant and I know, and it has to stay that way."

My nose wrinkles, and I look back at my locker. "Rosie already knows."

"You told her?" he asks, eyes narrowed.

I shoot him a half-hearted glare, taking out my film club journals. Our club meetings start when after-school tutoring ends at 4:00 p.m., so I still have some time to spare. "We're the co-presidents of the film club. We've watched your movies, dickhead. Even with your new dye job, you're pretty recognizable."

Emmitt's hands immediately go to his hair, a self-conscious

expression coming across his face, but both of his arms fall to his side when he notices me muffling my laughter. "Okay. You can't tell anyone *else*."

"Fine," I say, rolling my eyes. Just for that, I don't tell him that Anam, Nazifa, and Syeda also already know. It's not like he'll ever meet any of them.

"Fine," Emmitt says back, glowering at me, and I slam my locker door shut, hoping to startle the look off his face.

Suddenly the distance between us seems nonexistent, my arm nearly brushing against his chest. "I won't tell anyone and I'll help you with your photography contest, but *you* have to start coming to our film club meetings," I say, forcing myself to remain unaffected. "And you'll act in the role assigned to you by me and Rosie."

Emmitt leans down, his nose brushing against mine. I inhale sharply and almost take a step back but manage to stand my ground, peering up at him through my lashes. "It's a deal," he says.

I swallow roughly. "It's a deal." Then I shoulder past him, our elbows knocking into each other. "Come on, you don't want to be late to your first film club meeting."

Emmitt hums but follows after me, his confidence returning with every step he takes, before he flows into an easy gait at my side.

All the while, I try not to question my sanity for agreeing to this.

The film club meeting goes relatively normal. Rosie nearly jumps out of her seat when she sees me walk in alongside Emmitt. Grant gives both of us a look of disbelief, and I barely resist sticking my tongue out at him.

The rest of the club members look between us in bemusement, but they move on when I don't bother introducing Emmitt. Only Christina keeps watching me, but for an entirely different reason. I give her a small smile before launching into an explanation of what to expect when auditions start on Tuesday.

The last thing I want to do is bring attention to Emmitt's existence. This is film club, after all. It's more than possible that one of the others has seen one of Emmitt's indie films or heard about him starring in the upcoming Firebrand movie. I made a deal to keep his identity a secret, so putting him on blast is going to do me no favors.

At any rate, they'll see his face often enough when he stars in our film.

"How did you do it?" Rosie whispers after we're done explaining, and Emmitt has taken a seat beside Grant in the back.

"By selling my soul to the devil," I say, trying not to think too hard about the fact that those words feel like the truth.

Rosie raises her eyebrows before holding out her Hydro Flask, which she bought ironically because of TikTok and now uses almost constantly. "Cheers to the devil, then."

I sigh, clinking my *Mad Max: Fury Road* (2015) water bottle against hers. "Cheers to the devil."

11

"He *agreed*?" Anam asks, peering over my shoulder at where Emmitt is sitting with Grant, sprawled at one of the cafeteria tables as if it's a throne, rather than a plain blue bench. It's like a worse version of manspreading.

"Lower your voice," I say, gesturing vaguely. There's still twenty minutes before first period starts, and our school is buzzing with noise, despite the Monday morning gloominess outside. Rosie is running late, so I figured now was a good time as any to clue Anam in. "You're not supposed to know about any of this."

"Then you shouldn't have told me," Anam singsongs, but her eyes are wide as she takes him in. We're sitting near the exit, me on top of the table, and her on the bench below. There are people weaving in and out of the cafeteria, grabbing breakfast before class starts or heading straight for their lockers. "You really insulted a celebrity to his face, huh?"

"Apparently so," I say, sighing, before pointing a finger

at her in warning. "His movies are *banned* from our movie nights. I'm serious."

Anam turns to look at me, her mouth puckered. "Can we still watch the Firebrand one when it comes out?"

"Maybe," I say. "Depends how much he pisses me off the next five weeks."

"Fair enough." Anam stares at Emmitt in consideration. "You know, he's kind of hot."

"Don't start," I warn, elbowing her. "The last thing we need to explain to Ma and Baba is how you wound up with a celebrity boyfriend."

"I meant generally," Anam says, pouting. "Although if anyone is going to end up with a celebrity boyfriend, I think it's you."

"Shut up," I say, flicking her nose. One of Anam's volleyball friends coos at the gesture, and Anam waves her away. "In his dreams."

"He should be so lucky," she agrees, a grin coming to life on her face. She leans her elbow on the table, scattering half her APUSH notes. "But imagine you two taking over the film industry. The hate-to-love international implications of it all…"

"You spend too much time on the internet," I say, knocking her head lightly. "Go back to watching BTS music videos."

"My favorite group is TWICE, dumbass," Anam says, but there's laughter in her voice. Sometimes I think my sister is the human personification of the sun. "BTS is cool, though. I like their music."

"And they're gorgeous," I add.

Anam's eyes take on a mischievous glint. "You know, Emmitt kind of gives me a Taehyung vibe—"

"Shut up," I say again and hop off the table, leaving her giggling in my wake.

As I'm heading up the main stairway, someone taps my shoulder. I turn my head and meet Emmitt's brown eyes.

"What?" I ask.

Emmitt grabs my hand in response, startling me into almost dropping my phone, and pulls me into the mathematics hallway.

I nearly trip in my haste to follow after him, his hand warm in mine, even though his rings are cool to the touch. He leads us all the way to the main entrance, near the auditorium, although he looks a little lost the farther he progresses into the hall.

Our school is relatively large. It's one of the top schools in the city and students come from all over the boroughs—well, not from Staten Island, but Staten Island barely counts as a borough—to attend, given they have the grades and pass the mini entrance exam.

Our alumni have gone off to break records and win awards and all that jazz. There's a healthy flow of donations coming in, so we don't lack for much. Our halls are bright and open, our textbooks new and pristine, and our amenities large and expansive.

A lot of our school comes from low-income households, and our school accommodates them in the best way possible, providing any and every resource they might require. I often feel grateful for the chance to attend Astoria Academy of the Arts and Sciences at all, since a lot of my friends from middle school don't have the same experience at their own high schools.

At AAAS, we have three separate gyms—one for volleyball, one for basketball, and one for gymnastics, as well an outdoor track and a field for baseball and cricket. Similarly, our planetarium has all the latest technology, our library has hundreds and hundreds of books in great condition, and our botanical garden has excellent upkeep.

Even our auditorium was recently renovated, and Rosie and I often spend hours in there, brainstorming away for film club.

It's no surprise Grant came here. His dad is one of our most famous alumni. It's probably also why Emmitt was sent here—on what seems to be some kind of undercover mission to learn about American high schools—instead of somewhere else.

It's lucky that Emmitt is eighteen and can still pass for a senior. If he'd been just a year older and had his jawline been just a little sharper, I'm not sure that anyone would buy it.

At any rate, he looks like a child in a zoo when he finally falters in the middle of the hallway to look back at me. A hint of panic is hidden behind his long lashes. "We have to find a location today."

"*Today?*" I ask, blinking. He's still holding my hand, making me antsy for reasons I can't quite put into words. "I don't even know what the prompt is—"

Almost immediately, he drops my hand to pull his phone out of his back pocket, then shoves it in my direction.

I sigh, looking down at the screen. The clouds are clearing

through the windows of the main entrance, daylight finally streaming through the wide panels. I have to shift until I can avoid the sun's glare, but eventually I make out the words.

PROMPT 1: WAVE
DEADLINE: SATURDAY
GOOD LUCK!

"Is that it?" I ask, frowning at the prompt. "Just the word *wave*?"

Emmitt nods. When I look up at him, he still has an arrogant twist to his mouth, but his cheeks are rosier than usual. He's *flustered* over this contest.

Huh.

Maybe this is more important than I realized.

"Let me think on it," I say, pushing his phone back. An idea niggles at the back of my head, taking shape, not fully formed yet. "I'll figure it out by our stats class."

Emmitt nods, his jaw tight. "I'll find you then."

I shake my head, turning around and heading back toward the staircase. "We're going the same way, dickhead. AP Italian, remember?"

He makes a low noise, clearly insulted. "You know that isn't my name, right?"

I look at him over my shoulder. The light reflects off the studs in his left ear, casting shadows across his face. "Should I call you by your name, then?"

"Fuck off," he grumbles.

A smile tugs at my mouth as I face forward again. If I can

speak my mind while dealing with him, maybe the next few weeks won't be completely miserable. "You don't have to tell me twice."

12

I stare at my phone for the fifth time in two minutes. It's ten past three, and Emmitt promised to meet me at my locker after class ended fifteen minutes ago.

Rosie is at my side, fiddling with a piece of pink glittery paper. I think she's trying to make a crane—presumably for Sofia—but it isn't looking too good.

"How can it be this hard to show up on time?" I ask her, lolling my head to the side to meet her blue eyes.

She shrugs, still attempting to fold the paper. "He's probably used to showing up on set whenever he wants."

I sigh, rubbing circles into my temple. "Well, this isn't a film set, and he's not paying me to wait around for his sorry ass."

"Mina," Rosie admonishes without looking up, "we need his help."

"He can help us even if I lightly stab him," I say, musing on that thought for a while.

In the back of my head, though, a worry arises. I can stay out only so late before my parents start blowing up my phone, demanding an explanation. I'm used to handling the brunt of their disappointment, but it's not *fun* to deal with. I'm not eager to sit through one of their lectures tonight. If Emmitt subjects me to that fate, I really might stab him.

"Ten more minutes, and I'm going home," I say to Rosie, who sighs but doesn't protest. I nudge her shoulder, grateful she's keeping me company while I wait, and she smiles faintly, nudging back.

"Hey, auditions are tomorrow," I say, eyeing the end of the hall for Emmitt's impending arrival. "Do you think Sofia will get a part?"

Rosie rips the paper in half.

I blink at her, taking in her flushed cheeks. "Ro, all I said was her name."

"I'm fine," Rosie says, crumpling the paper into a ball and throwing it at the trash can across from us. She misses by a foot and I snort. "I'm *fine*," she repeats, stomping over to the balled-up paper. She drops it into the bin herself.

"Whatever you say." I offer her a slip of loose-leaf paper— it's not pink and glittery, but it'll have to do. She takes it with a disgruntled look on her face. "What do you think, though?"

Rosie hesitates a moment before nodding. "I think she'd be a good fit for the love interest."

"Noted," I say, playing out the film in my head with Sofia cast as the second lead. "I hope you didn't get too distracted while running lines."

The comment slips out without much thought, but Rosie stiffens, making me instantly rethink my words.

"Mina," Rosie starts to say, but before she can finish her sentence, Emmitt shows up, out of breath.

"Sorry. Let's go?"

I raise my brows at him, trying to force down the unease from the conversation Rosie was about to start. "No explanation?"

The corner of Emmitt's mouth creases. "I...had a phone call with my mother. It ran longer than I anticipated. And then I kind of got lost. I'm still not used to this place."

After hours researching Emmitt, it would be difficult to not know who his mother is. Claire Gong is a marketing executive at the UK branch of Twentieth Century Studios and has been waddling Emmitt into film auditions since he was in diapers.

His father, Alejandro Ramos, isn't in the picture—passed away when Emmitt was young—so it's always been just him and his mother. By the looks of it, they're not exactly on the best terms.

I wonder if she's in New York with him or if she's still in London, calling from five hours ahead. I wonder which he'd prefer.

And then I shake myself free of that line of thought. I don't care about Emmitt's life *that* much.

"Come on, then, pretty boy," I say, beckoning him forward as I head for the main staircase. "We're already late."

The lines of Emmitt's expression relax, settling into his usual condescending frown. "She never calls me by my name," he says to Rosie, like that's going to help anything.

Rosie offers him a consolatory smile and a pat on the shoulder. "You'll get used to it."

I sure hope he doesn't.

★ ★ ★

"So? Where are we going?" Emmitt asks, matching my stride as we start walking to the R train. He's back to his British accent, which is funny to hear after a day of listening to him pretend to be American. Every time we're together, he seems to revert back to it. I guess I'm one of the only people that knows who he is, but it's strange to hear him go back and forth between accents, putting on a fake persona whenever it suits him.

The weather has fully cleared up, so the sun beats down on us as we cross the street. It's early February, though, so it's still chilly enough that I button up my mustard coat before we even leave the building.

I blow onto my fingers, rubbing them together. My breath comes out as vapor in the frosty air, and I regret not bringing gloves. "I thought it would be a cool idea to do a different New York City borough for each one of the prompts. Five photos, five boroughs. We're going to Staten Island today."

Emmitt falters, staring at me with an intensity that stops me in my tracks, too.

"What?" I ask, my skin itching under his gaze.

He stares at me for another beat of silence, and just as I'm considering turning away, he says, "That's actually a good idea."

I narrow my eyes at the use of *actually*. "As it would turn out, I have brain cells I like to actively employ. You should give it a try on occasion."

He exhales out a breath, tucking his hands in his own coat pockets, but an aggravating smirk is hidden in the corner of his mouth. "I can't even pay you a compliment without some smart-ass remark."

I ignore him and keep walking. Ten minutes later, we arrive at the subway station, and Emmitt stares at the entrance in dismay.

"We're taking the subway?"

I give him an unimpressed look. "How else are we going to get around New York? Do you have a fancy driver to take us places?"

Emmitt's lips thin. "Surely we can call an Uber or Lyft?"

"And who's going to pay for that?" I ask, lifting a brow. Before he can answer, I shake my head. "Come on, let's not waste time. I'm not going to take a car into Manhattan when the subway is right there. Let's go."

Without waiting for his response, I hop down the stairs to the subway. There's a homeless man in a sleeping bag across from us, more or less knocked out, and Emmitt inhales sharply at the sight of him, bumping into my back.

"Oh my God, relax," I say, pushing him away from me with one hand. "I'm pretty sure they have homeless people in London, too."

I stroll down the pathway, and Emmitt follows me after a moment, far too close for comfort. I consider reaching out to push him away again, but it's too much effort.

When we get to the turnstiles, I pause. "I'm assuming you don't have a MetroCard."

"I didn't realize I'd be needing one," he says under his breath.

I press my lips together and walk over to one of the machines. If he does it himself, we're going to be standing here all day. "Come on, then. Do you have cash on you?"

Emmitt nods, taking out his wallet after looking around

suspiciously. I roll my eyes and take the twenty-dollar bill from his outstretched hand, then quickly click through the options for a regular MetroCard. He watches over my shoulder, eyes tracking my movements.

I insert the bill and wait for the machine to spit out a card. When it does, I offer it to him, then make my way back to the turnstiles and swipe my student MetroCard.

It takes him approximately four tries to swipe correctly. Everyone that passes through gives him a pitying glance, opting for a different turnstile instead of waiting for him to get it right.

I sigh and resist the urge to reach over and do it myself. The last time I had to deal with this was when my cousins from Canada came to visit three years ago, and I relegated most of those duties to Anam. I merely stepped to the side and glared at my parents for dragging me along on a ridiculous tourist venture.

Since then, Anam has grown to become uncannily like me when it comes to dealing with our parents' demands. I fear if our cousins ever visited again, they'd be getting the cold shoulder from both of us, not for any fault of their own, but rather because Anam and I would refuse on principle, to inconvenience Ma and Baba.

Offhandedly, I wish I could pass off my Emmitt duties to someone else, too, but life isn't quite that simple.

When he finally swipes through, he grins at me. For a moment, I'm thrown by the brightness of his smile.

I've seen it in movies but never in person. I always thought Emmitt Ramos, for all his personal flaws, had a really nice smile.

I didn't know it was far more beautiful in person. The blinding sight of it enrages me beyond reason. I can't even stand to *look* at him.

My face feels like it's on fire, so I pointedly turn away.

"Come on, let's go," I say, the words half-strangled. "We have to get on the platform."

And then I watch in bemusement as he starts walking in the opposite direction, toward the sign that says Forest Hills and Queens.

"The other way!" I call after him, skipping down the steps of the platform leading to Manhattan. "Signs are your friends!"

Emmitt meets me on the crowded platform a minute later, his expression dark. It appeases some of the lingering heat in my stomach, and my chest doesn't feel quite as tight watching him.

"You know, you could stand to be a little less rude," he mutters.

"Probably," I agree, before I shrug. "You could also stand to be a little less of a dickhead. Are either of us going to make an effort to stop? I highly doubt it."

He glares at me before looking away, eyeing the edge of the platform warily. A rat scuttles down below, and he blanches, knocking into me for the umpteenth time.

I sigh and resign myself to a fate of continually bumping into Emmitt Ramos for the next five weeks.

When the train finally pulls up, it's filled to the brim.

Emmitt grimaces contemplating the doorway. "Should we wait for the next one?"

"It's rush hour—they're all going to be packed," I say and

grab the collar of his jacket, dragging him inside the subway car with me.

What I don't account for is the way we're pressed against each other. My cheeks start to warm, and I pointedly look away from him, grabbing the nearest pole. He follows suit, his ringed fingers just above mine, his pinky brushing against my thumb.

"Now what?" he asks.

"Now I put in my headphones, blast Olivia Rodrigo, and you do whatever it is you want to pass the time," I say, pointedly waving my phone in the little space between us. "We're getting off at Whitehall Street, so we have a while to go."

Emmitt arches an eyebrow, eyeing the stops listed along the top of the subway car. "That's like fifteen stops away."

I shrug, putting in my earphones.

And almost immediately, the train lurches, and I practically sprawl all over Emmitt.

I clench my eyes shut, wondering who I wronged in my past life for this to be happening to me. "Sorry," I say and take a pointed step back, cursing the subway gods.

Emmitt gives me a knowing look, and I nearly stomp on his feet in response. It's a miracle I hold myself back.

Instead, I swelter in the heat of the bodies around me and think about how I ardently hate New York City.

California can't come soon enough.

13

"This is our stop," I say, flicking Emmitt's arm as the subway starts to pull in to Whitehall Street.

He glances up from his phone and looks almost bewildered by the near-empty train. "Is this the last stop?"

"In Manhattan, yes," I say, before inclining my head to the doors. "Come on."

The doors slide open and I quickly step out, looking for the nearest staircase. Emmitt trails after me slowly, his careful eyes taking in our surroundings. It doesn't look that different from any other subway stop, but I don't say that. As long as he's following me, he can stare at the empty station as much as he wants.

"Don't fall too behind," I say, climbing up the first set of stairs. He blinks as if my words startled him, but falls in line behind me.

When we get to the escalator, I lean against the railing and watch Emmitt idly for a moment, considering the arrogant tilt of his jaw and his observant eyes. He didn't say much for the duration of the subway ride, and I'm grateful.

I'm not eager to make small talk with a celebrity. I doubt we have anything in common, aside from our interest in the film industry—although his seems like less of an interest and more of a passing fancy. It's so unfair that he's the one with a career being handed to him on a silver platter of nepotism, while I have to struggle to win a single film competition.

But maybe it's not my place to judge. It's not as if I really know anything about him except for what he chooses to show me.

I grimace at the thought and turn away, looking forward as the top of the escalator comes in sight. Across from us is the ferry terminal, bold lettering on top of the building proclaiming it the *STATEN ISLAND FERRY.*

I glance at my phone, checking the time, but then my eyes bulge. *4:26 p.m.* We're going to miss the 4:30 ferry.

Without thinking about it, I grab Emmitt's arm and start pulling him up the escalator. "Hurry! We're going to miss the ferry."

Emmitt stumbles behind me. "What?"

"Hurry," I say, tugging more insistently.

After a beat, Emmitt follows, matching me for pace as I start tumbling up the stairs and then rushing across the street toward the terminal. "Mina, can't we—"

"Don't call me *Mina,*" I hiss, momentarily distracted. There's a crowd between us and the terminal, and with each passing moment comes the certainty we're going to have to board the next ferry.

I finally slump in defeat, letting go of his arm. Even if we make it in time, there's way too many people waiting ahead of us. I should've figured as much with rush hour approaching.

At my side, Emmitt's eyes are narrowed. "Is Mina not your name?"

I fold my arms across my chest. "No."

He purses his lips, the disbelief written plain across his face. "That's what Rosie calls you."

"Rosie is my best friend," I say with a raised eyebrow. "You are a stranger. Call me Samina, or nothing at all. You wouldn't like it if I called you Mitt, would you?"

Emmitt's mouth curls in distaste. "Mitt is a horrid nickname."

I offer him a sharp smile. "I think it's rather fitting."

He huffs, looking away from me. "Point made. I won't call you Mina."

I pat his shoulder amicably. "And I won't call you Mitt. The best of both worlds." I'm tempted to make some kind of joke about his blond hair and Hannah Montana, but we're not at that level of friendship and we never will be.

We wade deeper into the terminal, and I head for a row of seats, intending to plug in my headphones and wait out the next thirty minutes without speaking to Emmitt.

When I sit down, Emmitt stops in front of me, reaching in his bag and pulling out a slim black camera. I study it briefly, but I don't know enough about cameras to make any kind of relevant judgment. I briefly wonder what happened to the disposable camera he bought from the deli the day we met, before discarding the thought. It doesn't matter.

He hangs the strap around his neck so the camera rests against his chest as he takes in our surroundings, catching sight of the glittering blue bay through the glass walls. "The ocean?" he asks. "You meant literal waves."

I nod, tapping my fingers against the edge of my seat. "It works, right? The ocean seemed like a good backdrop for photographs."

A smile pulls at Emmitt's mouth, though it doesn't fully bloom to life like before. "It works," he agrees, his expression thoughtful as he looks around.

Then he lifts the camera to his face, the shutter clicking as he takes a photo of the terminal. I lean forward without thinking, watching him.

Emmitt doesn't seem to notice, his attention on whatever he's seeing through the lens of his camera. He adjusts the setting without looking up, the lens zooming in and out as he moves in a slow circle, observing the people around us.

There's something strange about this scene, as if Emmitt is separate from the rest of the world. His hair is bright in the afternoon sunlight, and every time he lifts his head to take in a sight, his brown eyes are glittering. He holds a million secrets in his gaze, and it's increasingly hard to look away.

No wonder he's an actor. Even in real life, he manages to captivate any audience.

When he's facing me again, he lowers his camera and arches his brows. "What? Why are you staring at me?"

My cheeks burn and I look away immediately, before he can call me out any further. This would be so much easier if his features weren't as striking as they are. "It's nothing."

Emmitt hums, a sound that implies far too much, and I curl my fingers into my palms to keep from making a sharp-tongued response.

He's about to drop into the seat beside me when he falters, sniffing the air. "What is that?"

I glance at him from the corner of my eye. His nose is wrinkled, his eyes scanning the row in front of us, as if it'll give him the answer he's looking for. "The smell of cinnamon?" I ask.

Emmitt's gaze immediately darts to me. "Yes. You smell it, too?"

I snort and tilt my head in the opposite direction. "Auntie Anne's. They sell pretzels."

Emmitt follows my line of vision, and his eyes light up at the sight of the small counter tucked away in the terminal. "It smells really good."

"Go knock yourself out, then, pretty boy," I say, shrugging my shoulders. "We have another twenty-five minutes before the ferry pulls in."

Without another word, Emmitt walks off in the direction of Auntie Anne's. I lean back in my seat and stare at the clock positioned on the wall, willing the minutes to go by faster.

It's because I'm staring at the time that I realize five minutes have passed and Emmitt still hasn't come back.

I glance at Auntie Anne's and see Emmitt leaned over the counter, a crooked grin on his face. The girl behind the register is blushing bright red and fumbling with change. My eyebrows rise of their own accord. It seems Emmitt Ramos lives up to his flirtatious reputation.

For no discernable reason, something uncomfortable tugs at my chest, but I quickly shove it down. Whatever. As long as he comes back in time for the ferry.

When Emmitt finally comes back with a cup of pretzel

sticks, I note the phone number written across the lid and shake my head slightly. He doesn't seem to notice, picking out one of the cinnamon sticks with an expression of glee.

"Happy?" I ask, but it comes out less snarky than I hoped for.

Emmitt smirks, taking the seat beside me. "Elated, love."

I roll my eyes and turn my attention to my phone, scrolling through Twitter, but the scent of cinnamon is even stronger now. I lick my lips, keeping my gaze on my screen.

My view is obstructed when Emmitt holds the cup out in front of me. "Want one?" he asks.

"No," I say, but at the most inopportune moment of all time, my stomach rumbles, giving me away.

Emmitt chuckles darkly. "Are you sure?"

I turn to him, my glare harsh. "Yes, I'm—"

Before I can finish my sentence, he shoves a cinnamon stick inside my mouth, and I falter incredulously.

Emmitt's lips are curled in amusement as he pokes one of my puffed cheeks. "You don't have to be so stubborn all the time."

I reach up and roughly bite off the piece still in my mouth. I would never admit it aloud, but the pretzel is *really fucking good*, and I immediately want another bite. "You are such a dickhead."

"I offer you food out of the kindness of my heart and I'm a dickhead?" Emmitt pouts far too dramatically, but there's still a sharp awareness in his eyes that I don't trust. "There's no winning with you."

"Shut up," I mutter, turning away. When he isn't looking, I take another bite of the pretzel stick.

It's clear I'm not as discreet as I think I am, because seconds later, Emmitt places the entire cup in my lap and walks away, whistling quietly. "All yours, sweetheart."

It seems he's slipped from asshole mode to heartbreaker mode, even with me. I can't say I have much of a preference for either one.

I stare after him with squinted eyes, but he only heads in the direction of the bathroom, absently toying with the strap of his camera.

By the time he returns, I've finished off the cup of pretzels, hungrier than I realized.

Emmitt flashes me a quick grin, and I flip him off in return, but it doesn't feel as hostile as the last time I did it. The thought leaves me disgruntled. I can't let Emmitt Ramos win me over with *pretzels*.

A few minutes later, they call on passengers for the next ferry, and we both gather our things and head for the entryway. There are too many bodies packed around us, and Emmitt holds his camera almost protectively as we press forward.

"No one is going to steal your camera right off your neck," I say, maneuvering my way through a gaggle of businessmen.

Emmitt slants me a look. "I know that. I just don't want my lens to get scratched."

I open my mouth to reply, but nothing rises to the tip of my tongue. I press my lips together, irked that he managed to leave me speechless.

In a matter of minutes, we board the Staten Island Ferry, and I lead Emmitt to the middle of the deck, where the windows lend a clear view out to the ocean. The weather is still bright, the skies clear of clouds. The waves sweep steadily against the side of the ferry, a rhythmic beat that exists on the edge of time.

"Knock yourself out," I say, setting my stuff down on one of the seats near the windows. The inside of the ferry reminds of me of a subway car, if it were expanded to fit hundreds of people. "I'll be here if you need me."

Emmitt nods, but it's as if my words go in one ear and exit the other, his eyes faraway as he stares out at the sea. I follow his gaze, taking in the Atlantic Ocean again. The water is ephemeral blue, glittering like diamonds in the blazing sunlight.

Sometimes, I forget how beautiful New York is. It's easy to get caught up in the rush of the bustling city, but in the quiet moments, there really is something picturesque about this place.

Eventually, Emmitt wanders away and starts talking to the passengers, which makes me sit up in surprise. I cock my head, trying to hear what he's saying. "...permission to photograph you."

Oh. I blink, looking on as a little girl nods with enthusiasm.

Emmitt grins widely—God, that *infuriating* grin—in return.

For the next ten minutes, he goes to different passengers and asks if they'll allow him to photograph them, and most of them readily agree. He even explains the contest to those who ask what the photos are for, and a few of the little kids wave eagerly at the camera, playing on the prompt. It seems he's unaware I'm watching him, because some part of his facade drops. There's something almost sweet about the way he talks to his photography subjects, infinitely more genuine than when he turned on the charm for the girl at Auntie Anne's.

I can't help but smile at the sight of a boy with his front teeth missing waving like it's the last thing he'll ever do. It's then that Emmitt turns his camera away from the boy and onto me.

Before my smile can slip, the flash goes off and the shutter sounds. My facial muscles are frozen for a moment, but my expression twists within seconds. "You didn't ask *me* for permission, dickhead!"

Emmitt laughs. "You look good in the light, love."

I huff in annoyance, but the knowledge that he's never going to use that photograph comforts me.

A few minutes later, Emmitt shows up in my vicinity again, staring out the window with wide eyes. "Is that the Statue of Liberty?"

I glance over my shoulder, spotting the green figure in the distance. My hand itches toward my phone, to record in the same way Emmitt is taking photographs. This might be one of the last times I ride the ferry before I go off to college. "The one and only."

Emmitt exhales, his expression caught between intrigue and…melancholy? "New York City is a wonder, isn't it?"

I frown. His words aren't that different from my earlier thoughts, but it's weird hearing someone say it aloud. "I suppose."

He stares at me for half a second, his expression scrutinizing. A strange chill passes over me—it's as if he's seeing more than he's supposed to—but then he looks away, turning back to the Statue of Liberty. I force myself to stop clenching my jaw and to open the camera app on my phone instead.

The rest of the ride goes by quickly and I keep filming

until we arrive at Staten Island. I grimace at the crowd wait-ing on the other side. We have to hurry if we want to make the ferry back.

"Come on," I say, tugging Emmitt's arm. He follows me readily, still taking photographs. The sound of the shutter has all but faded into the background now that I've heard it over a dozen times in the last ten minutes alone.

I try not to think too hard on that.

14

When we finally board the ship back, I slump in my new seat, exhausted. I expect Emmitt to keep taking photographs for the prompt, but he sits across from me instead and the camera flashes in my face.

I turn to him in surprise. "What are you doing?"

He responds by taking another photo of me.

"I'm going to throw something at you," I warn, pointing a finger at him. "I don't think your precious little camera will enjoy being crushed by my economics textbook."

Emmitt's mouth curls with amusement. "Sorry. I just needed photographic evidence in case you decided to push me overboard."

I roll my eyes. "Bold of you to assume I wouldn't toss your camera to the sharks after I'm finished with you."

"Oh, say it again, I'm close," Emmitt teases, a wicked light in his eyes. This time, I really do contemplate throwing my textbook at him.

"I don't know who told you your jokes were funny, but they were lying," I say darkly.

Emmitt laughs, throwing his head back. There's a beauty mark on his neck that my eyes are drawn to, but I quickly divert my gaze.

God, I wish I could put a paper bag over his head. Maybe then I'd have some peace in my heart.

Instead of focusing on that, I pull out a different topic from the hat of options in my head. "Why are you doing this contest anyway?"

Emmitt's humor dies immediately, and he stares at me with a flat expression. I blink at him, trying to make sense of the sudden mood change. He's so *strange*. It seems he can flip between personas as he pleases.

Sometimes he's bold and flirtatious, and other times he's cold and aloof. I can't tell which one of the personalities is his true self. I'm slowly leaning more toward the latter, even as he puts on a bright performance.

"I like photography," he says baldly.

"I figured that much," I say, raising an eyebrow. "That wasn't the answer I was looking for."

"Then you should ask more specific questions," Emmitt returns, his gaze unrelenting.

I furrow my brows, considering the stiff set to his shoulders. "Okay. Why is it a secret that I'm helping you with this contest?"

Emmitt's brown eyes are glacial, and I almost think he's going to remain silent, but then he says, "Because my mum can't know about it, and the more people that know, the more likely it'll get back to her."

"Your *mum*?" I repeat. That was the last thing I expected. It seems unfathomable that Emmitt Ramos could also have family problems like any other normal teenager.

His expression doesn't shift. "That's what I said. Where did those brain cells you were boasting about go, love?"

I make a face at him, unimpressed. And he calls *me* rude. "Why can't your mother know?"

Emmitt shrugs, the movement nonchalant, despite the intensity of his gaze. "She wouldn't approve."

But why not? I want to ask. I don't, because I can already tell he won't answer, not when his jaw is that tense. I can't help but resent the fact I've spent enough time with him to identify his emotions. "I see. And you're doing the contest anyway?"

He offers me a mirthless smile. "As I said, I love photography."

"Huh," I say, studying his expression. There's more to Emmitt Ramos than I anticipated. He has passions and dreams of his own, outside of what his family expects of him. It's weird to think we might actually have something in common.

Knowing that Shana Torres, the photographer running Emmitt's contest, is from Spain makes me wonder if this is some way to connect with his father, to keep the bond between them alive.

But maybe that's not my place to speculate.

"What about you?" Emmitt says, startling me out of an extended silence. "What about your little Golden Ivy competition? Why are you so adamant about winning?"

The truth gets stuck in my throat. *Because I have to.* "I'm the co-president of the film club. Why wouldn't I want to win?"

"I see both of us excel at evading questions," Emmitt says too lightly.

Before I can protest, he lifts a finger to his lips, his rings brushing against his mouth as he shushes me. I squint at him suspiciously, watching as he cocks his head. "Tell me about the short film."

"Do you even care?" I ask.

"Would I ask if I didn't care?"

"I wouldn't put it past you."

Emmitt releases a low laugh. "Ah, love, it seems you're learning my bad habits already."

"Not by any choice of my own," I say under my breath.

Still, Emmitt looks entertained by the notion. I restrain the urge to grumble further, though I dearly want to.

"Won't you tell me, Samina?" he asks, staring at me through hooded lids. "I've already asked twice."

"One of these days, someone is going to stab you, and I'm going to watch on pleasantly," I say, scowling.

A catlike grin stretches across Emmitt's face. "I won't ask again, Samina."

I hate the sound of my name in his mouth. He says it like it's more than it is, like it holds weight and meaning, like it's a weapon that he's eager to use.

"It's about these two girls that are best friends," I say after a moment, looking away from his smug expression.

"Like you and Rosie?"

I snort. "Decidedly not like me and Rosie. The main character—Charlie—is in love with her best friend, Vivienne. They've known each other since childhood. Charlie only realized her feelings a few months ago, and she's been trying to work up the courage to tell Vivienne the truth, but she's afraid."

Emmitt makes an agreeable noise. "Where does my character fit in, then? I'm assuming I'm not playing Charlie or Vivienne."

"No, you're playing Nick. He's the captain of the football team."

"Ah, a footie player," Emmitt says, nodding. "I see."

"Not footie," I say, raising an eyebrow. "Football. You're the quarterback."

Emmitt's nose wrinkles immediately. "Oh. I would've much preferred footie. Or soccer. Whatever you want to call it."

"You should take that up with the person who wrote the script," I say.

He almost looks like he's considering it. "Who wrote the script?"

I smile viciously in response.

Emmitt sighs. "You. You wrote it."

"Ding, ding, we have a winner! Would you like a medal or a trophy in recognition of having common sense?"

He gives me a pointed look, but it does little to dampen my mood. Pulling one over on him is oddly satisfying.

"As I was saying," I continue, "you're playing Nick. He's your typical asshole with a heart of gold trope."

"Interesting that you chose to cast me for his role," Emmitt says, tapping his ringed fingers against his knee.

"It wasn't much of a choice," I say. "If we want to win the competition, we need you to have screen time, and Nick is the only one who has a significant role in the film aside from Charlie and Vivienne."

Emmitt leans forward, still far enough that he can't reach me, but far too close regardless. "What is Nick's purpose in this film?"

"You'll have to come and watch our auditions tomorrow to find out," I say, offering him an icy smile. "We have a deal, after all."

He smiles back, equally as cold. "How could I ever forget?"

Twenty minutes later, I leave Emmitt on the subway platform, and he stares after me with a piercing gaze. As I board the subway car, he raises his camera to his face. He snaps a photo of me through the doors, right before the train pulls out of the station, and I flip him off.

On the ride home, the score to *Inception* (2010) blasting in my earphones, something peculiar occurs to me.

Those few hours I spent with Emmitt today, exploring New York City—it was the first time in months that my thoughts didn't stray to USC.

I stare at the ground in dismay. I'm *always* thinking about California. But the second we stepped onto the platform at Whitehall Street, it was as if all thoughts of a future far away from here vanished, disappeared in plain sight.

Strange.

I swallow uncomfortably and lean my head against the subway map behind me.

Emmitt's lilting voice echoes in my head. *New York City is a wonder, isn't it?*

15

Auditions start off with a bang.

A literal bang, because Grant thinks it's a great idea to try to set off firework sparklers in the auditorium, which is *definitely* a fire hazard. I'm surprised the bright red curtains don't go up in flames.

I hold my head in my hands. "Rosie, please collect him before I do. Fireworks do *not* help team morale, no matter what Grant says."

Rosie squeezes my shoulder. "It's fine, Mina."

The two of us are sitting at a table in front of the stage, three dozen applications before us. Most of the other film club members are seated behind the table, whispering to one another. Though Rosie and I make the final casting decisions, the film club has a tradition of allowing every member to vote for who they think should be cast in each role.

The freshmen are overly excited, whispering to one another as they examine the people waiting to audition. I'm glad to see Christina among them—it looks like she decided to stay in film club, after all. She and all her friends are staring up at the stage in awe. It's their first time, so I understand their bright eyes and wide smiles—Rosie and I were also incredibly eager during freshman year, but now that we're in charge... I'm more stressed than anything else.

The drama club is seated on the opposite end of the auditorium, along with a few stragglers that aren't a part of any specific club but wanted to audition anyway.

Half of the stage crew is fiddling around on the stage, working on sets for the spring play, but we don't need the entire stage for auditions anyway, so I don't pay them much mind. Even then, I can't help but sympathize with them since they look as inclined to smack Grant upside the head as I am.

Meanwhile, Emmitt is off to the side of the stage, chuckling as if all this is *amusing*.

I blow out a harsh breath.

At my side, Rosie is busy stealing glances at Sofia, but anytime their eyes meet, she twists her head back to the stage so fast I'm worried her neck will snap.

"Are you done yet?" I call to Grant.

Grant looks up, blinking innocuously. "What did I do?"

I narrow my eyes, and he quickly scampers off the stage, though he's laughing, and Emmitt offers him a high five as they disappear behind the curtains.

"Clowns," I say under my breath. "I've let *clowns* enter the film club."

Rosie nudges my shoulder. "At least people find the circus entertaining?"

I give her a flat look.

She laughs loudly, which lightens some of the weight on my shoulders. "Come on. We've got this."

With a sigh, I nod. "All right, let's manifest it. I'm speaking our success into existence."

Rosie grins, offering me one of her pinky fingers. "We are planting the seed."

"And we will see the harvest," I say, linking my pinky with hers.

"Next!" Rosie shouts.

Another sophomore climbs onstage, her expression hopeful. "My name is Zoe. I'd like to audition for the role of Charlie. I'll be reading from the eighth scene."

"Go ahead," Rosie says, offering her an encouraging nod. I lean back in my seat, absently chewing on my pen cap as I flip to the aforementioned page.

Zoe clears her throat, before looking up at us with an anguished expression. *"Vivienne... I'm sorry, I didn't think—"* She falters, her lips parted on a sharp inhale. *"I didn't realize it would get so messed up. I didn't—"* She closes her eyes, her fingers clenched tightly at her sides. *"I love you. I should have told you sooner."*

"How long?" Rosie asks, reading from the script, her voice monotonous, though her cheeks are flushed with color. We flipped a coin for who would have to read along with the actors, and I lucked out in picking heads. There's a reason the two of us prefer to be behind the camera. *"How long have you loved me?"*

Zoe opens her eyes, and they glisten in the overhead spotlights. *"I think I've always loved you."* She pauses, taking a deep breath and looking away, as if she can't bear to meet our eyes. *"Do you hate me? Do you want me to leave you alone?"*

"I could never hate you," Rosie reads. *"I could never hate you—how could you ever think that? I just wish you would've told me before…"*

My eyes dart away from Zoe's performance to Emmitt, where he's idly swinging his legs back and forth as he sits on the edge of the stage. He looks up, as if he can feel my gaze, and offers me a lurid grin.

I glare at him before looking back at Zoe, whose face has broken with painful relief. *"You love me, too?"*

"And scene!" Rosie says.

I start clapping first, genuinely impressed. It's been a while since I've seen an underclassman with such promise. Though we probably won't cast her for the role of Charlie, I can't help but make a note next to her name anyway, to include as one of the side characters. I have a feeling she's going to make a future film club president *very* happy.

"Thank you, Zoe," I say, offering her a small smile. "That was a lovely performance."

Zoe beams and bows, before she files off the stage. I lean my chin on my hands, my elbows braced against the table.

"She was really good," Rosie says in a hushed voice, staring after her. "I really believed her performance."

I nod in agreement, starring Zoe's application. "Maybe we could cast her for Emily's character?"

Rosie's eyes light up. "I like that idea. She'd be great beside Emmitt. I'll make a note, too."

I wrinkle my nose at the mention of Emmitt, though it makes sense. Emily's character is the younger sister to Nick's character, so Emmitt and Zoe would need to play off each other while we're filming.

Again, my gaze darts to Emmitt, who's now busying himself talking to some of the stage crew. More ridiculous is the fact they're indulging him.

I look back at my notes, willing myself to stop paying attention to him. I don't know why my eyes keep seeking him out, but I'm getting really annoyed with my own brain. As if it wasn't enough to plague me with an annoying voice that loves to spout my insecurities back at me, it's now seeking out an asshole celebrity for eye candy.

Rosie must notice because she pokes my cheek. "You keep looking at Emmitt."

I press my lips together, tugging on the end of one of my braids. "I'm not."

"You are," Rosie says, raising a brow. "Did you think I wouldn't notice?"

I huff, willing my cheeks not to warm. "Maybe I didn't. You spend most of your time looking at Sofia anyway."

Rosie blinks slowly, as she's processing the words, and then her expression falls. My heart constricts in sudden awareness of the fact she looks hurt by what I said.

"I'm paying attention to the auditions," Rosie says quietly. "I would never jeopardize the competition."

I shake my head, almost panicked. "I know. I didn't mean it like that. I—"

Before I can finish my sentence, Sofia comes up to audition, skipping to the center of the stage. "Hi, I'm Sofia," she says, offering us a crinkly-eyed smile. "I'd like to audition for the role of Vivienne. I'll be reading from the third scene."

Rosie's mouth opens but no words come out. I swallow past the lump in my throat and elbow her lightly, making her snap out of it.

"Go ahead," my best friend says, her voice hoarse.

I stare at her for an extra beat, my stomach twisting into knots, and then I force myself to turn back to the stage.

Sofia takes a deep breath, before a huge smile breaks across her face. *"Oh my God, Charlie, look. Look, look!"*

"What?" Rosie reads from the script, the tips of her ears turning red.

Sofia bounces on her toes, a look of wonder on her face. *"Someone left this note in my locker. It's...a pickup line?"*

"Oh?" Rosie reads, and I consider my best friend's expression, watching as some tension slips out of her, replaced by something warm.

Sofia nods, clutching a letter to her chest, her eyes wide. She even brought her own props—impressive. *"It says, 'I can't remember the other twenty-one letters of the alphabet. All I know is U R A QT.' It's addressed to me. What do you think it means?"*

Rosie coughs, pulling my attention back to her. *"Well, from over here it looks like you have a secret admirer."*

"No way, Charlie," Sofia says, scoffing, but then she hesitates, looking down at the letter. *"I mean, there's no way, right? Do you really think...do you really think someone likes me?"*

"Yeah," Rosie says, her tone slightly off, as if she's out of breath. I doubt anyone else can tell. *"I think someone does."*

"Huh," Sofia says, running a finger along the edge of the letter and worrying her bottom lip between her teeth. *"It doesn't feel real, you know? Like why would someone leave a note*

in my *locker? I'm just…me. I don't know."* She looks up, a soft smile playing at her mouth. *"I guess I never thought the day would come."*

"I always knew it would," Rosie says softly, before clearing her throat. "And scene!"

"Yay!" Sofia does a bizarre but enthusiastic celebratory dance. "Thank you so much!"

"You were wonderful," Rosie says, and each word seems to carry a weight. "Thank you."

As soon as Sofia hops off the stage, I turn to Rosie again. "Listen, I didn't mean—"

"Let's just forget it, okay?" Rosie says, tucking an auburn curl behind her ear. "It's fine."

I shake my head. "It's not fine, I wasn't—"

"It's *fine*, Mira," Rosie says, but she won't look me in the eye. "I think Sofia should be cast for Vivienne."

"Okay," I say.

Rosie's mouth twists. "Are you saying okay because you agree, or okay because you think I want you to agree?"

I stare at her hopelessly, willing her to just *look* at me. "Because I agree."

"Great," Rosie says, but her tone is flat. "Next!"

Auditions go by quietly from that point on, Rosie giving me short, to-the-point answers, while I sit there contemplating walking into traffic. Why don't I ever *think* before I speak?

This competition—it's everything to me—but I don't want to damage my friendship with Rosie because of it. I thought she'd understand, but the last few weeks, it seems like we're no longer on the same page.

Every day, it feels like the chasm between Rosie and me grows, and I'm terrified I might never be able to overcome the gap.

We take a ten-minute break halfway through auditions, and before I can try to talk to Rosie again, she stands up and walks across the auditorium, to where Sofia, Linli, and Kaity are talking to one another.

I sigh after her, slumping in my seat.

Naturally, my eyes land on Emmitt, standing at the back of the auditorium as he talks to a bunch of underclassmen from film club. Half of them are giggling at whatever he's saying—which I seriously doubt is funny—while the rest stare up at him in awe.

I don't know why it gets on my nerves so badly, but part of it is probably residual frustration over the situation with Rosie. Either way, seconds later I find myself moving across the auditorium to where Emmitt is, carrying a script in my hands.

When I approach the group that's formed around him, he's saying, "—but they weren't nearly as lovely as all of you," in a horrendous American accent. "Maybe one of you could show me around? I still haven't been able to find the planetarium. I swear, this school is a maze."

"Oh my God," I say in disbelief.

Emmitt turns to look at me, and his eyes gleam with delight. "Glad you could join us, sweetheart."

The underclassmen titter curiously, looking between us. Blood rushes to my cheeks, and Emmitt's amusement only heightens my irritation.

"Shut up," I say and slap the script against his chest. "Start memorizing Nick's parts."

Brighton perks up. "Ezra's auditioning for the himbo role?"

"Yes," I say, daring him to argue.

Instead, he raises his brows as he takes the script from me. "What's a himbo?"

"Do I look like Google?" I ask, placing my hands on my hips.

Emmitt considers me for a moment before turning a charming smile on Brighton. "Won't you tell me, darling?"

"Do *not*," I say, stepping bodily in between him and Brighton, shooting him a glare for even attempting to flirt with one of my film kids. I look at the underclassmen over my shoulder. "Stay away from his clown ass."

Christina frowns. "Mina, didn't *you* bring him to film club?"

Emmitt smirks. "Yeah, didn't you?"

I raise a finger in warning. "Fuck off," I say to him, and he snaps his teeth at me, making me pull my hand back immediately.

Brighton and Christina both giggle behind me, and I glower at them. They pointedly look away but keep side-eyeing me in a way that makes me want to scream.

"All of you deserve better than whatever all this—" I gesture to all of Emmitt "—is."

Emmitt takes a step closer, his arm brushing against mine. "What exactly is all *this*?"

I narrow my eyes at him. "Don't make me stab you."

"Kinky," he says idly.

"You are *incorrigible*," I say, pushing him away with one

hand. He goes easily, but there's an impish grin on his lips now. I swear to God, he's making a game out of pissing me off. "Stay away from the underclassmen. In fact, stay away from everyone in film club."

"Does that include you?" Emmitt asks, leaning a shoulder against the wall, his eyes dancing in amusement. *Dickhead.*

"It *especially* includes me," I say, before turning back to the underclassmen. "Back to the front of the auditorium! Come on! We only have a few minutes left in the break."

"Okay, Mom," says Andie, a sophomore. She turns a cheeky smile on Emmitt. "Bye, Dad."

"Andie," I say sharply, but she's running off with all the other freshmen, their laughter filling the room.

"Bye, dear!" Emmitt says, waving his fingers flirtatiously.

I jab my elbow into his ribs, grumbling under my breath, before following the underclassmen down the aisle.

I try not to look back, but my body betrays me anyway, and I meet Emmitt's dark eyes as he winks.

Ugh.

16

The next day, I miss half the school day alongside all the other seniors for the Senior Movie Event. It's one of the many events our school throws together every year in the spirit of celebrating our last year in high school. I think they must know most of us aren't exactly paying attention in classes anyway, so skipping a few periods for a movie won't affect any of our grades.

At least it'll give Emmitt some insight into what a normal American high school is like. I don't know if he's really *learned* anything since coming here, but if this is what Firebrand Studios wants him to do, then I'm not going to be one to question it.

The school event makes it so I don't have a chance to talk to Rosie in the morning. When I finally catch up to her, she seems to have all but forgotten the day before. She's all sparkly eyes and soft smiles as she waves for me to join her in the back of the auditorium.

"Horrible choice," she says, gesturing to the projector, where they're booting up the live action version of *The Lion King*.

I make a face at the screen. "They should've just played the animated version if they were going to go this route."

"Right?" Rosie looks up at the coffered ceiling, holding her hands out in front of her. "God, if you're out there, *please* stop letting our principal make decisions best left to film club."

"You're not even religious," I say, but something settles in my chest at her airy attitude today and the easy way she smiles at me.

"Not yet," Rosie says, tapping her cheek. "But if Principal Khan keeps this up, I might have to adopt Jesus into my life."

I snort and lean back in my seat as they dim the lights, and the movie flickers to life.

After the movie, I barely have a chance to speak to Rosie. I plan to during lunch, but she meets me by my locker, fluttering anxiously. When she explains she's going to the library to study for an AP Calc exam, I offer to join her, but she shakes me off, promising to catch me later.

By the end of the day, I exhale in defeat and accept that I'm just going to have to let this go. Especially if Rosie is pretending it never happened. Maybe she just wants to put this all behind us. I'm all for it, but I can't help but worry it's going to blow up in my face.

Anam meets me in the front of the school, her eyes roaming my expression. "What's wrong?"

I give her a warm look, immediately pulling her into a hug. "Nothing."

She laughs, squeezing my waist. "Something is definitely wrong, but I'll let you have it. Are you ready to go?"

I pull back, nodding. We made plans to go to Queens Center Mall a few days ago in preparation for midwinter break next week. Anam has a date—which she's still being super secretive about, blushing deeply anytime I ask—and begged me to help her choose an outfit.

"I'm still waiting on a name," I say as we walk toward the subway. Before we can get far, Emmitt appears in my line of vision.

He catches sight of me, his eyes quickly darting between me and my sister, before he grins obnoxiously and starts walking toward us.

Oh my God, absolutely not. I don't even want to imagine the chaos of him and Anam meeting.

"Do not *start* with me," I shout over Anam's head, pulling her behind me. "Go home, dickhead."

Emmitt falters halfway toward us, arching his brows. When I keep glaring adamantly, he raises his hands in surrender. "I just wanted to say hello to your beautiful—sister, is it?"

Anam peeks around my shoulder with wide eyes. "Is that Emmitt?"

I cover her eyes with one hand. "We have plans, remember?"

She snorts but doesn't try to push my fingers away. "There's always next time."

"We're leaving," I tell her before shooting Emmitt another dirty look. As if flirting with the film club members wasn't bad enough. "We're *leaving*," I repeat louder.

"Bye, gorgeous!" Emmitt calls, before wrinkling his nose dramatically. "And you, too, Samina, I suppose."

"I can't stand you," I say, flipping him off with my free hand. "Good the fuck *bye*."

He chuckles but doesn't follow as I slowly back away with Anam behind me. When we're a safe distance apart, I turn back around, releasing a deep breath. "Right. Anyway, what's your date's name?"

Anam stares at me with a fond expression. "I don't think my date is the one we should be worried about."

I bump into her shoulder roughly. "Their name is...?"

She keeps smiling but allows the change in topic. "Not yet. You'll scare them off."

"That's not true," I say, my lips turning down in a pout. "I can be nice."

She raises her eyebrows. "You threatened my last boyfriend with bodily harm."

"I should have threatened him with worse," I say. "Maybe then he would've thought twice before cheating on you *three times*."

My sister makes a disturbed face. "Yikes. Yeah. Okay, fair point." Then she offers me a sheepish grin. "My date isn't like him."

"That remains to be seen," I say, but squeeze her hand. "Come on."

Anam abandons me in Aldo, looking for a pair of strappy high heels that I wouldn't be caught dead in. I'm not particularly clumsy, but I'd rather not tempt fate by wearing shoes higher than two inches.

I browse through flip-flops instead, considering them with

a critical eye. New York summers get pretty warm, but I imagine California must be significantly worse.

I've never been a huge fan of the beach, but I think I could grow to love it. At any rate, I'm going to need much more beach apparel than I currently own.

If you get in, a treacherous voice whispers. To spite that thought, I grab the shoes I was eyeing and head for the register.

When Anam finds me again, I'm carrying a bag at my side, two pairs of flip-flops tucked away.

"Did you buy something?" she asks.

"Just some flip-flops," I say, looping my arm through hers. I'll get into USC and make use of these. I don't care what anyone says, not even the voice in my head. "Where to next?"

Anam pauses, giving me a strange look I can't decipher, before she shakes her head. "I was going to head to H&M. Good with you?"

"Sounds great," I say, and follow her, taking note of various window displays as we go. Anam keeps looking back at me, her eyes cloudy, and I give her an uncertain smile in return.

When we get to H&M, Anam sticks weirdly close to me, trailing me as I wander through the store. I falter, giving her a cursory look. "Do you need help picking something out? I thought we were going to do what we usually do, and you'd let me choose from options you picked out."

"I think I'll just walk with you for a while," Anam says quietly.

I furrow my brows. "If that's what you want."

We wander through the store, and I stop in front of the

swimwear section, reaching out and picking through different options.

"It's February," Anam says, her tone a little sharp.

I glance to the side, but her attention is fixed on a sun-hat
display. I turn back to a rack of shorts, looking for my waist
size. "I know, but I figure I might as well start shopping for
California. Plus, these are priced cheaper right now."

"Ma's not going to be happy if you buy those," Anam
mutters.

I laugh under my breath. "Since when do you care what
Ma thinks?"

My sister is silent for an odd amount of time, but then she
finally says, "You're right. You might as well buy the whole
store in preparation for USC."

I wiggle my brows at her. "I'm thinking about it."

Anam doesn't react, her gaze focused firmly on a rack of
sunglasses. My smile slips, and I consider her more earnestly.
Maybe she's more nervous about this date than I realized.

"Hey," I say, laying a hand on her shoulder. "It'll be okay."

She starts under my touch, looking at me with wide eyes.
"What?"

"Your date," I say, tucking a strand of blue hair behind her
ear. "It'll be great, and if it's not, I'll be home waiting for you
with a pint of ice cream."

Anam stares at me. "You'll be home," she echoes.

I nod. "I'll be home, and we can have a movie night. We'll
get through it together, like always."

"Together, like always," Anam says and looks away, a hoarse
laugh escaping her throat. "Right. Yeah. Sorry."

"No apology necessary," I say, booping her nose. "I love you, Anam."

She offers me an unsteady smile. "I love you, too, Apu."

Though the words sound true, there's something off about them—but I can't put my finger on what. I settle for throwing an arm around Anam's shoulders and leading her away from the swimwear section.

As I do, I ignore the pit forming in my stomach. It's nothing. Anam is just having an off day.

I shouldn't overthink it.

17

Auditions on Friday aren't as intense—I nearly beat Grant's ass when I saw him enter the auditorium with more sparklers— but I still sit on the edge of my seat, nervous that I'm going to say something wrong to Rosie again.

My muscles are tense and each sentence that leaves my mouth feels stilted. I'm careful to avoid the topic of Sofia entirely, instead only discussing the auditions taking place in front of us.

Emmitt is also nowhere to be seen, so my attention isn't momentarily stolen by his shenanigans, though a worry arises in the back of my head that he's ditching film club altogether— he hadn't mentioned anything about missing today's meeting, but that doesn't mean anything when it comes to him.

For all I know, he could be busy flirting with half a dozen girls outside the auditorium. Or maybe he's just lost again. I've found him wandering the hallways countless times this past week alone, looking bewildered by his surroundings. It's a distinct reminder that for all Emmitt blends in with the film club, he doesn't belong here. This is all a learning experience for him, so he can go off and play the main role in a blockbuster film for Firebrand Studios.

He's not like us. He's not like me.

And I still don't know if I can depend on him to come through and deliver on our deal.

As if my thoughts are being astral projected, Emmitt appears from behind the curtains, his expression cool.

I blink in surprise, but Rosie is smiling. "Next!"

Emmitt walks toward center stage and stops in front of us. "Hello, I'm Ezra. I'd like to audition for the role of Nick. I'll be reading from the second scene."

"Did you know about this?" I ask Rosie in a hushed voice.

She laughs under her breath. "Well, we can't just *give* him the role, right? We have to make sure it seems fair. He told me you gave him the script to study."

I blink, recalling my fit of irritation during auditions the other day. "Oh. I suppose I did do that."

"Before we start, can I ask for a quick favor?" Emmitt asks, and a flicker of a smirk passes across his face. An uneasy feeling rises in me, butterflies fluttering insistently.

Rosie raises her brows. "What is it?"

His eyes are glittering. "I'm a little too nervous to audition with you. You are a goddess descended from the heavens, and I am but a mere mortal. Could I audition with Samina instead?"

"Yes," Rosie agrees before I can shut it down.

I give my best friend an appalled look. "Rosie, I—"

"The competition is at stake," she says back, her tone sickly sweet. "We need him, Mina."

I scowl. "We flipped a coin!"

"He asked for you specifically," Rosie says with a shrug, her eyes lit up mischievously. "The sooner you go along with it, the sooner it's done."

"I hate you," I say darkly, but turn my script to the third page, meeting Emmitt's gaze. "Go ahead."

He shakes his head, before beckoning me forward with a finger. "I work better in person."

My lips part. "What? No. We're not—"

"Mina, go up!" calls Kaity across the auditorium. "It's only a few minutes!"

"Yeah, go up, Mina!" echo members of the film club behind me.

I glare harshly at them and some of the underclassmen wither beneath my gaze. The other seniors aren't cowed, still grinning at me obnoxiously.

"You are all going to regret this," I hiss, before giving Rosie a desperate look. She knows more than anyone how much I detest being in any sort of spotlight. "Ro, don't make me go up there."

Rosie pokes my cheek. "You're on your own, bubs."

Emmitt clicks his tongue. "How long are you going to make me wait, Samina?"

I turn a fierce glare on him but jerkily stand up from my seat, snatching my script as I go. I don't *need* it, having written it and memorized all the words long before any of these actors, but at least it'll be one more barrier between Emmitt and me.

I climb onto the stage, muttering insults under my breath. I have to push past the red curtains, but eventually I make it to center stage.

Emmitt huffs a quiet laugh when I'm in hearing range.

"You say the sweetest things," he says, before holding a hand out for me to take.

I pointedly ignore it, instead crossing my arms. "Start."

He grins—quick and self-assured—before his expression softens. *"Hi, Charlie."*

"Hi, Nick," I say back, forcing my voice to stay even.

In the script, Nick and Charlie are close friends, neighbors who grew up beside each other—and Nick has a bit of an un-requited, but ultimately innocent, crush on her. I'm already dreading Emmitt's interpretation of Nick's character.

Emmitt shifts closer, his eyes warm. *"Emily said you'd be waiting for me after football practice. Is everything okay?"*

I fidget slightly, wishing I could look away from his tender expression. *"Not really. I need your help with something."*

Emmitt's lips part, his brows furrowing with concern. *"What's wrong?"* he asks softly, reaching forward and laying a hand on my arm.

My eyes dart down to where his rings press into my skin. *"I—I have a crush."*

"Oh?" Emmitt says, his voice taking on a different tone. Then his other hand is reaching for me, his fingers tilting my chin up until his gaze locks on mine. *"On who?"*

Why is it suddenly so hard to breathe? *"I—don't be mad at me. Please."*

Emmitt takes a step backward, examining me more thoroughly, his eyes uncertain as they flit across my features. *"There's nothing you could do to make me mad, Charlie."*

I swallow. *"Vivienne. I have a crush on Vivienne."*

Emmitt stares at me for an extended beat of silence. *"Vivienne... Chen?"*

"*The one and only,*" I say, looking down. "*I'm sorry, I never told you I was pansexual, I should have, but I—*"

He grabs my hands, and the words die on my lips. "*Don't apologize to me, Charlie,*" he says fiercely.

We stare at each other for a quiet moment before he breaks it, laughing uncertainly and running a hand through his blond hair. "*Since you said Vivienne, I'm assuming pansexual doesn't mean attraction to pans.*"

A hesitant giggle escapes my own lips. "*Not quite. More like an attraction to all genders.*"

Emmitt blinks, then cocks his head. "*Huh. You learn something new every day.*" He reaches forward again, this time to flick my nose. "*Won't you please stop frowning, and tell me how I can help instead?*"

"*You'll help? Really?*" I ask, my eyes wide.

He smiles softly, leaning forward to press a featherlight kiss to my cheek. I inhale sharply in surprise, since that wasn't a part of the script. "*Always.*"

"And scene!"

I pull away from Emmitt so fast I nearly twist my ankle. I open my mouth to say something—anything—to draw attention away from my flushed cheeks, but thunderous applause fills the auditorium instead.

I look out at the audience, and everyone is on their feet, clapping enthusiastically. Even Rosie is watching us with her mouth hanging open, something like awe written across her expression.

And I know it's not because of me.

I turn to Emmitt, but he's back to an impassive expression, nothing like the gentle and kind character he adopted mere seconds ago.

Knowing Emmitt Ramos is a professional actor is one thing. Seeing it for myself, being pulled in by his acting to a point where I nearly forgot how much I detest him, is an entirely different thing.

He's good. He's really, really good.

And for the first time it occurs to me that we might win. We might *actually* win the Golden Ivy film competition. My future is no longer a far-off impossibility.

There is hope. There is more than hope.

A wide grin stretches across my face.

Across from me, Emmitt's nonchalance falls apart, his eyes slightly wider than usual as he looks at me.

"What?" I ask, but even he can't ruin my good mood right now.

Emmitt releases a quiet breath of air, his stare focused on my mouth. "I think this is the first time I've seen you smile like you mean it."

I blink, my grin faltering for a moment. Has Emmitt been watching me the same way I watch him, cataloguing my expressions and mannerisms?

Before I can think about it for too long, Rosie joins me onstage, pulling me into a one-armed hug. "We're going to win, I'm certain of it!" she says in my ear, shaking me in her excitement.

I turn to her slowly, finding it difficult to tear my gaze away from Emmitt, but then my smile blooms back to life at the stars in her eyes. "Yes, we are."

intermission

"All this time, I hid in the darkness.
All this time, I was the light."
— MINA RAHMAN
(SCREENWRITER, *YOU ARE THE LIGHT*)

18

Maybe a normal teenager would enjoy midwinter break, but I spend the entire time wanting to scream into the void. I hate being around my parents for extended periods of time. My depression is always worse when I don't have anything to do, and having them around doesn't help *at all*.

Even more, now that winning the Golden Ivy competition is in reach, I'm more anxious than ever about what decision USC will make.

What if I don't get in? What if I don't get in? *What if I don't get in?*

I feel like I'm about to go stir-crazy, my mental health taking a slow downward turn as I sit at home, waiting and waiting and waiting.

"Poppy," Ma says, blocking my view of *Thoroughbreds* (2017) on the television. "Are you listening to me? Poppy!"

I grimace and look up at her, an apron tied around her waist, and an empty colander in her hands. "What?"

"All you do is sit around and do nothing," she gripes, frowning at me. "Why don't you help me cook dinner today? I'm making your favorite, ilish pulao."

My nose wrinkles. It is my favorite, but Ma usually makes plain rice and calls it a day. Baba is the cook in the house. "Why?"

Ma's frown deepens as she wipes sweat off her forehead with her sleeve. "Do I have to explain everything to you now? It's not as if you tell *us* anything."

My mood immediately drops, an anchor weighing down any lingering curiosity I had. "I wonder why that is," I say.

"Poppy," Ma says coldly. "Don't be so childish. It's shameful. Imagine if someone saw you being so immature? Come now, help me." She turns her head in the direction of the dining room, where Anam is on FaceTime with a friend. "Anam, why don't you join Poppy and me? Afterward, we can all do a puzzle together. I just ordered a—"

"I actually have homework to do," I say, turning off Netflix with a press of a button. "And it looks like Anam is busy, too, so…sorry."

Without another word, I head up the stairs, ignoring my mother's pointed glare.

I shut the door to my room behind me and I groan, rubbing my temples. There's never any peace with my parents—it's always barbed remarks hidden behind pleasantries. If we had done Ma's puzzle, she would've eventually turned the conversation back to staying in New York for college like she *always* does. Their disappointment is like a steadily spreading rash across my skin, and I'm tired of itching myself until I bleed.

Ironically enough, my love of film came from my parents.

When I was younger, my parents would buy us tickets to the movie theater every weekend.

We'd catch the earliest showing in the morning because tickets were half off for the first show, but my dad would make up for the early hour by buying us popcorn and candy.

Anam always put too much butter on the popcorn—a habit my dad loved to indulge—so me and my mom would share a packet of Sour Patch Kids instead.

Week after week, I watched every single movie I could get my hands on and found myself falling in love with films as a storytelling medium.

My parents were more than happy to support my love for films when it was just a hobby—the same way that they were happy to support Anam's love for volleyball when it was a harmless game she played in her spare time—but when it became more than that, suddenly their support was all but nonexistent.

It's not like I'm unsympathetic to what they've been through. They're both immigrants who have sacrificed so much to ensure that their children have every available opportunity. They worked hard to build this life for us, and now they want us to attain every possible success in order to make their hardships worthwhile.

But they've taken it too far. At some point, they started caring more about our futures than about us as human beings.

There's a way to want the best for us without being cruel. There's a way to want the best for us without causing us pain.

Maybe they don't know even know they're doing it. Maybe they're doing the best way they can.

Or maybe I'm just making up excuses to make this situation seem less awful.

Less than a minute later, my door opens again, and I turn around, a sharp dismissal on my tongue, but it's just Anam.

She looks as haggard as I feel. "I'm going to lose my damn mind."

I laugh tiredly. "Join the club, dude."

Anam holds out something out, which I quickly identify as a volleyball. "Want to throw some around to get away from all this?"

Though I'm not the most athletic, throwing a ball to Anam isn't too difficult a task. And if it makes my sister smile, it's worth it. "Say less," I say, grabbing a jean jacket off the back of my chair. "I'm ready."

Our backyard isn't particularly grand. Aside from our shed, it's basically all cement—which is typical, given it's New York City and we're not ridiculously wealthy. The only greenery are plants my mom bought from Home Depot, lining the fence sectioning our backyard from the Ali family's.

A few chairs and a small circular table are hidden in the shade of the shed, toward the back of the yard, and closer to our house is a volleyball net. In middle school, my dad helped Anam set it up. It was back when our parents saw our passions as silly little hobbies, so Baba was more than happy to buy Anam everything she needed to create her own little volleyball court.

In fact, I recall him encouraging her to play in the first place. "It'll get you out of the house, Anam," he used to tease before he'd turn his attention toward me. "Maybe you could join her, Poppy."

"Or we could go to the movie theater again," I'd say, and all of us would laugh.

But that feels like a lifetime ago now.

Anam and I stand on one side of the net, and I throw her the ball while she practices sets.

The set of her lips is determined, her hair tied into a tight ponytail, though a few flyaway blue hairs still fall into her face.

"Are you nervous for your next match?" I ask, tossing her another volleyball. She moves instantly, meeting the ball with the pads of her fingers and sending it in a high arc. "You were great against Nazifa's team last week."

The ball hits one of the red plastic cups we set up along the length of the net. She exhales a breath of relief before turning to me and shrugging.

I take the nonanswer as a *yes, she is nervous.*

"You're playing against Durham, right?" I ask, reaching out to pick up the volleyball as it rolls back toward me. "Isn't their captain slated for Duke University?"

Anam heaves a sigh. "Yeah. They've been scouting her since freshman year. She's the best libero I've ever seen."

I toss her the ball. "I'm not worried. *You* are the best setter I've ever seen."

"You don't exactly watch a lot of volleyball games," Anam says, but there's a small smile on her lips as she sets the ball again.

"I watch enough," I say, watching the ball knock out another plastic cup. "How many games have you had over the years? Like fifty? I've been to all of them."

"Definitely not fifty," Anam says. The tension knotting her shoulders seems to release with each successful set. "Let's not talk about it anymore. How is your film competition going?"

I bite the inside my cheek. "It's going good," I say, trying not to think about the impending doom of receiving USC's decision *again*. "We're all meeting up tomorrow to finalize casting decisions."

Anam nods, glancing up at the sky, holding a hand over her eyes to shield her gaze from the sun. "Is the weather supposed to be sunny again tomorrow?"

"God, I hope so," I say, immediately pulling out my phone to check. "Yeah, about the same as today. A little warmer, actually."

"Ooooh," Anam says, taking out her own phone. "Maybe Nazifa is free. I don't want to stay home alone with Ma and Baba if you're going to be out."

In the last year, Anam has been expressing that sentiment more and more often. A desire to be away from our parents, especially when it's clear I won't be at her side.

The protective instincts I hold in regard to my sister are iron hard. I'd do *anything* for her, and I've always suffered the brunt of our parents' expectations so she wouldn't have to.

It hasn't exactly been easy, since Anam's much more rebellious than I am. Where I choose not to engage and use our parents' disappointment as fuel to propel me forward, Anam chooses to get *angry* and throw their disappointment right back at them.

When my parents say "Don't do this," I ignore them and do it anyway.

When my parents say "Don't do this," Anam says *fuck you* and does something even worse.

I can't say I don't understand. I think if I were a little bolder, I'd be the same way.

But I'm just so *tired*. I don't see any point in fighting with them anymore. All I want to do is escape.

"If Nazifa isn't free, I can try to come back early," I say, a hesitant offering. I'm not eager to spend more time home than I have to, but if she asks this of me, I will do it.

Anam clicks her tongue, quickly tapping out a message, before her eyes light up. "No need, she's free. We'll probably go to the Halal Guys near school. Where are you guys going to be?"

"We're going to Astoria Park. I should be home around eight, though, if you want to meet on the subway home?"

She looks tempted, but then she shakes her head. "I'll probably be home later."

I raise my eyebrows. "Don't let Nazifa drag you into too much trouble. You know our curfew is earlier than hers, and even if she breaks hers, Mishti Auntie and Farhan Uncle will forgive her. Ma and Baba…well."

Anam sticks her tongue out. "I know, I know. Toss me another ball, would you?"

I huff fondly and reach for the volleyball.

Later in the afternoon, I get a text from an unfamiliar number as Anam jumps rope in front of me, doing her daily workout routine.

I would join her except I think I'd last only two minutes before calling it quits. I have this text to deal with anyway.

okay so the prompt is LIE this week

I sigh when I remember Emmitt insisted we swap numbers at the end of last week, ahead of midwinter break. Normally, I would've said no, but then he reminded me about his photography contest. Now I have no choice but to humor him.

ME: LIE? that's it?

EMMITT RAMOS: yeah just one word like always...

I glower at the ellipses, but then the perfect idea blooms in the back of my head.

ME: it's a loose interpretation right? so it could be like when you lie down? like on your bed?

EMMITT RAMOS: interesting that you choose to mention beds...

ME: shut up oh my god how are you still this annoying over text!!!!!

EMMITT RAMOS: it's a talent ;)

EMMITT RAMOS: but yes lie down on an object works

EMMITT RAMOS: do you have somewhere in mind ??

EMMITT RAMOS: are you just going to take me to bed bath and beyond

ME: why would I...you know what nvm I don't even want the answer to that you clown

ME: anyway I was thinking along the lines of like camping

EMMITT RAMOS: like the woods? that doesn't sound like a half bad idea. could get some good nature shots in

ME: the WOODS?

EMMITT RAMOS: yeah the woods...?

ME: where tf do you think you're going to find WOODS for CAMPING in new york city?

EMMITT RAMOS: ur the one who suggested it I was merely going with the flow

EMMITT RAMOS: so no to campgrounds then?

ME: uh yeah dude. there are no forests around here

EMMITT RAMOS: I thought you lived in forest hills?

ME: ....names of places =/= literal meaning

ME: anyway we can figure out details during the film club meeting tomorrow stop bothering me xoxo

EMMITT RAMOS: wait so when are we actually gonna go??

ME: we can't go until thursday if you want good shots

EMMITT RAMOS: what's on thursday

ME: you'll see!

ME: now stop texting me ok BYE!!!!!!!!!

EMMITT: BUT WHY THURSDAY

I close out of iMessage, rolling my eyes, but I can't help but feel a little smug at leaving him in suspense. Anam is now Hula-Hooping, for no apparent reason as far as I can tell, and if I don't have a video of it, did it really even happen?

"Smile for the camera!" I say, switching apps, and Anam laughs loudly, throwing her head back.

Click.

19

"Well?" Grant asks, rubbing his hands together and blowing on them. "Can we start yet?"

I raise my brows at him. It really isn't that cold. Global warming is as alive as ever, and it's above fifty degrees outside. And anyway—*your* friend is the one who's missing."

Grant grumbles, something about Emmitt running late and also being an asshole, and I have to hide my smile behind my clipboard.

The other members of film club loiter near us, clumping into groups. Not far from us the RFK Bridge towers, a perfect backdrop for a lot of the Instagram pictures some of the seniors are taking. Astoria Park is beautiful in its simplicity, with a track field for people to run, and a swimming pool for the warmer months. Right now, it's enough to stand around on a grassy field with the rest of film club and enjoy the fresh air.

As I look around, I can't help but feel a deep sense of pride. Living in New York City, it was inevitable that our club would be diverse in nature, but knowing how *white* the film industry is, it always fills my heart with joy to see us pushing forward from all our different cultures and backgrounds.

Whether it's because I'm Bangladeshi, or Grant is Nigerian, or Andie is Brazilian, we all bring a different perspective to film club.

This club is a carved-out safe space where we can just be ourselves. At first, I was drawn to film club because I've always loved watching and dissecting movies, but after freshman year, I realized I was even more excited about potentially creating them myself. To be able to write a script and see it play it out on the big screen, to know there are stories within stories hidden in every frame, to be the beating heart of something bigger than myself...it's all I've ever wanted to do.

And to do this alongside the rest of the club makes it so much better. Having people who understand my vision and my storytelling desires is a gift in and of itself. We all see and understand one another in ways no one outside of the film world ever will.

We all share one dream, even if we're going about it in different ways.

When another five minutes pass idly watching pigeons peck at the ground, I ask Grant, "How long is he going to be?"

Grant sighs, running a hand over his buzzed head. His hair is growing out slowly, and I figure it's only a day or two before he shaves it again. It used to be grown out during freshman year, but he's since taken to buzzing it all off—in what I think is an attempt to look like his father. "He's not answering my texts anymore."

As soon as Grant says the words, though, Emmitt comes

jogging up to the track field, wiping sweat off his brow with the bottom of his shirt.

I try not to gape at the sight of his abs, much less the snake tattoo winding across his rib cage, *quickly* diverting my gaze.

"Holy shit," whispers one of the juniors behind me. "Chloe, are you *seeing* this?"

"Oh my God, he's so hot, Sadia," the other junior says breathlessly, as if she's somehow winded from the sight of Emmitt. "Oh my *God*."

"Stop it," I say to both of them, thwacking them upside the heads. "This is not the time to thirst over the new kid."

Chloe pouts at me. "You only say that because he likes you."

"I—*what*?" I shake my head, though my cheeks are suddenly too warm. "He flirts with everyone. Don't feed into random gossip."

"Random gossip," Chloe mocks, exchanging a look with Sadia. "Whatever you say, Mina."

One of these days, I'm going to be convicted of murder. It's inevitable at this point.

Chloe and Sadia must sense the homicidal energy radiating off me because they quickly scamper away just as Emmitt approaches Grant and me.

"Sorry, my mom—" Emmitt frowns, running a hand through his blond hair. "Sorry."

Some of the strange heat building in my stomach disappears at the mention of his mother. This isn't the first time he's been late because of Claire Gong, and for some reason, I doubt it'll be the last.

"It's fine," Rosie says, propping her chin on my shoulder. "Let's get started?"

I nod, absently patting her cheek. "Let's all form a circle."

Once everyone sits down on the large picnic blanket Grant brought, I gesture to my clipboard. We counted all of the votes cast by the film club for who should be in the film, and most of it was in league with our own decisions.

Except… "The decision we're most torn on is the casting of Vivienne," I say, looking around at all the familiar faces around me. "The votes were very close between casting Sofia Dhital or casting Manuela Ureña."

"Who did you vote for?" Grant asks, rubbing his mouth, his gaze uncertain. He was one of the few people that voted for a third option.

"I—"

"Sofia," Rosie says, and I immediately seal my lips together.

It takes a second, but I force myself to relax my facial muscles and smile. "Yeah. We wanted to do another round of voting, for anyone who might have voted for someone other than Sofia and Manuela, and then go from there."

"Sounds good," says one of the other seniors, and everyone else nods.

"Raise your hand if you would like to vote for Sofia," I say, and Rosie's hand shoots up beside me. I don't know why it makes me want to sigh.

Instead of doing that, I stand up and start counting heads, walking slowly around the circle to make sure I don't miss anyone.

As I'm taking count, Emmitt's hand shoots out, wrapping around my ankle. I falter, looking at him.

"Surely you can act better than that, sweetheart," he whispers. "Your smile is as flimsy as this blanket."

I scowl at him, flicking the back of his head. "Be quiet," I say under my breath and keep counting.

When I'm done, I say, "And for Manuela?"

Different hands shoot into the air, and I manually count them as well, taking care to walk widely around Emmitt. When I finish, Sofia has won by six votes, and I announce as much.

Rosie grins widely. "Love that for us!"

I tug one of her red curls as I sit down. "Don't bring out the sparklers."

There's a beat of silence, and then Rosie huffs, turning away from me. "All right, Mina."

I blink, slightly taken aback. I didn't think I said anything bad. "It was just a joke, Rosie."

Though Rosie won't look at me, there's a frown on her face, clear as day. "*Was* it?"

I stare at her in disbelief. "Yes?"

"Ladies, ladies, let's not argue," Grant says, holding out his hands in a placating gesture. I shoot him a dark look, but for the first time, he doesn't look daunted. "It's settled, then. Sofia for Vivienne. No need for a catfight."

"Mind your business, Grant," I say, and turn back to Rosie. "I was *joking*, Ro. I didn't mean anything by it."

"Okay," Rosie says, but she doesn't sound like she believes me.

My mouth curls unpleasantly. "It was a joke. Come on."

Rosie doesn't say anything, and everyone falls silent. It feels like a dozen people are staring holes into the side of my head, and I just… I don't even understand what just *happened* here.

Rosie and I have never felt the need to hold back when it comes to each other—what's a joke between best friends?

The silence continues.

Forbidden. That's what a joke is, apparently.

"Are you serious right now?" I ask her. "I'm sorry. I didn't mean anything by it. It was just a silly little comment."

Rosie firms her lips, still adamantly silent.

The weight of everyone's eyes on my skin feels heavier and heavier, as if it's going to sink me down to the bottom of the East River.

"Jesus Christ," I say and gather my things, standing up. "Whatever. Sorry again."

Without another word, I march off, my face burning red. A wave of shame crashes over me, and I feel resentment toward not only the whole situation but also myself.

How am I supposed to fix this if Rosie won't even let me talk to her about this, much less accept my apology? And why would she start a fight in front of the whole film club, of all places?

I keep walking until I come across a set of metal benches and sit down, my breaths rattling around uncertainly inside my chest. The bench is too cold through the thin material of my leggings, but my options are limited right now. I'm afraid if I stand, my knees will give out.

Was I in the wrong? Was it wrong of me to joke about Sofia?

The longer I think about it, the more frustrated I grow. It isn't fair that Rosie is taking this out on me without giving me a chance to explain myself; it isn't fair that she's mad at me at all when she *knows* me, knows I would never try to purposely hurt her. We're supposed to be best friends. We're supposed to be better than this.

A group of children run by, laughing as they blow bubbles at one another. The noise startles me enough that it breaks through my train of thought.

I stare at them and exhale a quiet sigh. One of the kids stops and smiles at me, and my lips curve in response.

She laughs, and I immediately take out my phone without thinking much of it, turn to the camera app, and flick the screen until I switch to video mode.

The little girl winks at me before running off to play with her friends. I smile after her faintly, still filming.

I turn my phone, taking in the rest of the park. The trees are still bare of leaves, but that doesn't make the sight of them any less beautiful, the branches twined together with the RFK Bridge looming in the background. As I go through the motions, my head quiets, some of my frustration melting away. The world is still turning. Things will be okay in the end. Rosie and I will work this out one way or another.

I tilt my phone, adjusting until I get the lighting right, trying to use the sun to my advantage. As I'm slowly turning counterclockwise, Emmitt appears on my phone screen.

I look up to where Emmitt is walking toward me, eyebrows raised. "I've noticed you filming quite a bit these past few weeks," he says, eyeing my phone.

"Have you?" I ask dryly.

A sharp smile passes across Emmitt's face, fleeting and barely there. "You'd be surprised how observant I can be."

I consider him for a moment. His eyes are always analytical, carefully watching. I've noticed it from the moment we met. Even when he chooses to flirt and tease and joke, there is always a hidden shrewdness present in the depths of his gaze. Only recently did I realize he watches me as much as he watches his surroundings. "No, I don't think I would be, actually."

He cocks his head. "Perhaps." Then he's back to his charming self, grinning obnoxiously. "Come back with me."

I scoff. "They sent *you*, of all people, to come get me?"

Emmitt holds his hand out, wiggling his fingers in offer. "Yes."

My nose wrinkles. Even though my frustration has receded, I'm still not quite ready to face Rosie yet. "Not yet," I say, before I wiggle my own finger, spinning it in a slow, mocking circle. "Why don't you do a few twirls for the camera in the meantime?"

For some reason, Emmitt's smile only grows more suggestive.

"Or you could drop dead on camera," I add, resisting the urge to tug on my braid. "That's also acceptable."

Emmitt chuckles and drops his hand. "Come on, Samina. You're holding up everyone."

I sigh, slumping my shoulders. I don't want to inconvenience the others. "Fine."

As I walk past him, he pauses, giving me a curious look. "Hey, we're still meeting at two on Thursday, right? At the Thirty-Sixth Street station near AAAS?"

I poke a finger at his chest, trying not to think about the tattoo that lingers not far beneath my hand. "It's not pronounced *Ace*. It's *A-A-A-S*. And yes. Don't be late."

"Ace sounds cooler." Emmitt loops his finger with mine, his grip slightly too tight. "And I wouldn't dream of it."

I almost mention my cousin Karina's boyfriend is named Ace, but Emmitt doesn't need to know any more about my personal life than he already does. Instead, I pull away, rolling my eyes. "Whatever, dickhead."

20

When I get to Thirty-Sixth Street, Emmitt is already there, sitting on one of the wooden benches, toying idly with his camera.

My skin is still crawling from my encounter with my dad this morning, when he caught me awake at five in the morning. I have reoccurring insomnia because of my depression (not that my parents believe me—"Just go to sleep. How hard can it be?"), and I often lie awake staring at the ceiling, my mind numb.

Today, instead of staring despondently at the wall, I decided to sit in the living room and watch some bad television instead, hoping it would trick me into falling asleep. *Cats* (2019) was the most boring film I could think of, but even that didn't work.

Baba saw me on the couch on his way to the bathroom and didn't even say anything to me. He just gave me the heaviest look of disappointment and sighed, before turning around and leaving behind the bannister.

As he went to the bathroom, I heard him mutter, "Shouldn't be surprised." I can't stop thinking about it. It's not like this is the first time I've spent the whole night awake, trying to get my brain to shut off, but having my dad say those words in such a grave tone, like I've spent my entire life constantly letting him down… It's plaguing my every thought.

I'm not sure how old I was when I realized my parents were never going to love me the way I wanted them to—that their love was conditional, dependent on my own behavior and whether I fit their definition of success. Maybe it was my fifth birthday party, when Ma refused to let me wear the dress I wanted because it didn't fit her color scheme. Maybe it was Valentine's Day during third grade, when my crush rejected me and I spent the entire night crying, only for Baba to scorn me for talking to boys. Maybe it was the summer of sixth grade, when I was invited to my first sleepover, and Ma told me that if I went, I shouldn't bother coming back home. Maybe it was first semester of eighth grade, when I was applying to high schools, and my parents refused to drive me to the interview for my top choice.

Maybe it was all the times they yelled at me instead of sitting me down and talking to me. Maybe it was all the times they looked at me in disgust and outrage, instead of love and compassion. Maybe it was all the times I tried to be the daughter they wanted, and they still insisted it wasn't enough.

Each one of these by itself isn't so bad. If they were isolated events, maybe I could forgive my parents. But all of these put together…

It's not like we haven't had good times, too. We have. I have fond memories of going to Six Flags and riding roller coasters with my mom, of learning how to cook the most delicious rasmalai with my dad during Ramadan, of taking family road trips to visit my cousins across the country, stopping at fun little tourist destinations along the way. Once upon a time, I was their pride and joy. Once upon a time, they "loved" me.

But then I started disappointing them. Then I started being someone other than who they wanted me to be, who they expected me to be.

And things changed.

When I was younger, I thought that maybe their expectations were an integral part of our culture and our religion— but now that I'm older, I know that's not true. It would be foolish to blame it on those things, when the real root of the issue is my parents themselves.

There are so many other families who look like mine but don't treat their children the way my parents treat me and Anam. Nafiza and Syeda's family is a perfect example of that— the unconditional love they all have for each other haunts me late at night if I think too much about it. So many people get to have amazing, supportive, loving parents.

But there are no happy endings in my story.

And now, because of my parents, I feel such a *disconnect* from my identity. Sometimes I feel like I'm not Bangladeshi or Muslim enough because there's so much I don't know— being diaspora is a huge part of that, but even bigger is the fact I can't sit down and have a heart-to-heart with my parents like other kids get to have with theirs. There's only so much I can learn peripherally and from the internet.

Maybe one day, when I'm out of this house, I'll be able to reconnect with my Bangladeshi roots. Maybe I'll be able to improve my relationship with Allah. I *want* both of those things so badly it hurts. I hate feeling like a stranger to my own beliefs. I want to know more and learn more and *be* more.

I just hate that I have to do it alone.

I roll my neck in a stiff circle, trying to get rid of the tension building between my shoulder blades. There's a time and a place, and this isn't it.

"Hey," I say, and Emmitt looks up.

There's a moment of silence where we just stare at each other, his eyes taking in my haggard expression. I wait for him to make some kind of ill-timed comment, but he doesn't say anything.

Instead, he quietly rises to his feet and meets me at the edge of the platform. "So where are we off to, love?"

"Rockefeller Center," I say, checking Google Maps for when the next R train is arriving. Two minutes away. "We'll walk from the Forty-Ninth Street station."

Emmitt furrows his eyebrows, absently toying with the three earrings lining his left ear. "We're going to…lie down at Rockefeller Center? On a Thursday?"

I turn to him in exasperation, some of my discomfort melting away. "Can you just be patient? And trust me?"

A hazy smile curves his lips. "Only if you trust me in return."

Before I can reply, the subway pulls up, hot wind blowing my pigtails back. I grimace, picking out a strand of hair from my mouth.

It's even warmer today somehow. I stuffed my sweater in

my backpack within five minutes of waiting for the R train at Forest Hills.

Emmitt is wearing a brown coat, a black hoodie peeking out from the top. I don't know how he's *not* warm. He's never dressed correctly for the weather.

"Come on," I say, pulling him by the lapels of his coat inside the train. It's pretty empty, considering it's only two in the afternoon on a Thursday, so we quickly find seats.

I sit down first, expecting him to take the seat beside me, but he sits across from me instead. I shrug to myself, unbothered, until I see his fingers reaching for his camera.

No wonder he sat over there.

The camera shutter goes off, a *click* sounding in the otherwise silent subway. I flip him off in response.

A woman a few seats away smiles as she looks between me and Emmitt. "You two are so cute."

My mouth falls open, certain I heard that wrong. "Me? And *him*?"

Emmitt scoffs across from me. "You should be so lucky."

I turn my glare on him. "I *will* throw something at you."

"You never live up to your threats, sweetheart," he says, waving me off.

For a minute, I genuinely contemplate crumpling a piece of paper and lobbing it at his head, before I realize the woman is still staring at us, a soft smile on her face.

Ya Allah.

Next time, I mouth, pinning Emmitt with daggers.

He only blows me a kiss in return.

21

Once we're out of the subway, I take lead, weaving my way through the tourists heading for Times Square. "Don't fall behind, pretty boy," I call over my shoulder.

Emmitt, busy staring at the billboards and bright lights of the heart of New York City, startles at the sound of my voice. There's so much traffic, yellow and green cabs honking left and right, that I'm surprised he heard me at all.

After a belated moment, he falls in step beside me. "Will you explain to me what we're doing here now?"

"We're going to the standby line for *Saturday Night Live*," I say, tucking my fingers in my jean pockets.

A wrinkle forms between Emmitt's brows. "Why?"

I smile faintly, recalling a particularly daring escapade of mine involving the *SNL* line. "Because people camp out for days in order to get standby tickets."

Emmitt falters, staring at me aghast. "On the *sidewalk*?"

I nod. Last year, Rosie and I spent three days in sleeping

bags in anticipation of Saoirse Ronan hosting *Saturday Night Live*.

I had to lie to my parents and say I was attending an overnight lecture at Princeton University with Rosie to pull it off, but I still have no regrets to this day. Usually, my parents would never let me go, but the mention of Princeton and how it would look good on college applications won them over.

Rosie's mom is a trouper who agreed to cover for us as long as she was allowed to check in on us in line. After a brief discussion, Rosie and I decided seeing Saoirse was worth the embarrassment of having her mother babysit us.

From befriending the Tishman security guards (whom we now fondly call the Tish*men*), to eating the absolute best avocado breakfast burritos at Toasties, to running into three different celebrities by accident—it was arguably the most chaotic and exhilarating experience of my life.

And I got to experience it with Rosie, which is the best part of all.

There's a sour taste in my mouth all of a sudden, and I swallow it down. Focus. *Focus.* "The line usually starts on Thursday, which is why we had to wait to go later in the week. Sometimes, for bigger celebrities, people line up from Monday or Tuesday, but I didn't want to risk it."

"So they sleep on the street from *Monday* to *Saturday*?" he asks incredulously, clearly struggling to comprehend why anyone would want to.

I want to point out that it's the superior version of camping, because there's restaurants lined up all down Forty-Eighth Street and easy access to restrooms, but instead I shrug a shoulder. "It's not that bad. I got the best sleep of my life on the street. Hard surfaces are good for your back, you know?"

Emmitt's jaw somehow dips even lower. "*You* did that?"

"And I'd do it again," I say, raising my brows. "I'd work on that attitude. I'm sure your fans will be lining up on the street for you in a few years, too. You don't want it to seem like you're judging them for their devotion toward you."

His expression is doubtful, but with how attractive he is and the films lined up on his IMDb page, I'm certain of it.

"Come on, it's on the next street," I say, waving him forward.

Emmitt follows me slowly, his eyes searching out the *SNL* line. We spot it pretty quickly once we reach Sixth Avenue.

He inhales in surprise, and even I'm slightly taken back by the length of it, wrapping around the block.

I scramble for my phone, eager to commemorate this. At my side, Emmitt is still taking the sight in, his hands clenched tightly around his camera. "They're really going to sleep here until Saturday?"

"Yup," I say, popping the *p*. Even as I record the line, I turn to look at him. "Does this work for your prompt?"

After a beat, Emmitt nods, his eyes narrowed with focus.

I nod in satisfaction. "Great." Then I walk away, moving down the street. There are a lot of girls my age lined up, tucked into their sleeping bags and talking to one another quietly.

When I'm across from DELIS 48, I rest my arms against the barricade, leaning forward curiously. "Who's on *SNL* this week?"

Two girls look up at me, taking me in. I remember being annoyed when people consistently asked us what we were waiting for, but it seems I may be one of the first to ask, because they don't seem too bothered. "Ariel Nova."

I stare at them for a long moment, unsure if I heard correctly. "Ariel Nova," I repeat, my voice half-hysterical. "As in, Oscar-award-winning actor Ariel Nova? From *Amaryllis* and *In The Shattered Places*?"

"Yeah!" one of the girls says eagerly, gesturing to her shirt, where Ariel Nova's face is plastered. "He's promoting his new movie with Firebrand Studios."

Oh God.

Of all people, *why* did it have to be the most famous actor in Emmitt's upcoming film? Ariel is playing the villain, opposing Emmitt as the main character. There are already pictures of them floating across the internet, from early promotional materials.

Behind me, Emmitt stiffens. Out of the corner of my eye, I see him slowly pull up his hood, shadowing his face from view.

"Thanks," I say to the girls, offering a pleasant and slightly forced smile, before walking back to Emmitt. He was taking pictures of the line while I was talking, but now he looks hesitant.

"They're not going to recognize you, inshallah," I say quietly, but I'm not too sure. "You can keep taking photos."

Emmitt searches my face, and I don't know what he finds— maybe he's choosing to trust me, like I asked him to earlier— but he nods. "Can you ask them for permission?"

"Yeah, definitely," I say and return to the barricade once more, offering them another apologetic smile. "Is it okay if my—" I pause, trying to find the right word "—*friend* takes pictures of you guys? It's for a photography contest."

The girls look over my shoulder to where Emmitt is holding his camera to his face, taking a picture of the street signs.

"Sure," one of them answers, her eyes drinking Emmitt in. I resist the urge to step in front of her. "But why didn't he ask us himself?"

"He's shy," I say, though I've never met someone as forward as Emmitt is. "But thank you for your permission. Really."

I turn and walk back to Emmitt. He looks at me in inquiry, and I nod. He gives me a grin, and someone behind me whistles lowly.

When I reach his side, I realize the girls I spoke to before are looking at us now. And so are the girls beside them.

I bite my thumb, eyes darting back to Emmitt. He keeps lowering his camera to check the photos, so his face keeps coming into view, as shadowed as it might be.

The girls are whispering now, quietly enough that I can't hear them, but a chill passes over my skin all the same, especially since they keep inconspicuously looking back at us.

I subtly move closer to Emmitt, attempting to hide him from sight.

He falters from taking photos, raising his brows at me. "You're blocking the shot."

I grimace, opening my mouth to explain, but he raises his camera again, taking a picture of me instead. A sigh escapes me. I should have expected that.

"What?"

"Nothing," I say, rolling my eyes.

But after Emmitt takes a few more pictures of me, he lowers his camera again. "Love, as much as you're a pleasant sight, I *am* trying to win a contest."

Immediately, I hear a loud whisper of "Did he say *love*?"

And the sound of a camera shutter goes off again, but from behind me this time. Welp. That's not good.

"I think we have to run," I say, wincing.

Emmitt is distracted by his camera, looking through the film. "What?"

I put my hand on top of the screen, blocking his view. "I think we have to run."

Then I grab his hand and start tugging him toward the building beside us, where we can quickly escape into Rockefeller Center. Our feet pound against the pavement, and I maneuver us around pedestrians with an ease that comes from navigating New York City on a daily basis.

As we start moving, though, the girls also begin to move, shedding their sleeping bags and getting to their feet.

"Oh, fuck," I mutter, before I grip him tighter. *"Run."*

I sprint toward the building, and Emmitt curses under his breath as he runs after me, still holding my hand. More and more people look at us curiously as we run by, past the Nintendo store and Rockefeller Plaza.

We pass through the glass doors beside a Citibank, and I immediately lock in on the escalator leading down to the Rockefeller concourse. "Come on, we have to hurry."

Emmitt nods, and we sprint toward the escalator, though I take the stairs beside them instead, not wanting anyone to slow us down. He follows me readily. When we reach the bottom, the concourse bathrooms are in front of us.

I turn in the opposite direction, dragging him toward the

ice skating rink, until we reach one of the opposing hallways
that wraps around the other side of the concourse. There, I
pull him quickly up a set of stairs that lead to the observa-
tion deck.

I glance behind us, and it looks like no one is following
us for the moment—or they haven't caught up yet, at least.

"Take off your coat," I say, pulling down his hood so his
blond hair is in view. Light filters in from the glass doors
near us. Through them, I can see various world flags cir-
cling around The Rink. No sight of any fans from that direction, either.

Emmitt blinks at me but immediately starts unbuttoning
his coat. As he does that, I pull my sweater out of my bag,
quickly slipping it over my head. Hopefully that will throw
off anyone pursuing us.

"Here," Emmitt says, reaching for my pigtails and tugging
free the hair ties. I nod, running my fingers through my dark
waves and airing them out.

Then I reach forward, unhooking his earrings quickly. He
startles at the touch but bends so I have easier access.

I tuck the earrings in my pocket, shove his coat in my bag,
and start to run in the direction of the Rainbow Room. But
he suddenly reaches out to stop me, his fingers tight around
my wrist and his gaze intent behind me.

Emmitt's eyes meet mine again, his gaze warm and steady.
"Can I kiss you?"

My mouth falls open. *"What?"*

Emmitt keeps staring at me. "Can I kiss you?"

When I don't respond, his eyes flicker over my shoulder
again, a hint of panic in them.

Oh. He's trying to—*oh*.

"Yes, you can," I say, though I can hardly believe the words.

Emmitt swoops forward in the next moment, burying his fingers in my hair, whirling me around so my back is against the wall and his is to the people passing by.

His lips meet mine, soft but frenzied. My own hands hang uselessly in the air, but he reaches down with one hand, leading them to his collarbone.

I wrap my arms around his neck accordingly, even though I have to stretch on my tiptoes to maintain our kiss. At least I have something to do with myself.

There's a low burning in the pit of my stomach, something sharp and jagged running through me, knifing along my ribs.

"Do you see him? Are you sure it was really *Emmitt Ramos*?"

"I could have sworn—"

Emmitt's lips shift lower so he's kissing the edge of my jaw instead, giving me a moment to breathe. My heart skips an uncertain beat, my hands trailing up to cup his cheeks, shielding him further from view.

"He had three earrings," the first voice insists. "It had to be him."

"Maybe he's still downstairs," the second voice says, far too close for comfort. "Wasn't he with some girl?"

A nervous jitter runs through me, and I tilt Emmitt's head up, meeting him for a kiss again. His lips taste like pomegranates, which is something I never thought I would know.

Again, something pierces my gut, sharp and prickly.

"Yeah," the first voice says. "Maybe we should check near The Rink?"

"Good idea," the second voice says, and they're already moving farther away.

I give it another thirty seconds, trying to ignore the lightning rushing through my veins as Emmitt's tongue brushes against my lips.

Then I finally pull away, lowering myself to the flats of my feet.

Emmitt's hair is slightly mussed, and his brown eyes are blown wide as he stares down at me, pupils dilated. His lips are red, kissed raw, and his cheeks are splotchy with color.

My own face is burning, and I distract myself by running a hand through my hair, brushing it out of my eyes. "I never understood why that worked in the movies."

A pause—and then Emmitt laughs loudly, throwing his head back. The knife in my stomach climbs higher, puncturing my heart instead.

"Thank you, love," Emmitt says, offering me a loose grin. "I owe you one."

I forcibly gather myself, tucking my hair behind my ears. "Don't you forget it, *love*."

22

After we go the NBC store and find Emmitt a suitable disguise, we return to the concourse. I lead him toward the main Starbucks, since they have a sectioned-off seating area with outlets, and I can charge my phone. It's the only place in the entirety of Rockefeller Center I've ever been able to plug my charger in.

We sit down, me carrying a blueberry muffin, him holding a black coffee. As I take my seat, I pull out my phone to film our surroundings, and Emmitt considers me with a tilt to his head.

There's something different in the air between us—something unspoken that I can't put a name to. It's as if we've reached some sort of truce. I guess faking a make out with someone is something you can't exactly take back.

"Why are you always filming?" he asks.

I stop picking at my muffin, looking up at him. I consider snapping that it's none of his business, but for some reason,

I can't bring myself to. "My dream school is the University of Southern California," I say, my gaze dropping back to the table. "When I'm in California, I'm sure I'll feel home-sick. So I thought I'd spend senior year recording the world around me, so I can remind myself what New York City is like—and remember that California is the right place for me at the end of the day."

Emmitt makes a low noise. "What's wrong with New York?"

I shake my head. "You wouldn't get it."

"Try me," he says, shifting closer and resting his hands on the small table in front of us.

I glower at his fingers and reach forward, plucking them off the table one by one, holding my phone in one hand. "New York is just so—it's *gross*, dude. It's too congested, and there's so much filth, and it's so loud, and you have to wait five years for a bus to come and another ten for the subway, given your train isn't on an entirely different route. Wherever you go, there are people giving you dark looks for *breathing*, and no one ever offers a helping hand, and..." I stare at Em-mitt's pinky, the last finger remaining on the table.

"And?"

"And I don't feel at home here," I say quietly, setting my phone down on the table. "I can barely breathe in this city. I turn eighteen next week and I still don't have *any* freedom. My parents think I'm too incompetent—"

I cut off, a lump rising in the back of my throat. I don't know how to finish that sentence.

Emmitt doesn't say anything, but then his pinky moves along the length of the table, nudging against mine.

"You're so annoying," I say, staring at our hands, our fingers touching just barely. My words hold no heat whatsoever.

He smiles faintly. "I know. You are, too."

Though he doesn't push, I can tell this conversation isn't done here. There's a sense of doom looming over me, in anticipation of the day I'll have let everything go and finally be honest about the chaos leashed inside my chest.

I'm finishing up my Nutritional Science homework, a huge packet assigned for midwinter break, when Ma sits down across from me at the dining table, wearing her glasses and holding a fashion magazine. Anam is out on her date tonight, but throughout the rest of the break, we've been spending our evenings holed up in her room, both of us scrolling through our phones.

Sometimes Anam goes off on rants about her classmates, and I sit by, nodding along. Admittedly, I occasionally tune out, but for the most part, I try to listen between scrolling through my Twitter feed. Her life is far more dramatic than mine, but that isn't saying much, as I tend to focus on film club and little else.

Since my sister was headed outside today, I decided to do my homework in the dining room, but I'm beginning to regret that decision now.

Ma looks tired, probably from her shift at Michaels. Her and Baba's room is always a mess of arts and crafts, so she must think the benefits of working there outweigh the costs. With Baba's job as a dentist, we're not exactly low on funds.

I can't help but resent that she *clearly* finds joy in the arts, but when I want to make a career out of it, I'm the one being ridiculous.

"I was talking to your Chachi, and she recommended this magazine for graduation dresses," Ma says by way of explanation when I keep staring at her blankly. "Do you want to look through it?"

I frown, trying to suss out if there's any underlying motivation. Chachi, my paternal aunt, is my favorite relative aside from Dadu, my paternal grandmother, mostly because Chachi and Mishti Auntie from next door are more alike than Ma would ever admit. With that in mind, I decide to give my mom the momentary benefit of the doubt and hold my hand out for the magazine.

Ma passes it over to me, and I start flipping through. Though there are nice outfits in the magazine, my mom has marked the blandest of the bunch. Chachi would probably roll over and die if she saw Ma's choices. If I were Anam, I'd throw this magazine right back in my mom's face and march upstairs in a hysterical fit.

At any rate, I don't have the energy—nor do I care enough—to fight with my mother about what I wear. Graduation is the last time she'll have a say in my outfits anyway.

"I dog-eared the ones I thought would suit you," Ma says, reaching across the table to tap an example. "You could also wear it to Baba's forty-second birthday party—"

"I'm not going to be here for Baba's forty-second birthday," I say, without looking up, though the embers of anger are starting to spark in my chest. "It's in September, so I'll be at college."

"Poppy, be serious," Ma says, shaking her head at me. "You know how foolish—"

"I'll choose later," I say, dropping the magazine on the table and grabbing my homework packet. "I'm going to bed."

"How long are you going to keep running from us?" Ma asks, her voice carrying across the living room as I trek toward the stairs. "You'll have to talk to us someday."

I grind my teeth together but don't bother responding. There's no point.

I hate that there's a small part of me that wishes my parents would change their tune, would support me wholeheartedly again, like they did when I was young and directionless. When I had no dreams or ambitions of my own, and happily went along with whatever they asked of me.

But I can't be that person anymore. And I just wish they could love this version of me, too. The cursed voice in the back of my head insists I'm obsessing over this competition *because* of them. Because I want their approval and understanding.

The voice in my head also loves to remind me that no matter what I do, it'll never be enough.

That I'll never be enough.

I keep hoping it'll get easier as the years go by, but it hasn't yet. Time doesn't make this any less painful, especially when I lack closure.

I wish I knew why they were like this. I wish there was a simple explanation behind their behavior, beyond society's expectations. I wish there was a way to sit them down and demand some kind of answer for all the damage they've done. *I wish there was a way to ask why I'm not enough as I am.*

But I know there's no easy answer. Not one any of us can put into words anyway.

We're raised to see our parents as infallible, to believe they're incapable of making mistakes—but what about when they do? What about when they keep making them? What about when their mistakes *hurt* us?

I used to blame myself. I thought it was my own fault. I thought I deserved it.

Now I know that's far from the truth. I didn't realize until Anam started blaming herself, too. That's when I found the flaw in the system. How could my sister—my lovely, brave, beautiful, kind sister—be responsible for my parents' actions? And if it wasn't her fault, then how could it be mine?

Knowing the blame lies entirely on my parents doesn't stop it from hurting. No matter how much I bury it beneath the surface, their lack of love is an ache I don't know how to heal from.

But I can hide it—I can cover it up, the same way the movies do.

23

Monday brings yet another incident of Rosie pretending our minor altercation didn't happen. I want to rip my hair out in frustration when I see her in front of my locker. She's carrying a can of Pringles, her favorite snack, even though it's barely eight in the morning—but more importantly, she's smiling like nothing is wrong.

I hate not knowing what I can or can't say to her, and the feeling heightens with each passing week.

"Hi," I say, coming to stand before her.

Rosie reaches over to fiddle with the end of my braid. "Apparently NYU is going to send out our decisions in the next few weeks," she says, nearly bouncing in her spot. "We'll probably hear back soon."

I raise my eyebrows, previous worries forgotten. Though I also applied to NYU, I'm more concerned about Rosie's application than mine. "Really? Have you been checking online?"

She nods, toying with her own hair a moment later. "Nothing yet. But a lot of people with SAT scores and GPAs similar to mine on Naviance marked their applications as accepted around the same time last year."

I've refreshed the USC page on Naviance—our high school's website for tracking college applications—a hundred times myself, so I'm not surprised that Rosie's been doing the same.

"I hope they're preparing a parade in honor of your acceptance," I say, offering her a small smile as I turn to the dial on my locker.

Rosie grins. "And I hope USC is doing the same for you."

Then we fall into an awkward silence, Rosie holding her binder closer to her chest while I sift through my locker.

When it becomes unbearable, I offer an olive branch, turning to her once I'm done gathering my things. "So, uh. Remember how I'm helping Emmitt with his photography contest? So we've been going to the different boroughs?"

She angles her head curiously. "Yeah. Why? Did something happen?"

I tuck a loose strand of black hair behind my ear, unable to meet her gaze. "Well… I mean, it's kind of hard to explain. Long story short, he kissed me?"

"What?" ask a group of freshmen behind me.

I swivel around in surprise. Brighton and Christina are staring at me with wide eyes while a handful of other freshmen trail after them with their mouths open. Christina is holding out a film club folder in her hand, as if she meant to hand it to me, but my words stopped her in her tracks.

"What?" Rosie repeats at my side, her can of Pringles falling to the ground and rolling at our feet.

"Who?" ask the freshmen, pressing in around us. *"Who?"*

I wince. "Don't be so loud."

Rosie is spluttering, her face turning increasingly red. "He—he kissed—"

Kaity stops in the middle of the hallway, on her way to her locker, just a few feet down from mine. "*Ezra* kissed you?"

"No," I say immediately, but my own cheeks are flushed with heat now. I can tell by the way everyone is looking at me that no one believes me. "No, it wasn't—"

"Oh my God," Kaity says, taking a slow step back. There's a bright, yet wicked, look in her eye. "I'm about to win so much money."

"Wait, but I—"

Before I can finish my sentence, Kaity turns around and heads in the opposite direction of her locker, toward the main staircase. There's even a skip to her step.

At the same time, Christina shoves the folder at me. "Congrats, Mina!"

I gape at her. "Why are you *congratulating* me?"

Brighton grins. "It's okay. We won't tell Ezra you kiss and tell."

"I do *not* kiss and tell!" I turn to Rosie in dismay, but she's still staring at me in unadulterated shock. "Rosie, can you please tell them—"

"They've already left," she says as her hand reaches out to grip my arm.

I twist my head, seeking out the freshmen, but they've all disappeared.

"Tell me everything, Mina." I look back at Rosie, who

has gathered herself, her manicured nails digging into my skin. "Now!"

"We didn't *kiss* kiss," I say, hiding my face behind my hands. "Some Firebrand fans recognized Emmitt so we had to run, and then we needed a distraction, and he just—he asked to kiss me and I was panicking and...it just kind of happened?"

Rosie's silence speaks volumes. I peek between my fingers, and she's staring at me incredulously. "I thought you hated him?" She starts poking my chest. "You two are running clown nation over there, huh?"

"Don't start," I mutter and drop my head on her shoulder.

She runs a gentle hand over my braid, before giving it a sharp tug. "Don't be an imbecile. Even my gay ass knows you don't just 'randomly' agree to kiss people you hate."

"Shhh," I say, pressing my hand against her mouth. "Don't manifest it."

Rosie snorts. "At this rate, I don't think I need to manifest anything."

I hate that I'm starting to think along the same lines.

24

When I walk up to my Italian classroom with Rosie, Emmitt is leaning a shoulder against the doorway, absently toying with the rings on his fingers.

"There you are," he says. There's an arrogant tilt to his mouth as per usual, but in the morning light, his eyes look—softer? "I've been looking for you."

Rosie lifts her brows. "I will leave you two to it, then."

"Wait," I say, but Rosie slips free of my grasp, disappearing into the classroom after shooting a grin at me over her shoulder. I glower after her before turning to Emmitt.

His eyes scan my expression, but his tone doesn't change as he says, "The prompt for this week is memory."

Two of our classmates pass between us, walking into the room, but not without giving me a pointed look. I stare after them, wondering what I could have *possibly* done to deserve special attention from them. Kaity and the freshmen couldn't have spread the news that fast. Right?

Emmitt is still watching me expectantly, and I shift uncomfortably under his intense gaze. "You know, you could just text me the link. Then I could find out the prompt by myself and you wouldn't have to tell me."

And then people wouldn't see us together more than necessary and draw ridiculous conclusions, I think.

His cool expression slips somewhat, and he runs a hand through his messy blond hair, almost self-consciously. "Oh. Yeah. I mean... I don't mind telling you."

I shake my head, a thin smile on my lips. "It's fine. Just send me the link."

Emmitt nods slowly, taking out his phone and typing a quick message. My bag buzzes faintly as the text delivers.

"Thanks," I say, looking away from him. Everyone in the classroom is watching us, but they turn their heads when they catch my eye. "I'll try to think of a place by the end of the day."

Emmitt opens his mouth as if to say more, but I swivel on my heel and head inside the classroom. As soon as I do, people start quietly whispering to one another.

I glance briefly over my shoulder, and Emmitt's dark brows are knitted together as he looks around the classroom. I move before he can ask me anything, quickly taking my seat and ducking my head.

"I told you so," Rosie singsongs, poking me. I smack her arm away and try not to groan.

This is just great. Only *I* would accidentally start a rumor about myself.

As I leave my last class of the day, English, I see Emmitt waiting for me once again, leaning against my locker this time.

He raises his eyebrows at me, and a sense of dread crawls down my spine before he even speaks. "I keep hearing people whisper our names. What's going on, love?"

"I don't know," I say curtly, moving past him to spin my locker's dial—*32, 15*—but then his fingers press against mine, halting my motions.

"Don't you?" he asks, taking a step closer so my shoulder is brushing his chest. "Your cheeks are awfully red."

"It's hot," I say without pause, spinning the dial again.

Emmitt huffs a laugh, close enough that his breath is cool against my face. "You are horrible at lying."

I elbow him as I open my locker, and he lets out a grunt of surprise. "You are a nuisance."

He lifts his hands into the air in a sign of surrender, watching me pack away my things. "Whatever you say." When I lift my arm to elbow him again, he easily sidesteps it. "Have you thought of a place yet?"

I sigh, shutting my locker. "Yes, I did."

He inclines his head. "Which borough are we off to today?"

"Brooklyn," I say, shifting past him, ignoring the feeling of his body's warmth pressing against my side. "It's going to be a long ride, so I hope you have time to spare."

Emmitt shrugs, hooking his fingers into the strap of my backpack and following after me. "It's not as if I have anything else to do."

I give him a flat look. "Shouldn't you have like...actor things to do? Surely they didn't send you here *just* to attend school?"

"They kind of did," Emmitt says, his fingers slipping underneath the straps, cool through the fabric of my sweater.

"I honestly have no idea how anything at this school works. What's a Regents exam?"

"A New York state exam," I say, shaking my head. "Don't worry, I doubt they'll put that in your script."

"You never know," Emmitt muses. "So it's basically like an A level?"

My nose wrinkles. "Uh...sure."

Emmitt hums. "I'll get the hang of it eventually. I'm almost certain I know where most of my classes are now."

"Good job, pretty boy," I say, rolling my eyes. "It's not like most of us figure that out within the first two days of school."

"You have *three* separate gyms," Emmitt grumbles. "It's hardly my fault I keep getting lost."

"Whatever you say." I give him a cursory glance as we walk down the stairs, toward the main entrance. "Are you sure you don't have interviews to attend? Press junkets? Film auditions? *Something?*"

"Grant's father has been very lenient with my schedule in light of this arrangement," he says, but the line of his mouth is crueler somehow. "Though if my mother had a say in it, I'm sure I'd have a packed schedule."

"Oh?" He never talks about his mother at length, but the internet proclaims Claire Gong a workaholic. It makes sense that Emmitt would have to learn to accommodate that lifestyle. "Where is she anyway?"

"Back in London," he says, tapping his fingers in an uneven pattern along my back.

"Do you miss her?" I ask, watching him carefully. "You never talk about her."

Emmitt offers me a mild smile. "You act as if we speak about our lives with one another often, Samina."

For some reason, that stings more than it should. It's not as if Emmitt and I are friends. He might flirt with me all the time, but that doesn't mean anything. He flirts with *everyone*.

Still, I thought something changed last week after we… I flush at the direction of my own thoughts and shove them to the back of my head. "I just meant—even around Grant, you don't… I don't know."

"There's enough about me online," Emmitt says after a pause. His expression is more guarded than I'm used to. "I tend to protect what little privacy I have left."

"I never thought about it like that," I say, fidgeting with the end of my sleeve.

"I imagine most people don't," Emmitt says, a bitter twist to his lips. "But to answer your question, I do miss her…but I also don't. It's complicated."

I wonder if that's how I'm going to feel once I go off to USC. I can't imagine missing my parents, but an uneasy part of me worries that I might not sing the same tune when I'm across the country.

If I even get in, says a tiny voice for the umpteenth time.

Emmitt and I head out of school together, walking the familiar path toward the subway. Last week's good weather has carried into this week as well, and the sun shines high in the sky, a few puffy white clouds occasionally blocking its rays.

I take a deep breath of fresh air, letting it spread through me before I exhale. The world is still turning, and it will continue to do so.

Things will work out the way they're supposed to.

25

It's not until halfway through our commute, when half the train unloads at Union Square, that Emmitt and I snag two seats. They're at the end of the train, two seats beside each other, pressed against the doors interconnecting the subway cars.

Emmitt gestures for me to sit first and then lowers himself beside me.

"Thanks," I say, taking out one earphone.

He offers me a half smile, but his eyes are still dark. I chew on my bottom lip, wondering if it's because I asked him about his mother.

If she's away in London, it must be awfully lonely for him out here in New York City. And yet he never shows any sign of it—always maintains this *facade* that seems impenetrable.

There's so little I actually know about him, aside from his reputation for stealing hearts and disrespecting the press. I've seen both at play, whether it's the underclassmen in the film club fawning over him or his sharp tongue when he feels caged in. But I have no idea why his expression is oddly somber, why his fingers are tapping a nervous beat against the metal pole attached to our bench.

I don't even know where he's going to *go* at the end of the day. Is he staying with Grant? Does he have a relative nearby? Is he fine dining in the penthouse of a classy hotel?

"Where are you staying?" I ask, the words tumbling out without permission.

Emmitt glances at me, his face closed off. "What?"

I clear my throat, tugging at my braid. "While you're in New York, where are you staying? Are you living with someone or…?"

"Oh. I leased an apartment in Brooklyn," he says mildly, looking away from me. "It's not too bad. I'm used to living alone when I'm filming in new locations. Such is the life of an actor."

For some reason, my heart drops lower in my chest at the despondency in his voice.

Not for the first time, I get the sense that he doesn't like acting. But I still don't understand how that can be true—not when he's Emmitt Ramos.

"So do you just ride the R train all the way home?" I ask instead. It's odd seeing him withdrawn, and I don't want to contribute to it more than necessary.

He shakes his head, rubbing the back of his neck. "I usually take a Lyft."

"Oh my God," I say, bumping my shoulder into his. "What's wrong with taking the subway? Surely after all our rides together, you've gotten a handle on how to swipe a MetroCard."

"I mean, yeah," Emmitt says, and some of the tension seems to ease from his expression. "But it's easier with you by my side. New York City isn't as intimidating when you're with someone who knows it inside out."

I snort. "You make me sound like some kind of New York City expert."

He cocks his head. "Aren't you?"

I start to protest, but... I realize I might be. Just a little. Living here my whole life, growing up on these very streets, I know the ins and outs.

I lean back in my seat, staring blankly at the subway map across from us. "Yeah. I suppose I am."

I come to a stop in front of Green-Wood Cemetery, one of my favorite spots in Brooklyn, and look back at Emmitt. "So? Does it work?"

He doesn't even respond, already raising his camera to his face, his eyes lit up as he looks around.

I smile, trailing behind him as he wanders through the cemetery. It was the first thing that came to mind when I thought of *memory* in terms of a location.

The cemetery consists of cathedral architecture, brilliant arches rising high above our heads, stone mausoleums with a thin layer of dust upon them, and iron statues watching us with disquieting eyes. It's hauntingly beautiful.

"There are tours, I think," I say, my gaze catching on some of the other tourists milling the area. "We can ask around."

Emmitt shakes his head, adjusting the settings on his camera. "You're the only tour guide I need."

"All right, Casanova," I say, rolling my eyes. At least we're back to normal.

He shoots me a small grin and turns the camera on me. At this point, I'm used to it so I just ignore him, looking up at the elegantly designed arch coming up ahead instead.

As we traverse the city, I can't help but feel a strange sense of nostalgia. These sights are only an hour's commute right now, but when I'm in California, they'll be three thousand miles away. I pull out my phone, recording my surroundings, even as an offbeat emptiness tugs at my chest.

It's natural to feel sad, I tell myself. I'm saying goodbye to the only city I've ever known. It would be stranger if I *didn't* feel some kind of loss.

Emmitt's camera keeps clicking behind me, until a sudden beat of silence followed by a yelp. *"Fuck."*

I turn on my heel, eyes wide, and then promptly burst into laughter.

There's a frog on his head.

A frog.

On his head.

"Oh my God," I say and point my phone at him, recording without missing a beat. "Oh my *God*."

"How do I get it off me?" Emmitt asks, his entire face turning red. "How—"

The frog ribbits.

I laugh again, the sound so loud it startles even me.

"Samina," he says, but there's a reluctant smile on his face now, too, as if he didn't intend for it. "Please help me."

Another giggle escapes me, but I oblige, moving forward until I'm in front of him. "Only because you said please."

I lean onto my tiptoes, wrapping my fingers around the frog. It's slimy in my grip, and I kind of want to gag, but I imagine it would feel *much* worse if it was sitting in my hair. "Got it," I say, and abruptly realize how close my face is to Emmitt's.

He stares at me, his eyes warm, and I'm immobilized, my breath caught in my throat.

Emmitt's gaze drops to my mouth, and for a delirious moment, I sway closer. He catches me by the waist, his hand warm through the flimsy fabric of my T-shirt.

"Love," he says quietly, and it almost seems like he's going to lean in—

The frog ribbits again.

We both jump apart, and the frog wriggles in my grip. I release my hold on it, and it hops away, croaking as it goes.

I laugh nervously, willing my face not to warm. I don't think it's working. "Hopefully no more frogs jump on you."

"Yeah," Emmitt says faintly, but his cheeks are also bright with color. Whether it's leftover from before or new because of the...incident, I can only guess. "Hopefully."

An awkward silence ensues.

I turn around, walking toward the arch instead, wondering what the hell I'm even *doing*. Why was I just about to kiss Emmitt? Why was I about to let Emmitt kiss *me*? Have I dropped into an alternate universe?

Behind me, Emmitt resumes taking photographs, his camera whirring loudly in the quiet.

"Oh my God, are you Emmitt Ramos?" a shrill voice says.

I blink and slowly turn around again. A girl with platinum-blond hair is looking up at Emmitt with wide eyes, her fingers tight around the iced drink in her hand.

Not too far from us, a family of four—with the same platinum blond hair—watches on curiously.

Emmitt sighs, lowering his camera. "Yes. But I'm not taking any pictures at this time."

For some reason, my eyes narrow into slits. It seems I'm not the only person he says that to.

The girl doesn't look bothered. "That's okay. It's an honor just to meet you." She grins, reaching up to twirl a strand of her hair around her finger. "You're even more handsome in person."

Emmitt offers her a smile—one I can clearly read as fake—and says, "Thanks, love."

Love?

The girl giggles, shrugging. "It's true. And your hair looks even better blond. Is it for a movie?"

I put a hand on my hip, raising an eyebrow at Emmitt, though he hasn't looked at me since the girl's arrival. Still, I can't imagine he's going to tell the truth.

Except then Emmitt laughs quietly. "You could say that. Your hair is also a lovely color. Kind of like starlight."

Some part of me bristles in disbelief. There's no way he just used a *Howl's Moving Castle* (2004) pickup line on some random fan.

The girl's expression brightens further. "So, are you here by yourself? I can show you around if you—"

I clear my throat.

Emmitt's eyes flicker toward me, and he quickly scans my expression. Then a smirk tugs at his mouth, unbelievably condescending.

I scowl at him.

His smirk deepens, until a dimple is pressing into one side of his cheek, and he cocks his head in question.

I open my mouth to tell him to stop being such a *dickhead*, but then the girl finally notices me.

She looks between us, her brows furrowed. "Are you here with her?"

Emmitt doesn't look away from me. "I don't know. Am I?"

"What's wrong with you?" I ask, shaking my head. "It's not that hard to say yes or no."

He shrugs. "What do you want me to say, sweetheart?"

I cross the distance between us, taking his camera from him, unwinding the strap from around his neck. He lets it happen, watching me with sparkling eyes. "If you're not here with me, I'm sure you won't be needing this," I say.

"It's all yours," he says, inclining his head. "Take good care of it."

"Are you guys dating?" the girl asks, frowning.

I blink. *Dating?* A scoff escapes me. "No. Why would anyone want to date him?"

His grin somehow grows even cockier. "I think anyone would be lucky to date me."

"As if you have enough brain cells inside that thick head of yours to even make that judgment."

Emmitt makes a low noise of amusement. "Would you like to come and check? Knock around to see if you can hear anything?"

"You'd like that, wouldn't you?"

"I like a lot of things."

"I'm sure you'll like it when I stick my foot up your ass."

"If that's what you're into, love."

Before I can retort, the girl stomps her foot, huffing. "Are you seriously ignoring me right now? You *are* a douchebag!" Suddenly, time seems to still, everything moving in slow motion, and I watch in disbelief as she throws her *drink* at Emmitt. Holy shit. "I defended you on Twitter so many times, and for what? For you to pretend I don't even exist?"

Emmitt gapes at her, some kind of coffee concoction dripping down his face. The drink pools along his collarbones, running in watery lines across his skin, staining his shirt and soaking into his jeans.

The girl turns on her heel, muttering insults as she walks back to her family.

I can't help it. I burst into laughter, pressing my fingers to my mouth to contain the noise.

Emmitt gives me a look of betrayal, coffee dripping from his lashes, but I can't stop myself. I clutch my sides as I crouch on the ground, laughter wracking my body until I can hardly breathe.

"Oh my God," I say, tears springing to my eyes. Did that really just happen? "She threw her drink at you! Oh my *God*."

"I can't believe you're laughing right now," Emmitt grumbles, wiping his face with his sleeve. "This is *your* fault."

"My fault?" I ask through giggles. "I think you underestimate how much of an asshole you can be."

"Really, love?" he asks, clearly unimpressed.

"At least your camera is safe," I say, rising to my feet now that my laugher has finally subsided. "I'd give it to you but… you're kind of wet."

Emmitt looks down at his camera, still held in my grasp, and relief flashes briefly across his face. Then he exhales, pinching the bridge of his nose. "I need a shower."

"Can't help you there, buddy," I say.

"Park Slope is nearby, right?" he asks instead.

I nod slowly. "Yeah. Why?"

Emmitt grimaces, taking off his jacket and wringing it out. His shirt is sticking to him, his snake tattoo visible through the plain white material. My eyes wander there of their own accord, but I quickly direct them back to his face.

"I can walk from here to my apartment, then." Emmitt pauses, giving me a hesitant look. He starts to reach out, but the movement drips coffee down his forearm, pooling near my shoe.

"Ya Allah," I say, shaking my head with a grin. "Look at you. You're an absolute mess."

Emmitt makes a face at the puddle of coffee at our feet. "I shouldn't touch my camera while I'm soaked. It would probably be better if you took it home with you." He shifts uncomfortably, refusing to meet my gaze. "Unless...you wanted to come with me?"

I consider his forlorn expression and a swell of pathetic fondness springs up between my ribs before I can quell it. I sigh and incline my head toward the cemetery's exit. "Lead the way."

26

The amount of people that stare at us as we walk through the Brooklyn streets are far too many. At least it's because Emmitt is drenched in coffee and not because they've recognized him as a celebrity.

When we get to his block, he leads me to a cute little brick building and punches in a code on a black keypad.

Emmitt falters on the steps, looking at me. "Do you want to wait out here? My apartment is a disaster. I'll only be like twenty minutes."

I shrug. "Sure," I say and sit down on the stone steps. "Take longer than twenty minutes, and I'll sell your camera on the black market."

He scoffs. "No one would buy it."

"Wouldn't they?" I raise my brows. "I've seen people buy Harry Styles's vomit."

Emmitt's entire face screws up. "Maybe you have a point."

I wave him off. "Go take your shower, dickhead."

He nods in acquiescence, then hops up the stairs and heads inside the apartment building. I busy myself on Twitter, typing Emmitt's name into the search bar.

Emmitt Ramos Updates @EmmittRamosUA:
Emmitt Ramos was spotted in NYC earlier today by a fan. He is reportedly filming for a new movie.

crystal @emmittsramos:
omg was emmitt really with a girl??? do we know who she is

fariha @anakinskywalked:
A FAN THREW A DRINK AT EMMITT? IM CRYING ASKFJALFAF

gen @cosmicmoonlight:
oh my god why are some of you SO ENTITLED WTF emmitt is allowed to hang out with a girl without you ASSAULTING HIM?????? fucking weirdos

mana @shatteredplaces:
OK WAIT WHAT IS THIS ABOUT EMMITT BEING BLOND I'M ABOUT TO D WORD

lav @emmittluvr:
omg emmitt was taking pictures????? when I say he's the softest boy on the planet I'm <3 <3 <3

kris @tomhollandoscar:
okay but WHOMST was the girl with emmitt omg. a costar. a gf. what goes on my dudes

michelle @lisasemmitt:
HELLOOOOOO DID SOMEONE SAY BLOND EMMITT
WE FINALLY WON LADIES #EMMITT1STWIN

val @bisexualramos:
alexa play that_should_be_me.mp3 I WANNA GO ON A
DATE WITH EMMITT RAMOS IN NEW YORK CITY whose
dick do I have to suck to make this happen

I close out of the app after reading that one, my eyes wide in alarm. A *date*?

I push that thought away, instead focusing on what's more important. While there are no pictures of Emmitt circulating the internet, the information that he's in New York City paired with him being blond doesn't bode well for keeping his identity a secret.

I suppose it was just a matter of time anyway. He's been around for almost three weeks without getting caught— barring the *Saturday Night Live* incident—which is already more than I expected. I'm more surprised that no one else in film club has realized.

Except…now that I'm thinking back on the way some of the students in film club watch Emmitt, I'm doubting myself. They often hang on to his every word, swarming him when they have the chance, almost hero-worshipping him. I had it down to his charismatic personality, but…

I groan, holding my head in my hands. Of course they know. How did I expect any different?

Behind me a door opens. I turn to see Emmitt standing there, rubbing a towel through his wet hair. Then my eyes drop to his bare chest and my mouth goes dry, even as he says, "Did I make the twenty-minute mark, or have I lost my camera forever?"

I can't look away from his snake tattoo. Oh my God, I need to look away from his snake tattoo, but *I can't look away from his snake tattoo.*

It's red and yellow, inked down his rib cage with one beady black eye staring at me as its forked tongue trails against the edge of Emmitt's hip bone. Why is it suddenly so hard to breathe?

"Sweetheart?" Emmitt says, startling me into meeting his eyes again. "Did you hear me?"

"Oh. Uh." I check my phone for the time, willing myself to focus. "Two minutes early. Impressive."

He grins. "This is the only time I've ever been early."

"I know," I say, letting out a forced chuckle. Without my permission, my eyes dart down again, and this time I give in to the impulse to ask, "Uh...your snake tattoo. Is there a story behind it?"

Emmitt looks down at his chest in surprise. "Oh. I didn't even realize you could see it. There is a story, but it's not that interesting." He shrugs, resting his towel around his shoulders. "My dad grew up in Spain before he moved to England for university. During one of his summers in Spain, he was bitten by a snake. It wasn't poisonous or anything, so he was fine, but he got a really cool scar from it. I used to ask him about it when I was little, and every time he told the story, he made it sound like this incredible adventure. It's one of my favorite memories of him, so when I turned eighteen last year, I decided to get this tattoo. Since both Spain and China have red and yellow in their flags, the colors felt like a fitting homage to both of my parents. Combining both parts of my identity, no matter how different they are."

I gape at him. "That's *not that interesting*? Are you kidding? That's such a lovely and meaningful reason to get a tattoo."

Emmitt shrugs, idly running his fingers over the snake. "I've never told anyone about that before. Mum just kind of knew why I did it when she saw it."

Something in my chest warms. "Thank you for telling me, then. I promise to take it to the grave."

Emmitt offers me a small smile in return. "I'll hold you to it."

I grin and stand up, ready to pass over his camera when Emmitt stops me, holding a hand out.

He looks almost self-conscious as he clears his throat, and that's what fully draws my attention away from even the thought of his tattoo. "I ordered Chinese takeout, if you wanted to stick around. I have a really nice rooftop view."

I stare at him for a long moment, trying to parse out his true meaning. It's clear he's not saying everything he wants to say. I study the curve of his shoulders, the way his chin is ducked, his brown eyes steady but—hesitant.

And again, I think about how lonely it must be to live in a foreign city all by yourself, a city where you have to hide who you are, a city where you feel adrift.

"Okay," I say, nodding slowly. "I won't say no to free food."

Emmitt smiles, but it's nothing like the outrageous grins he wears for everyone else. It's small, soft, private. I've never seen it before. "Come on."

I follow Emmitt up two flights of stairs before he stops briefly at his apartment to abandon his towel. When he comes back out, he's holding a bottle of soda in one hand and a bed-sheet in the other. We head up two more flights of stairs and he pushes open a battered door with one shoulder. I step onto the roof and glance around, looking out on the New York City skyline.

"It is a nice view," I say and hold my hand out for the bed-sheet. He passes it over readily and helps me lay it out on the ground.

All the while, I stare at him, trying to pinpoint what about him is different because something *is* different. But what?

Emmitt's phone buzzes and he glances at it briefly, before looking back at me. "I'll grab the food and be right back," he says.

I nod, watching him go. It's right on the tip of my tongue, but I don't know how to put it into words. Something has shifted.

I can't help but wonder why I even agreed to this. If some-one asked me a few weeks ago if I'd spend time with indie film star Emmitt Ramos of my own volition, I would laugh at them. He's arrogant, too confident for his own good, and he wears a fake smile most of the time.

Yet here I sit, on a rooftop with peeling paint, the sun beating down on my back, staring out at New York City and waiting for him to return. Maybe even looking forward to it.

27

Emmitt comes back a few minutes later, and I help him spread out the food, taking stock of which cartons don't have pork—and quickly realize none of them do. I wonder if he remembered I was Muslim and chose accordingly, but then I shake my head at myself. There's no reason he'd think of my preferences while ordering food for *himself*.

"Can I get my camera?" he asks once we're done setting up.

I reach for my neck, pulling the strap over my head before handing him the camera. "Here."

There's something strange in his stare, as if he's finally dropped his analytical guard and just let himself *exist*. A nervous flutter rises in my stomach, though I firmly ignore it.

Instead, I reach for the shrimp lo mein and fork some out onto a plastic plate. I'm about to start eating when I notice that Emmitt isn't touching any of the food, his eyes focused on his camera instead.

I lean back on my hands, peering up at Emmitt through

my lashes as he flicks through the photos. His eyes are glittering, so bright it almost hurts to look at him. "You're different like this," I say, the words coming out unbidden. "You're not putting on a show for anyone."

A smile flickers at the corner of Emmitt's mouth. "Maybe I am. A show for two."

My heart stutters uncertainly. "For you and your camera?"

Emmitt holds my gaze and the silence stretches taut between us. He breaks it, his voice quiet as he says, "For me and you."

My breath hitches, and I feel like I'm sitting on the precipice of something bigger than myself. As if I'm dangling my legs over the edge of the roof and preparing myself for a steep fall.

"For me and you?" I repeat softly, but it comes out as more of a question than anything else.

Emmitt keeps staring at me. The quiet is louder than if he were screaming, louder than if the wind was roaring in our ears and thunder was cracking down on our heads.

"Maybe I should buy a seasonal pass," I say and let the words hang in the air.

Slowly, slowly his mouth widens into a grin, a dimple pressing into his cheek. "I can get you a discount on a yearly pass instead, if you want."

"We'll see," I say, but my own lips curve into a small smile. "Now eat your *food*."

Emmitt laughs quietly, reaching for a plate of scallion pancakes and a carton of shrimp with broccoli.

As we eat, a thought occurs to me, and I scrunch my nose. "Did you get enough photos for this week? We didn't spend that long at Green-Wood Cemetery."

"I'm sure I took at least one decent shot," he says, shrugging a shoulder and lifting some noodles with a pair of chopsticks. "Memory is probably the best prompt so far. And I think the cemetery location will subvert expectations, while still fitting the theme. We'll be fine."

He refers to us as a we. As if we're a team.

The words *a show for two* echo in my head once again.

"I just thought a graveyard would be chock-full of memories," I say, toying with a piece of broccoli.

Emmitt nods. It's golden hour, and he glows in the sunlight. The curve of his nose, the line of his jaw, the flutter of his lashes. "I don't remember a lot about my dad, but when I visit his grave, I can still feel the weight of the memories we *did* share together. The stories he used to tell. The smell of his cologne. A smile, a laugh. Warmth and kindness. That kind of stuff."

"You must miss him a lot," I say softly.

"I do," Emmitt says, sighing. "One of the last trips we took before he died was to visit Spain for the first time, and he took me to the beach and taught me how to swim. He told me he would buy me all the tapas in the world if I made it farther than ten feet by myself."

I give him a curious look. "Did you?"

A faint smile touches Emmitt's lips. "Of course. Anything for fresh tapas."

My eyes trace his features again. He doesn't look sad, but there is a wistful quality to him. "How old were you when he passed away?"

"Six," Emmitt says, his eyes focused on his food again. "You know, I thought about taking Spanish when I came to

AAAS, since I never got to pick it up from my dad, but since Grant takes Italian, I didn't really have a choice in my language elective."

I frown. "Maybe you could switch? I'm sure the school faculty would understand. It's not like you're really being graded while you're here."

Emmitt shakes his head. "It's okay. Maybe I'll download Duolingo or something. Have the owl yell at me until I finally pick up Spanish. Connect with my roots somehow."

"Yelling does seem to work pretty effectively with you," I tease lightly, but lower my gaze from his. "I know our situations aren't the same, but... I also feel disconnected from my roots. From my culture. I know it's a part of me, but some days, it doesn't feel that way. Me and my parents don't really get along, so I feel like there's so much I'm missing out on. I just don't feel like...enough."

Emmitt furrows his brows, his expression growing serious. "You know that's not your fault, right?"

"I know," I say, heaving a deep breath. "But it doesn't stop me from feeling that way."

There's a slump to his shoulders as he spears a mushroom. "If only we could control our feelings."

I give him a bitter smile. "If only. But I guess we just have to make the most of what we have. At least I have my sister. At least you have your mother."

The corner of Emmitt's mouth twitches. "Honestly, sometimes it feels like it's just been me and my mum my whole life. Always her hand on my shoulder, that kind of thing."

"It must have been cool growing up with someone like her as a mother," I say. "She has such an amazing job."

"It is an amazing job," he agrees, but it doesn't sound like a good thing. "I wouldn't be here today without her."

"You don't look too happy about it," I say slowly.

Emmitt's gaze catches mine, and he sighs, scrubbing a hand over his face. "It's not that I'm not happy about it. It's just... tiring, I guess. To have to meet her expectations all the time. To be what she wants me to be."

My heart suddenly feels like a boulder. "Do you not want to be an actor?" I ask, even though it feels almost sacrilegious to say the words aloud.

I expect him to deny it, but he's quiet for a long time.

"I don't mind," Emmitt finally says. "But I...liked it a lot more before."

"Before what?"

"Before it started to define me," he says tiredly. "Before I became known as Emmitt Ramos the actor, rather than Emmitt Ramos the person. Sometimes it seems like my mother just sees me as one of her projects."

"I'm sure that's not true," I say, but then I think of my own parents and I'm not too sure.

Emmitt laughs, the sound hoarse. "You'd be surprised, love. I think after my dad died, she just kind of threw herself into her work and forgot I was there."

The space between us is too vast all of a sudden. I want to reach out, to lay a hand on his arm and tell him I'm sorry, but it feels like moving will break the strange, honest atmosphere we've managed to create.

"There are good parts to life as a celebrity, though, right?" I say lightly.

"I guess, yeah. It's nice knowing that I've touched people

with my work. But... I'd rather do that with something I've created myself, you know?" He swallows, his throat shifting with the movement. "Rather than because I'm pretending to be someone I'm not."

My eyes drop to his camera. "Is that why you took up photography?"

He nods slowly, his fingers lingering on the edge of the lens. "Yeah. It started as a hobby, but it's grown into something... *more.* Especially recently, with all these new career changes on the horizon... I don't know. I guess some people would see the Firebrand movie as an incredible opportunity. And I'm not ungrateful, I know how amazing it is, but it also seems like a cage in some ways. Like if I don't make the most of my time now, I might not ever have it again. Shana Torres's contest feels like it might be my last chance to really make something of myself as a photographer and live the life I want."

I offer him a weak smile. "How'd you find out about the contest anyway?"

Emmitt laughs quietly. "Funnily enough, through my dad. He must have bought one of Shana Torres's photos at the beginning of her career, because we have one framed in our apartment back in London. She was one of the first photographers I ever looked into. When I saw she was hosting this contest... I knew I had to apply. Everything inside me was screaming at me to do it."

"You love it, don't you? Photography?" I ask, but I can read the answer plainly on his face. The air around me is suffocating, awareness buzzing in my ears. We're more alike than I ever thought possible.

As if he reads my mind, Emmitt says, "The same way you

love films." A shadow of a smile touches his lips. "I heard you, you know. That day you were giving advice to Christina."

Blood rushes up to my cheeks, until it feels like my face is baking in the sun. "I—I didn't think anyone was…"

"I know," he says, looking down at his lap. "And I'm sorry. It wasn't for my ears. But, as awful as this sounds, I'm glad I overheard you." He shrugs. "We got off on a really bad foot, and I had no intention of helping you with your short film. Then I heard what you said to Christina and I realized…this short film is to you what this photography contest is to me."

My throat is choked with some unnamed emotion, butterflies cramming themselves into my chest until my ribs threaten to snap. I think about how much I want to win the Golden Ivy competition, how much I *need* to win it, and realize I have yet another thing in common with Emmitt. "You could never give up on it?"

"Something like that," he says, biting his lip. "This isn't a hobby for you either, is it? It means everything to you."

I nod, swallowing loudly. "Yeah. It's kind of like…the world is super shitty sometimes, right? It feels like there's no winning, no matter what we do. But for me, movies are the one ray of light in the darkness. They give me hope for something bigger and better and *brighter*."

"Light," Emmitt echoes, and there's something strange in his gaze.

I offer him a helpless smile. "Is that what photography is for you? The light?"

He shrugs, glancing at the New York City skyline. "More or less. Sometimes, taking photos is the only time I feel like myself. It's the only time I don't have to hide." He offers me a sidelong grin. "No putting on a show."

Tension builds in my gut for no reason I can fathom. "Only the truth."

"Exactly. Nowhere to run, nowhere to hide. Just the world as it is, real and honest." Then he sighs. "I've been—acting out, I guess, for lack of a better term, in interviews and the like. My publicist wants to strangle me for my reputation as a prick, but..." He tugs his earrings, something I'm beginning to recognize as a nervous habit. "I don't know how else to tell Mum about all of this."

"Has your mom seen your work? Maybe you could try explaining your dreams to her through your photographs." *And hope it doesn't go as badly as it did with my parents.*

Emmitt shakes his head. "Mum will see it as a distraction. That's why I can't tell her about this contest. She has this single-minded focus that makes me want to rip my hair out. She always says anything else outside of our goals is a disruption, and that anyone who serves as a block in our vision is someone we didn't want by our side in the first place." His expression is sour. "I don't want to be one of the people in her way."

I stare at him hopelessly, wishing there was an easy answer. But I don't have one. "I'm sorry," I say. "I'm really, really sorry."

He offers me a grim smile. "If I win this contest, then maybe I'll finally be able to prove my silly little hobby has its worth. That's what I'm hoping anyway."

"I hope you win," I say and I mean it. This common link between us is growing stronger, a fraying thread lengthening into a solid rope that ties me to him in a way I can't deny. And maybe I don't want to, not anymore, not when he *understands*, not when he sees more than I ever expected him to.

We're the same, he and I. Both chasing after our dreams, despite what it might cost us.

"No, love." Emmitt's gaze is steady. "I hope we win."

28

By the time I get home, it's late at night. Much later than I expected. Emmitt and I sat on the rooftop past sunset, the city lights illuminating our view.

And now it's past 10:00 p.m. and I'm shuffling down my driveway, already wincing in preparation for the shouting that's bound to come.

As expected, as soon as I turn my key and step into the foyer, I see both Ma and Baba sitting in the living room. They glower at the sight of me and I sigh, shutting the door behind me.

Let's hear it. I don't say it, but I might as well have.

"Do you know what time it is?" Baba asks, staring me down.

I lift my shoulder in a vague gesture before unlacing my boots and stepping out of them.

"Past my bedtime, that's for sure," he says. "But your mother was so worried something happened to you that I couldn't sleep."

Sure. Worried. We'll go with that, I say again in the safety of mind. In person, I just offer them a blank gaze and shrug off my jacket, hanging it up on the coatrack.

"Where were you?" Ma demands, her voice sharp. It feels like needles pricking my skin. "You have no idea what kind of dangerous things can happen at this time of night. You are the most irresponsible—"

"Keep it down!" Anam shouts from upstairs. "I'm trying to study!"

My mother's expression darkens further. "You see what you've done? You've set such a horrible example for your sister that now she doesn't think twice before disrespecting us."

I try not to let my incredulity show on my face. As if I'm the reason Anam hates them.

I tug my hair tie, releasing my unruly locks. I work my hands through my braid methodically, untangling knots and letting the dark waves hang loose against my back.

"What have we done as parents to deserve this?" Ma asks, shaking her head. She looks to Baba, who rubs circles into his temples. "We're good people. We gave you everything. And you choose to repay us by being disobedient?"

My gaze narrows. They always do this—play the part of the victim, as if I'm the one being malicious. *We're your parents, we're good people, we raised you, we sacrificed so much for you, we have done nothing but love you.* Even though I recognize and appreciate all the effort they've put in to ensure Anam and I have a good life, it's still ridiculous to act like that gives them the right to dictate our futures. The older I am, the more I resent the implication that it's my responsibility to repay them for my existence.

"You've been staying out late a lot these last weeks. Do

you know how it makes you look, Poppy? And how it makes us look as parents? You have no common sense. Some days, I wonder if the world is punishing us by giving us a daughter like you," Ma says, lips pressed into a thin line. "Every day, I pray for you to be a better person, and still, you remain as you are."

My eyes burn. I wish they didn't, but they do. It's just not *fair*. Why couldn't I have parents who are more understanding, more sympathetic? Don't I deserve parents who view me as more than a burden, as more than a mistake for them to fix?

"Are you going to stay silent?" Baba asks, his jaw tense. "Do you have nothing to say for yourself? You aren't even going to apologize?"

When I don't say anything, my gaze dropping to the carpet, Baba huffs an angry breath. "You know what happens to children who don't listen to their parents, don't you? They're failures in life. Is that what you want for yourself?"

The words brand themselves into my memory, and I taste bile on the back of my tongue. Both of my parents look at me with so much resentment, yet still disguise it as concern.

"Poppy, look at us," Ma asks sharply, and my head jerks up without permission. "Do you think you're all grown up now, too smart to listen to us?"

Only silence prevails. Baba finally turns toward me, pinning me to the spot with a harsh glare. "Be better than this. Right now, you are nothing but a disappointment."

Then he stands and makes his way to the stairs, leaving me with only my mother.

A lump is rising up my throat, slowly but surely. Whether it's born of anger or frustration or sadness, I don't know, but I feel the distinct urge to cry.

Ma walks over to me and grips my chin with tight fingers. "You think your stupid university in California will want you when you act like this? You can't even behave properly around your parents." Her nails dig into my skin. "You're a shame upon this family."

She lets go of me and follows after my father.

I stare after her, my breath coming out in harsh pants. Then slowly, piece by piece, I gather myself and walk up the stairs, head into my room, and shut the door.

In the mirror, my face looks back, but it feels separate from me, from who I really am. There are faint crescent marks on my cheeks, from where Ma's fingernails dug in. They're fading, but I can still feel the heat of her on my skin.

I had such a good day. I laughed more than I've laughed in months. My heart was at ease. I didn't even think about how USC might reject me, or how we might not win the film competition, or how a million things might go wrong. I was happy.

But it doesn't matter. Not when there's a heaviness descending on me now, burying my heart in rubble. I recognize the signs of an upcoming depressive episode, but I can't bring myself to change my thought pattern, to find the cognitive distortions and remind myself of what truly matters.

My door opens, and I don't move, not until I see Anam behind me in the mirror, her face wet with tears.

Something cracks inside me.

And in a split second, I force myself to pull it together, shutting down the volatile emotions raging war within my chest. I have to stay strong for Anam.

"Don't cry," I say, pulling her into my arms, stroking a hand down her blue hair. "It's okay, Anam."

"Apu," she croaks, her tears soaking through my shirt. "What's going to happen when you leave? I don't know if I can…"

I hush her, holding her head against my shoulder. "You'll be okay, Anam. One day, they won't be able to hurt us ever again. We can make it until the end."

"I can't do it alone," she whispers, fear palpable in her voice. "I can't do it without you."

"You can," I say fiercely, even as my throat aches from holding back tears. "You are capable of so much more than you know."

Anam keeps crying, her arms tight around my waist, and I rub circles into her back, all while reminding myself to breathe and keep it moving. My eighteenth birthday is in four days, and I will *not* spend another year in this city. I refuse to.

My ticket out of here is the Golden Ivy film competition. I have to win, no matter what it takes. There is no other choice.

There's no room to falter, to hesitate. I have to focus on the competition and make our short film the best it can be, so I can finally *leave*. If I want freedom, this is how to get it.

And one year later, Anam will follow me, and we'll both leave behind this wretched place for good. We'll be happy in California, whether it's at USC or Stanford. We'll be okay.

I have to believe that.

29

Castings go live the next day. I pin the sheet to the bulletin board in front of the auditorium and step back, making sure it's not crooked.

It tilts slightly to the left, but I decide it's good enough.

"Well?" Emmitt's voice comes from behind me. "Did I get the role?"

I gesture half-heartedly to the paper but don't say anything.

He comes to stand beside me, his eyes scanning the sheet, though we both already know he got the role. This film hinges on his performance. Sofia's ex-boyfriend also auditioned for the role of Nick, and maybe if Emmitt wasn't here, he would've gotten it.

But Emmitt is here, so there's no point wondering about what would have happened.

What matters is the future ahead of us.

Emmitt turns to me, a smirk on his face, but it disappears as soon as he takes me in. "What's wrong, love?"

"Nothing," I say quietly.

I turn my back on him and start walking toward my locker, ignoring the flurry of drama club members I see heading for the bulletin board, speaking in loud, excited tones.

A moment later, Emmitt wraps his hand around my elbow, stopping me in my tracks. I look at him, waiting for whatever it is he wants to say.

He stares at me, his eyes roaming my face, before his other hand rises, his fingertips brushing underneath my eye. "Did you get any sleep last night?"

"I need to go to my locker," I say. "Please."

It looks like he's going to protest, but then he lets go of me, taking a step back. His voice is unsure when he says, "I'll see you in Italian, right?"

"Yeah," I say and head for my locker again. As I walk down the hallway, I feel Emmitt's gaze following me, right until I turn the corner.

A breath locked away inside my chest releases in the form of a deep exhale.

The competition. I need to focus on the competition.

By the time film club rolls around, I'm exhausted. I want nothing more than to lie down for a few hours, maybe listen to some sad music, maybe cry at videos of cute animals.

But this isn't something I can avoid. In fact, this is the last thing I can afford to skip out on.

When I reach the classroom, Ms. Somal is standing near the doorway, monitoring all the students filtering in.

"More stragglers than usual, Samina?" she asks when she

sees me, gesturing to all the actors that have made themselves at home in her classroom.

"We're starting the short film," I say by way of explanation. "Today is an introductory meeting."

"Already?" Ms. Somal blinks. "Time passes so quickly."

"And yet not quickly enough," I mutter to myself. Ms. Somal gives me a bemused look but doesn't ask me anything as I pass her to enter the room.

Rosie is already seated on the desk, and I join her, setting down my book bag and pulling out my short-film journal.

This is the first time I've had a chance to properly speak to Rosie all day. We had an Italian test this morning, and she was busy studying in the library when I arrived at school. The responsibility of pinning the cast list fell to me for that very reason.

"Can you lead the meeting?" I ask, clicking my pen absently.

She looks at me in surprise, but nods. "Yeah, of course. Are you good?"

I shrug. "My parents are being...my parents."

Rosie's face softens in understanding. She's seen this enough times before. "Oh." She reaches between us, grabbing my hand and squeezing. "Let me know if you need anything. I love you."

I manage enough strength to squeeze back. "Love you."

Emmitt and Grant enter a minute later, laughing about something uproariously. My heart only grows heavier at the sound, and I rub my hands over my arms as goose bumps form along my skin.

The bell rings and Rosie claps her hands excitedly. "Hi,

everyone! Welcome to our first joint film club meeting of the year. If we could all go around and introduce ourselves, that'd be great. Please include your preferred name, pronouns, and what your favorite movie is."

When no one takes the initiative, Rosie sighs. "I'll start. I'm Rosie Hardy, I use she and her pronouns, and my favorite movie is *The Handmaiden*."

She looks to me, and I nod. "I'm Mina Rahman, I use she and her pronouns, and my favorite movie is *The Umbrellas of Cherbourg*."

"I'm Grant Njoku, I use he and him pronouns, and my favorite movie is *Get Out*."

"I'm Andie Zavala, I use she and her—"

The circle goes around the room, everyone introducing themselves until we finally end at Emmitt.

"I'm Ezra Rivera, I use he and him pronouns, and my favorite movie is *Foul Lady Fortune*." As he says it, he aims a cocky grin my way, obviously alluding to the fact he played the male lead.

The rest of the room titters in amusement, more or less confirming they know Emmitt's true identity, but I can't bring myself to feign laughter.

For the second time that day, I watch his smile fall.

Rosie looks between us, biting her lip, but eventually clears her throat. "Grant, can you pull up the website for the Golden Ivy student film competition? We'll go over rules and regulations."

As Grant moves toward the computer, the makeshift circle breaks apart and people start clumping into groups.

I grab my stuff, moving for my usual seat, and Rosie follows me. Every so often, her eyes flicker toward Sofia, but for the most part, she seems focused.

I hate that a part of me is grateful for that. I can't help but feel slightly selfish, but I know I can't do this without Rosie at my side. I need her to match me in giving a hundred percent to this competition.

"Ro," I say, once we sit down. "I think we should change the schedule and increase our weekly meetings to make sure everything is prepared leading up to the deadline."

Rosie frowns, considering my expression, before she sighs and opens her planner. "Which day do you want to add?"

Her tone is reluctant, but it's an acceptance all the same. "Wednesday would probably be best. And then we can adjust closer to the deadline to see if we need four days."

Rosie pencil halts, and she gives me a sidelong look. "Mina…"

"What?" I ask.

She sighs again. "Nothing. Yeah, we can adjust closer to the deadline if necessary."

I nod and lean back in my seat. "I'll announce it."

Rosie gestures for me to go ahead, and I stand, calling attention to myself. "In effort to make sure the competition runs as smoothly as possible, we will now be meeting three times a week. Tuesday, Wednesday, and Friday. If you are unable to attend on Wednesdays, let me or Rosie know in advance. Otherwise, I'll see you all on Wednesday evenings going forward."

Everyone in the room looks surprised, looking at one another, but the freshmen nod eagerly. Christina even rushes to grab her planner, penciling the meetings in.

"Thank you," I say and sit back down, pulling out my own phone to make note of the meetings.

Emmitt suddenly appears, plopping into the seat beside me.

"So does this mean I can call you Mina now?" he asks, resting his hands on my desk.

I look down at his hands. His fingers are long, the slopes of his knuckles slightly bruised, rings assorted on half of his fingers. I look back up at him. "What?"

Emmitt arches his brows. "When you introduced yourself, you said Mina Rahman."

"Did I?" I ask. Though it was only twenty minutes ago, I don't even recall.

He nods, tapping a beat out on the desk. "So? Does this mean we can drop the formalities?"

"Sure," I say tiredly. "Whatever."

Emmitt furrows his brows, and his gaze shifts from me to Rosie. He tilts his head in question, but my best friend only sighs.

"Was there anything else?" I ask.

He slowly shakes his head, then stands and walks over to Grant. I don't watch him go, but in the corner of my eye I see him whispering something in Grant's ear.

It doesn't matter. None of it matters.

All that matters is winning.

30

I almost wish my birthday was like any other day. Instead, I wake up on March 1 to the sound of my parents screaming.

For a minute, I contemplate shoving my pillow over my head and drowning out the sound. Maybe I can fake my death.

Except then I hear them yelling Anam's name, too.

I grudgingly climb out of bed, checking the calendar as I go. It's a Friday, which means as soon as I make it through today, I'll have the weekend to finally sleep and block out the world.

I close my eyes, willing myself to remember that for the next few hours. It'll be over soon.

By the time I come downstairs, dressed for school, my parents are sitting at the dining table, and Anam is huffing in the kitchen doorway.

"What happened?" I ask her, reaching forward to tie her hair back with the tie on my wrist. "Are you okay?"

"I was trying to make you a birthday breakfast, and Baba

lost his mind because I put a paratha in the toaster oven instead of frying it. I know you like them more crispy, which is why I—"

"Oh, of course, make us look like some kind of big bad villain," Ma snaps. There are dark circles under her eyes, not unlike my own. It seems her migraines are keeping her up. "You're going to neglect to tell your sister that *smoke* was coming out of the toaster oven?"

Anam makes a low growling noise, and I wrap my fingers around her wrist to keep her from acting without thinking. "Well, it's not like *you* were going to do anything for her birthday."

Baba blows out a breath. "You two are acting absurd. This is not some kind of war that we have to constantly fight. You're sixteen and eighteen, and yet you act like toddlers. You know we just want what's best for you."

My sister scoffs. "What did you get Apu for her birthday, then?"

A long silence follows. My head is buzzing faintly with white noise, but I tune it out. "It's fine, we'll make breakfast together some other time," I say, pressing a kiss to Anam's forehead. "Thank you."

Anam grimaces but wraps me in a tight hug. "Happy birthday."

I give her a weak smile and grab a banana off the table. Baba used to pack us a breakfast when he was leaving for work, but in the last few months, he's neglected to do it, as some kind of misplaced punishment. I can't help but recall when he said cooking for us brought him more joy than anything in the world. I guess things change.

Anam takes off her apron, heading up the stairs to grab her book bag, squeezing my arm as she goes.

I'm sifting through the closet when my mom appears in the corner of my vision. "What?" I ask, without stopping my search.

She walks closer and stands there, an obtrusive presence, one I have no choice but to acknowledge. I reluctantly pick out a jean jacket before facing her. "Yes?" I ask.

Ma holds out a fifty-dollar bill. I stare at it wordlessly. When I don't automatically take it, she shoves it into my hand, frowning at me. "Take it. I don't want to hear you complain we gave you nothing for your birthday."

I almost shove it right back at her, but I don't have the strength to have this argument today of all days. "Thanks," I say shortly, my fingers curling around the bill.

There used to be a time when they put in loads of effort for my birthday, throwing me ostentatious parties, showering me with gifts.

Those memories only make this last-ditch effort hurt even more.

Anam watches from the doorway, her arms crossed, shaking her head.

"Don't spend it on anything silly," Ma says, turning away from me. She sees Anam staring at her judgmentally and pauses, looking at me over her shoulder. "Happy birthday, Poppy."

And yet I feel further from happiness than ever.

31

When I get to school, a brief flash of gratitude runs through me at the sight of my locker. It's covered in pictures and memes and proclamations of birthday wishes.

Rosie pops out from behind the row of lockers, carrying an armful of balloons. They're red and gold, the USC colors. I shouldn't have expected anything less from my best friend. "Happy birthday, Mina!"

I manage to dredge up a real, honest smile for her. "Thank you, Rosie."

She captures me in a bear hug, squeezing until I can barely breathe. "You're an adult now!" She pulls back, eyes bright. "Let's hitchhike to Canada and load a duffel bag with alcohol."

I shove her shoulder lightly. "That's what your older brother is for."

"Luke isn't good for anything," she mutters, but her eyes are still sparkling as she hands me a bright pink gift bag. "Don't open your present until you get home, okay?"

I nod, pressing a kiss to her cheek in thanks. "I won't."

Rosie grins, looping her arm with mine. "One step closer to freedom, right?"

I ignore the bittersweet tug in my chest. "Exactly."

After I open my locker, confetti raining down on me while Rosie laughs, we head to Italian together. I'm unsurprised to find Emmitt waiting near the doorway, but I am surprised to see him holding out a small box, wrapped in gold foil.

"Happy birthday, love," he says.

I'm surprised he remembered it was my birthday. I only mentioned it offhandedly last week. Maybe Rosie told him?

Either way, I take it slowly, testing the weight of it in my palm, before looking back at him. "Thank you."

He smiles at me, reaching forward to tuck a strand of hair behind my ear. "I hope it's a good one."

It's not the worst one, I decide. It's not the best by any means, but there are people who are trying, who care enough to wish me well and give me gifts, and that counts for something.

And next year will be better.

During film club that afternoon, I sit and watch the actors run lines. Linli and Sofia are Charlie and Vivienne, and have incredible chemistry from years of being best friends. They work off each other in ways that resonate even more strongly through a camera.

As they're rehearsing the first scene, Rosie directs their body language and expressions. Grant is framing the shot, messing around with different lighting options. I think if his dad saw him, he'd be proud. On a better day, I might voice the thought aloud.

Instead I sit at my desk, glancing between the actresses and the script. Linli is known for her improvisation, and I want to make sure I catch any instances she ad-libs that work better than the actual scripted lines. I'm of the firm belief that a screenplay is adjustable if an actor has a better way to bring the scene to life, evoking the right emotion.

Emmitt's scenes aren't being rehearsed today, so he comes to sit beside me, though he leans against the edge of the desk rather than properly situating himself in a seat. "Hey."

I don't look up from the script, my head tilted as I listen to Linli and Sofia. "Hi."

"What are you doing after the meeting?"

I glance briefly to the side, taking in his hesitant expression. "Why?"

He shrugs in a blasé manner. "Just because."

I turn back to my script, making a small note. "Oh. Well. Going home, I guess," I say, though I'm already exhausted at the thought.

Emmitt wraps his fingers around my arm, halting my pen, his thumb pressing against my pulse. "Can you spare me half an hour?"

For a brief moment, I consider saying no. I don't know if I have the energy to deal with people.

But the thought of dealing with my parents is so much worse.

"Yeah," I say, nodding slowly. "Sure."

Emmitt squeezes my wrist, his fingers warm against my

skin, contrasting the cold metal of his rings. "I'll be right back."

I watch as he walks over to Rosie, ducking so he can whisper something in her hair. Rosie falters for a moment, cocking her head as she listens to him, before her face brightens.

"Lin, Sof, come here for a second," she says, waving them over. Both of them falter midscene, but oblige. "Kaity, you too!"

Meanwhile, Emmitt goes over to Grant, bumping fists before he starts speaking again in a hushed tone.

I look back down at the script. A minute later, everything returns to normal as Sofia and Linli start rehearsing the next scene.

A sliver of suspicion rises in me all the same, but it's drowned out by how tired I am. Whatever Emmitt's doing, I'm sure I'll hear the details soon enough.

32

I expect Emmitt to drag me somewhere after school, but instead I find a horde of people waiting for me once I'm done packing up. There's Rosie and Sofia talking to each other quietly, gesturing at the script although they're both flushed like they've run a marathon. Emmitt and Grant are fooling around, poking and prodding each other. Kaity and Linli are joined by the latter's boyfriend, Noojman, who's smiling good-naturedly as Kaity ribs him.

"Are you guys waiting for something?" I ask as I make my way to Emmitt, shrugging on my jean jacket.

"You," Emmitt says, grinning crookedly. "Are you ready?"

I blink. "Wait, *all* of us? Where are we going?"

"You'll have to wait and see," he says, tapping my nose. Then he reaches down, grabs my hand, and tugs me along. I'm too surprised to protest, not that I would have if he'd given me proper warning.

He leads me outside, and there's an SUV already waiting

for us. The rest of our classmates follow us, laughing at my bemusement.

"What's going on?" I ask.

Emmitt presses a finger to my lips, effectively shutting me up as he climbs into the SUV. "Patience, love."

I sigh but allow him to help me up, taking the seat beside him. Everyone else climbs into the back, Kaity taking the other seat beside me.

She wiggles her eyebrows at me suggestively, and I shake my head, but she doesn't let that deter her.

"Does *everyone* know where we're going except me?" I ask, turning to glance at the back row.

Rosie grins back at me. "Have I ever led you astray?"

"*Many* times."

"Well, this isn't one of those times," she says, before poking my forehead. "Turn around and buckle your seat belt."

I grudgingly turn back around, but when I go to reach for my seat belt, Emmitt is already there, tugging it down for me.

His face is suddenly too close to mine as he pulls it across my chest and down to my lap. His fingers brush against my waist, and a chill runs through me despite the heat blowing from the ventilation system. "I've got you," he says quietly, his breath ghosting against my cheek.

I nod slowly, my eyes lingering on his, even as the seat belt clicks into place and he no longer has an excuse for being as close to me as he is. "Thank you," I whisper in the liminal space between us.

Rosie whacks the back of my head, and I shift forward, turning my head at the very last second. His mouth brushes against my cheekbone, though he quickly pulls back.

"Sorry," he says, his cheeks a warm shade of pink.

"You shouldn't be the one apologizing," I assure, before turning to glare at Rosie. She's laughing under her breath, her face tucked into Grant's shoulder. I turn my glare on him, but he raises his hands placatingly.

I sigh and face forward, trying not to recall the feeling of Emmitt's soft lips on my skin. "Let's get this over with."

A carnival. Emmitt has brought us to a carnival.

In big, bold letters, *FRESH MEADOWS WINTER CAR-NIVAL* is painted across a stark red banner.

"How did you even find out about this place?" I ask, reaching for my backpack strap to fiddle with before I remember it's not there. We left our stuff in the SUV, which Emmitt proclaimed safe since he apparently *rented* it just for this occasion. In light of that, all we have with us are our phones and Emmitt's camera.

Emmitt shrugs. "Grant helped me."

I look to Grant, and he offers me an almost nervous smile in return. I suddenly feel horrible for all the times I've been unnecessarily abrasive toward him.

"Thank you, Grant," I say softly.

A small smile graces Grant's lips, before it widens into a large grin, his teeth bright against his dark skin. "You're welcome, Mina."

My eyes dart around the different booths ahead of us and the crowd weaving in between them, before returning to Emmitt, who stands with his hands tucked into his pockets. He's even wearing a beanie to hide his blond hair from view, which is almost ironic since it was initially meant to disguise his identity.

Rosie grabs my arm, pulling me past the entrance before I can say anything more. "Come on!"

I shake my head, letting her drag me along. "Wait, but why are we—"

Emmitt claps a hand over my mouth. "Talk less, smile more."

"Okay, Aaron Burr," I mutter, before biting his pinky finger. I expect him to pull his hand back, but he only raises an eyebrow at me in challenge.

I stare back, realizing I'm out of moves. I think that even if I licked his palm, he'd remain unbothered. Eventually, I just reach up, gently prying his fingers away, and he allows me it, if only to raise my hand to his mouth, pressing a soft kiss against my fingertips.

I flush in surprise. I wasn't expecting such a gentle touch from him, but the more I think about it, the more I realize he's been increasingly tactile as of late. Maybe it's because we've finally settled into a friendship.

I try my best to hide my reaction, looking anywhere but at Emmitt. Rosie lets go of my arm, moving ahead to one of the booths, and I manage to focus on her and Grant as they offer money to the girl behind the counter in exchange for plastic rings.

Grant takes the first throw, but his lands almost a foot away from the bottles. He makes a quiet noise of despair and gestures for Rosie to go ahead.

Rosie laughs, tossing her own ring, which lands neatly

around the bottle neck. Grant pouts, knocking his hip into hers to push her aside.

A small smile flits across my face. "Your friend is really bad at this," I say, as another one of Grant's rings fall short.

Eventually, Grant seems to give up, because instead of throwing his rings, he tries to distract Rosie instead.

"I know," Emmitt says, and his voice is affectionate. I glance up at him and see his private smile again, directed at none other than Grant. "It's a shame, since he probably would've given me the prize."

My nose wrinkles as I eye the prizes in question—huge stuffed animals sitting on the shelves behind the girl running the booth. "Why would he give *you* the prize?"

"Who else is he going to give them to?" Emmitt asks, offering me a sharp grin. "I picked this group strategically."

I feel the urge to roll my eyes for the first time in days. "Shut up."

"Make me," he teases.

I stare at him for a long time before leaning up on my toes. Emmitt's eyes go wide as I balance myself on his shoulders, but his hands move to accommodate me, resting on my waist and steadying me.

"What are you doing?" he asks, his voice hoarse.

"Making you," I say quietly, and then my hands slide farther up, wrapping around his neck until I can squeeze, though there's no real strength behind my hands. *"Dickhead."*

Emmitt splutters with sudden laughter. My nerves settle at the return to our normal bickering—even if it's more playful now than anything else. "How is it you always manage to surprise me?"

I land flat on my feet, dropping my hands to my side, though his are still on my waist, warm through the layers of clothes I'm wearing. "I'm a girl of many talents."

Emmitt makes a fond noise. "I suppose that is true."

"Suppose?"

"Suppose," he repeats, mirth lining his eyes.

I flip him off, turning my attention back to Rosie and Grant. The weight on my shoulders feels lighter than it has in days.

When Rosie wins the round, she points to a fluffy penguin on the middle shelf. "That one, please."

I'm not surprised when she holds it out to Sofia afterward, her cheeks bright pink. "For you."

Sofia smiles warmly, taking the stuffed animal into her arms. "Penguins are my favorite."

Rosie digs her toe in the ground, toying with an auburn curl. "I know."

I take in her expression, more enamored than I've ever seen before, and feel a painful sense of distance. When did this development happen? When did Rosie's feelings grow this intense? I thought it was a schoolyard crush, but this—this looks like more than that.

Emmitt's voice draws my attention away as Grant claps him on the back.

"There's no way," Grant is saying, shaking his head. "You have the hand-eye coordination of a toddler."

"Smack talk before we even begin? You wound me, Grant," Emmitt says, holding a hand to his heart. "I could run circles around you."

"As if," Grant says, waving him off. "My *grandmother* could do better than you."

"Is that a challenge?" Emmitt asks, a wicked grin on his lips as he slides the plastic rings along the length of his arm. "You're on."

And then, because Emmitt Ramos apparently has not an ounce of shame, he walks up to the counter of the booth and leans forward, talking to the girl running it.

The girl—who can't be more than a few years older than us—becomes increasingly flustered, visible in the way she starts fidgeting, her cheeks flushing and her eyes sparkling as she looks up at him.

I sigh, shaking my head. The flirting never ends with Emmitt.

But I realize why he went over a minute later, when he climbs onto the counter on his knees.

"Bro, the fuck?" Grant protests, pooling his plastic rings in one hand to swat Emmitt on the arm with his other one. "That's not fair. Come on."

Emmitt shrugs. "It's not my bloody fault you didn't think of it first."

Grant turns to me, gesturing wildly to Emmitt, as if I somehow missed the spectacle occurring in front of me.

I look back at him in bemusement. "What?"

"Collect your man!" he says, pointing at Emmitt with way too much conviction for the words coming out of his mouth.

"He is not my man," I say, lifting a brow.

Grant levels me a look of disbelief. "Who exactly do you think he's winning that prize for?"

I shrug a shoulder, refusing to read into that implication.

"Don't know, don't care. And if you can't collect him as his friend, I can't collect him, either."

Grant gives me a look of despair. "This is the worst kind of betrayal."

Meanwhile, Emmitt has tuned us out, throwing the rings with ease, watching as they land securely around the bottle necks with a smug smile on his face.

"Worry less about me, and more about convincing that girl over there to let you climb on the counter," I suggest, my eyes tracking the movement of Emmitt's rings.

Grant groans at my side as Emmitt's last ring neatly circles around a bottle neck. "This is so unfair."

Emmitt climbs off the counter, brushing his knees off, before offering the girl a bright grin. My heart seems to both shrivel and grow at the sight of it. "I want the black wolf," he says, pointing at the top shelf.

The girl moves to grab it, all the while flushing deeply. She hands it to Emmitt a minute later, and I watch him unsubtly slide her a fifty-dollar bill in return.

Again, I shake my head at him.

But then he turns to me, holding out the giant wolf. "Happy birthday, Mina."

My lips part in surprise—and Grant gives me an *I told you so* look—as I stare at the stuffed animal. "Are—are you sure?"

Emmitt's mouth turns up in one corner. "I've never been more sure of anything in my life."

My chest warms, sunflowers blooming to life between my ribs. "Thank you," I say, clutching it tight to my chest.

Grant makes a retching noise, and Emmitt punches his arm without looking away from me.

I'm the one who breaks our stare, looking down and running my hand over the soft fur. "It needs a name."

A beat of silence, and then Emmitt says, "Well?"

I make a low noise of consideration, tweaking a fluffy ear. "I'll let you know when I decide on one."

Emmitt lifts the wolf's tail, brushing my nose with it. "I look forward to it."

I don't know why, but that sounds like a bigger promise than it is.

33

When Emmitt leads me to the Ferris wheel, it's with his camera in hand. The others have gone their own way, Linli and Noojman as one pair, Rosie and Sofia as another pair, and then a surprising duo of Grant and Kaity as the final pair. Before we split up, though, we wandered through together, playing at different booths, buying cotton candy from vendors, running through the fair with laughter following our every step.

And my heart…it feels almost lightweight.

Emmitt is taking photos every few minutes, and I can't blame him. The carnival is beautiful, silver streamers and off-white paper lanterns strung high above us. All of the booths are set up in cream-colored tents, fairy lights twined through, and even the Ferris wheel looks as if it's made of pure snow.

Set against the darkness of the night, it seems to glow.

"Next!"

Emmitt and I move forward, and the person running the Ferris wheel leads us to an empty seat. I eye my wolf plushie with unease. There's no way I can hold it in my arms, which means it'll have to sit beside me. Which also means Emmitt and I will be thigh to thigh, arm to arm, unless I want to awkwardly place it between us.

Emmitt doesn't seem to notice, readily taking a seat.

I hesitate a moment before blowing a breath out and forcing myself to move. I've kissed Emmitt before, for God's sake— there's no reason for me to make a fuss over our legs pressed against each other.

They seal us in, and I try not to be hyperaware of his warmth, of the lines of his body.

"Did you name it yet?" Emmitt asks, reaching over me to give the wolf a pat.

I shake my head and jolt in surprise when the Ferris wheel starts moving. A smile flickers on Emmitt's face, though he manages to contain it. "Why, do you have suggestions?"

He shrugs, before holding his hands up to his face. "I think I'd be a great person to name him after."

I give him an unimpressed look. "No."

Emmitt sighs, dropping his hands. "It was worth a try."

This time I'm the one who has to hold back a smile.

"What about Chip?" I ask, patting the wolf absently. "Short for Chipotle."

Emmitt snorts, shaking his head. "Only you would come up with that. Can it have my last name, then?"

"Chip Ramos?" I tilt my head, considering it. "I suppose it doesn't sound awful."

"You're horrible at giving compliments," he says, but there's laughter in his voice. "My dad will be honored to have the family name live on."

The Ferris wheel comes to a halt. I look down, where the rest of the carnival twinkles beneath the night sky. I inhale quietly in awe and I hear Emmitt take a photo.

Then a pause, followed by another click. When I turn to look at him, the camera is facing me, rather than the view below.

"Your poor camera," I say, holding a hand out in front of the lens. "It's seen far too much of my face."

Emmitt hums, peering at me over the top of the camera. "Or not enough."

I roll my eyes, gently nudging the camera away. He lowers it to his lap, and suddenly, there's nothing between us anymore. It's just me and him, staring at each other quietly at the top of the world.

"How is your birthday so far?" he asks, his eyes passing over my features with careful consideration. As if he sees more than he's supposed to, as if he sees *me*.

I shrug, my cheeks warm. "It's…better than I hoped. Thank you," I say and offer him a timid smile. "You didn't have to do all of this."

"Of course I did. You deserve to be happy today." Emmitt leans closer and our noses bump into each other. "You deserve to be happy every day."

My breath hitches, and I stare at him, unsure what to say. The air is thick with palpable tension and I'm afraid to break it, afraid of what all of this *means*. In a few months, I'll be leaving NYC behind and hopefully running off to California. I should be worrying about the film competition, I should be worrying about my *life*, with my parents watching over my shoulder and my dreams on the line.

I shouldn't be worrying about *Emmitt Ramos*, a known heartbreaker. I can't let myself get caught up in his flirtations—

but is that what this is? The look in his eyes is earnest, unfaltering, and his words resonate deep inside me, echoing and echoing and echoing.

"Mina," Emmitt whispers. "I—"

The Ferris wheel jerks, our position in the sky shifting back a few feet. My body sways away from Emmitt's, giving me a chance to take a deep breath.

When I look back at Emmitt, there's a rueful grin on his face. I open my mouth to ask what he was going to say when he reaches into his pocket, pulling out something small and rectangular.

A flame blinks into existence, and I realize it's a lighter.

Emmitt looks at me, and the stars are alive in his dark gaze. "Make a wish."

I blink slowly, the heat of the fire warm against my face. "A wish?"

He nods, still watching me evenly.

I lower my gaze to the flame, watching as it flickers in the light wind. "You know it's a lighter, right? It's not going to blow out."

A low chuckle escapes his lips. "Love, you can absolutely blow out a lighter."

"What?" I examine the lighter more closely. "Really? Are you sure?"

He lifts it to his own mouth and blows. The flame vanishes in an instant, before he lights it again and holds it out to me. "Well?"

I raise my hand, touching the lighter with hesitant fingers. "Is this some kind of special lighter?"

"Mina," Emmitt says, exasperated. "Make a wish."

I sigh, but a faint smile touches my lips as I close my eyes. What do I wish for? What can I ask of the universe?

I think of the weight in my chest, the heaviness on my heart. I think of my parents looking at me in disappointment, of our school constantly losing the Golden Ivy student film competition. I think of Anam looking at me with tears in her eyes, of Rosie looking at me with quiet anger in hers.

I think about everything I want, and everything I know I will never have.

I should wish to win the competition. It's all I've wanted for the last year. It's the one thought that consumes my every waking moment. It's the only thing that makes sense.

Before I purse my lips, I open my eyes again, only to find that Emmitt is still staring at me. His face is patient, his eyes are bright, and his cheek is dimpling with a sweet smile.

When I'm with him, I don't think about how I need to win the competition, even though I should. I don't think about how my life hinges on someone else's judgment.

I don't think about anything. I don't have to put on a show for anyone. I just exist.

Real, honest, true.

A show for two is what Emmitt said, and the more I think about it, the more it makes sense.

When it's just him and me, we don't have to be anything but ourselves. Is that enough?

I wish for happiness, I think instead, *in whatever form it might be.* And then I blow.

When I get home, I sit on my bed and look at the fifty-dollar bill Ma gave me.

It's like carrying the weight of the world in my palm, carrying the weight of my parents' shame and disappointment and frustration.

My fingers slowly go slack and the bill flutters away. The moment it touches the ground, a sob escapes my throat.

The noise jars me, enough that tears spring to my eyes. They hang there for a minute as I hold my breath.

The pain inside me begins to build, rising up and up until it's choking me.

And I decide to let go. I let go of the bitterness and the anger and the resentment and the heartache and the grief.

I blow out.

And I *finally* let myself cry.

Tears stream down my face, unrelenting, and the pain buried inside me rises to the surface, blooming like flowers on my skin.

Or maybe they're thorns.

I cry, and I cry, and I cry.

Locking up all these emotions for so long has bred insidious thoughts inside me. But with each tear, I pluck away another dead dream, another dead hope. I deserve to be happy. *I deserve to be happy.*

The longer I let myself sob, the better I feel. It's almost healing.

When I finally tire myself out, I crawl into bed, still sniffling. I stare at my ceiling, and a movie poster of *Grease* (1978) looks back at me.

I have to pull it together. I have to manage my mental health better. I know I'm going to live with my depression forever, but my coping habits need be less unhealthy. I can't let myself bottle everything up until I hit a breaking point.

At USC, I'll use school resources to get therapy, but for now, I have to be there for myself. That's the only way I'm going to get through the next few months.

So for the rest of the weekend, I let myself wallow, listening to sad music, taking a brief hiatus on social media, watching my favorite films, and eating comfort foods.

On Monday morning, I wake up, and take a deep breath.

I am Mina Rahman. I will succeed, no matter what it takes.

closing

"Home is where you find love."
— MINA RAHMAN AND EMMITT RAMOS
(CO-SCREENWRITERS, *A SHOW FOR TWO*)

34

I greet Rosie with a grin on Monday. "Thank you for the birthday gift. I loved it."

Rosie brightens in response. "Really?"

I nod. She made a scrapbook with scenes from all the movies we've watched together, including ticket stubs and pictures of us. The last picture was a commissioned art piece of the two of us at a red carpet premiere for our own joint film, ten years down the line. "It was lovely," I say and wrap one arm around her neck, pulling her in for a hug. "Thank you, Rosie."

She shrugs as if it was no big deal, but the way her eyes are shining tells me otherwise. "What did Emmitt get you?"

I raise a hand to my neck, where a small pendant rests. "This."

Rosie shifts closer, eyeing with raised eyebrows. "Is that an inscription? What does it say?"

"You are the light." I brush my thumb over the words, inspired by a quiet rooftop conversation between two kindred

souls. The picture inside the pendant is one of my shadow against the pavement, taken while we were at Rockefeller Center.

Rosie exhales a quiet breath. "Maybe he's not an asshole after all."

I hold the pendant between my fingers, considering it with a small smile. "Yeah. Maybe not."

Emmitt is missing from Italian class. I give Grant a curious look when Rosie and I walk in, but he shrugs in response.

Huh.

After class, I check my phone, but there are no texts from Emmitt. I decide to click into the photography contest website instead, sorting through the information until I come across the prompt.

FLIGHT.

Immediately, I know where to go. But Emmitt isn't here, so it doesn't really matter.

I pause to send him a quick text: are you running late to school???

Within seconds, I have a response.

EMMITT RAMOS: funny story?

EMMITT RAMOS: my mum flew in for the week without telling me bc she has some business stuff to handle in NYC so she's staying with me rn and she's booked my entire day

EMMITT RAMOS: I don't know why I have to attend this meeting with these film producers but mum doesn't seem to care about my complaints so...

ME: oh noooo

ME: so ur not coming to school then?

EMMITT RAMOS: afraid not :(soz xxxx

ME: ahhhhh ok ok well I just wanted to say thank you for the gift. I finally opened it and it was A+

EMMITT RAMOS: only A+? I think it deserves A+++ at least

ME: oh my god I can't stand you

EMMITT RAMOS: <3

ME: dickhead

ME: anyway see you tmrw?

EMMITT RAMOS: hopefully but I'll keep you updated

EMMITT RAMOS: also the prompt is FLIGHT

ME: I saw! I checked the website lmao

EMMITT RAMOS: oh

EMMITT RAMOS: did you see anything else or...

ME: no...should I have??

EMMITT RAMOS: nope nvm

EMMITT RAMOS: anyway I have to dick into this meeting

EMMITT RAMOS: *duck

ME: freudian slip?

EMMITT RAMOS: who can say?

EMMITT RAMOS: have a good day mina xx

ME: you too dickhead

ME: *duckhead

I start to put my phone away but then pause, wondering what it was on the website Emmitt thought I saw. I open Safari again, clicking into my previous tab.

After nosing around, I finally find a leaderboard. I spy Emmitt's username immediately—ramostomorrows. He's ranked third on the list right now, and when I press on his username, it leads me to a portfolio with his contest pictures.

Three photos look back at me. The first is a young girl waving, the ocean in the background, and the Statue of Liberty peeking around the corner. The second is four girls lying on their sleeping bags, gesturing to their phones, though the lighting obscures their faces. The third is a spiderweb on a mausoleum, and in the corner, a family of three kneels at a grave.

His photos are amazing. I guessed as much, but confirming it really puts into perspective how much talent Emmitt truly has. His passions define his life as my passions define mine, and it feels so *good* to know we've grown from the same roots. Almost like his soul echoes mine.

I wonder why he didn't show me these earlier. Was he nervous?

I'm tempted to text him and tell him I love his photos, but I don't want to distract him while he's in a meeting. Especially if his mother is looking over his shoulder. At any rate, I'm sure I'll have a chance to tell him later.

He's not going anywhere, and neither am I.

35

The next day is a whirlwind of events. During Nutri Sci, half the juniors weave in and out of the room, taking senior pictures.

As I watch them go, I lean my chin on my hand and reflect on the year that's passed. It feels like just yesterday that Rosie and I were taking our own photos.

But then the anxiety sets in, festering in the pit of my stomach. This time next year, I'm going to be a freshman again, but in *college* instead.

And I still don't know whether I'll be accepted into USC. I've been stalking the USC tag on Instagram, Twitter, TikTok, and Tumblr. All I've seen is a post of Dr. Stewart and a bunch of other admissions counselors showing up in person to tell Californians about their acceptance.

I feel an ounce of resentment, wishing I lived in California—but then the thought makes me falter. If I lived in California, would USC be an escape at all?

In an alternate universe, am I praying I get accepted into NYU instead?

The thought makes my head spin unnecessarily, and I push it away.

Rosie looks as anxious as I feel, her pencil tapping rapidly against her binder, though I'm not sure why.

I lean forward, nudging her. "What's wrong, Ro?"

She glances at me through a curtain of auburn hair. "Nothing. Nothing. It's just—Sofia's ex-boyfriend, Matt, has been acting really weirdly and I'm just a little worried about her."

For a moment, I'm not sure how to respond. Rosie's face starts to close off, so I hurry to say something. "Is she okay?"

Rosie hesitates but then nods. "Yeah. She seemed upset this weekend, but I think she's better today. Hopefully she'll be fine by the time film club rolls around." A bitter smile passes over her face. "After all, we wouldn't want her performance to suffer for it."

I blink, not sure how to take that comment, but Rosie turns back to her notes, sighing deeply, so I decide to leave it be. I don't want to fight with her unnecessarily.

I don't know much about Sofia's ex-boyfriend, but I know he's also in the drama club, and they apparently had a really bad breakup. Kaity has ranted about Matt during statistics class over half a dozen times, and Linli has dragged the shit out of him on her Finsta even more often than that. Sofia has been oddly silent on the topic, but her friends are more than willing to take the lead when it comes to defending her.

I'd do the same for Rosie, so I'm not that surprised. But I *am* surprised that her ex-boyfriend is still pestering her.

I look at Rosie and nearly open my mouth to tell her to

pass my well wishes on to Sofia, but I don't know if it would be well received.

I match Rosie's deep sigh, watching as another junior rises and leaves the classroom to take their senior photos.

I arrive to film club first, though Emmitt arrives soon after me. His eyes fasten on my pendant, and he smiles at me warmly.

I smile back, toying with the chain. "You're back."

He walks over, taking a seat beside me. "So I am. What's on the agenda today, sweetheart?"

"We're filming Sofia and Linli's love confession," I say, pointing at the scene in the script. "We always start filming off with a high, to set the tone for the film."

Emmitt nods, his eyes trailing over the page.

"You're not in this scene," I say, raising a brow.

"I know," he says, leaning an elbow against my desk. "But Mum and I would read the script thoroughly front to back anyway. She said it was good to know the weight of every scene, whether I was in them or not."

I file that away in the back of my head. It's the first time he's spoken of his mother without resentment coloring his tone. "How did your meetings go yesterday?"

"Well enough," he says, but he starts tugging his earrings. "I would've rather been here."

"You'd rather be at *high school*?" I ask, slightly incredulous.

Emmitt tilts his head. "High school has you," he says, as if it's that simple.

I stare at him, unsure how literally to take that. Emmitt is always flirtatious by nature, so it's difficult to parse out the true meaning of his words.

"Whatever you say," I eventually reply. "Is it nice seeing your mom again? It's been a few weeks, hasn't it?"

"It's always nice at first." Emmitt taps his fingers against my desk, an offbeat rhythm I can't quite predict. "Mum, for all her flaws, is a really lovely person. But I hate being micromanaged. It feels like I can't breathe without her watching me over my shoulder, telling me to tuck in my shirt or smooth down my collar."

I frown. "I'm sorry," I say, because there isn't really anything else *to* say. "At least she let you come back to school today?"

"Barely," Emmitt says, shaking his head. "I have to figure out an excuse for tomorrow evening. If she finds out what I'm actually doing..." He draws his thumb across his throat in the gesture for death.

"You could use the lie I tell my parents," I offer, nudging his arm. "School projects are of the utmost importance."

Emmitt snorts, nudging me back. "I can hear Mum's voice in my head already." He pitches his voice higher. *"You're not there to study, you're there to learn! Yes, those are two different things, Yangyang! You know what—you've already been there for a few weeks. Surely, you've learned enough about NYC high school students by now. Maybe we should take it off your calendar. Can you pass me my agenda?"* He makes a face, wrinkling his nose. "Yeah, no, I'll need a better excuse."

I pause, smiling despite myself. "I know this isn't the point but...young?"

He rolls his eyes, but there's a matching grin on his face now. "Yangyang," he corrects. "It's my small name. My full Chinese name is Gong Wenyang. Mum's side of the family insisted. Well, my great-grandpa specifically. He wanted our names to share one of the same Chinese characters."

"What's his name?" I ask curiously.

"Liwen," Emmitt says almost fondly. "Apparently Mum threw a fit when he tried to name me, but Dad wanted to get into her family's good graces, so he immediately agreed to it."

"Can't blame your dad for wanting to win points with the in-laws," I say, laughing quietly. "And either way, it's a lovely name."

"It's what I use as my hotel alias," Emmitt says, his smile widening until his dimple appears.

"Not Ezra Rivera?" I tease.

"Maybe next time," he says, his eyes bright with amusement.

I squeeze his wrist. "You know, Bangladeshi people have this thing called a dak nam, which is a similar concept to a small name, I think. Mine is Poppy."

"Also a lovely name," he says, before tilting his head in consideration. "Yangyang and Poppy. Sounds like a rom-com waiting to happen."

"You *wish*," I say, shoving him away half-heartedly.

Emmitt laughs, throwing his head back. "Am I wrong?"

"Be quiet." I wave him off, turning back to the script. "I'm trying to focus."

He hums, resting his head against my arm and reading along with me. I consider shaking him off, but that's more effort than it's worth.

After a moment, he leans over, using a pen to scratch something onto the page. "Yangyang," he says in explanation.

I raise my brows but slowly jot down something beside it.

Even though I don't know how to read or write in Bengali, I have the characters of my own name memorized. "And Poppy."

龚文阳 + পপি

"I told you they look good together," he says smugly.

I roll my eyes fondly and return to reading the script. Ms. Somal is the next person to arrive, and she looks at us with a raised eyebrow. As usual, she remains blessedly silent as she heads to her usual seat in the back of the classroom.

Other club members start filing in soon after, joining us. Linli comes over to me, pulling out her script.

"Hey, Mina, I had a question about this line," she says, pointing to a highlighted portion of the script. "Do you think it would make sense to portray Charlie as feeling shame? I know it's not written into the text, but I was talking to Noojman about it, and before we started dating, I felt really bad about having feelings for him, because he was my best friend. It felt like I was breaking an unspoken rule, you know? Like I was breaching the contract of our friendship. I felt ashamed of myself for not knowing better, for endangering what we had as friends. So I thought maybe I could channel that?"

I nod immediately, making a note in my own script. "I think that's a great idea, Lin. And it definitely makes sense. Confessing your feelings runs the risk of ruining your friendship."

Linli snaps her fingers, pointing at me. "Exactly. I thought Charlie might be feeling some of that shame, especially since she resorted to anonymous notes."

"You're brilliant," I tell her, squeezing her hand. "Just run it by Rosie first, so she also knows what you're trying to evoke."

Linli pauses. "But Rosie isn't here?"

"What?" I look up and my head turns in a slow semicircle, scanning the room for my best friend and coming up empty-handed.

Rosie has never been late to any of our film meetings. A nervous sweat breaks out on the back of my neck, but I tell myself I'm just overreacting. I take out my phone to text Rosie: where are you?

At the same time, I realize I have two unread texts.

ANAM RAHMAN: what time are you coming home

ANAM RAHMAN: ma and baba are being uhhhh

I reply quickly. after film club!!

Then I turn to Linli. "I'll take over directing for now," I say, standing up.

At my side, Emmitt is watching silently, but he offers me a supportive smile when we meet eyes.

But we quickly come to the realization Sofia is missing, too. All of the club members start whispering, trading looks. Linli gives me a hopeless look and Noojman comes up behind her, rubbing her shoulders.

I check my phone again, but there's no response from Rosie. There is another text from Anam, though.

ANAM RAHMAN: do you think you can come home earlier??

I furrow my brows. sorry, we're filming a big scene today but I'll be home right afterward!! promise.

Then I text Rosie again. I wait a minute, and when there's no response, I dial her number, raising my phone to my ear.

It goes straight to voice mail. Is her phone *off*?

I stare at my screen incredulously and try calling again. Voice mail. Again. Voice mail. Again. Voice mail.

Anxiety rises like a wave over me. We always start filming with a bang, and Rosie and I have been planning this for weeks. How can she bail on such an important day of film club?

More than that, where is Sofia? Are they *together*?

"Does anyone know where Sofia is?" I ask aloud.

Kaity and Linli shake their heads, also attached to their phones, presumably calling Sofia the way I'm calling Rosie.

My phone buzzes, and my nerves jump in anticipation. Then I realize it's just another text from Anam.

ANAM RAHMAN: are you sure you can't come early???

I pinch the bridge of my nose, trying to manage my irritation. It's not Anam's fault that Rosie is apparently off gallivanting with her crush.

ME: I'm rlly sorry I can't but I should be home in 2 hrs!!

Another call to Rosie. Voice mail.

My phone starts ringing, and I have my hopes up for all of two seconds, until I see Anam's picture flashing across the screen.

I blow out a harsh breath and pick up. "What's up?"

Anam coughs. "Apu, are you sure you can't come early?"

I grimace. "Sorry, Anam, but today's a really important

day for filming." If only Rosie remembered that. "But I'll be home right afterward."

There's a long moment of silence and I check my phone to make sure the call hasn't dropped. I bring it back to my ear just as Anam says, "Apu, I'm really— Ma and Baba are just…"

"Ignore them," I say quickly. "You know how they are. As long as you don't engage, they won't, either. It'll be fine, I promise. Just lock yourself in your room. Or see if you can go over to Nazifa's. I'm sure Mishti Auntie won't mind."

"I don't think that's going to work," Anam says, her voice uncertain. "I really wish you were here."

I sigh, scrubbing a hand over my face. "I'm sorry, Anam. I can't. I'm kind of running the show here. But I'll be home soon, okay?" Another wave of panic rushes over me when I see Linli frowning at her phone. "Listen, I have to go, but I'll see you later, all right? Just ignore them."

"Apu—"

"Love you, too, Anam," I say quickly into the phone before hanging up and walking over to Linli. "What's wrong?"

She holds her phone out toward me. "Sofia's Snapchat location is still at school."

My blood starts simmering under my skin, anger creeping into my veins. "Okay. Let's go find her, and then we'll see if we can find Rosie."

My phone buzzes again, and when I check, it's three texts from Anam.

With the way my skin is itching and a sharp retort is sitting on my tongue, I know it's better not to reply right now. I don't want to say something I'll regret to Anam.

Instead, I turn my phone off. It's not like Rosie is going to call me at this rate anyway.

"Let's go," I say, gesturing for Linli to come with me. I look back at the room, all the club members' faces reading of concern, and I turn to Grant. "Take over until I get back?"

Grant's eyes widen but he nods. "Yeah. Of course."

At the same time, Emmitt comes up to my side. "Do you want me to come with you?"

I shake my head. Emmitt still doesn't know the school building well enough to help. "Stay here with Grant. I'll be back."

I grab Linli's hand and head for the door. She takes the lead once we're in the hallway, leading us past a row of sea-foam-green lockers until we reach the stairs.

"I think she's near her locker," Linli explains, as we climb up to the third floor. "Or at least that's what it looks like according to the Snap Map."

"I'll take your word for it," I say, though my eyes are quickly scanning every hallway we pass for any sight of Rosie's red hair.

When we finally reach Sofia's locker, there's no one there.

I slump my shoulders in defeat and resist the urge to start ripping my hair out. This is so ridiculous. Even if Sofia doesn't know how important it is for us to win the Golden Ivy student film competition, Rosie does.

Her admission to NYU *depends* on the scholarship that comes with it, the same way I depend on my parents' funding my admission on the basis of our win. So how can she treat it like it's no big deal, like we can just miss meetings without even *telling* each other?

"Maybe we should—"

Linli's sentence is cut off by the sound of someone—a boy?—yelling.

We both slowly turn in the direction of the sound, giving each other bemused looks. Could this day get *any* worse?

36

The voice is deep, somewhat familiar, though I can't place it.

"Why are you *lying*?" the person says, and Linli's eyes narrow into slits. A sense of foreboding runs through me. "I'm sick and tired of your bullshit!"

"That's Matt," she says, moving forward immediately, and I follow her. I didn't recognize it at first since I haven't spent that much time with Matt, but now that I'm listening, it's obviously him.

"Do you think Sofia is with him?" I ask, tugging on my braid.

Linli hesitates. "I hope not," she says, but there's an underlying grimness to her voice, as if she's already accepted that's the case.

We arrive to the choir room, and my eyes immediately lock on Rosie, who's standing protectively in front of Sofia.

Matt turns at our entrance. His face is bright red and his forehead is bulging with thick veins. "Oh, great, more people. Are we having a tea party? Jesus Christ, Sofia. You just love attention, don't you?"

"I didn't ask anyone to come," Sofia says, her voice trembling.

Some of my anger dissipates at the sound of her voice, replaced by concern.

"Get a hint, you absolute waste of space," Linli says, marching forward without pausing. I'm taken off guard by her confidence but then remember this is why we cast her as the main character in the first place—the way she commands every stage. "How many times have we told you to leave Sofia alone?"

Matt scowls. "You know she's lying, Lin. I never cheated on her. I—"

"Bro, shut the fuck up," Linli says, holding up a hand. "I don't want to hear it. Leave Sofia alone, or I'm going to get my dad involved, and I *promise* you're not going to like it when he slams you with a restraining order. I wonder how Cornell will feel about that. I can't imagine it'll look good. Maybe they'll even rescind your early admission."

Matt's face drains of color. "Lin, come on."

Linli raises an eyebrow. "Fuck. Off. I mean it, jackass."

A moment that feels like an eternity passes before Matt finally backs down, turning away from us to gather his stuff. He's grumbling under his breath, words too quiet to make out, but when he leaves for the exit, passing by me, I hear him calling Sofia a bitch.

Wow. What a piece of shit.

My foot pops out, and he stumbles over it, sprawling onto the floor.

"What the fuck?" he says, but I don't give him a second look, shutting the door behind him.

Linli rushes over to Sofia, enveloping her in a tight hug. "I'm sorry, Sof. Are you okay?"

Sofia nods, wrapping her arms around Linli's neck. "Yes, I'm—yes. Jesus Christ, he's such an asshole. But I'm okay now. Thank you for coming."

I release a sigh of relief, leaning against the doorway. "I'm so sorry you had to deal with that, Sofia. Thank God you're all right."

Sofia offers me a watery smile before burying her face in Linli's hair. "I'm just glad he's gone."

That's when Rosie turns to me, blinking as she takes me in. And my anger returns, simmering underneath my skin. It's not Sofia's fault her ex-boyfriend is clearly the worst, but it *is* Rosie's fault for not telling me anything. If she had just explained, I would've understood, but letting me worry, letting me stress—

"Do you have a minute, Ro?" I ask. "Can we talk?"

Rosie's lips thin, and she nods, gesturing for the door.

I open it, looking out into the hallway for any sight of Matt, but he's gone, so I safely step outside.

Rosie follows me a minute later, crossing her arms. "What is it?"

I give her an incredulous look. "I texted you and called you so many times. Why didn't you pick up? I was worried out of my mind. You know we had an important scene to film today—"

"How are you thinking about the film right now?" Rosie

asks in disbelief. "Sofia is in there *crying*, and all you can do is complain about—"

"I didn't say anything about Sofia!" I protest, throwing my arms up. "I'm asking you why you didn't *tell* me if you were going to confront Sofia's boyfriend. We're supposed to be best friends! I would've understood—"

"Oh, really? Would you have?" Rosie asks, rolling her eyes. "All that matters to you these days is this stupid competition! Who gives a fuck, Mina?"

I gape at her. "We *both* wanted to win this competition. We were in this together. How can you even say something like that? Of course I would've fucking understood. I'm not some kind of sociopathic bitch that's incapable of empathizing with people. But how am I supposed to do that if you won't even *tell me* what's going on?"

"Because I know it wouldn't have made a difference!" Rosie shouts. "You already think I'm distracted because I spend time with Sofia, though you spend just as much time with Emmitt, and I never say anything! Because I *know* people can care about more than one thing at once."

"I spend time with Emmitt because *you* told me we had to do whatever it took to get him in our film," I remind her sharply.

"All right, Mina, whatever you say," Rosie says, shaking her head. "I'm over it. Sofia is going through some shit, and I'm not going to stand out here and fight with you about this."

Rosie turns on her heel, heading back inside the room without another word.

I stare after her, my lips parted in disbelief. I—I can't believe Rosie thinks so little of me. I can't believe she wouldn't just *tell me* what was wrong, instead of letting it blow up in our faces like this.

I care about this competition more than anything, but that doesn't mean I don't care about her and our friendship, *too*.

My arms fall limply to my sides. Okay. Fine. If it's going be like this, then *fine*.

I start walking, heading for the stairs. Within a minute, I return to our film club classroom, my fists clenched at my side.

Everyone looks at me in anticipation, and I ignore the anguish threatening to choke me by pasting on a fake smile. "Sorry, guys. It looks like we're going to have to cancel the club meeting today. We'll refilm today's scenes tomorrow. I apologize for wasting your time. If I'd known in advance, I would've warned you."

The entire room seems shocked into silence. We've never canceled a film club meeting before, not unless academic circumstances forced us to. This is unprecedented territory.

"What happened, Mina?" Andie asks uncertainly.

I shake my head. "Don't worry about it, guys. We'll meet again tomorrow, okay?"

Emmitt is frowning at me, but I can't deal with that right now. I can't deal with any of this.

"You can all pack up," I say, nodding at them, before I move to gather my own things, letting it serve as a call to action.

Slowly, the other club members begin packing up their things, but not without casting me surreptitious looks when they think I can't see.

Emmitt comes up beside me. "What happened?"

"I don't want to talk about it," I say and rub my eyes when

I feel stray moisture threaten to leak out. "Can we— Can we postpone our photography outing until Thursday? We're going to have to go overtime during film club tomorrow to make up for today."

He nods, and then his thumb comes up to brush my cheek, where a stray tear has slipped free. "Are you sure you don't want to talk about it?"

I nod, wiping at my own face hastily. He stops my hands, his touch gentle, and carefully brushes away all my tears. "Okay. Take care of yourself, love."

I don't respond. Taking care of myself is a lot easier said than done.

And clearly, I can't do anything right.

37

When I get home, I head to my room, ready to crash on my bed and yell into the void aka scream into a pillow. Except, when I open my door, Anam is sitting there, her shoulders shaking. Even her hair is in disarray, as if she's run her fingers through it one too many times. When she looks up at me, her expression is tear streaked.

I open my mouth, but nothing comes out. Regret rushes through me like a waterfall. I shouldn't have brushed off Anam earlier.

"What's wrong?" I ask, setting my book bag down on my chair.

"Ma and Baba found out about the summer volleyball camp I signed up for," Anam says, rubbing her runny nose. "The one in Washington, DC."

I furrow my brows, sitting down beside her. "What summer volleyball camp?"

Anam looks up at me, her brown eyes wide—in betrayal?

"What do you mean? I told you. I know I told you. Nazifa and I applied during midwinter break."

My lips part, but I'm not sure what response to give. "I… I don't remember, I'm sorry."

My sister's cheeks bloom with color, but it's not from embarrassment—it's an angry flush, one I've seen many times before during her fights with our parents.

"Apu, I *told* you. Do you even listen to me when I talk?"

"Of course I do," I say, but now I'm wondering if I tuned out such an important conversation without realizing. I must have, if she's this upset about it. "I'm really sorry, I must have been distracted—"

Anam scoffs, her eyes wet with tears again. "Of course you were. When *aren't* you distracted? I texted you like twenty times, and even called you, but you didn't listen to me. All you care about is California and your film competition and getting away from here—away from *me*."

"*What?*" I ask. My own cheeks are burning with heat now. This is the second time I've had this accusation hurled at me today, and I don't understand. I don't understand why I can't make mistakes, I don't understand why no one will accept my apologies, I don't understand *anything*. "That's not true, Anam."

She snorts derisively. "Sure, Apu. All you ever talk about is how much better things are going to be when you get away from here. What about me? What am I supposed to do when you're gone? You're going to leave me here with Ma and Baba, when you *know*, you know what they're like—"

"You make it sound like I'm abandoning you on purpose," I say, shaking my head. "This isn't about you—"

"No, it's about *you*. It's always about you. Everything in the world revolves around you and your problems."

My entire body feels numb. "I care about you. I care about what happens to you and—"

"No, you don't! You're so selfish!" Anam shouts, standing up, running her hands through her hair again, as if she means to rip out the strands. "You never think about anyone other than yourself. And I'm sick of it. I wish you could go back to who you were before you found out about USC."

"Anam," I say, reaching out to wrap my fingers around her wrist. My eyes burn with the effort I'm expending to hold back tears. "I'm not trying to leave you—"

"It doesn't matter if you're trying or not," she says sharply, shaking me off. "What matters is that you *are* leaving, and I'm going to be here alone when you're gone."

She walks out before I can call her back, slamming the door to my room so loudly that my bones feel like they vibrate with the reverberations.

There's an emptiness inside me, a hole that's gaping. *Selfish?* My sister thinks I'm selfish?

I thought we both wanted to get away from New York City. I thought we both understood that we would do what it would take to survive in this household, where every day feels like a battlefield.

If I could take her with me, I would, but I *can't*. Am I meant to sacrifice my future away from here for her? Am I meant to stop focusing on the film competition for Rosie?

Is it wrong to want things for myself? Is it wrong to want a future away from all of this?

Tears stream down my face, and I scrub them away with the rough fabric of my sleeve. Is wanting to survive so wrong? I don't have the answer, but I wish I did.

38

On Wednesday, we film the scenes we missed the day before. Rosie and I don't talk to each other—a stony silence that everyone can feel, given the furtive glances they keep shooting our way.

Emmitt gives me a searching look halfway through the meeting, as Rosie directs Linli and Sofia into position. I can read the question on his face: *Do you want to talk about it?*

I shake my head, but my lips turn up slightly of their own accord. At least this one part of my life isn't spiraling horribly out of control.

At home, Anam ices me out just like Rosie has. She leaves in the mornings before I do, then spends her evenings at Nazifa's house. When she is home, she locks her door and blasts K-pop music so loud that my parents ask *me* to tell her to lower it.

That night, Baba knocks on my door. "Can you tell Anam—"

I give him a flat look. "She's your daughter. Ask her your-self."

And then I shut my door on him, despite his glower. At least I keep *my* music contained to my earphones.

The next day, I meet Emmitt after school. It's colder out-side today, and the wind ruffles Emmitt's blond hair.

"Ready?" he asks, offering me a smile.

"Ready," I agree, matching his pace as we walk to the sub-way station. It's strange to think about how much has changed in four weeks, from something as small as me preferring to walk ahead of Emmitt before…but preferring to walk at his side now.

"Your Italian presentation was great today," he says, nudg-ing me.

I shrug. Miss Turano assigned this project weeks ago—groups of four have to present a lesson for the entire class, acting as if they're the teacher. It was fun to plan it, but less fun to actually present our lesson, given recent circumstances. "It could've been better."

"You mean because of Rosie," Emmitt says, a muscle jump-ing in his jaw. "Are you sure you don't want to talk about it?"

My lips press together tightly. "What is there to talk about? My best friend thinks I'm a selfish bitch."

Emmitt inhales sharply. "She *said* that?"

"She might as well have," I mutter, climbing up the stairs to the subway entrance.

Emmitt follows me, but his expression is cold now, almost cruel. It reminds me of the few times I've seen him without his mask on, before he trusted me. This is the Emmitt Ramos that the press calls an asshole.

Yet, just by looking at him, I can tell it's a protective instinct. And the person he's protecting today is me.

"Why would she do that?" Emmitt asks, his voice low and scratchy. "You know it's not true, right?"

I shrug, swiping my MetroCard through the turnstile. We're heading to the Bronx today, so we're going to have to switch to the 4 train halfway through our ride, but a transfer should cover that.

"That's not an answer," Emmitt says darkly, swiping his own card through in one go and following me. "Mina, you know that isn't true, right?"

"Rosie has known me for four years," I say instead, heading for the Manhattan side of the station.

Emmitt shakes his head, trailing after me as we walk onto the platform. "She's mad at you," he says, though his cool expression wavers for a brief second, bemusement flitting across his face. "She probably said things she didn't mean in the heat of the moment."

I laugh bitterly. "No. I'm pretty sure she meant it." The R train starts to approach, hot wind blowing in every which way. It doesn't annoy me for once, which is confirmation I'm losing my mind. "Let's not talk about it anymore, okay?"

Emmitt looks like he might protest but then ultimately decides not to. We both grab the same pole, my pinky nudging his index finger. One of his rings brushes against my skin, and I find that doesn't bother me, either. Yeah, I'm definitely losing my mind.

There are too many people crowded in the train to have any kind of productive conversation, but once we switch to the 4 train at the Fifty-Ninth Street station, a seat opens up.

Emmitt gestures for me to take it, so I do, and he busies himself standing above me. I lean my head back, closing my eyes, and hear the telltale click of a camera. I open one eye to look at Emmitt.

He releases a low chuckle and takes another picture, even though his camera is positioned oddly due to our close quarters.

I close my eye again.

Emmitt takes another photo. And then another. And then another one.

I sigh, blinking the opposite eye open. "Can I help you?"

He shifts closer, sliding into the space between my knees, and leans over me. His eyes are half-lidded, his lips parted in a devilish grin. "Can you?"

I cross my arms. "That doesn't work on me."

Emmitt tilts his head. "Maybe that's why I like you."

I rest my hand on his chest, pushing him back. He moves without a fuss, but his grin just deepens in amusement. "I'm sure you like me just as much as you like any other girl I've seen you flirt with."

He shrugs, standing straight again. "And yet you're the only one I'm taking photos of."

I hum, unimpressed. I decided a long time ago not to take Emmitt's flirtatious remarks at face value, and I don't plan to change my mind now.

"How'd you manage to convince your mom to let you go out anyway?" I ask. "What was your excuse?"

Emmitt gives me a look like he knows why I changed the subject—which is bold, since *I* don't even really know why—but he answers anyway. "I told her I had a date."

I blink. "A *date*?"

"A date," he confirms, his grin back in place. "If anyone asks, you're my girlfriend."

"You are out of your mind," I say, shaking my head. "I am not fake dating you for the day. This isn't a movie, dickhead."

"Isn't it?" Emmitt asks, raising an eyebrow. "Don't worry, it's not as if Mum is going to pop around the corner. She's in meetings all day."

I give him a wary look, and he offers me his most angelic smile. "If you say so."

Then I close my eyes again, suddenly tired. There's so much to do and so little time, and my brain is whirring with all the things I don't want to think about. I hear Emmitt sigh quietly, but he doesn't say anything.

The next time I open my eyes, daylight streams through the subway windows. We're aboveground again, and our stop is next.

"We get out at the next stop," I say.

Emmitt nods, lowering his camera. He must have been taking pictures of the view through the windows. I glance over my shoulder, looking out at the streets of the Bronx.

The subway comes to a halt, and when I turn around, Emmitt is holding out his hand for me to take.

I rest my palm in his, and his fingers wrap around mine, pulling me to my feet. We weave through the crowded entrance as one, and by the time we exit the station, we're still holding hands.

Emmitt doesn't let go, not until I pull away. Then he releases me slowly, staring at our hands with a strange look on his face.

My hands feel the absence of his, and I curl my fingers inward to get a hold of myself.

I can't rely on anyone else, only myself. That's the way it always has to be. Using Emmitt as a crutch is a bad idea. Being around him always lightens the load on my shoulders, but I can't expect this to last. This is temporary, like everything else in New York City.

Why is it my brain doesn't seem to understand that?

39

As we start walking toward our destination, following Google Maps, my phone buzzes. I look down at my screen. Baba.

For a brief moment, I consider declining the call. I know that talking to him is only going to worsen my mood, but...

With a grimace, I slide my thumb across the screen to pick up. Emmitt watches me with mild interest, but I ignore him, walking in the same general direction as before. "What, Baba?"

Baba huffs on the other end of the line. "Is that any way to address your father? Every day, you grow more disrespectful."

I scowl at the ground, but keep my voice even as I say, "Okay. As-salaam alaikum. There. Is that better?"

I can practically feel his glare in the silence that follows. "Poppy..." He takes a deep breath. "What time will you be home tonight?"

"Late," I say, tugging the end of my braid. "I have a school project to work on. I told you that already."

Baba makes a displeased noise. "You keep coming home late. It's incredibly irresponsible. You should learn to manage your time better, or people will start to look down on us—on you."

People, by which he means the subsection of judgmental elders in our community that have nothing better to do than gossip about children in their spare time. As if I care what they think about me.

Sometimes I feel like one of Ma's vases. My only purpose is to sit and look pretty, empty of any depth or character.

One single crack, and the entire thing loses value.

"Yeah, well, I have a lot of schoolwork," I say, swallowing the bitterness coating my throat. "I don't know what you want me to tell you."

Another long silence, full of judgment. "Do you know what time Anam is coming home? She's not picking up her phone."

"No," I say sharply. "I'm not her babysitter. Is there anything else you need?"

"That is enough, Poppy," Baba snaps back. I flinch, unable to help myself. "Sometimes I think I could die tomorrow and you wouldn't shed a tear."

I don't offer him a response, my cheeks burning with unjustified shame. It's a guilt trip. I *know* it's a guilt trip. It doesn't make it any easier. I hate that they try to make me feel bad for being unwilling to put up with their constant derision.

Baba grumbles, before saying, "Don't be home too late."

The call drops, and I switch back to the Google Maps app, my jaw tense as I force myself to take a deep breath. Emmitt's look has shifted from intrigued to concerned.

"You dislike them," he says, startling me.

I blink up at him, looking away from the map on my phone. "Uh…who?"

Emmitt bites his lip, considering me. "Your parents. What did they do? I know you said you don't get along, but this is more than that, isn't it?"

The air is suddenly too thick. It feels like it's pressing all around me, suffocating me.

I pull on my braid, forcing myself to snap out of it, and only falter when pain blooms in my skull. I immediately let go, grimacing at how red my palm is. "What haven't they done is probably a better question."

Emmitt keeps staring at me, waiting for me to answer. His eyes are so genuine that my treacherous walls fall down inch by inch, making space for him to climb over.

"They think so little of me," I say in a small voice. "They think I'm incapable of succeeding. It's like they want me under their thumb for the rest of my life. Every time I do something my own way, they look at me like they're ashamed of me. Like I'm constantly disappointing them by being my own person."

He frowns, brushing a hand against my cheek. I immediately scrub my face for tears, but there are none. I look back at Emmitt and realize he reached out as a means of comfort.

I swallow loudly and look away from his heavy gaze. "They're just really controlling. They want me to live my life a certain way, because it's what society expects of me. But what about what I want? What about my dreams? They matter, too." I clench my fingers around my phone. "When I told them I wanted to go to USC, they *laughed* at me. My mom said me getting accepted was as unlikely as me winning the Golden Ivy competition."

"Jesus," Emmitt mutters. "Have they always been like this?"

"It feels like that sometimes," I say, and I can't help the way my throat aches as memories of the past flood my brain. "But no, not always. They used to be better before."

"What changed?" Emmitt asks quietly as we reach the stairs that lead up to High Bridge, the spot I chose, and start climbing them steadily.

Though Emmitt doesn't falter in his step, it seems he's all but forgotten his surroundings, his entire attention focused on me.

"I don't know," I say, gripping the handrail tightly. "I guess I just stopped making them proud. You know, I don't even know if I'd be in film club without them, which is what makes this really funny." I laugh weakly, but the sound is wretched to even my own ears. "If my parents didn't take me to the movie theater all the time when I was younger, maybe I wouldn't even be on this path. Maybe I wouldn't even know what the Golden Ivy film competition is."

"Hey..." Emmitt says, but I shake my head.

"It's still my favorite place in the world despite everything," I say. At his bemused expression, I add, "The movie theater. They'll never be able to take that away from me. My love for films is always going to exist, whether or not they think I'll never amount to anything."

"You will, though," Emmitt whispers, reaching out to touch my arm. "They're wrong about you."

"Yeah," I say, but the word comes out flimsy. "I try to tell myself that. But it's harder than it seems. They even said if I won the Golden Ivy competition, they'd pay for me to go to USC themselves. That's how little they believe in me."

I hesitate before reaching into my pocket and pulling out my wallet. I tug out the signed note from the inside flap and hand it over to Emmitt just as we approach the entrance to High Bridge.

Emmitt stops walking, unfolding the piece of paper. I pull him slightly to the side, so we don't block anyone else at the top of the stairs. We retreat to the metal railing that keeps people from accidentally falling into the Harlem River. He doesn't notice, his eyes skimming over the words before immediately flashing back to me. "Mina..."

"I know," I say, taking the paper back, tucking it away again. The voice in my head quietly spits vitriol at me, a reminder that a part of me still wants their love and approval, even though they make me more miserable than anything else. "It's fucked up."

"I'm sorry," he says quietly, his fingers sliding down to squeeze my wrist. "I'm really sorry."

"It is what it is," I say, shrugging a casual shoulder to hide the tug-of-war my emotions are playing inside me. "All I can do is get away at this point. I have to win this competition and I have to get into USC. Then I can finally get away from this horrible city and live my best life."

Emmitt furrows his brows, something complicated passing over his face. "Is this city so horrible?"

"Yes," I say without missing a beat, but my chest pangs uncertainly.

His expression twists, his mouth creasing. "What's so horrible about it? Why do you hate it so much?"

"I—" My mind goes completely blank, even though I was able to list off ten things the last time he asked. "Well, I…"

There's a loaded silence weighing down the air around us, impossible to ignore.

A wistful smile crosses Emmitt's face. "I don't think you hate New York City at all. What do you really hate?"

"You," I say, but saying that feels even more wrong.

He shakes his head. "I don't think you hate me, either."

"You don't know what you're talking about." The words are weak.

Emmitt tilts his head, looking me up and down slowly, and my skin feels like it's being set alight by the weight of it. It's so different from the first time we met—now his eyes are understanding, compassionate, *tender.* "You know, you remind me of a bird."

"A bird? Why a bird?" I ask, despite the fact there's an entirely new voice in my head telling me to back away slowly and then never stop running. It's almost as loud as the one that picks at me endlessly.

He shrugs, lifting a hand to brush a lock of hair behind my ear. "You look like you might fly away at any second. I don't know if that's a good or a bad thing."

My mouth is too dry. "Don't have any wings."

Emmitt shakes his head, his fingers trailing down my shoulder until he can give my braid a light tug. "I don't think you need any."

I don't have anything to say to that, my heart pounding unevenly. Emmitt doesn't seem to mind, instead taking a step back and looking around. "This is a good place for the prompt," he says lightly, lifting his camera to take a quick photo of me against the railing. "I'll be back in a few, love."

He wanders off, taking photos as he goes, and I stare after him, the word *flight* flashing in my mind like a broken neon sign.

40

Emmitt must sense my reluctance to go home, because he comes back twenty minutes later, holding his phone to his ear.

"Yeah, thank you, that'd be great," he says. When we meet eyes, he offers me a wink. "Absolutely. We'll see you later."

He hangs up, and I give him a questioning look. My volatile emotions have settled in our time apart, enough that I feel comfortable flicking him on the arm. "What was that about?"

"Can I take a picture of you?" he asks instead.

"Oh, you're asking now?" I raise my brows. "I suppose. But only if you tell me what that phone call was about."

Emmitt silently contemplates that for a moment, before he nods. "Deal."

He holds his hand out for me to shake, and I take it slowly. The feel of his rings is almost familiar against my skin now. The moment we let go, I feel a strange sense of...longing?

I shove that thought out of my head and start walking ahead

of him, my fingers trailing against the railing, trying to erase the memory of his touch from my skin.

Behind me, I hear the shutter of his camera. I falter, glancing over the edge of the bridge, where the Harlem River glitters below. It's beautiful, the slow tug and pull of running water. I lean up on my toes, trying to get a better view, and Emmitt's camera clicks again.

"Are you sure there aren't better things you could be taking pictures of?" I ask, fingers hooking into the links between the fence. "I'm not even dressed that nicely."

Emmitt laughs quietly and takes another picture.

I ignore him again, taking out my phone to record the river below. I shift a moment later, capturing Emmitt on film, followed by an elderly couple passing by, walking their dog.

They look between Emmitt and me fondly, and the tips of my ears warm in response. I turn around and keep walking, filming as I go.

I only falter when I hear Emmitt's voice speaking in low tones. I turn, phone in hand, and see him crouching, petting the couple's dog with a bright grin on his face.

Somehow, the sight only makes me more flustered. Emmitt Ramos is charming, even when he doesn't mean to be. Maybe even more so.

I take a deep breath, swiveling around to face forward. The click of Emmitt's camera sounds a minute later, and I keep walking, my phone still recording.

Eventually, we reach the Manhattan side of High Bridge, looking out over Washington Heights. I cut him a look over my shoulder. "Now what?"

Emmitt smirks as he saunters over to me, his hands tucked

into his pockets. I want to roll my eyes at his display of confidence, but I can't bring myself to. "Let's get some food. We have plans later."

"We?" I repeat. "Since when?"

"That's what my phone call was about," he says, before he starts walking down the ramp. I follow after him as he leads us into Highbridge Park. I can't imagine he knows where he's going, but I let him take the lead anyway.

"You called someone to make *plans*?" I ask, reaching his side. He's toying with his camera again as we start walking down a gravel path, trees and shrubbery on either side of us.

Emmitt nods, taking a quick picture of a large rock on display. And then another picture of me.

I wave him off, finally putting my phone away. "Answer properly, dickhead."

"It's a surprise," he says back, before he beckons me forward with a finger. "Let's get food."

I sigh and resign myself to dealing with his clownery. "All right, let's go. There are probably twenty halal carts right outside."

He blinks. "What's a halal cart?"

A smile flits across my face. There's still so much of New York he's yet to see. "Come on, I'll show you."

Twenty minutes later, we sit in the park with two platters of street meat in our laps. Emmitt took way more hot sauce than anyone sensible would, and keeps staring at my platter—with only white sauce atop lamb and rice—wistfully.

"Here," I say, rolling my eyes and offering him a cold water bottle. "I told you not to get that much."

He sighs, uncapping the water bottle and tilting his head back to take a long swig. I try not to watch the way the moles on his throat shift as he swallows. "Maybe I should listen to you more often."

"Yeah, maybe," I agree, but offer him a forkful of my own food. He grins at me, opening his mouth accordingly. "So where are we going afterward?"

"Thirty-Fourth Street," he says, which is more specific, but still not specific enough. "Near Penn Station. Are there any subway stations nearby that will take us there?"

"Wow, willingly seeking out the subway? I never thought I'd see the day."

He grins and opens his mouth for another forkful of food. I snort and indulge him. Every minute we spend together, more of my defenses break down. One of these days, I won't have any walls left at all.

I don't know if I dread or anticipate it.

"No more," I say, pointing a finger at him in warning, and take a bite of my own food.

Emmitt makes a low noise, and I look at him in question. He's staring at my mouth. "You've got a bit of sauce on..."

I wipe my face, but he shakes his head. Then he moves forward on his own, his thumb brushing against the corner of my mouth, lingering a beat too long.

I clear my throat. My sweater feels like it's overheating me to a crisp. Maybe the weather got warmer? "Did you get it?"

Emmitt nods slowly, lifting his thumb to his own mouth, licking the white sauce off it.

I stare at him wide-eyed, before quickly redirecting my

gaze. Oh my God, what am I *doing*? I need to stop letting him distract me so easily.

The rest of our meal goes by quickly and without much of a conversation, an almost physical tension sitting heavy on my throat. From the way his eyes keep dropping to my mouth when he thinks I'm not looking, I'm assuming he feels it, too.

Absolutely not, I tell myself before the voice in my head can. *Don't even think about it.*

We throw our platters out, and I use Google Maps to find the closest subway. As we board the A train, Emmitt looks distracted, his cheeks bright with color, which is strange. I can count on one hand the times I've seen Emmitt flustered.

"Why do I feel like you did something you shouldn't have?" I ask, poking his rib cage. "Your expression looks guilty."

He laughs, but it's arguably the fakest one I've heard from him yet. "I have no idea what you're talking about."

"You're supposed to be a good actor," I say, leaning my head against the subway pole.

That earns me a real smile and he reaches over, tweaking my nose. "You've insulted me too many times. It just rolls off me now."

"A pity," I say. "I'll have to get more inventive."

His eyes are warm. "I look forward to it."

41

"You had to *call* someone to get us in here?" I ask and raise a brow at the AMC theater on Thirty-Fourth Street, even though my entire body is warming from the inside out. It was only a few hours ago that I told Emmitt how much movie theaters mean to me, and he immediately made plans for us to come to one. "You know you can just buy tickets on Fandango, right?"

"Be patient, love," Emmitt says, flagging down a movie attendant the moment we step inside.

The boy looks up at Emmitt with wide eyes. "Uh—Mr. Ramos..." He clears his throat. "Right this way."

My eyebrows lift even higher, disappearing into my hairline. "You told them who you are?"

"Come on, Mina," Emmitt says, a hint of a grin blooming in the corner of his mouth.

I follow after him, but not without taking stock of the other AMC employees. Most of them are whispering as we pass, some of them giggling at Emmitt, others staring at me curiously.

"Here you go, sir," the boy says, gesturing to one of the theaters. "Snacks and drinks can be bought at the counter."

"We're good," Emmitt says, offering the boy a nod. "Thank you so much."

"Of c-course," he says, cheeks flushed a deep shade of red. "Enjoy your movie."

The moment he's out of hearing distance, I turn another pointed look on Emmitt. "Did you really need an escort?"

He shrugs, grabbing my hand and pulling me inside the dark theater. I follow after him, shaking my head. When we get inside, though, the theater is empty of another soul.

"Are we early?" I ask, looking around in dismay.

Emmitt laughs. "No, we're right on time."

The projector starts up, familiar musical notes playing, and I turn around, my jaw dropping. "No fucking way." Then I immediately slap my hand over my mouth, remembering that we're in a movie theater.

He reaches for me, gently prying my fingers away from my lips. "I rented out the theater, love. Make as much noise as you want."

I look at him incredulously, but my heart is beating so fast—too fast—in awareness. "They're playing *The Umbrellas of Cherbourg*," I say. "My favorite movie."

He smiles, though his jaw is tense, as if he's still nervous. "I know. I heard Tom Holland did it before, so I thought I might give it a whack."

"Oh?" My chest floods with warmth, with something that

is undeniably affection for this foolish, foolish boy. "Did you do this for me?"

Emmitt nods, running a hand through his hair restlessly. "You seemed upset earlier, and you said this was your favorite place in the world."

God. *God.* He's ridiculous.

I lean forward, stretching on my toes to brush my lips against his cheek in a soft kiss. My own face flushes as I pull back, but I can't bring myself to regret it. "Thank you, Emmitt."

He looks down at me, his eyes suddenly bright. I belatedly realize it's the first time I've used his given name. "You're welcome, Mina. I'd do it all over again if it meant getting first-name privileges from you."

I drop back to my feet, shaking my head, but there's an unmistakable grin on my face. I pull him into a seat in the back for the best view, and he comes easily. I lean back in my seat just as one of the main characters, Guy, comes on the screen, singing in a low melodic tone.

Within a few scenes, Emmitt leans over, whispering, "Is it true this movie inspired *La La Land*?"

I nod, before giving him an exasperated look. "Why are you whispering? There's no one else here."

"It's all about the vibe," he says, but his cheek is dimpling.

And then a few minutes later: "Does that mean this movie won't have a happy ending, either?"

"Emmitt, be quiet." I flick the side of his arm and resist the urge to keep my hand there, lingering on his skin. "Pay attention."

He huffs a laugh but falls silent again.

Again, minutes later: "I can act better than that guy. Get it. Guy?"

I loll my head against the seat to level Emmitt my most unimpressed face. "A pun? Really?"

He grins and mimes zipping his lips shut.

Throughout the rest of the movie, Emmitt keeps making silly comments, even taking to mocking the actors on occasion. Yet I can't stop smiling. He's almost more entertaining to watch than the movie.

At any rate, it lifts my mood, and I forget about the rest of the world for a few hours. And I think that might have been his plan all along.

When we leave finally leave the movie theater, we're greeted with the sight of Madison Square Garden to our right and the Empire State Building only a block ahead of us. The city is filled with glittering lights, bright against the backdrop of the late winter evening.

New Yorkers bustle past us, talking, laughing, *living.*

This city is so alive, it's like a pulsing heart, beating louder and louder until it drowns out everything else.

"This city is so beautiful," Emmitt says quietly, voicing my thoughts aloud. He has his camera out again, taking a picture of the stores lined up down the block.

I look at him, his eyes reflecting the lights of New York City, and something clicks into place in my head—he's also beautiful. Maybe just as much as this city.

Oh. *Oh.*

"Yeah," I say breathlessly, and I don't know which I'm talking about anymore. "It is."

Emmitt turns to look at me and whatever he was going to say dies on his lips, his entire attention focused on me.

For a moment, the world quiets. There is no one else except for me and him, him and me, at the heart of a city that's more beautiful than words can ever describe.

It's him reaching for me, his fingers brushing against my cheek as he tucks away an errant curl of hair. It's me resting my hand atop his, halting his movements if only for a bare second. It's us swaying toward each other, sharing the same air, taking a breath at the same time.

It's him tilting my chin up, me closing my eyes, us leaning closer and closer and closer—

—and then he's *kissing me*.

It's just the barest touch of our lips, easy in its simplicity, until someone says, *"Yangyang?"*

I jump away, holding a hand to my chest in sudden fright. A woman is staring at us in question, her eyes wide.

My jaw works as I try to respond but I don't remember how to speak, much less form a coherent sentence.

"Mum?" Emmitt asks, his cheeks flushed. I don't doubt mine are as dark as his, if not worse. "What are you doing here?"

"You said you would be home by six," Claire Gong says, blinking at us in clear surprise. She's dressed in a pantsuit, her hair pulled into a tight bun, but there are warm laughter lines around her eyes. "I was worried, so I—"

"Oh my God, Mum, you did *not* track my phone again," Emmitt says, groaning. "I've told you before, that's a huge invasion of privacy. I'm an adult, I can handle myself without you hunting me down because I didn't answer your texts for a few hours."

"Don't take that tone with me, Yangyang," his mother says, batting him on the arm. "If you would take a bodyguard with you when you go outside, I wouldn't have to worry so much."

"I'm not having this conversation with you again," Emmitt says, scrubbing a hand over his face.

His mother's face pinches. "Why do you always—" She cuts off suddenly, looking over at me, before she sighs, shaking her head. "Are you going to introduce us, at least?"

Emmitt gives me a helpless look and I give him an encouraging smile in return. It seems to bolster him somewhat because he straightens his shoulders, meeting his mother's eyes. "I told you I was out with my girlfriend. This is Mina Rahman."

I jolt, remembering that we're pretending to *date*.

"Mina," his mother says, holding out her hand. "It's nice to meet you. I'm Emmitt's mother."

I force myself to move, shaking her hand lightly. "It's an honor to meet you, Mrs. Gong. I'm a huge fan of your work."

"Call me Claire," she says, offering me a smile. Then she gives Emmitt a curious look. "You went to the movie theater. You hate going to the movie theater."

Emmitt's jaw tenses and he looks away, his eyes on the ground. Some part of me is frozen in shock—he hates movie theaters but he still came here for me. The rest of me recognizes Emmitt is upset, so I force myself to get it together and reach over, taking his hand in mine.

His fingers immediately squeeze mine, and I return the

gesture. "Mina loves films," he says quietly, and my heart bursts into butterflies inside my chest.

When Claire Gong looks at me again, her gaze is entirely different, more assessing and...more approving? "I see. Maybe she'll be a good influence on you, then."

I try not to make a face at those words, especially when Emmitt's grip tightens on my hand. "I think he's the one who's a good influence on me," I say, my voice light. "He's taught me so much about capturing the world on film."

At my words, Claire's gaze drops to the camera hanging around Emmitt's neck, her eyebrows furrowed in something akin to bemusement.

Emmitt doesn't seem to notice, his expression soft as he looks down at me. "You don't have to say that, sweetheart."

"Of course I do. It's true," I say.

Claire observes us for a moment, a thoughtful quality to her gaze. "It seems you two are well suited, then." She takes a step back, gesturing to a black car farther down the street. "However, we should call it a night. Yangyang, you have business calls in the morning."

Emmitt sighs, running a hand through his hair. "All right. Let me walk Mina to the subway, and I'll be back. Give me ten minutes?"

It seems like Claire is going to refuse, but then she gives me a long, lingering look. Finally, a small smile curves her lips. "Don't take too long."

She leaves a moment later, and I let go of Emmitt's hand, turning to look at him. I scratch my head, uncertain what to say now that we're standing here in the awkward aftermath of a *kiss* and *meeting his mother*. The feelings in my chest are heady and strong, but I don't dare to put them into words.

"I guess we should head to the subway, then," Emmitt says, offering me a hesitant smile.

I breathe out, exhaling the air pent up in my lungs, and nod. "Let's go."

Minutes later, we're waiting for the F train at Thirty-Fourth Herald Square. Even though I told him not to waste a subway fare on me, he insisted. I think he's hoping to avoid his mother as long as possible, and I don't blame him.

At any rate, Claire Gong seems like she loves him. That's worth something, even if it seems to come with a handful of expectations that chafe against Emmitt's dreams. I'd trade near everything to be in the same situation, but it's out of the cards for me at this point.

"Hey," I say, bumping my shoulder into his. "Are you going to be okay?"

Emmitt laughs hoarsely and then, suddenly, I'm being swept into a hug. I stiffen at first but eventually relax into his embrace, resting my head against his chest.

"Is this your answer?" I ask softly, wrapping my arms around his waist. "It's a little concerning."

"I wish the world would stop for a minute," he whispers, his lips brushing against my hair. "I wish we could stay in this moment forever."

I lean back, offering him a shrug. "That's what pictures are for. Living in memories, even when they're gone."

Emmitt's gaze is wistful. "Maybe one day we won't have to live in the past. Maybe one day we can both stop hiding and be true to ourselves."

I peer up at him through my lashes, unsure what to say. He doesn't look like he expects an answer. Maybe he knows that there's nothing I can say in response that wouldn't lay me open, my bleeding heart on display for everyone to see.

When the subway arrives, I pull away painstakingly, moving toward the double doors, but Emmitt tugs me back by my elbow. I blink in surprise, watching as he lifts my hand to his lips, pressing a gentle kiss to the back of my knuckles.

"See you tomorrow, Mina."

My breath hitches. "See you tomorrow, Emmitt."

He lets go of my hand, and I get on the F train. I watch him through the closing doors, and when he raises his camera to take a picture of me this time, I smile.

42

When I get home, a wisp of a smile still on my face, I find Anam in the living room with Nazifa. The two of them are watching a recorded volleyball competition, holding scribbled notes in their laps. I give them a cursory glance and start to head for the stairs when Anam's voice calls me back.

"Pretty late to be coming home," my sister says darkly, and my shoulders tense. "Has Emmitt been keeping you out all night?"

Baba, who's in the kitchen, leans his head around the corner. The pleasant smell of piyajus, Anam's favorite snack, wafts through the room. "*What?* Who's Emmitt?"

I glower at Anam. She definitely did that on purpose. Even Nazifa is looking at Anam in surprise, her eyes darting between my sister and me in clear trepidation.

"No one, Baba," I say, turning away from Anam's challenging stare. I'm not going to fight with her, especially not in front of an audience.

Ma appears at the top of the stairs, staring down at me with narrowed eyes. My skin burns beneath her gaze. "Were you outside with a boy?"

I huff a frustrated breath, marching up the stairs, maneuvering past her to get to my room. I refuse to deal with this right now.

My mom grabs my arm, her expression incensed, and I know it's because Nazifa is witnessing this conversation. It always comes back to what other people think, what other people say.

I consider snapping that Nazifa isn't going to tell her family about this—because she isn't, aside from maybe Syeda—and even if she did, Mishti Auntie and Farhan Uncle wouldn't *give a shit*. No one cares as much as my parents do.

"Poppy, tell me right now, were you with a boy? You know you're not allowed—"

"It was for a school project," I say, shaking her off. I shut my door with a slam, cutting off any conversation that might have progressed.

In my room, I slump onto my bed, groaning. Really? This is how it's going to be? My sister is going to throw me under the bus for a brief flash of vindication?

Anam and I have always been a team, holding a strong front when it came to our parents.

Apparently that time has come to an end.

Most of my bad mood dissipates by the morning, even though I have to pass Rosie in the cafeteria to get to my locker upon arriving at school. Warm memories of last night float through my head, comforting me despite everything else.

I quickly gather my things and head for Italian, taking my usual seat in the front. Miss Turano offers me a bemused smile, but I've done this thrice this week, so she turns back to the whiteboard less than a second later.

Busying myself, I take out one of my journals, outlining a new script idea that's been roaming around in the back of my head.

As I work, a sliver of anxiety runs through me, reminding me that the USC decision is nearing closer and closer. One of these days, I'm going to wake up with an email from them, and it's going to be an acceptance or a denial.

If it's an acceptance...

My pencil falters, and I furrow my brows. If it's an acceptance, I'll have to leave behind New York City. I'll have to leave behind Rosie and Anam. I'll have to leave behind Queens, Manhattan, Staten Island, Brooklyn, and the Bronx. I'll have to leave behind halal carts, the MTA, bright city lights, diverse faces all around me, and a world I know like the back of my hand.

I lick my lips, trying to push away that train of thought, but it proves to be a lot more difficult than it should.

Los Angeles will have most of those things. It'll be fine.

But will it be the same? whispers that awful voice in my head.

Before I can think too long on that, Emmitt appears in my line of vision, leaning against the edge of my desk, sitting without fully putting his weight against the feeble plastic.

Then he reaches out, tracing letters into my arm.

I smile softly. "Hi to you, too. You know you're kind of ridiculous, right?"

A crooked grin takes over his own face. *T-H-A-N-K-S*, he spells out on my arm.

"You're welcome," I say, biting my lip.

Emmitt's fingers trail up the length of my arm, until he reaches the edge of my collarbone. Then they move farther up, gently sweeping up my neck, then brushing lightly over my lips.

"Where are your manners?" I ask, but watch in mild interest, nearly going crossed-eyed as his fingers shift to the curve of my cheekbone. My skin is overheating beneath his touch. Now that I'm aware of my attraction to him, it seems my body is insistent on reminding me at every possible opportunity.

I don't know if we're going to talk about that kiss—if it meant anything, or if we were both just caught up in the moment—but I don't want to add more weight to his shoulders, especially with his mother in the city.

I also don't know if *I* have the mental bandwidth to talk about it, to put my feelings into words, to give this relationship between us the time it deserves. Not until the Golden Ivy film competition is submitted, at the very least.

"I left them behind with my shame," Emmitt says as his fingers finally reach my forehead, skimming my hairline.

And then his mouth replaces his fingers, his lips brushing gently against my temple. My heart stutters, falling into sudden half beats. "Behave yourself," I say, but make no effort to push him away.

He leans back anyway, his teeth flashing as he laughs in dark amusement. "If that's what you would like. I'm helpless to your command."

"Okay, Shakespeare," I say, though my heart is still attempting to recover from the initial shock.

"Did my heart love till now? Forswear it, sight! For I ne'er saw true beauty till this night," Emmitt says, sliding off the desk to dramatically bow before me. "O Mina, Mina—"

"Be quiet," I say, smacking his arm. "You have *Romeo and Juliet* memorized?"

He shrugs, his eyes bright. "Mum thought it would help with memorizing scripts."

The casual mention of his mother takes me aback, because I thought he'd be upset with her for longer, but he's clearly moved past yesterday night. I shake my head, unable to deny my burgeoning delight. Emmitt has countless layers, not unlike a movie, and I'm slowly peeling them all back, revealing the bare soul underneath.

And it's not just his face that's beautiful.

I've always said I loved movies because of what they can hide, but the more I think about it, the more that doesn't feel quite right. Do movies reframe the ordinary or was the ordinary always phenomenal?

"I'm taking away your rights," I say, instead of pursuing that line of thinking.

The bell rings, startling me, and I glance to the side to find Rosie watching us, her expression even. I remember what she said earlier this week—*you spend just as much time with Emmitt, and I never say anything.*

A hot flash of guilt rushes through me, and I direct my gaze down to my desk. Emmitt doesn't seem to mind, giving one of my pigtails a light tug, before he makes his way to the back of the room, where Grant is sitting.

I lift my head only when Miss Turano is speaking and try not to think too much about the fact Rosie hasn't looked at me since Emmitt left.

I don't succeed.

43

Before film club, Emmitt runs up to me at my locker, a grimace on his face. "I can't come to film club today," he says, hanging his head. "I'm sorry."

I blink, considering the despondent curve of his shoulders. "What happened?"

Emmitt lets out a heavy breath. "Mum called and said I have to do some interviews downtown. She wants me to leave right away so I can meet her there."

My nose wrinkles, and I reach forward, brushing away a strand of blond hair curling on his forehead. "It's okay. We'll film one of the scenes without you today, then. Have fun at the interviews."

Emmitt's expression screws up. "I doubt I will." Then a flicker of a cold smile. "I doubt they will, either. Maybe Mum will get a hint then."

I worry my bottom lip between my teeth, hesitating for half a moment. I've been thinking about Emmitt's situation for quite a while. After last night, I can't help but think that Emmitt should be up-front about his feelings toward the film industry—that he should consider telling his mother the truth.

Not wanting to overstep, I quietly ask, "Maybe you could tell her you don't want to go? Instead of just acting out during the interview?"

Emmitt shakes his head. "It wouldn't have the same effect."

I try to catch his gaze. "I know you said school projects aren't enough of an excuse, but...maybe if you said you're participating in a school photography contest as part of your research? You can say you have to take photos today, because you're on a deadline. It's not technically a lie." I place my hand on his arm, willing him to look at me. "I'm sure Grant would be happy to back you up if you needed it."

"She won't listen to me. She never does," he says, but he finally meets my eyes. A small but genuine smile passes across his face. "I'll see you on Monday. I'm sorry again."

I nod slowly and squeeze his wrist. I want to say more, maybe try to encourage him further, but I can tell when a conversation is done. "See you Monday."

When I tell the club Emmitt had a family thing to attend, Rosie cuts me a sharp look but doesn't say anything. I can read it plain on her face, though—*it's okay when he does it, but not when I do it?*

I wish I could scream that wasn't the issue between us in the first place. If Rosie had just told me the truth, I wouldn't have been upset.

But saying that feels useless at this point. Instead, a heavy weight sits in my chest, swinging its legs idly, as if it's having a leisure day out in the sun, and not trying to steadily sink my heart.

Two hours later, I unlock my front door.

Baba is home, given the Rolling Stones music drifting through the living room. It's unusually early for him, since he keeps his private practice open until 7:00 p.m.

I shut the door behind me, put my stuff away, and wander into the kitchen. Baba is cooking something, and it smells great. I glance inside the pan and see he's making tehari.

"When is it going to be ready?" I ask, moving around him to open the fridge, pulling out a cold water bottle.

"Oh, you're speaking to me now?" Baba asks, and my hand tightens around the bottle. "It's a modern-day miracle. God must have been looking out for me today."

I take a deep breath and slowly unclench my fingers. "When is it going to be ready?" I repeat.

"When it's ready," Baba says, reaching for a can of salt. "Isn't it annoying when the person you're talking to refuses to give you a straight answer?"

"You're supposed to be the adult," I remind him coldly. Every word that comes out of my parents' mouths is so passive-aggressive, and it makes me want to *scream*. "But if you want to act like a child, fine. Leave me out of it."

I grab a carton of ice cream and leave the kitchen. I try not to think about all the times in the past when I've asked Baba what he was cooking and instead of telling me, he showed me, walking me through all the steps with a patience that I haven't seen in years.

But then comes the memory of the time I told Baba he should become a chef and open his own restaurant, and he looked at me as if I were insane for suggesting such a thing. Even his own happiness isn't a priority—why did I ever think mine would be?

Sometimes, between facing off against my parents and protecting Anam, it feels like I had to grow up too fast to survive in this house.

I wonder what it's like to be a normal teenager. One with a loving household, filled with laughter and affection and warmth.

My heart sinks in my chest as I realize that's a luxury I'll never experience. This house is my own personal nightmare, and every day is somehow worse than the last.

But can you leave? asks the voice in my head.

I don't know if there was ever any other choice.

44

Monday morning, I receive a text from Emmitt before I even arrive to school.

EMMITT RAMOS: the prompt is HOME

I don't respond immediately, busy catching the subway, but my mind starts whirring at the possibilities. *Home* is such a broad word, and there's a million things that could fit the prompt.

I'm still musing on it when I walk into the cafeteria, swiping my student ID card. I'm so lost in my thoughts that it comes as a surprise when Rosie stops me in the hallway, just as I'm about to approach my locker.

I blink, taking her in. Her expression is grim, her blue eyes dimmed, and her auburn hair pulled back from her face for once, in a braid like mine. It's strange and perplexing, to say the least.

"Yeah?" I say uncertainly.

"Can you postpone your thing with Emmitt today?" Rosie asks, fidgeting with the strap of her tote bag. "I really need to talk to you after school. It's important."

I stare at her in bemusement, wondering what spurred this. Are we finally going to talk about what's happening between us? Is this her effort to reach out?

After a moment of observing her anxious countenance, I nod. "Of course. Where do you want to meet?"

Rosie licks her lips, her eyes flicking between me and her hands, where she's twiddling her thumbs. There's a palpable tension in the air, thick and buzzing. "Let's meet near the auditorium. At three?"

I nod again. "At three."

She leaves a moment later, and I watch her go. I can't help but feel danger encroaching on me, warning me that this won't go the way I want it to.

But it will. I'll say whatever it takes. I just want my best friend back at this point. I'm tired of fighting with Rosie.

I send Emmitt a quick text, explaining I have to talk to Rosie after school today, so I won't have time to take him anywhere. He replies in an instant, even though we'll see each other in class in only a few minutes.

EMMITT RAMOS: it's fine no worries

EMMITT RAMOS: I'm glad you guys are sorting things out

ME: we'll see I guess lmao

ME: does thursday work better for ur contest?

ME: since we have film club on tuesday and wednesday

EMMITT RAMOS: I have something film-related on thursday :(it's mum's last day in the city and she wants to get soup dumplings in flushing afterward

EMMITT RAMOS: maybe friday instead?? but we have film club then too so idk it's ur pick

ME: friday is best!!!

I don't explain that I chose Friday because it's more acceptable to my parents if I'm home late on a day I don't have school the next day. Not that they'll be happy regardless.

I wish I could stop fucking caring about their approval.

I take a deep breath, leaning against my locker. Another wave of trepidation runs though me, disquieting and uncertain.

No. Things are going to be okay. They have to be.

I'll make sure of it.

As soon as English class is done, I grab my things from my locker and head to the auditorium, seeking out Rosie's red hair.

I find her quickly, waiting near the entrance, chewing on the end of a pen. She sets it down when she sees me, squaring her shoulders as if for battle.

My mouth creases, knowing that isn't a good sign. "What's up?" I say when I'm close enough for her to hear me. "You wanted to talk?"

Rosie's chest moves up and down with a deep breath before her eyes meet mine, blazing with determination. "You've been a horrible friend lately, Samina."

The words are like a slow train wreck. I watch it happen, unable to stop the collision, though I dearly wish I could. "What?"

I wasn't expecting this. Maybe I should have.

"You've been prioritizing the Golden Ivy competition above the people in your life, and it's really fucking shitty. We all care about you and know what winning this competition means to you, but that's not an excuse to treat us like we're expendable as long as you somehow win."

"Rosie," I start to say, but I'm not sure how to finish that sentence. Still, I try helplessly. "That's not true—"

"Isn't it?" Rosie's voice is quiet, which is worse than if she were screaming. "Then can you explain all your little snide remarks? Your unhealthy obsession with winning? Why you judge the rest of us for not making this competition our *everything*, as if we can't care about more than one thing at once?"

"I didn't mean anything by any of those comments," I say, swallowing past the lump in my throat. "You know I was joking. I would never try to hurt you on purpose. You know that. You know me."

"Well, these days, it feels like I *don't* know you," Rosie says, but her lips are quivering. "And it's not just me. Anam thinks so, too."

And just like that, all the hopes I had of fixing this today dash out the window.

"*What?*" I ask, my voice growing sharp. "You've been talking to my sister behind my back? What the fuck, Rosie?"

"We're worried about you," Rosie says, but her eyes are

almost unsure now, as if she's only just realized she's crossed a line. "You've been acting—"

I sneer, taking a step back. My heart feels like it's breaking in my chest, and anger is the only thing I have in the face of this betrayal. "Worry about yourself, Rosie."

There's so much more I want to say. I want to scream at the top of my lungs, demand to know why she betrayed me, why she and my sister are colluding behind my back, but I don't have it in me. All my energy has been depleted, sucked in by a black hole that never fucking *ends*.

Some days are better for my mental health, and some days are worse. Unsurprisingly, today is the latter.

I turn around, ignoring Rosie's protest. If I stay a moment longer, I'm going to start bawling, and I can't—I won't do that here.

I hold my head high and leave school.

It's only when I'm on the R train home, tucked away in the corner of the train with my head ducked low, that I allow myself to cry.

Maybe I should have gone somewhere else. Somewhere that wasn't home. The world is taking a shit on me today, and I should've known better.

Anam is sitting on our doorstep when I arrive, and when we meet eyes, anger roars to life in my chest again. I can see Ma in the backyard, talking to Mishti Auntie as she waters the plants woven through our mutual fence, so I decide not to say anything. The last thing I want is for my parents to be involved in this.

Anam doesn't seem to share the same reservations. "Apu, Rosie said—"

"Rosie said, did she?" I say darkly, stepping around her to jack my keys into the lock, my hand moving in abrupt, jerky moves as I open the front door. "I'm so glad you two are still talking to each other behind my back, while simultaneously ignoring me."

"What about us?" Anam protests, tugging my arm. I don't look back, instead shoving the door open with a shoulder. "You've been ignoring us for *months*. We've been trying to tell you, but you never listen!"

My fingers clench around my keys, the metal digging into the skin of my palms. "I have *always* listened to you, Anam. When Ma and Baba ignored you, I always sat down and heard you out. I always fought on your side. But when it matters, you won't fight on mine, will you?"

"What is your side?" Anam pushes her way in front of me as I take off my shoes, nearly hurling them onto the ground. "Is it the side where you leave us all behind and finally be happy in California?"

"So what if it is?" I ask, setting my jaw as I pull off my coat, throwing it at the rack. I walk into the living room, but Anam is quick on my heels.

"Do you even hear yourself?" Anam asks, following me all the way up the stairs. "You've put California on such a pedestal, and for what? How do you know you'll be any happier there than here? Yeah, Ma and Baba won't be there, but neither will we!"

"Maybe that's better!" I say, turning back to her right as I approach my door. "Why would I want to be here when you all talk behind my back? You, more than anyone, should get why I want to leave so bad!"

"Of course I get it!" Anam says, waving her hands. "But it doesn't change the fact you've become so obsessed with California that you've left the rest of us in the dust. How is that fair, Apu? Do you not care about us anymore? Are we just stepping stools on your journey to success?"

My pulse is beating almost painfully in my neck. "If you really think that low of me, I have nothing to say to you."

With shaking hands, I open the door to my room and close it on Anam, trying to forget the hurt written across her face.

My phone buzzes in my hand and I stare down at it. An Instagram post notification from *uscadmission*. I don't even click into it, instead throwing my phone onto my bed.

I can't think about what will happen if I don't get into USC. I can't be stuck here.

California is where my future is. It has to be.

45

I start to ignore Rosie. I don't have any other choice. I think my heart would rip itself apart if I had to talk to her again, to have her look at me like I'm some kind of selfish monster.

Emmitt watches me throughout Italian and statistics, but he doesn't say anything until we're walking to film club together. "So how did it go between you and Rosie?"

I suck my bottom lip into my mouth, shrugging.

His eyes are too quick, too aware to not know what that means. "What happened? What's wrong?"

I shake my head.

Emmitt sighs, running his hands through his hair. The roots are starting to grow out, hints of black bleeding through the blond.

I stare at him for a beat too long, tracing the lines of his face—the angle of his jaw, the line of his nose, the curve of his cheekbone. I like him. I really, really like him.

But I can't do anything about it, at least not right now. And

I'm still unsure where we stand—what if he doesn't return my feelings, not to the same extent? What if this means more to me than it does to him?

There's so much we have in common that sometimes I wonder if it's not the same heart beating in our chests.

But then there are also things that separate us into entirely different worlds. He's a *celebrity*. One day in the near future, he's going to attend movie premieres and have paparazzi tailing his every move. There will be screaming fans popping around every corner, chanting his name over and over. He's going to be a star, which is nothing less than what he deserves, but I'll still be here, as normal as ever. Just Mina Rahman, a girl with a dream that may or may not come true. Even though I have no idea if we have a future beyond his brief stay at AAAS, I can't deny that I want one, so much it hurts.

I look away from him.

Focus, Mina, I tell myself. *Focus.*

At film club the next day, I'm still ignoring Rosie, and Emmitt is still casting me looks of concern. Even Grant looks worried, his fingers tapping rapidly against the side of his laptop.

The underclassmen look almost afraid to take a side. I want to tell them they don't have to. Our fight shouldn't affect the rest of film club, especially not when we have a deadline rapidly approaching. Only two and a half weeks left until we have to submit our short film, and each minute counts.

I don't bother trying to put on a bright and cheery demeanor. Everyone would know I'm faking it within minutes. I've never been an actor and I doubt I'm going to start now.

Instead, I keep it short and simple, directing everyone's attention to their work.

Emmitt and Linli are running lines together right now, and they have an easy chemistry together. Even when the cameras aren't rolling, they've taken to lightly flirting with each other, for no other reason than they can.

Noojman watches from my side with an amused grin, more than used to Linli's loud personality. I think I'm beginning to acclimate to Emmitt's flirtatious personality, too.

I try not to think about it too much. At some point, while Noojman is helping a few other seniors with the costume design for the next scene, I see Linli making a kissy face at Emmitt.

A fond huff escapes me despite myself, making her turn to me. "What? Jealous, Mina?"

I raise my brows, and I see Kaity perk up in the corner of my vision. "Not exactly. I'm more worried about Noojman, actually. What's he going to do without you to support his budding rapper career?"

Linli rolls her eyes, a grin curling her lips, but Emmitt falters, his eyes squinted. "Wait, *Noojman* wants to be a *rapper*?"

I shake my head, mouthing *Don't*, at the same time Linli sighs. "Why does everyone say it like that?"

Emmitt quickly schools his expression back to one of nonchalance. "No reason. Noojman would be a great rapper." And then, under his breath, he adds, "If the rap industry is adopting cinnamon rolls."

I choke in surprise, covering my mouth to hide any stray laughter. Kaity doesn't bother, giggling uproariously. Linli just waves us off, going over to give her boyfriend a kiss on the cheek.

It settles something in me, though. Rosie might be mad at me, but she must not have told Sofia, Linli, or Kaity. They still look upon me with a warm gaze.

A small part of me is holding out hope that that our friendship is still salvageable. The rest of me reminds me that in order to be salvageable, both parties have to want to salvage it.

Later, Emmitt comes up beside me as Linli and Sofia run lines. "Noojman doesn't really strike me as the rapper type. Is he any good?"

I smile mildly. "You'd be surprised. It's always the ones you suspect the least."

Emmitt tilts his head. "That sounds like someone I know—"

I bump my shoulder into his. "Be quiet, dickhead."

"I thought we matured past the dickhead stage," he teases, nudging me back.

"We're never going to mature past the dickhead stage," I say. "In fact, I think—" I cut off when Rosie walks back into the room, carrying a letterman jacket in her arms.

"This is for the next scene," she says to Emmitt, holding it out without sparing me a glance.

I keep my face impassive, refusing to look at her except out of the corner of my eye.

She starts to walk away and I'm startled when Emmitt moves, trailing after her, the space at my side empty.

My eyes follow him and see him lean down to whisper to Rosie. She falters for half a moment, her head tilted as she listens to him.

Then she leans up, covering her mouth from view so she can whisper back to him.

I frown, unsure what to make of it. Emmitt comes back a few minutes later, wearing the letterman jacket.

"What was that about?" I ask quietly.

He flicks my nose. "Just homework. No worries."

That doesn't feel like the entire truth, but I don't have it in me to poke holes at his explanation. Instead, I nod and turn my eyes back to Linli as Brighton comes up behind her, braiding her hair for the next scene.

There's a time and place for trivial concerns like this, and it's after we've applied to the Golden Ivy student film competition.

46

On Friday, we finish filming Emmitt's last scene. There are a few left with Linli and Sofia, but it's still a milestone to celebrate.

For the first time in a while, I feel a hopeful light in my heart, like maybe things will work out after all.

Maybe that's why after the club meeting is done, I turn to Emmitt, tugging the end of my braid. "Before we go to the location, I have somewhere I want to show you."

Emmitt arches his brows but nods. "Lead the way, love."

We go in the opposite direction of the subway, which earns me a bemused look. He still follows me anyway, and we walk for only a few minutes until Kaufman Studios comes into sight. We stop just before, arriving in front of the Museum of the Moving Image.

"This is one of my favorite places in the world," I say, turning to him with a bright grin. Even the text Baba sent me a few minutes ago, asking what time I'll be home, isn't enough to dampen my mood. There is hope in the world, and I'm reaching out to grab it with both hands. "I thought you might like it, too."

Emmitt looks around, a faint smile on his lips. "Let's go in, then."

On Fridays after 4:00 p.m., tickets are free, so Emmitt and I bypass paying entirely, though we do linger on the first floor for a minute, admiring the architecture.

"I don't think you're allowed to take professional pictures here," I say after a moment, biting my lip. "But our actual location is pretty close to here. Like twenty-five minutes? I hope that's okay."

"Of course it is," he says, his fingers coming up to brush a strand of hair away from my face. He falters, eyeing me curiously. "Can I untie your hair?"

I blink. "My hair? Why?"

"I like it down. It suits you." He shrugs, looking almost self-conscious. "You look happier when you let loose."

My stomach somersaults, and I nod slowly. Emmitt hums, reaching for the hair tie at the end of my braid, pulling it free. Before I can reach up to run my hand through my hair, he does it for me.

Emmitt's fingers are gentle as they card through my dark waves, and he pulls one lock between his fingers, skimming down the length of it before he lets go. "You're beautiful," he says softly.

And for once, I don't think it's his charisma speaking on his behalf. His gaze is even, steady, and his lips are parted in something like quiet awe.

I believe him. I believe him, and I don't know what to make of it.

★ ★ ★

We wander through the museum for an hour, me pointing out some of my favorite pieces, and Emmitt absently taking photos on his phone instead of his camera. I join in, filming as we go through the galleries.

There are a multitude of exhibitions. One that dives into the creative and technical process of producing, promoting, and presenting all kinds of digital media. Another that dives into Jim Henson's impact on the film and television industry, from *Sesame Street* to *Labyrinth* (1986). Even more, unpacking the behind-the-scenes of *A Space Odyssey* (2001), *The Simpsons*, and *The Dark Crystal: Age of Resistance*.

I'm wide-eyed as I take in all the details I missed the last time I was here. Even though I'm looking at the art, I can feel Emmitt looking at me. He doesn't even pretend to redirect his gaze when I catch him staring.

"There are much more interesting things to look at," I say, poking his rib cage.

His lips curve in amusement. "I don't know about that, love."

"Whatever," I say, reaching out to tangle our fingers together and pull him toward the exhibit. "Come on."

He doesn't protest, but he does tilt his head quizzically. "You seem cheerful today. Did you receive good news?"

I shake my head. "No. I'm just in a good mood. You did really well in your scenes for the short film. USC decisions come out soon. Big things are happening, you know? And if everything works out, my parents will pay my tuition. I'm excited for everything to come."

"Ah," he says, and his smile takes on more of an earnest touch. "I'm glad to see you in high spirits."

"Let's hope it lasts," I say, crossing my fingers with my free hand. "Inshallah."

He follows suit, the lights above glittering against his rings as he intertwines his pointer and middle finger. "What you said."

47

For the rest of the museum visit, Emmitt is quiet and obser-vant, taking a lot of photos, more of me than the pieces on display.

Before we leave, Emmitt asks me to stand in front of the glass doors at the entrance of the museum, and I indulge him, rolling my eyes. He takes his camera back out to take the pic-ture, crouching slightly for a better angle.

"You have way too many pictures of me," I say later, as we walk to the M train.

Emmitt shrugs, flicking through the photos on his cam-era. "You keep saying that, yet it could not be further from the truth."

"You are way too confident in yourself," I say. Our hands keep bumping into each other, his rings cool against my knuckles. "Like, *way* too confident."

"You love it," Emmitt says back, blinking down at me languidly.

"You wish," I say, but I think it might be true. He doesn't need to know that, though—he'll just get a bigger head. "I think you need to come back down to earth."

I can tell by the look in his eyes that he has some kind of smart-ass remark to that, so I press my index finger to his mouth. "Shhh. Let's enjoy the silence."

He laughs against my finger but nods, pressing his lips together pointedly.

When we finally get to Gantry Plaza State Park, the stars are high in the sky and the Manhattan skyline is bright across the East River.

Emmitt inhales quietly, looking around with sharp eyes, taking in the piers and the grassy plains and the large signs hanging over our heads. It might not be Manhattan, but it's the epitome of New York City for me.

I bite the inside of my cheek, offering him a smile. "I thought that since New York has been your home for the last few weeks, this place would be fitting for the last picture. You can see so much of the city from here, but the photo will still be taken in Queens, where you've been going to school. What do you think?"

"It's perfect," Emmitt says, his voice soft. "Thank you, Mina."

I nod, wrapping my arms around myself and walking in the direction of the East River. He follows me, taking a few photos here and there. We reach the edge, overlooking the river, and walk side by side down the expanse of it.

If every night was like this, I think I'd be at peace. Having Emmitt beside me, his gaze warm, taking photographs with a small smile on his face is all I could ever ask for. My feelings for him grow by the minute, as if they're vines wrapping around my heart protectively, squeezing on the rare occasion.

Everything about tonight is quiet and lovely. I can't think of anywhere I'd rather be than here.

After a short trip to an ice cream truck, Emmitt and I continue walking down the length of the pier. He's holding a mint chocolate chip cone, his camera hanging on his chest. I carry a strawberry cone in my own hands, licking it before it melts down the sides.

"Do you think you'll win?" I ask Emmitt, glancing at him from the corner of my eye. "The photography contest?"

He shrugs, licking some ice cream off his thumb. "I'm not sure, honestly. I'm in third place right now."

"So you could win," I say, excitement building inside me. Maybe we'll both win our competitions and go on to thrive and succeed and be *happy*. "Shana Torres is going to love working with you! How are you going to tell your mom about everything?"

His brows furrow as he chases another drop of ice cream down his cone. "I'm not sure. I've been thinking, and I honestly don't know if it'll be enough to convince her. I think I might have placed too much faith in it... No matter what, I'm still going to have to do this Firebrand movie. No matter what, things are going to change. At the end of the day, this is just a silly little contest."

"Hey, it's not silly," I say, jabbing his side. "I put in too much work picking locations for you to downplay how much work *you* put in."

Emmitt huffs quietly, his expression inexplicably tender as he looks back at me. "Sorry."

"You should be," I mutter, licking my cone again. I'm nearly done at this point, though Emmitt still has a lot of ice cream left on his cone. "So? I guess it makes sense that you can't really stop being an actor because of contracts and stuff, but do you think your mother could at least lessen your workload? Maybe you can slow down the pace a little after the Firebrand project. I know I didn't really talk to her a lot, but she seems like she really cares about you. Maybe she'd be amenable to it."

"Who knows," Emmitt says, kicking a pebble in our path as I crunch down on the rest of my cone, until all that's left is a napkin in the palm of my hand. "My hopes aren't too high."

"Well, raise them," I say, and lean over to take a lick of his ice cream before he can protest. Though, he just watches me with dark amusement, so maybe he wouldn't have said anything regardless.

I pull back, smiling up at him, and his jaw goes slightly slack. His ice cream cone hits the ground and his eyes track my every movement as I shift back.

"You just wasted five dollars," I say, but he doesn't answer, still staring at me. "What?" I ask, moving to tug my braid, only to remember my hair is loose.

"It seems you have a habit of getting messy, love," he says, his thumb brushing my lower lip, revealing a drop of ice cream on the pad of his finger.

I nearly stop breathing when he moves closer, so we're just barely a step apart. I can feel Emmitt's breath ghosting along my cheek. "Mina…"

I nod slowly, not trusting myself to speak.

"I'm glad I'm here with you," he whispers. "I'm glad it's you and not anyone else."

His eyes are so brown up close, darker than chestnuts and sweet like honey.

"I'm glad I'm here with you, too," I say quietly, searching his gaze for the answer to a question I'm afraid to ask. Even though the moon lingers above us, being around Emmitt is like breathing in the sun. "Did you get the perfect picture yet?"

Emmitt shakes his head, and his nose brushes against my cheek, making me shiver in surprise. "No," he says, and when he reaches for my waist, I don't move away, even though his hands are so cold they nearly burn.

He tugs me forward lightly, until I'm as close as I can be without being pressed up against him. My heart is racing, taking off at a speed I'm not sure I can keep up with.

"What are you doing?" I ask.

Emmitt is quiet for a moment. His fingers feel like they're burning through the fabric of my sweater, as if his touch is sacred, as if there's a new beginning being pressed into my skin. Then he asks, "Can I kiss you?" and the words hold so much *weight*.

He's not asking for the casual brush of lips at Madison Square Garden, he's not asking for the frenzied panic at Rockefeller Center. He's asking for something bigger, something more, something *real*.

I should say no. I have to focus on the competition. I have to focus on California. I have to focus on a million other things, and not Emmitt Ramos.

But he's still watching me, a hopeful light in his eyes, and I think I'd give him the world if he asked.

I surge forward.

Our mouths meet, my arms slipping around his neck. A soft gasp escapes Emmitt, but then his fingers tighten around my waist and he leans into it. Not a single thought exists in my head except for *EmmittEmmittEmmitt*, and in this one moment, I'm okay with that.

I lean on my toes, giving myself more leverage to run my fingers through the soft blond hair near the nape of his neck. Emmitt presses against me in return, winding his fingers into my dark waves, kissing me with a passion that goes beyond words.

My entire body feels like it's on fire, raging with the flames of a thousand burning suns. Emmitt is a blizzard, with cold hands that chill me to the bone. It's hot and it's cold and there's no in-between.

When I pull away, it's because I'm near dizzy, as if I'm intoxicated on Emmitt's kiss alone. I don't think I've ever felt like this before.

I take one look at Emmitt, whose eyes are still dark as he watches me, licking his lips. Without thinking, I pull him close, pressing our lips together again, but in a chaste kiss this time.

He's the one that shifts back, his fingers gentle as he cups my face, his thumb brushing against my cheekbone. "Are you even real?" he asks.

I laugh breathlessly. "Ask your camera."

Emmitt leans back again, breaking away from me only to lift his camera to his face. The flash goes off, blinding me for half a second. When I blink my eyes back to normal, he's watching with me with a warm, honest smile. "Now I have the perfect picture for the prompt."

I raise my brows. "But the prompt was home..."

His smile widens until a dimple appears in his cheek. "I know."

48

When we start walking back to the subway, our fingers are firmly interlaced. It's a nice and comforting weight at my side.

"The city looks brilliant at night," I say offhandedly, staring out at the Manhattan skyline. "I love seeing all the lights. I used to try to count them when I was younger."

Emmitt laughs quietly. "Did you ever manage to finish?"

I shake my head, smiling ruefully. "My parents always cut me off before I could. Maybe one day, but it'll probably have to wait until I'm back from California. At least they won't be able to distract me then."

There's a strange silence, and I turn to see Emmitt staring at the skyline with a frown on his face.

"What?" I ask, poking him with my free hand. "Are you counting, too?"

"Mina," Emmitt says slowly, turning to look at me. "Where is home for you?"

I pause, furrowing my brows. "What do you mean?"

He stops walking entirely, pulling us to a standstill. "The prompt. Home. Where is it for you?" he asks again, his voice a little more hesitant.

"What do you mean?" I ask again. "It's—" I falter, unable to come up with an answer that feels right. I shake off the uncomfortable feeling, tugging on his hand. "Well, it doesn't really matter, does it? Come on, let's go."

A range of emotions flit quickly across Emmitt's face, uncertainty the one that sits on his features the longest, before he seems to steel himself. "I... I feel like you keep running away from everything."

My hand goes slack in his. "What?"

Emmitt squeezes my hand, but I don't squeeze back, trying to decipher his expression. "Your dream of going to California...what's wrong with New York City? Why can't this be home for you?"

"Don't," I say, taking a shaky step backward. I can't do this with him, too. "I don't want to talk about this."

"Why?" he asks, almost pleading. "I don't understand, Mina. You love New York City so much. I see it every time you take me somewhere new. This city screams your name louder than anything else."

"Emmitt, you don't get it," I say, tugging my hand out of his grip. My blood has turned to ice. "My parents—"

"They're still going to be with you, whether you're here or across the world," Emmitt says, and my heart drops to the pit of my stomach. "You can't outrun them."

"I can try," I say. His hand is still outstretched between us, and I feel like I'm going to be sick. "I *will* try. I'm going to win this film competition and I'm going to get into USC and I'm going to move to California."

Emmitt blows out a breath, looking down. "You talk about this competition like it's the only thing that matters."

"It is," I say fiercely, ignoring the way my fingers are trembling. "It's my ticket out of here. I thought you understood that. You said that your photography contest meant the same thing to you."

"But you're *so* focused on it," he says, finally dropping his hand. "You remind me of my mother sometimes. You have this overwhelming intensity that makes you forget the world around you. You're neglecting so many of the people that love and care about you—"

"That's not fair," I say, shaking my head. "I can't do this anymore, Emmitt. I can't live in this city and be around my parents and constantly live in worry of their judgment. That's not what a home is."

"I know, Mina," he says, his voice heavy. "But home doesn't have to be with your parents. Home can be your friends, your sister, this city. Home can be yourself. Don't you get it? Home is where you find love."

I start crying. I can't help it. My eyes gloss over and tears fall down my cheeks, wet and warm. Being happy is always just out of reach. Maybe it's never going to be in the cards for me.

Emmitt reaches for me, but I take another step back. "You don't understand. They'll kill my dreams."

"They don't have that power," he says, his hands twitching at his sides as tears continue to stream down my face. "Don't give it to them."

"Easy for you to say," I snap, my defensive guard finally

kicking into gear. How could he start this fight? He was the one part of my life untouched by all this misery. "What about you? You won't even follow your dreams. You're letting your mother dictate your life and your choices. Your future hinges on the outcome of a *contest*. How can you judge me?"

Hurt flashes across Emmitt's face. "That isn't the same thing."

"It's just as bad," I say, wiping my cheeks hastily. "Maybe I'm running away, but at least I'm following my dreams. You'd rather sit by idly."

Emmitt's jaw tenses, his lips firmed. "I'm not sitting by idly. My mother is just like you—she sees things on the outside as a distraction. It would just be another thing to come between us."

"You keep saying she and I are so similar—but how could you *ever* think that I'd force you to give up your dreams for mine?" My voice cracks, and we both wince. "I would never do that, and she wouldn't, either. I saw the way she was looking at you that night. She *loves* you. She would understand if you took the time to explain. You're not giving her enough credit."

Emmitt's face pales, but he doesn't back down. "She might love me, but it's not enough. It comes with terms and conditions. Her career is already in the way of our relationship. I'm not adding one more thing to the list without definitive proof of my talent."

I scoff, even though the noise hurts my throat. "And who determines that? Some random panel of judges? A ridiculous ranking? This whole contest is just an excuse not to tell your mother, because you're banking on the fact that you won't win. If you love photography, that's all that should matter. Even if your mother doesn't approve, it's your *dream*. You deserve to chase after it. Why are you waiting around for outside validation to do what you should've done ages ago?"

"As if you've sat down with your parents and had an honest conversation about what you want," he says sharply. "You can't point a finger at me."

For a moment, I'm thrown back to our first meeting, the scathing remarks, the vicious undercurrent of emotion. But this is so much worse, because he knows me now, and I know him, and we *see* each other, but it's not enough. Even after everything, it's not enough. I can almost hear my heart breaking, a slow, painful crack that vibrates inside me. All our shared memories, all our shared dreams fade until there's nothing left but a throbbing ache.

"There's nothing to talk about, Emmitt! My parents will never look at me the way your mother looks at you, so don't pretend you understand what I'm going through. I told them what my dreams are and they dismissed them, so now I have to live with that. And I'm *trying*, but all of you keep acting like wanting to live a life without them is a crime."

"It's not a life without them, Mina. It's a life without *all of us*," Emmitt says, his eyes narrowed to slits. "How much are you willing to sacrifice for your dreams?" *Too much.*

I shake my head, laughing hoarsely. "How much are you willing to sacrifice for yours?" *Not enough.*

Only silence prevails, both of us breathing heavily, looking at each other without an answer.

Finally, I turn on my heel and start running, heading for the subway. As I go, I pray he doesn't follow me, because I don't know what I'll do if he does. I fear I might break apart at the lightest touch of his fingers.

When I get to the station, I swipe my card through the turnstile and run into the first train I see. It's local and nearly empty, and as soon as I take my first trembling breath aboard it, I start crying again.

I press my sweater against my lips to muffle any sounds that might escape my mouth, but my shoulders are still shaking uncontrollably.

I have nothing left. I don't have Anam, I don't have Rosie, I don't have Emmitt, and I don't have this city.

All I have are my dreams, and I'm beginning to realize that might not be enough.

49

The moment I close my bedroom door behind me, my knees buckle and I hit the ground with a quiet thud. Ma and Baba aren't home, which is the only relief in the midst of all the overwhelming panic crowding my chest.

I draw in a ragged breath, my hands curling helplessly at the carpet.

What am I supposed to do to mend the hole in my heart? Is there even anything I *can* do?

Why is everyone pushing me away? Why are my dreams standing in between us? USC was supposed to make things *better*, not worse.

Going to California was supposed to mean being free. Going to California was supposed to mean being happy. USC has been my dream for so long now, a light at the end of an awful tunnel, and now I'm questioning if there was ever any light at all.

Why won't this nightmare end?

Another sob escapes me, and I shake my head, forcing myself to *stop thinking*. I stand and walk to my bed on shaky legs, even though every step seems to widen the empty cavern between my ribs. I make it only halfway there before I have to stop, gripping the back of my chair, my knuckles straining with the effort not to break something.

USC flyers and pamphlets and information brochures are splayed across my desk, and I look at them blankly, trying to make sense of the words swimming in my vision.

How can going to USC be worth it if I'm this miserable before I've even gotten my application status back?

I close my eyes, trying in vain to stop the onslaught of tears. There has to be something I can do to fix this—*there has to be*.

But there isn't.

How is that fair? Why is everything so hard? Why can't there be an easy answer? When will it finally be my turn to live the life I deserve, one where I get to thrive and chase my dreams and keep everyone I love at my side?

And suddenly, I'm so *angry*. Why can't I be happy? Why is that asking so much of the world?

I grab one of the USC flyers, crumpling it in my fist. It satisfies some of my rage, but not enough to stop the water still pooling in my eyes, not enough to stop the shallow sobs escaping my lips.

I pick up another USC pamphlet and I rip it in halves, in fourths, in eighths. I destroy everything in sight, ripping and tearing and shredding, until my room is covered in scraps of red-and-gold paper.

I stare at the mess, my chest heaving with all my spent

effort—but none of it fucking means anything—and I *scream*, a shriek so loud I can barely hear my own thoughts past it.

"What the hell?" someone calls across the hall, and I don't have enough time to gather myself before Anam is bursting into my room, her eyes wide in alarm.

When she finally catches sight of me in the middle of the room, kneeling in front of my bed, she sags in relief. Then her eyes take in the mess on the floor and the tears streaming down my cheeks, and an awful expression passes over her face.

"Did you get rejected?" she asks, her voice small.

"No," I say hoarsely, unable to meet her gaze. "I don't have my results yet."

"Then what the fuck is this?" Anam asks, regaining some of her normal attitude. "Why did you just *scream*?"

I don't have an answer, my throat aching with everything left unsaid between us. I open my mouth, but all that comes out is another pathetic sob.

Anam doesn't react for a long time, and I finally chance a look up, wondering if she's left me to fend for myself. But she's still there, a torn expression on her face as she watches me.

I look away when we lock eyes, but suddenly she's shutting the door behind her, walking over to me, and pushing aside the mountain of scraps. "Apu, look at me."

I shake my head, staring at my hands, both of them shaking.

"Apu, look at me," Anam says again, more insistent. She grabs my hands, steadying them in hers. I slowly lift my head, staring at her blankly, and she sighs, her shoulders slumping. "Listen, I don't know what's wrong, but it's going to be okay, all right?"

I press my lips together to keep them from quivering. "It's

not. I've ruined everything. How can everything be okay when you won't even *talk* to me?"

Anam releases a heavy breath, her own eyes bright with unshed tears. "Apu, it's not—" She cuts herself off. "That's not what you're upset about," she says instead. "Don't make this about that."

"But it is," I say hysterically. "It's—it's you, it's Rosie, it's Emmitt—I just—I don't know what to *do*. I don't want to leave any of you behind, I don't—" I shake my head, taking in another ragged breath, letting it rattle around inside my chest. "I'm sorry. I'm *sorry*, I'm so sorry. I'm sorry, I'm sorry, I'm sorry—"

Anam pulls me into her arms, her arms tight around my neck, nearly choking me. "Apu, *stop*," she says, but her voice is thick and wet now. My fists curl into her shirt, hopelessly trying to keep her here, at my side.

"I never meant for things to get this messed up," I say, the words barely coherent through my sobs. "I—I'm supposed to be your big sister, I'm supposed to look out for you, but I *fucked up*. I wasn't trying to abandon—"

"I know, I *know*," Anam says brokenly, her fingers tangling in my hair. "I should have—I should have told you sooner, I didn't—" She makes a low sound in the back of her throat. "Apu, please don't cry, *please*, I'm sorry, too. I'm *sorry*."

"I should've paid more attention, I should've realized something was off between us. I didn't mean to dismiss your worries about Ma and Baba, but I—I got so caught up in leaving, in being free from them, and I wasn't thinking about how *you* might feel, and I—"

"*Stop*," she says, pulling back to meet my gaze, her face tear streaked and pained. "I was being selfish, it wasn't fair of me to ask you to stay here when I know how bad Ma and Baba are. I just felt so alone. It felt like you were leaving me behind, while I had to stay here and keep suffering, but I shouldn't have put that weight on you when it's not your fault. I'm just so scared—"

"I *know.*" I can barely see Anam through the haze of my tears. "I'm scared, too, I just don't let anyone see it. I—I focused it all on the competition, and I shouldn't have. You're more important than any competition could ever be. You're my sister, I love you more than anything, and I should have told you how I felt sooner so you knew I understood where you were coming from. Instead, I ruined everything, I ruined *us.*"

"*Apu,*" Anam says, her voice cracking. "I love you, it's okay. You could never ruin us. It's okay, it's going to be okay, I promise."

"I'm never going to leave you behind," I say, holding her gaze, willing her to understand my frenzied desperation. "No matter what time of day it is, you can always call me, and I will *always* answer. I'm sorry I wasn't paying attention before, but you have to know that I hear you and I see you and I'm here for you."

Anam sniffles, wiping her nose. "What about when you go to California?"

"Even then," I say, reaching up to cup her cheeks, even though my fingers are still trembling against her skin. "*Especially* then."

"Do you promise?" Anam asks, reaching up to hold one of my hands, clutching it tightly enough to cut off circulation. Both of us let out another weak sob at the touch.

"I swear," I say and rest my forehead against hers. "It's always going to be you and me, Anam. That's never going to change, no matter how far apart we are."

Anam lets out a shaky breath. "Then we'll get through it."

I close my eyes, trying to hold on to those words. "Then we'll get through it," I echo.

I lie in bed that weekend, cocooned in blankets, trying to stifle the heartbreak in my chest. Even with Anam's tentative forgiveness, I feel lost, untethered. As if I'm at risk of drifting, and there's no rope left to anchor me. There used to be so many things tying me to California, but they've all disappeared.

I don't know what I want anymore. I don't know where I'm flying to.

Sunday morning, I flip open my laptop, looking for a comfort movie. I'm about to type in *Matilda* (1996) when I notice that I have a tab open to the website for Emmitt's photography contest.

I hesitate, but my curiosity gets the best of me, and I click into the rankings, scanning for Emmitt's username.

#2: ramostomorrows.

He didn't win.

I exhale a heavy breath, sinking into my sheets. He lost. God, this is so fucking awful. He worked so hard, and he was going to tell his mother, and…

I press my lips together, moving to text him, because even if I'm mad, even if I'm upset, it doesn't change that this was something he cared about. And he's someone *I* care about.

As I move, though, my elbow accidentally clicks on his username, pulling up his entire collection of photos.

And staring back at me on the screen is my own face.

My mouth falls open, my gaze dropping to the caption. *Home is where the heart is. Taken in Queens, New York.*

Then I look back at the photo. It's me with a bright smile on my face, my brown skin rosy with color, my dark eyes brighter than the night sky. The Manhattan skyline is visible behind me, but the focus of the photo is undeniably me.

I know he said the picture of me was the perfect photo for the prompt, but I didn't think he meant it.

The longer I stare at it, me set against New York City, the more I start to realize I'm wrong. I've been wrong this whole time.

My heart climbs up my throat, the beat growing louder and louder until it's all I can hear, echoing in my ears. How could I have missed it? Why did it take Emmitt saying it for me to realize the truth?

This place is my home. These people are my home.

I have memories in the cracks of every sidewalk, good and bad. Everywhere I go, I'll see the faces of people who have hurt me and people who have cherished me. I can run and run and run, but I'm never going to escape.

It's obvious now that it was never a physical place I was running from. It's something I will always carry with me, something that will haunt me whether I'm here or on a beach in California. Trauma isn't something that I can elude, no matter how far I go.

Setting all my hopes and dreams on USC was just a way for me to avoid accepting that, the same way focusing on the student film competition let me hide how scared I was, how scared I *am*—of being stuck for the rest of my life.

I thought going to California would fix all my issues. I thought going to California would make me happy. I thought going to California would mean I was free.

Looking at this picture, though, I'm realizing that it was never New York City that was the problem. It was always my parents, who defined the word *home* for me. But I was wrong.

Home is where you find love, and I am loved by this city and the people in it more than anything. I don't want to leave it behind.

I want to stop running. I want to find happiness with the people who have always been there for me and supported me, even when I wasn't at my best.

I want to learn and I want to grow and I want to be a better person—a person who is worthy of these people and worthy of this city.

And maybe I'll do that in California, maybe I'll do that in New York City, maybe I'll do that on Mars. It doesn't matter where I am. It matters who I want to be, and what I intend to do about it.

Anam, Rosie, Emmitt—they were all right. They knew my heart better than I did.

"I fucked up," I whisper to the picture of myself. "I'm sorry."

I don't know who I'm apologizing to. The people who care about me or myself. Maybe both.

The weight on my shoulder lifts in increments, until I'm able to sit up straight, my head held high. I'm going to become the person I'm meant to be. And I'm going to start by taking action, by repairing the things I've broken. There's a path forward here, if I'm brave enough to take it.

The first thing I do is send a text to Emmitt. I'm sorry you lost. and I'm sorry about everything else too. if you need anything, I'm here.

It's only one step, but it's a start. And I'm going to see it through all the way to the end.

50

On Monday morning, I find Rosie at her locker. When she sees me, her shoulders tense, and my chest tightens. My best friend shouldn't feel defensive around me.

I walk up to her and hold out a can of Pringles. She looks down at it in surprise, her blue eyes wide, before she meets my gaze again. "What's this?"

"Part one of my apology," I say, pressing it into her hands. "I'm so sorry, Rosie. You were right. I was being selfish. I should've realized it sooner, but I've been so mad at my parents, and I got caught up in the competition."

Rosie opens her mouth as if to speak, but I shake my head. I have to get this all out in one go.

"That's not an excuse, I know. I should have been a better friend. I know you were giving this competition your all, just like I was, and it wasn't fair of me to treat you like that wasn't the case. I should've been more supportive about your crush, not making snide comments. More than that, I

shouldn't have prioritized the competition over our friendship." I sigh, looking down at my shoes. "I wish I could take
back the last few months, but I can't. I hope you can forgive
me, but I understand if you need more time."

"Shut up," Rosie says, and I look up just as she crashes into
me, her arms tight around my waist as we fall against the lockers. I don't care that people are staring at us, not when I'm
holding my best friend in my arms again. "You're so ridiculous, Jesus Christ. Of *course* I forgive you."

I bury my face in her hair. I can't begin to explain my
gratitude in coherent words. "I'm so sorry. I'm going to be a
better friend from now on, I promise."

"Don't be an idiot," Rosie says, her fingers bunching up
my sweater. "It's not like we didn't both play a part in this.
I'm sorry, too. I shouldn't have talked to Anam behind your
back, especially when I knew you were going through a lot
with your parents. I should've been more conscious of that."

I shake my head, pulling her closer, until we're basically
melding into one person. "It's okay. I missed you so much,
you have no idea."

Rosie huffs a weak laugh. "I missed you, too. Do you even
know how much I hated not being able to talk to you?"

It's almost painful how much relief crashes into me upon
hearing that. I wasn't the only one who struggled without
having my best friend at my side. She missed me just as much
as I missed her, and that means *everything*.

"Never again," I say vehemently, pulling back to look her
in the eye. "I'm so sorry for everything I missed. I should have
been there for you, but I wasn't. We almost lost—"

Rosie shakes her head. "Don't even finish that sentence. Our friendship is strong enough to survive anything, Mina."

My lips are trembling, even as they curve into a smile. "I'm going to do better, I promise." I hold my pinky out. "I love you forever."

Rosie grins, her cheeks warm with color as she holds out her pinky. "So am I. I love you forever."

We reach for each other at the same time again, laughing wetly as we sway in an endless hug.

Things are going to be okay. There is light in the world again.

You are the light.

Now I just need to talk to one more person.

In Italian, I look for Emmitt's blond head, but don't find it beside Grant. I frown, glancing at the doorway. Maybe he's running late.

I don't know what to say to him. He was right and he was looking out for me, but—I also wonder if I wasn't a little right, too. I wish he'd chase after his dreams without worrying about ruining his relationship with his mother.

In retrospect, I can tell it's because he's scared, the same way I've been scared. We put so much of ourselves into our dreams that we risk being left with nothing if it doesn't work out.

Even though I think Emmitt deserves to pursue his photography passion, I shouldn't have phrased it the way I did. I was angry and upset and I let it out in the heat of the moment, when I should have approached the conversation a lot more gently.

Either way, I owe him an apology. He never responded to

my text from yesterday, and I don't blame him—he lost something important to him. If it were me, I probably wouldn't be jumping to reply to anyone's texts, either.

A minute later, the bell rings, and there's no sight of Emmitt. I swivel in my seat to look at Grant, but he's diligently taking notes.

I wrinkle my nose, turning to glance at Rosie, but she seems similarly bemused at Emmitt's absence. A deep sense of gratitude rushes through me at the fact I even *can* look at her—that we're back on the same brain waves of understanding without needing to speak.

The period passes by with me fidgeting, glancing at the doorway every few seconds like Emmitt will magically appear, and being disappointed every time he doesn't.

I haven't let myself think about our kiss in the park and what it might mean for our future. I also haven't let myself think about the picture he uploaded and what it might mean that he equates home to love.

If I do, I'm afraid I'm going to burst into flames.

As soon as Italian is done, I pack my things and flag down Grant. "Wait up!" I call, jogging down the hall.

Grant picks up the pace.

I gape at him, nearly sprinting to catch up. When I finally do, he's grimacing, refusing to meet my gaze.

That's not a good sign. "Do you know where Emmitt is?"

"Nope," Grant says, laughing nervously. "I have absolutely no clue. He could be anywhere. Who knows! Not me!"

I level him a flat look. "Really?"

"Really," he says, nodding far too enthusiastically.

For a brief moment, I consider threatening him with bodily

harm, because he's *obviously* lying. Then I remember I'm try-ing to be a better person and I step back, scowling to my-self. "Okay."

"Okay?" Grant says, nearly squeaking.

I roll my eyes, waving him away. "Yeah, okay. Don't be late for class."

Grant nods, slowly backing away, but the way he's eyeing me suspiciously says he doesn't believe I'm willing to leave it at that.

I sigh, wiggling my fingers in a goodbye, before turning around and heading to my own class for second period.

As I walk, I shoot Emmitt a text. are you around? I know we left things off on a less than pleasant note and… I want to apologize but not over text. you deserve better than that. let me know when we can talk. hope you're doing okay with the con-test and all <3

51

Emmitt doesn't show up to school for the whole week. I have to take several deep breaths a day to keep from bothering Grant until he gives me answers.

It must be something film related. I don't know what else it *could* be.

After our weekly movie night on Friday, Anam and I muse on Emmitt's disappearance, but neither of us can come up with a plausible explanation.

There's still some tension between my sister and me, but there's also so much *love* it's almost overwhelming. She's right—we're going to get through this, one way or another.

Then Anam earnestly offers to send Emmitt hate mail and I have no choice but to thwack her with a pillow. "Do *not* do that."

"Okay, okay," Anam says, laughing as she flees my room. "But the offer has no expiration date!"

After she leaves, I lie in bed, flipping through my photos. There are so many videos, too many to count, and in so many of them I see Emmitt.

His sharp eyes, his world-famous smirk, his sweet dimple, his bright laugh. Whether he's flirting with me or acting like an absolute clown, all of it puts a smile on my face.

And suddenly, the last piece in the puzzle clicks. Films don't hide the truth—they reveal it. They open our eyes, allowing us to see that something we thought was ordinary has always been phenomenal.

Nowhere to run, nowhere to hide.

The world doesn't look better when it's caught on film. It looks best when we experience it ourselves, and film gives us the chance to share that phenomenon with others.

I laugh in disbelief, shaking my head. Emmitt said it so many times, in so many ways, and it still didn't make sense to me until now.

But I finally understand.

I move to text him my newfound discovery, before I remember I can't. I falter, staring at the still image of him on my phone.

I miss him more than I care to admit. And the longer I go without hearing from him, the more I feel a deep sense of regret at my last words to him.

I still don't want to apologize over text—it feels flimsy—but as I flip through the videos on my phone, an idea spurs to life in my head. A film. A compilation of all our memories together.

A show for two.

★ ★ ★

I'm sorting through songs on Spotify, trying to find the perfect song to overlay on the short film for Emmitt, when my phone buzzes with an email notification.

Your NYU Admissions Decision

I stare at it, almost too terrified to click on it. Suddenly this all feels too real. College has always been too far away, but now it's too *close*. I'm not ready. I don't know if I'll ever be.

It turns out I don't have to be right away at least, because my phone buzzes again, this time with an incoming FaceTime call from Rosie.

I slide my thumb across the screen and am immediately greeted with a piercing shriek.

"Oh my God, oh my God, *oh my God*! Mina! Mina, I got in! Oh my God, oh my God, Mina, I got in! I got accepted into NYU! Holy fuck, oh my *God*," Rosie screeches, her phone shaking as she jumps up and down. "I got in!"

My heart soars in excitement and I immediately launch off my bed, jumping with her. "Oh my God, Rosie, that's *amazing*! Your dream school, holy shit!" Rosie lets out another high-pitched scream, and I burst into laughter. "I'm so happy for you! This is fucking incredible!"

"I can't believe this!" Rosie giggles hysterically. "I got *accepted*! To *New York University*!"

"It's what you deserve!" I say, beaming. Her cheeks are

flushed with fervor, her eyes sparkling with unshed tears. "I'm so, so happy for you, Ro. Really."

"Thank you," Rosie says, her smile nearly splitting her face in half. "I can't wait to freak out with you when you get accepted to USC."

But looking at Rosie, seeing how excited and happy she is, I don't know if we'd be freaking out the same way. I don't know if USC is the future I want anymore.

"Yeah, me either," I say anyway, smiling thinly. "Did you tell your parents yet?"

Rosie's eyes widen to the size of saucers. "Oh my God, no, I still have to tell Mom. I was with Dad and his girlfriend when I got the email, so they know, but I wanted to call you first. Mom's gonna kill me if Dad tells her before I do, though. I gotta go, talk later, okay? Love you!"

"Love you! Congrats again!" I say, waving as Rosie hangs up. Her face disappears, leaving behind only the NYU email notification on my phone.

I take a deep breath, bracing myself. It's fine. It's not a big deal. I slide my thumb across the screen, opening the email.

Dear Samina,
On behalf of the admissions committee, it is my honor to share with you that you have been admitted to the Tisch School of the Arts at New York University. Congratulations! I could not be more excited to welcome you to NYU.

I stare at my email in disbelief, and a tremor runs through me. I—I hadn't even really thought about whether I'd be accepted or not, but now that I have been, a decision lies ahead of me.

California or New York City?

I don't know the answer.

52

For hours, I pace in my room. I haven't even gotten a decision from USC yet, but that doesn't change that my head feels like static.

New York or California?

California or New York?

Even though I know I don't want to let go of New York City entirely, that California doesn't mean immediate happiness—I still don't know what my decision is. I've spent so long focusing on USC and it's the best film school in the country. Am I ready to let go of that?

Home is where you find love.

I run my fingers through my hair, loose for once. The way Emmitt likes it.

"Apu!" Anam calls from her room, and I look up at my open doorway. "Come here for a minute."

I sigh but head for her room all the same. She's crouched on the ground, looking for something, but she waves me forward without pause. I step inside, looking around briefly. There are posters of TWICE, Blackpink, and ITZY up on the walls, and dozens of albums lined up on her shelves. Her notes are scattered haphazardly on her desk, and two stray volleyballs roll on her floor.

"There we go," Anam says, taking out a third volleyball from underneath her bed. Then she shoots me a grin. "Want to throw one around? Might help distract you from your boy troubles."

I want to say yes, but I can't find my voice. When I don't reply immediately, Anam gives me a look of concern. "Are you okay?"

"I got into NYU," I say, the words choked.

"What? That's amazing!" Anam says, standing up and moving forward to give me a quick hug. "Congratulations!"

"Yeah," I say weakly, taking a seat on the edge of her mattress. "Congratulations. Right."

She raises her brows. "Is…is this a bad thing? Did you want them to reject you? I know it's not USC, but it's still good to get an acceptance, right?"

"Yes, it's…good," I say, biting the inside my cheek. The sharp tang of blood fills my mouth, which is fitting. "I—I guess I just didn't think about what would happen if they said yes."

Anam tosses the ball up in the air, her brows furrowed. "What do you mean?"

I pull my knees up to my chest. "I only let myself think about USC accepting me. I didn't think about what might happen if UMich or Wesleyan and Emory or—" I take a deep breath. "I just never took it into account that I might have multiple options."

Anam falters midthrow and the ball falls to the carpeted, ground with a light thud. "Does your acceptance to NYU *change* things?" she asks slowly, coming to stand in front of me.

My teeth press into my lower lip almost painfully. "I don't know. I think it might."

A loaded moment of silence follows, but then Anam places her hands on my shoulders, leaning down so she can meet my eyes. "Apu, you should do what's right for you. And the rest of us will be here to support you, no matter what it is you decide."

"But what if I don't know what to choose?" I ask, my voice small. For the first time, I feel like the younger one between us two. "What if I make a mistake?"

"You won't," Anam says, squeezing my shoulders. "Do what's right for your heart."

Home is where you find love.

I nod, swallowing the blood coating the inside of my mouth. "I'll try," I say, shifting forward to give her a hug.

Anam rests her head on top of mine, holding me without a word, before she pulls back again. "Good luck."

"Thank you," I say, each word weighted heavily. Having her in my corner means more than I can ever convey. With a subdued smile, I lean down to retrieve her volleyball, handing it to her.

She accepts it, offering me a smile in return. "Congratulations again, Apu."

★ ★ ★

I go downstairs.

Both of my parents are sitting at the dining table. Baba is peeling garlic and Ma is sorting through puzzle pieces, but they both look up at my arrival.

"What?" Ma asks, eyes narrowed. I try not to sigh at the defensive tone of her voice. "You never come to talk to us willingly unless you want something."

I take a deep breath, reminding myself this is not the time to start a fight with them. "I want to talk about college."

Ma snorts, turning back to her puzzle. "Have you won your little film competition yet? You should've told us earlier. Baba would have gotten out the checkbook."

I curl my fingers into fists but take a seat at the table anyway. "No. It's not that." I bite my tongue, reluctant to say the words aloud. *This isn't for them,* I tell myself. *This is for you.* "I got into New York University."

Baba stops peeling.

I start counting backward from ten in my head, trying to work up the courage to say what I need to say.

Looking at them, though, it's almost easier. Seeing Ma's cold, cutting gaze and Baba's darker glower. My parents will always expect the worst of me. No matter what, I'm never going to be enough for them. I'm never going to be what they want me to be.

And that's okay.

I don't need their acceptance. I don't need their validation.

They are not my home.

I'm my own home.

Home is where you find love.

"If you want me to stay in New York City, I will," I say, meeting their eyes without flinching. That feels like a win in and of itself. "But I'm living on campus."

"On campus?" Baba repeats slowly, setting down the garlic in his palm. His movements are slow, unaccepting, but that doesn't deter me.

I nod and set my shoulders. There's no going back now. "On campus. In a dorm."

My words finally seem to register with my mom. "In a *dorm?*" she says, nearly screeching. A puzzle piece snaps in half between her fingers, loud in the sudden silence. "Are you out of your mind?"

I withhold the urge to wince. I've made my decision, and there's nothing they can do to convince me otherwise. I'm going to do this with or without their permission, but I'd rather avoid the infighting that comes without their permission. I have countless pamphlets ready, a PowerPoint on deck, and cousins that attend NYU on hand to plead my case if necessary. But I'm already preemptively tired and want to avoid it if I can.

I'm going to stay in New York City. I'm going to live thirty minutes away, and I'm going to come back here on occasion, for Anam and Anam only, but still—I'll be around. They'll see me more than they ever would if I were attending USC.

But they can no longer define my world. They can no longer keep me caged.

"I'll still be in New York," I say, my voice quiet. "I'll be nearby, and I'll be attending one of the best schools in the country. They gave me a full scholarship, so you won't even have to pay for it. Isn't that what you wanted?"

"You *know* that isn't what we wanted. How can you be so selfish, Poppy? All you ever do is think about yourself!"

I press my lips together. "Is that so wrong?" I ask, and the words come out stronger than I thought they would. "Is it so awful of me to want something? To build a life for myself?"

"Don't turn this around like we're trying to sabotage your future," Ma says, shaking her head. "There is no reason for you to live in a dorm. What will people think? You're going to make the whole family look bad—"

"Who cares?" I ask, throwing my hands up. "Why do you care so much what other people think? Why can't you care about *me* instead?"

"Don't be ridiculous," Ma says. "You know we care about you. We've raised you your entire life, how can you say we don't care? We put this roof over your head—"

"And now I owe you my life in repayment?" I ask quietly. "I'm your *child*, Ma. Not one of your belongings. Why am I not enough as I am?"

"Fahim, do you hear this? Poppy has lost her mind," Ma says, sneering at me. "Tell your daughter—"

Baba holds out a hand, silencing her.

My eyes widen of their own accord, not expecting him to interrupt her mid tirade. She looks as surprised as I do, her mouth hanging open in dismay.

"Fine," he says, and the whole world seems to stop.

"Fine?" I repeat in disbelief. "Fine what?"

"Fine, you can stay in a dorm," Baba says, and the words

are *frigid*. "You can do whatever you want. Clearly, we have no say in what you do. You have already made your decision."

I stare at him, my heart pounding erratically in my chest. That's a yes. A fine is a yes. He's saying *yes*, even if he's saying it in the cruelest way possible.

Ma turns to look at Baba incredulously. "How can you accept this? You're spoiling her! There's no reason for her to—"

"Look at her," Baba says, his eyes locked on mine. As always, there is disappointment written across his face, but at this point, I'm over it. If I win in the end, he can be ashamed of me all he wants. "She will make our lives hell if we force her to stay. This is not a fight worth enduring. I no longer have the energy. Do you, Yara?"

My mom looks less than pleased with that explanation, her eyes darting between my dad and me. "She is using our love for her against us, Fahim," Ma says darkly. "She knows we would do anything for her to stay."

I resist the urge to grind my teeth. To call this love, as if it's not their overwhelming need to keep me under their thumb and put on a performance for others, to make me into some twisted version of myself that carries out their every whim and desire, even at the cost my own hopes and dreams...

But I know the truth. That's all that matters. "If you want me in New York City, this is the only way I will stay," I say, refusing to let my voice waver. "In a dorm, or not at all."

I'm tired of giving them power over my future. At the end of the day, it's mine. It's always been mine.

Nothing they say can hurt me anymore.

"Fine," Baba says again, before looking at my mom pointedly.

She clenches her jaw, refusing to even look at me. "Fine."

The tension seeps out of me all at once.

I got what I wanted. I can stay here in New York City, without having to live here with them. I can go to the same university as Rosie, I can see Anam on a weekly basis, I can follow my *dreams*—and I can do all of it in the city that loved me, even when I didn't love it.

They don't get to control me anymore. They never will again.

"Fine," I say, and for the first time in years, I smile at them.

53

The day before we submit our short film, I get an email from USC, alerting me about my application status.

I stare at it for too long, wondering what to do with it. I've already made my decision, but a small part of me hesitates at the reminder of my past dreams.

I painstakingly click into the email.

Dear Samina,
We have arrived at the end of our application review period, and I am sorry to say that we are unable to offer you a space in this year's incoming class.

And all I feel is relief.

54

As I'm sitting outside the film club classroom, waiting for everyone to arrive so we can submit the short film together, my finger hovers over Emmitt's contact.

I want to tell him the good news. About NYU and about staying and about—well, *everything*. But it's been two whole weeks since our fight, and he still hasn't come back to school.

Even worse, I still haven't heard from him.

Underclassmen pass by me, heading into the room, but not without stopping to say hello. Christina even leans down to give me a quick hug before she goes inside. I offer her a small smile and nod at the rest of the club members, but the one person I hope to see never appears.

Rosie shows up, holding hands with Sofia, and ruffles my hair on her way in. I give her a smile, squeezing her ankle as she heads inside.

But it's still not Emmitt.

With a low groan, I resign myself to the fact that I might

not have a chance to apologize in person. Bearing that in mind, I finally click into our text thread and pull up the short film I made for him.

I watch it back first.

It's every memory I have with Emmitt playing across the screen. Him staring out at the ocean on the Staten Island Ferry, his fingers resting on a table in Rockefeller Center, his coffee-stained shirt as we walk from Green-Wood Cemetery, him leaning down to pet a dog atop High Bridge, him taking a lick of mint chocolate chip in Gantry Plaza State Park.

Him holding out his hand toward me, him offering me an awful wink, him throwing back his head and laughing brightly, him taking photos of me over and over and over again.

All set to the lyrics of a song that capture my feelings more than I could ever hope to.

Dear Emmitt,
I'm really sorry about everything that happened. I hope you can forgive me and I hope you decide to come home someday.
Love,
Mina

I press Send and lean my head against the wall with a sigh of defeat, staring up at the row of lockers ahead of me.

Down the hall, a familiar tune starts playing. "Cornelia Street" by Taylor Swift.

My neck nearly snaps with how fast I turn my head.

Emmitt is standing at the end of the hallway, as beautiful as the first day I met him. His hair is black again, longer than the last time I saw him, a few strands falling onto his forehead. But he's still the same somehow. And more than that, he's here.

He's *here.*

Emmitt's eyes are locked on his phone as the chorus of the song starts to play. I rise to my feet, slowly walking toward him, as if I'm caught in a fever dream.

I wonder if he understands what I'm trying to say: that I don't want to lose him, that I don't want this to end, that every street of this city will remind me of him, no matter how much time passes.

I keep walking closer and closer, but he still hasn't looked up, his lips parted as he stares at his phone screen.

It's only when I start to reach out that Emmitt lifts his chin, meeting my eyes. My hand falters, standing still in the space between us, a mirror of the last time we were together.

The moment stretches, long beats of silence, as he studies my expression, as I study his. The music fades to a hum, until all I hear is the sound of my own heart beating in my chest.

"Emmitt," I say, and it comes out as a whisper. "Hi."

He blinks once, twice, and then he murmurs, "Hello, Mina."

A small hope starts to rise within me. Emmitt doesn't sound upset. Maybe what I said wasn't unforgivable. Maybe we can find the fine line and walk across it, finding a way to be together despite everything that's happened.

"You came back?" I ask, the words hesitant.

Emmitt looks down, examining the hand outstretched between us, and then he reaches out with ringed fingers, slowly intertwining them.

Butterflies burst to life in my stomach, flapping insistently, flying into my chest and swarming my heart. The hope in me is growing and growing and *growing*.

"I'm sorry I took so long, but I'm here," Emmitt says, lifting my hand until he can brush his lips against my knuckles. "I came home to you."

The hold on my heart releases, the butterflies turning into flurries of gold—of light, of warmth, of happiness and everything good in the world. This is what it feels like to be home.

I move forward until I'm so close that I have to tilt my head up to look at him. "I'm sorry. I'm so sorry. I shouldn't have said—"

"You don't have to apologize," he says, pressing his forehead against mine, our noses bumping gently. "I'm the one who's sorry. You were right."

"No, you were right," I say, offering him a shaky smile. "This city is my home. My friends are my home. *You* are my home. And I am my own home."

Emmitt's mouth curves in a soft, sweet smile. My free hand rises to poke the dimple in his cheek, and his smile only widens. "You were right, too. I told Mum the truth about my love for photography. I shouldn't have let my fears stand in the way of my dreams."

"Really?" I ask, my mouth dropping open as I pull back to get a good look at his face. "Emmitt, that's amazing! What did she say?"

He shrugs almost bashfully. "I knew I couldn't explain over the phone, so we arranged for me to fly out to London to see her. That's why I didn't respond to your texts, and I'm so sorry for that. But me and Mum sat down and talked, and I told her about the photography contest and everything else. It was a long and painful conversation, but she promised to balance her work life and personal life better in the future after I showed her some of my photos. And I promised to be honest and up-front with her about what I want, rather than expecting her to catch on when I act like an asshole in interviews."

A breathless laugh escapes me. He did it. He actually did it. It couldn't have been an easy decision, but he made it anyway, for himself and for his future.

"I'm sorry you won't get to work with Shana Torres," I say, brushing a thumb across his cheek. "But I hope you know your dad would be so proud of you. I know I never had the chance to meet him, but I don't doubt he would have hung up your pictures on the wall, too. Just like he hung up Shana's."

He leans into my touch. "I know. But Mum will hang my pictures up for both of them."

"That's what you deserve." I'm nearly vibrating with overwhelming pride for him. "So what happens now?"

"Now I get to pick and choose what films I want to work on in the future. I'm still going to be in Firebrand's upcoming project, but I'm kind of looking forward to it now. I can finally put all my AAAS knowledge to use." His smile is full of mischief and I can't help my breathless laughter. "And on an even brighter note, Mum said she'll let me decide what is and isn't too much in the future, and that I'll have more free time to pursue my passions." His smile grows. "And more time to spend with a girl that makes me happier than anything else."

"Be quiet," I say, but the way I'm beaming undercuts my demand. I don't think I could make myself sound serious if I tried. "You think you're so smooth, don't you?"

"A little," Emmitt says, reaching out to pull a lock of my hair through his fingers. I've been wearing it loose more often than not these days. "What about you? What happened? Did you get into USC?"

"No," I say, and his face falls.

"Mina, I'm so—"

"It's okay," I say quickly, squeezing his wrist. "I'm glad, honestly. I think this is the way it's meant to be."

Emmitt scans my expression for a sign I'm lying, but he must not find any, because he tilts his head in confusion. "Really? What changed?"

"I got into NYU," I say, tapping my thumb against his pulse. It speeds up underneath my touch. "And I realized that this is where I want to be. Home is where you find love, right?"

A pause, and then Emmitt softly says, "Right."

"Just kiss already!" Kaity shouts, making me jump in surprise, bumping into Emmitt's chest.

I turn my head to see half of film club standing in the doorway, the freshmen jumping to see us over the heads of the seniors. Rosie is smiling at me warmly, and even Grant has a wide grin on his face.

"Kiss, kiss, kiss," Linli starts chanting, elbowing Noojman to join her. *"Kiss, kiss, kiss!"*

"Oh my God," I say, covering my face with my hands, though I let myself peek between my fingers. "What's *wrong* with all of you?"

"Just kiss!" says Sofia, clapping her hands together in delight. Behind her, Christina and Brighton nod eagerly.

"I'm gonna end it all," I whisper to Emmitt, and he laughs, pressing his lips to the top of my head. "And once I'm done ending it all, I'm going to come back from the dead and end all of *them*."

Emmitt shift slightly, blocking me from sight. Then he turns a look on them, an eyebrow arched. "Privacy, if you will?"

I can't see Linli, but I can hear her. "You're a celebrity—aren't you used to invasive paparazzi?"

He flips them off, but his eyes are glittering with amusement. He even switches back to his usual British accent when he says, "Paps are usually called by PR teams, actually. My publicist didn't mention any of you lot to me?"

"You're such a dickhead," Rosie says, but I can hear the grin in her voice. "Mina was right."

"It happens on occasion." Emmitt flicks my nose. "Now if you'd all kindly *go back inside*?"

The club members grumble, but I hear rustling as they all return to the classroom, and then the sound of the door closing. Despite my death threat, I can't help the fondness bursting to life inside my chest.

I love being a part of film club so much, and I wouldn't be here, in this moment built of dreams and magic, without it.

Emmitt turns back to me, his mouth curling in the corner. "You were saying?"

"I don't remember," I say, my own lips curving in response. "Maybe that you were a dickhead?"

"No, I don't think it was quite that," he says, his hands cupping my cheeks. "Something about home?"

I shift forward slightly, our noses bumping again. "I can't seem to recall."

He huffs a fond laugh, his breath cool against my face. "I have something that might help you remember."

I expect him to kiss me, but he pulls back entirely, pulling something out of the slim black messenger bag at his side. It looks kind of like a portfolio, but when he hands it to me, I realize it's a photo book, not unlike the one Rosie gave me for my birthday.

"For you," he says, his cheeks flushed with color, a rare sight. One I treasure more than anything else. "Consider it my apology. I don't have a Taylor Swift song to go with it, but…"

He pulls out his phone, tapping into a Spotify playlist titled *M*. Before I can comment on that, "Shine" by Years & Years shows up on his screen, a steady rhythmic beat playing quietly.

My brows furrow, and I flip the photo book open. The first picture I see is from the deli down the street. It's the one Emmitt took with a disposable camera, focused on a sign in the back of the shop. But in the corner of the photo is a familiar figure, staring at a pack of Oreos with a thoughtful expression—me.

I flip to the next page, and it's me sitting on the Staten Island Ferry, a small smile on my face. I flip to the next page, and it's me leaning over a barricade at the *SNL* line, talking to the girls. I flip to the next page, and it's me on a subway platform, laughing as the wind plays with my hair. With each page, another photo of me appears.

And in each photo, I'm presented in a different light—Emmitt has somehow captured all the sides of me I didn't even know existed. I glow, and I burn, and I shine.

I look up at him, speechless.

Emmitt's eyes are hopeful, even though he still looks nervous. "You see me. You see past the show I put on for everyone else. And I wanted you to know I see you, too."

I laugh, the sound choked. "You see me."

Only the truth, I said to him once upon a time. *Real and honest*, he said in return.

"I do. I love what I see," he says quietly. "And I love you."

I make an incoherent noise, barely breathing.

Emmitt chuckles and finally crosses the distance between us, his fingers slipping into my hair as he pulls me into an impassioned kiss.

Nothing has ever been easier than kissing him back, than melting in his arms. I haven't felt his lips against mine in two weeks, and it almost feels like I can breathe again. I move closer, until our hearts beat as one.

When I pull away, it's to rest my forehead against Emmitt's and whisper, "And I love *you*."

His eyes are bright enough to set cities aflame. "Even if I'm a dickhead?"

"Especially when you're a dickhead," I say, and my cheeks hurt from how wide my smile is. "Who else is going to keep you in line?"

There's a lot we still need to talk about—a future we need

to figure out, not to mention a short film we still need to submit. But in this moment, I'm content with the knowledge that it's all going to be okay.

I think that might be all the reassurance I'm ever going to need.

55

There are three things that people waiting for the Golden Ivy student film competition to announce winners should know.

One: the background music for their livestream is absolutely atrocious.

Two: winners are never announced at a consistent time, so closing out even for half a moment is a risk.

Three: having friends by your side, crossing their fingers with you, is *always* a good idea.

The entire film club is watching the makeshift whiteboard screen with wide eyes. The projector doesn't have the best quality, but it's *enough*. I'm sitting on the floor, Rosie's hand clutched tightly between mine, and Emmitt's legs bracketing my shoulders.

"I'm going to start screaming any second," Rosie says, biting her nails. "Why is this going on *forever*?"

"It should be considered a crime against humanity," I say, tugging on a lock of hair. Emmitt reacts instantly, combing through my dark waves with gentle fingers from where he's sitting in the seat above me.

I allow myself a brief smile, pressing a kiss to his knee, and ignoring Rosie when she mutters, "Heteros."

When I turn back to her, though, she's grinning. Sofia's sitting on Rosie's other side, her eyes fond as she snacks on pink licorice.

Most of the film and drama club are stuffed into the room, and even Ms. Somal is watching attentively, her latest graphic novel set aside. None of us know what the outcome will be, but my heart is hoping, praying, *manifesting*.

The livestream starts buffering, and we all groan. Grant curses under his breath, tapping around on his computer, linked up to the projector. "I hate AAAS's Wi-Fi so much. It should not be *this* hard for us to watch something without interruptions."

"You're asking too much of this hellhole," Kaity says, banging her head against the desk behind Rosie.

"When do they usually announce winners?" Christina asks, scratching her head. Her foot is tapping anxiously, and I sympathize. Freshman year, Rosie and I were barely able to sit still in our seats.

"Only the Lord knows," I say, shaking my head. "It could be five minutes from now or in another thirty minutes."

"Do you think I could get on the judging panel?" Emmitt asks idly. "None of these pricks would know a good film if it slapped them in the face. Pending our results, of course."

I tilt my head up to look at him, seeing his face upside down. "Probably. You should've planned ahead. You could be sitting on our screen instead right now."

He raises an eyebrow, a sliver of a smile passing across his face. "I rather like where I am right now."

"I bet you do," I say, pinching his leg without any real intent.

Emmitt chuckles, leaning down to press a kiss to my forehead.

"Are the two of you quite finished?" Grant asks, wrinkling his nose. "The livestream is working again."

I shrug, and my heart skips a beat when Emmitt winks at me, sitting back upright. "I suppose we are."

We turn back to the screen as they give out an award for the film with the best cinematic score. I resist the urge to scowl—who has a score for a fifteen-minute film?

My phone buzzes, and I pull it out from between my legs to look at the notification.

ANAM RAHMAN: ur finding out soon right??

ANAM RAHMAN: good luck !!!!! love you

ME: yes thank you sm love you !!! I'll see you when I get homeee

ANAM RAHMAN: I already have tonight's movies picked out <3 tell my brother in law he's invited if he brings me chocolate

ME: I will do no such thing!!! text him yourself if ur willing to risk ma and baba's wrath

ANAM RAHMAN: they're going to chachi's house again we are temporarily freeeeee

ME: well I guess nothing is stopping you then!!

Recently, my parents have been leaving the house more and more often. As if they can't stand to be in the same place as me and Anam. In an ironic way, it's like we've finally won, but this victory is bittersweet at best.

I set my phone down, and behind me, I feel the vibration of Emmitt's phone buzzing. When I glance back at him, he's grinning at his screen.

He and Anam have taken to each other alarmingly well ever since I officially introduced them. I think it's the chaotic energy in both of them.

At any rate, Emmitt types out a quick reply, then tugs my earlobe lightly. "I'll be seeing you tonight?"

"Only if you're ready to run at a second's notice," I say in return, well aware of my parents' specific brand of boy-induced outrage from the time Anam got caught with her ex-boyfriend and nearly *died*. "We have a back door."

"Duly noted," Emmitt says, his voice heavy with amusement. "I've gotten quite a lot of practice running from fans, I'm sure it'll be fine."

I snort, looking back at the screen as they give an award for best costume design. I'm slightly offended we aren't the winners for that category, since Noojman and his team did an amazing job.

Linli pats Noojman's thigh across the room, a sad smile on her face. He rolls his eyes in response, wrapping an arm around her shoulders. "At least my rap career is still an option." He presses a kiss to her cheek. "And there will be other awards."

I wish the rest of us could have the same energy for the short-film award, but I doubt that'll happen. Even now, when my future doesn't hinge on it, I still want to *win*. It's our senior year, we gave this film our all, and we deserve it.

My determination drowns out even the small voice in the back of my head. It's probably never going to go away, but I'm learning to handle it—and my mental health—better. I'm going to keep moving forward, step by step by step.

"Here we go! It's starting!" Rosie says, drawing my attention back to the screen. She's squeezing my hand so hard I'm sure I'll hear the bones crack any second now. At this point, I don't even think I'd care.

The announcer starts droning on and on, dragging out the livestream for *no* reason, until he finally says, "In third place, we have Griffiths High School with *Stay Gold*."

A collective sigh releases across the room. Okay. Not third. That could be good or bad.

Hopefully good. Inshallah.

Again, the announcer rambles on and on. Rosie physically throws a crumpled paper ball at the screen, as if it'll do anything. "*Come on*, dude! Just say it!"

"In second place, we have Alamo Preparatory School with *We Could Be Enough*."

Now there's an unspoken tension in the room. Last year we were second place, and this year... I don't have the answer.

Emmitt leans forward, his hands on my shoulders, squeezing in comfort. He doesn't say anything, but his touch is more than enough.

I take a deep breath, clutch Rosie's hand, and pray.

"And in first place..."

...

...

...

"... We have Astoria Academy of the Arts and Sciences with *What If*."

Silence.

And then *pandemonium.*

"Oh my *God!*" I shout, jumping to my feet. "That's us! *That's us!*"

Rosie is screeching incoherently in my ear, slapping my arm. "We won! We *won!*"

I don't even know what to focus on, what to look at. Bodies pile on top of Rosie and me, wrapping us in the world's biggest group hug.

"We did it!"

"We won!"

"Holy shit, holy shit, holy shit."

"We fucking did it!"

"Is this real? Are we all dreaming?"

"Oh my God!"

Somehow, we did it. Our hard work paid off. We won the Golden Ivy student film competition for the first time *ever.* The short film Rosie and I created from scraps, from nothing but a dream, won first place.

It doesn't feel real. But it is.

An overwhelming, powerful wave of pride washes over me as I look out at the rest of film club. I did it. We did it.

Rosie is crying into my sweater, mascara streaking down her face, and I laugh helplessly, wiping her cheeks with my sleeve.

"We won! We really won!"

We really did.

After a quick subway ride to Forest Hills, Emmitt and I start walking back to my house. He keeps looking around, taking in my neighborhood, and I can't stop smiling. Our hands swing between us, back and forth like a steady pendulum.

"We really won, huh?" I ask, still trying to process the last few hours. It feels so surreal, yet it grounds me in reality as much as Emmitt's hand does.

He looks back at me, his eyes warm. "You won, love. I'm so proud of you."

"We couldn't have done it without you," I say, nudging his shoulder with mine, though it jostles the plastic bag brimming over with chocolate between us. "*We* won."

Emmitt shrugs, tugging the handle of the bag farther up his arm so it's no longer in the way. "I don't know about that. I think you could have. I've seen how passionate and driven you are. You could take over the world if you wanted to."

"It's lucky I don't want to, then," I say, grinning at him. "However, I won't say no to taking over the film industry."

There's a twinkle in his eye. "I can see your name in lights already."

"Is that right?" I feel almost giddy, talking about the future like this.

He nods. "Soon, I'll be known as your arm candy. Mina Rahman and her beautiful boyfriend walk the red carpet."

"Oh?" I say, my voice bright with amusement. "Well, you *are* a pretty boy."

"Why else would you keep me around throughout your entire career?" he asks, his lips pulling into a devilish grin. "I have to provide incentive."

My heart is bursting at the seams. "Throughout my *entire* career, huh? That's a long time."

"I'm playing the long game," Emmitt says easily, his cheek

dimpling. "Making sure I get a shout-out when you win your first Oscar."

"I think you might win one first," I point out, laughing. "What with you being an actor already."

Emmitt tilts his head, considering that. "Then I'll thank *you* in my Oscar speech, and prepare myself accordingly for when you win one shortly afterward. By which I mean, iron my best tux."

I stop walking, squeezing his hand. "You really think we'll still be together then?"

"I certainly hope so," Emmitt murmurs, his other hand coming up to touch the pendant resting at the hollow of my throat.

"Me too," I say, my cheeks warming as he toys with the chain, his fingers brushing along my collarbones. "I'm glad we're on the same page."

"My publicist is going to have a field day," Emmitt says, a wicked gleam in his eyes. "No more heartbreaker reputation."

"As long as she doesn't reveal my name," I remind him, though I'm sure he remembers. "Otherwise my parents are going to have a conniption, and I'm going to *die* before we get to our first Oscars."

"No worries," he says, lifting our joined hands to press a kiss against the inside of my wrist. "It just means I get to keep you to myself for a few more years."

I want to shush him, but I can't bring myself to. Not when he's looking at me like that, his eyes soft, his mouth curled into a small smile, completely unmasked.

"Sounds like a plan," I say, and reach up to press a kiss against his cheek.

"The first of many," he says, his eyes glittering as we start walking again.

There's a future here, ahead of us. And I'm looking forward to every minute of it.

five years later

zahra @tomorrowsramos:
OMG THE PICTURES OF EMMITT AND MINA ON THE
RED CARPET ARE WE ALL SEEING THIS

juliana @emminastan:
when I tell you mina and emmitt are my parents who raised
me I mean they literally birthed me

nandini @buckybxrnes:
I can't get over how cute emmitt and mina are like? IS
THAT ALLOWED? IS THAT ALLOWED?

rocky @blondemmitt:
so tempted to draw fanart of emmina on the red carpet
and I've seen one (1) singular picture

lydia @romeonjuliet:

when emmitt dedicates his oscar win tonight to mina then what. then what!

lorena @jnkemmitt:

omg omg omg I rlly hope emmitt wins and points to mina in the crowd CAN THESE COMMERCIALS END ALREADY?

shan @emmittsmina:

how many pictures of mina do y'all think emmitt has taken tonight. my bet is 50

sara @minasemmitt:

no offense but why are emmina the cutest couple at these white ass oscars. if emmitt doesn't win I'm beating someone's ass

holly @emmittrcmos:

not to be That Bitch but can emmitt move over. mina be my gf challenge!!! that dress is GORGEOUS on her

raisa @ramosholland:

EMMITT WON HIS FIRST OSCAR HOLY SHIT AND HE THANKED MINA FIRST??? I'M GONNA CRYYYYY

sabyne @moonlighting:

anyone else thinking about how when mina wins an oscar in a few years she's gonna thank emmitt first too? QUEEN

406 • TASHIE BHUIYAN

OF WRITING SCREENPLAYS can't wait for her to take over hollywood

emily @ramosquad:
okay wait do emmitt and mina have matching tattoos. what the fuck is on their arms SOMEONE PULL UP THE HQS??????

hannah @carolineklaus:
HOLY FUCK EMMITT AND MINA HAVE MATCHING TATTOOS THIS IS NOT A DRILL

EMMITT RAMOS UPDATES @EmmittRamosUA:
Emmitt Ramos and his girlfriend Mina Rahman reveal matching "HOME" tattoos on their right and left wrists respectively, following Emmitt's first Oscar win. Via Instagram.

★ ★ ★ ★ ★

acknowledgments

And the Oscar goes to…my readers! Welcome to my annual acknowledgments section—I am so glad to have you here. I want to start by thanking you for reading Mina's story and for investing time into my words. It's so, so appreciated. I hope it brought you some comfort and joy.

The next Oscar goes to my amazing agent, JL Stermer, for always being in my corner. You're the epitome of everything I adore about New York, and I couldn't do any of this without you!

And another Oscar for my old editor, Rebecca Kuss, for understanding the heart of this story and loving Tom Holland beyond words. Both those things bring me so much joy, and I'm grateful for your existence. An additional Oscar for my new editor, Claire Stetzer, who also loves Tom Holland (clearly, all my editors have incredible taste) and has been an incredible support on this journey. More Oscars for the wonderful Inkyard team: Bess Braswell, Brittany Mitchell, Laura

Gianino, and Linette Kim—you deserve it and more. Thank you to Gigi Lau and Valentina Fernandez for such a beautiful cover. It's exactly how I imagined it.

I'll stop the Oscar metaphor now, but every single person I'm about to list deserves their own individual award because they mean the world to me. To my someone supportives—to Fari Cannon, Kris Urbanova, Chloe Gong, Genesis Mendoza, Holly Hughes, Z. Ahmadi, and LinLi Wan, for never hesitating to pick up my calls. I could not have written this book without you.

To my favorite angels—to Lorena Valenzuela, Sofia Tulachan, Kaity Findley, Hannah Vitton, Nina Petropoulos and Alyssa Cavallaro, for being there through thick and thin, even across the world.

To the people who make New York City home—to Pietra Ibrisimovic, Kadeen Griffiths, Rachel Koltsov, Akvinder Kaur, Juliana Ogarrio, Helen Urena, Zuzu Bicane, Sophia Monsalve, and Syd Martinez, for always having my back. (Bonus points to Juliana for helping with nearly every single film reference in this book!)

To the writers who make publishing a brighter place—to the Gen Z girlies: Christina Li, Zoe Hana Mikuta, Racquel Marie (and Chloe again), for all the serotonin. To Tahereh Mafi, for being so generous with her time and blurbing this novel. To Leah Jordain, Avi Lewis, Emily Miner, and Shana Targosz, for showing my words infinite love and support.

To my bookish pals—Anam Sattar, Claire Malchow, Andie Gomes, Valerie L., and Michelle Bader, for reading this book and screaming about it with me. To Lydia L. and Silke Alina, for supporting my career along the way.

To my family, especially my Dadu, for believing in my dreams—and to Zareen Khan, Fabia Mahmud, and Shannon Ali, for being my touchstone.

To S and T, for everything always.

And finally, to Tom Holland, for inspiring this idea in and of itself. Like I said in the author's note, Emmitt Ramos is remarkably different from Tom Holland (although both are iconic!), but he exists in part because of him. Thank you for coming to Bronx Science and thank you for giving me a fictional story to spin out of the surreal circumstance of meeting you, Tom. I'll forever be grateful.

And that's a wrap! Thank you all for tuning into the *ASFT* Oscars! Have a wonderful night!